Incredible Acclaim for Jeffery Deaver

THE SKIN COLLECTOR

"Outstanding...the endgame remains in doubt to the end. Deaver proves himself a grandmaster of the genre as each surprise leads to an even bigger surprise, like a series of reverse Russian nesting dolls."

—*Publishers Weekly* (starred review)

"Deaver's ability to tell the reader everything and still manipulate the story with diabolical twists is the sign of a master at work. Readers unfamiliar with Lincoln Rhyme will find a detective that rivals Sherlock Holmes, and fans will enjoy the familial and reflective aspects of previous cases." —Associated Press

"Jeffery Deaver has brought a unique voice to the thriller genre, mixing high-energy action into novels about a brilliant criminalist...Lincoln Rhyme has become one of the genre's most iconic characters."

—*South Florida Sun Sentinel*

"Like all of his books, the storytelling is intricately plotted, with plenty of feints, misdirections and endgame twists to keep the reader guessing."

—*Raleigh News and Observer*

"For those who have never read a Deaver book, this is definitely the time to start. Once you are hooked you will find yourself searching for everything he has written in the past, and that is plenty. He is one of the premiere writers of mysteries and each and every one of his books is a reading pleasure from beginning to end. So get a copy of *The Skin Collector* and settle yourself in for hours of reading satisfaction." —*Huffington Post*

"Another suspenseful and twist-filled entry in this always-exciting series." —*Booklist*

"[A] page-turner full of Deaver's signature moves: frantic pacing, forensic minutiae, blindsides, gotchas and hairpin plot turns...a true return to classic form for Deaver." —*Winnipeg Free Press*

"'Deavotees' will expect and gratefully receive the many twists and sudden turns...No one is better at narrative misdirection. Just at the point you think 'That's impossible!' Deaver demonstrates the exact opposite...Once again the depth of his research and characterisation has created a superb example of modern American Gothic." —*The Evening Standard* (UK)

THE STEEL KISS

"Deaver is a genius when it comes to manipulation and deception. Stellar plot twists are in full abundance in *The Steel Kiss*, and the story line veers in several unpredictable directions." —Associated Press

"Deaver doesn't disappoint. With an unmatched ability to create the perfect characters...Deaver takes fans to the edge in this one and dangles them over the cliff... One of the best books of 2016." —*Suspense Magazine*

"Darkly witty...unsettling."

—*New York Times Book Review*

"Fiendishly inventive...all the usual thrills, which are worth every breathless minute." —*Kirkus Reviews*

"The plot twists are clever and unexpected, the dialogue is colloquial and natural, and the characters...are vividly realized. Highly recommendable." —*Booklist*

"Clever...entertaining...Convincing characters and an unexpected closing twist will remind readers why Deaver is one of today's top thriller writers."

—*Publishers Weekly*

"Deaver delivers another heart-stopping thriller in his Lincoln Rhyme series...The action, suspense and horrific crimes continue unabated." —*RT Book Reviews*

"Deaver at his best and when you are Jeffery Deaver this means the best of the best." —*Huffington Post*

"Fans will marvel at the creative manner in which Deaver incorporates current technological and societal trends into the plots of his thrillers." —*Library Journal*

"[*The Steel Kiss* is] like a master class in how to perfectly balance plot and character...A terrific novel."

—*Connecticut News*

"A gripping thriller...As with any thriller by Jeffery Deaver, *The Steel Kiss* is full of plot twists, misdirections, characters whose discourse is less than truthful, and contradictions that seem beyond explanation... still the reader is shocked by the final explanation, the straightening of the twists and turns of the plot. One will wonder 'How did I miss that?' "

—New York Journal of Books

"If you're looking for a pedal-to-the-floor thriller with reversals and twists, this is the novel for you."

—The Big Thrill

"Loaded from first page to (almost) last with suspense of one sort of another... *The Steel Kiss* is a terrific novel." —BookReporter.com

SOLITUDE CREEK

"What do we truly fear, and how would we react in a crisis? Would we fall apart and claw our way to safety? Or would we help someone else? Deaver forces the reader to tackle these questions, then adds his own brand of twists to play with expectations, delivering another outstanding and unpredictable thriller." —Associated Press

"Numerous surprises are in store for Kathryn Dance (and the reader) in bestseller Deaver's stellar fourth novel featuring the California Bureau of Investigation kinesics expert... Deaver's meaty thrillers are as good as they come." —*Publishers Weekly* (starred review)

"One of Deaver's most diabolical villains."

—*New York Times Book Review*

"Riveting...[Deaver] is definitely the Master of Suspense." —*Crimespree Magazine*

"Deaver once again meets and exceeds his own high water mark for surprises with *Solitude Creek.* Antioch March is a chilling and unforgettable antagonist...It's a story you will not soon forget." —BookReporter.com

"Deaver is a genius...The cat-and-mouse elements of this story are Deaver at his best." —Huffington Post

THE OCTOBER LIST

SELECTED AS ONE OF THE BEST FICTION BOOKS OF THE YEAR BY *KIRKUS REVIEWS*

"Don't skip ahead to the beginning and spoil the fun that's guaranteed for anyone interested in a thriller that forces readers to use their brains in a creative way... Deaver is a master of manipulation and *The October List* is [a] powerful book." —Associated Press

"Brilliant...might well be Deaver's most fiendish thriller ever...as the pace quickens and the story continues to backtrack, solid evidence, established plot points, and sturdily built characters all begin to come undone, until what started out as an interactive game becomes a truly unnerving exercise in deception."

—*New York Times Book Review*

"[Deaver] delivers a clever, demanding standalone...As the ingenious plot folds back on itself, the reader has to reevaluate and reinterpret the constantly shifting 'facts' in the case. The finished picture finally emerges with a shock of recognition. This is brilliant craftsmanship in a vastly entertaining package."

—*Publishers Weekly* (starred review)

"Elegantly clever...The novel takes a mischievous delight in misleading the reader, without ever outright cheating. It offers a delightful game of wits...Deaver wraps the novel up with breathtaking success."

—*Columbus Dispatch*

"Perhaps the cleverest of all Deaver's exceptionally clever thrillers. If you've ever wished you could take the film *Memento* to the beach, here's your chance."

—*Kirkus Reviews* (starred review)

"[A] mind-bending novel with twists and turns...a masterful race-against-the-clock mystery." —*BookPage*

"Intriguing and enjoyable...If any author could pull this off, it is Deaver. This is because he has the intelligence and skills to do anything and everything...It is a book like no other you have read." —Huffington Post

"The premise is clever, but Deaver's ability to execute it successfully makes this experimental novel even more impressive. Revealing the ending first, he still manages to surprise with a few twists, constantly challenging readers' understanding of the story. Read it backward, forward, once or twice, to see how all the pieces fit together—just be sure to chase down this List yourself."

—*Shelf Awareness*

"An absorbing read... Deaver skillfully patches together a compelling story that is filled with his trademark twists." —*Oklahoman*

THE KILL ROOM

"Fast and furious... an ace thriller [by] a master magician with words." —Associated Press

"This is Deaver at his very best and not to be missed by any thriller fan." —*Publishers Weekly* (starred review)

"Chillingly effective... Equal parts *Marathon Man* and top-notch political thriller, this is Deaver at the top of his game. Rhyme remains the most original hero in thriller fiction today... Not to be missed."

—*Providence Sunday Journal*

"Well-researched, expertly written, and nicely paced... Deaver makes it all work, with style."

—*Columbus Dispatch*

"A thrill ride... will keep readers guessing... The endless twists and turns in *The Kill Room* come so fast that, by the novel's end, the reader will be dizzy—and clamoring for more." —*San Jose Mercury News*

"Another well-crafted, unpredictable novel from a master of the genre." —*Booklist*

"*The Kill Room* will knock your socks off... If [it] doesn't get your pulse racing, your head spinning, and your adrenaline pumping then nothing will... If you are a person who enjoys a tight, twisted, terrific crime thriller which also has a personal story woven into it then you have to read Jeffery Deaver. He is one of the best writers on the scene today." —Huffington Post

"Deaver, who can't resist any opportunity for ingenuity...keeps mixing fastballs, curveballs, and change-ups." —*Kirkus Reviews*

"*The Kill Room* is full of his trademark twists, breathless suspense, and ironic humor. It is a thriller [that] never cheats the reader, so that the only response can be sighs of satisfaction and admiration."
—*Evening Standard* (London)

"Deaver delivers a dark tale of espionage, patriotism, and egos as his clever detective puts the pieces of an intricately drawn jigsaw together while a killer targets his investigation." —*RT Book Reviews*

"*The Kill Room* is very powerful in its exploration of current issues...This book is a page-turner with nothing as it seems to be, culminating in many surprise endings." —*Military Press*

"Entertaining and suspenseful...Deaver's best book to date." —BookReporter.com

"Fans will appreciate Deaver's customary detailing of each plot sequence, thereby heightening their anticipation of the upcoming clincher. Thriller aficionados will be lining up for this one." —*Library Journal*

The Skin Collector

Also by Jeffery Deaver

*The Steel Kiss**
*Solitude Creek***
*The Skin Collector**
The Starling Project, an original radio play
Trouble in Mind, Collected Stories, Volume Three
Ice Cold, Tales of Intrigue from the Cold War (Editor)
Books to Die For (Contributor)
The October List, a Thriller in Reverse
*The Kill Room**
*XO**/**
XO: The Album (Music CD of original songs)
Carte Blanche, a James Bond Novel
Edge
*The Burning Wire**
Best American Mystery Stories 2009 (Editor)
The Watch List (*The Copper Bracelet* and *The Chopin Manuscript*) (Contributor)
*Roadside Crosses***
The Bodies Left Behind
*The Broken Window**
*The Sleeping Doll***
More Twisted: Collected Stories, Volume Two
The Cold Moon/***
*The Twelfth Card**
Garden of Beasts
Twisted: Collected Stories
*The Vanished Man**
*The Stone Monkey**
The Blue Nowhere
*The Empty Chair**
Speaking in Tongues
The Devil's Teardrop
*The Coffin Dancer**
*The Bone Collector**
A Maiden's Grave
Praying for Sleep
The Lesson of Her Death
Mistress of Justice
Hard News
Death of a Blue Movie Star
Manhattan Is My Beat
Hell's Kitchen
Bloody River Blues
Shallow Graves
A Century of Great Suspense Stories (Editor)
A Hot and Sultry Night for Crime (Editor)
Mary Shelley's Frankenstein (Introduction)

*Featuring Lincoln Rhyme and Amelia Sachs
**Featuring Kathryn Dance

The Skin Collector

A Lincoln Rhyme Novel

Jeffery Deaver

GRAND CENTRAL PUBLISHING

NEW YORK BOSTON

This book is a work of fiction. Names, characters, places, and incidents are the product of the author's imagination or are used fictitiously. Any resemblance to actual events, locales, or persons, living or dead, is coincidental.

Grand Central Publishing
Hachette Book Group
1290 Avenue of the Americas, New York, NY 10104
grandcentralpublishing.com
twitter.com/grandcentralpub

Originally published in hardcover and ebook by Grand Central Publishing in May 2014
Reissued Edition: November 2016

Grand Central Publishing is a division of Hachette Book Group, Inc. The Grand Central Publishing name and logo is a trademark of Hachette Book Group, Inc.

The publisher is not responsible for websites (or their content) that are not owned by the publisher.

The Hachette Speakers Bureau provides a wide range of authors for speaking events. To find out more, go to www.hachettespeakersbureau.com or call (866) 376-6591.

ISBNs: 978-1-4555-9516-7 (mass market), 978-1-4555-1711-4 (ebook)

Printed in the United States of America

OPM

10 9 8 7 6 5 4 3 2 1

For Dennis, Patti, Melissa and Phillip

The Skin Collector

The creatures I had seen were not men, had never been men. They were animals—humanised animals—triumphs of vivisection.

—H. G. WELLS,
THE ISLAND OF DOCTOR MOREAU

TUESDAY, NOVEMBER 5

I

THE OUT-OF-PRINT BOOK

CHAPTER 1

NOON

The basement.

She had to go to the basement.

Chloe hated it down there.

But they'd sold out of sizes ten and twelve Rue du Cannes—the tacky little floral number with scalloped hemline and plunging front—and she needed to replenish the racks, fill 'em up for the grazers. Chloe was an actress, not a retail fashion expert, and new to the store. So she hadn't fathomed why, in a November impersonating January, these particular dresses were selling out. Until her boss explained that, even though the store was in alternative SoHo in Manhattan, the ZIP codes of the purchasers situated them in Jersey, Westchester and Long Island.

"And?"

"Cruises, Chloe. Cruises."

"Ah."

Chloe Moore walked into the back of the store. Here the shop was the opposite of the sales floor and about as chic as a storage unit. She found the key among those dangling from her wrist and unlocked the basement door. She flicked on the lights and studied the unsteady stairs.

A sigh and she started down. The door, on a spring, swung shut behind her. Not a small woman, Chloe took the steps carefully. She was also on Vera Wang knockoffs. Pseudo-designer heels and hundred-year-old architecture can be a dangerous combination.

The basement.

Hated it.

Not that she worried about intruders. There was only one door in and out—the one she'd just come through. But the place was moldy, damp, cold…and booby-trapped with cobwebs.

Which meant sly, predatory spiders.

And Chloe knew she'd need a dog roller to remove the dust from the dark-green skirt and black blouse (Le Bordeaux and La Seine).

She stepped onto the uneven, cracked concrete floor, moving to the left to avoid a big web. But another one got her; a long clinging strand clutched her face, tickling. After a comic dance of trying to brush the damn thing off and not fall over, she continued her search. Five minutes later she found the shipments of Rue du Cannes, which may have looked French and sounded French but came in boxes printed largely with Chinese characters.

As she tugged the cartons off the shelf Chloe heard a scrape.

She froze. Tilted her head.

The sound didn't repeat. But then she was aware of another noise.

Drip, drip, drip.

Was there a leak?

Chloe came down here often, if reluctantly, and she'd never heard water. She stacked the faux French garments near the stairs and turned to investigate. Most of the inventory was on shelves but some cartons rested on the floor. A leak could be disastrous. And while, yes, Chloe was eventually headed for Broadway she nonetheless needed to keep her job here at Chez Nord for the foreseeable future. Stopping a leak before it ruined ten thousand dollars' worth of overpriced clothes might go a long way in keeping those paychecks dribbling into Chase.

She walked to the back of the cellar, determined to find the leak, though also on serious spider alert.

The dripping grew louder as she moved toward the rear of the room, even murkier than the front, near the stairs.

Chloe stepped behind a shelf, containing a huge supply of blouses so ugly even her mother wouldn't wear them—a major order by a buyer who, Chloe believed, had made the purchase because he knew he was going to be sacked.

Drip, drip…

Squinting.

Odd. What was that? In the far wall an access door was open. The sound of water was coming from there. The door, painted gray like the walls, was about three feet by four.

What did it lead to? Was there a sub-basement? She'd never seen the doorway but then she didn't believe she'd ever glanced at the wall behind the last shelf. There was no reason to.

And why was it open? The city was always doing construction work, especially in the older parts, such as here, SoHo. But nobody had talked to the clerks—her, at least—about a repair beneath the building.

Maybe that weird Polish or Rumanian or Russian janitor was doing some repairs. But, no, couldn't be. The manager didn't trust him; he didn't have keys to the basement door.

Okay, the creep factor was rising.

Don't bother figuring it out. Tell Marge about the drip. Tell her about the open doorway. Get Vlad or Mikhail or whoever he is down here and let him earn his salary.

Then another scrape. This time it seemed to be a foot shifting on gritty concrete.

Fuck. That's it. Get. Out.

But before she got out, before she even spun an eighth turn away, he was on her from behind, slamming her head into the wall. He pressed a cloth over her mouth to gag her. She nearly fainted from the shock. A burst of pain blossomed in her neck.

Chloe turned fast to face him.

God, God...

She nearly puked, seeing the yellowish latex full-head mask, with slots for eyes and mouth and ears, tight and distorting the flesh underneath, as if his face had melted. He was in worker's coveralls, some logo on them she couldn't read.

Crying, shaking her head, she was pleading through the gag, screaming through the gag, which he kept pressed firmly in place with a hand in a glove as tight and sickly yellow as the mask.

"Listen to me, please! Don't do this! You don't understand! Listen, listen..." But the words were just random sounds through the cloth.

Thinking: Why didn't I chock the door open? I thought about it...Furious with herself.

His calm eyes looked her over—but not her breasts or lips or hips or legs. Just the skin of her bare arms, her throat, her neck—where he focused intently on a small blue tattoo of a tulip.

"Not bad, not good," he whispered.

She was whimpering, shivering, moaning. "What, what, what do you want?"

But why did she even ask? She knew. Of course she knew.

And, with that thought, Chloe controlled the fear. She tightened her heart.

Okay, asshole, wanna play? You'll pay.

She went limp. His eyes, surrounded by yellow latex like sickly skin, seemed confused. The attacker, apparently not expecting her collapse, adjusted his grip to keep her from falling.

As soon as she felt his hands slacken Chloe lunged forward and grabbed the collar of his coveralls. The zipper popped and cloth tore—both the outer garment and whatever was under it.

Her grip and the blows aimed at his chest and face were fierce. She pumped her knee upward toward his groin. Again and once more.

But she didn't connect. Her aim was off. It seemed such an easy target but she was suddenly uncoordinated, dizzy. He was cutting off her air with the gag—that was it maybe. Or the aftermath of the shock.

Keep going, she raged. Don't stop. He's scared. You can see it. Fucking coward...

And tried to hit him again, claw at his flesh, but she now found her energy fading fast. Her hands tapped uselessly against him. Her head lolled and, looking down, she noticed that his sleeve had ridden up. Chloe caught sight of a weird tattoo, in red, some insect, dozens of little insect legs, insect fangs but human eyes. And then she focused on the floor of the cellar. A glint from the hypodermic syringe. *That* was the source of the pain in her neck—and of her fleeing strength. He'd injected her with something.

Whatever the drug, it was taking effect in a big way. She was growing exhausted. Her mind tumbled, as if dipping into and out of a dream, and for some reason she found herself obsessing over the cheap perfume Chez Nord sold by the checkout counter.

Who'd buy that crap? Why didn't—?

What am I doing? she thought as clarity returned. Fight! Fight the son of a bitch!

But her hands were at her sides now, completely still, and her head heavy as stone.

She was sitting on the floor and then the room tilted and began to move. He was dragging her toward the access door.

No, not there, please!

Listen to me! I can explain why you shouldn't do this. Don't take me there! Listen!

Here in the cellar proper, at least there was still some hope that Marge would look down the stairs and see them both and she'd scream and he'd scramble off on his insect legs. But once Chloe was deep underground in his bug nest, it would be too late. The room was growing dark but an odd kind of dark, as if the ceiling bulbs, which were still on, were not *emitting* light but drawing in rays and extinguishing them.

Fight!

But she couldn't.

Closer to the black abyss.

Drip, drip, drip...

Scream!

She did.

But no sound came from her mouth beyond a hiss, a cricket click, a beetle hum.

Then he was easing her through the door into Wonderland, on the other side. Like that movie. Or cartoon. Or whatever.

She saw a small utility room below.

Chloe believed she was falling, over and over, and a moment later she was on the floor, the ground, the dirt, trying to breathe, the air kicked out of her lungs from the impact. But no pain, no pain at all. The sound of dripping water was more pronounced and she saw a trickle down the far wall, made of old stone and laced with pipes and wires, rusty and frayed and rotting.

Drip, drip...

A trickle of insect venom, of shiny clear insect blood.

Thinking, Alice, I'm Alice. Down the rabbit hole. The hookah-smoking caterpillar, the March Hare, the Red Queen, the red insect on his arm.

She never liked that goddamn story!

Chloe gave up on screaming. She wanted only to crawl away, to cry and huddle, to be left alone. But she couldn't move. She lay on her back, staring up at the faint light from the basement of the store that she hated working in, the store that she wanted with all her soul to be back inside right now, standing on sore feet and nodding with fake enthusiasm.

No, no, it makes you look sooo thin. Really...

Then the light grew dimmer yet as her attacker, the yellow-faced insect, climbed into the hole, pulled the access door shut behind him, and came down the short ladder to where she lay. A moment later a piercing light filled the tunnel; he'd pulled a miner's lamp onto his forehead, clicked it on. The white beam blinded and she screamed, or didn't scream, at the piercing brilliance.

Which suddenly faded to complete darkness.

She awoke a few seconds or minutes or a year later.

Chloe was someplace else now, not the utility room, but in a larger room, no, a tunnel. Hard to see, since the only illumination was a weak light above her and the focused beam from the masked insect man's forehead. It blinded her every time he looked at her face. She was on her back again, staring upward, and he was kneeling over her.

But what she'd been expecting, dreading, wasn't happening. In a way, though, this was worse because *that*—ripping her clothes off and then what would follow—would at least have been understandable. It would have fallen into a known category of horror.

This was different.

Yes, her blouse was tugged up but only slightly, exposing her belly from navel to the bottom of her bra, which was still chastely in place. Her skirt was tucked tight around her thighs, almost as if he didn't want there to be any suggestion of impropriety.

Leaning forward, hunched, intent, he was staring with those calm eyes of his, those insect eyes, at her smooth, white belly skin the way somebody would look over a canvas at MoMA: head tilted, getting the right angle to appreciate Jackson Pollock's spatter, Magritte's green apple.

He then slowly extended his index finger and stroked her flesh. His yellow finger. He splayed his palm and brushed back and forth. He pinched and raised peaks of skin between his thumb and forefinger. He let go and watched the mounds flatten back.

His insect mouth curved into a faint smile.

She thought he said, "Very nice." Or maybe that was the smoke-ring caterpillar talking or the bug on his arm.

She heard a faint hum of vibration and he looked at his watch. Another hum, from elsewhere. Then he glanced at her face and saw her eyes. He seemed surprised, maybe, that she was awake. Turning, he tugged into view a backpack and removed from it a filled hypodermic syringe. He stabbed her again, this time in a vein in her arm.

The warmth flowed, the fear lessened. As darkness trickled around her, sounds vanishing, she saw his yellow fingers, his caterpillar fingers, his insect claws, reach into the backpack once more and carefully remove a small box. He set it beside her exposed skin with the same reverence she remembered her priest displaying as he'd placed the silver vessel holding the blood of Christ on the altar last Sunday during Holy Communion.

CHAPTER 2

Billy Haven shut off his American Eagle tattoo machine to save the batteries.

He squatted back. He examined the work so far.

Eyes scanning.

Less-than-ideal conditions but the art was good.

You always put everything you could into your mods. From the simplest cross on a waitress's shoulder to an American flag on a contractor's chest, complete with multiple folds and three colors and blowin' in the wind, you inked like Michelangelo laboring away on the church ceiling. God and Adam, finger skin to finger skin.

Now, here, Billy could've rushed. Considering the circumstances, nobody would have blamed him.

But no. The mod had to be a Billy Mod. What they called it back home, in his shop.

He felt a tickle, sweat.

Lifted the dentist's face guard and with his gloved hand wiped sweat from his eyes, put the tissue into a pocket. Carefully, so no fibers would flake off. Telltale fibers that could be as dangerous to him as the inking was to Chloe.

The face shield was cumbersome. But necessary. His tattoo instructor had taught him this lesson. He'd had Billy slip one on before the boy had even picked up a machine for the first time. Billy, like most young apprentices, had protested: Got eye protection. Don't need more. It wasn't cool. Wearing a dorky mask was like giving newbies, in for their first inking, a pussy ball to squeeze.

Tat up. Get over it.

But then his instructor had Billy sit beside him while he inked a client. A little work: Ozzy Osbourne's face. For some reason.

Man, the blood and fluid that spattered! The face guard was as flecked as a pickup's windshield in August.

"Be smart, Billy. Remember."

"Sure."

Ever since, he'd assumed that each customer was ripe with hep C and B and HIV and whatever other sexual diseases were popular.

And for the mods he'd be inking over the next few days, of course, he couldn't afford *any* blowback.

So, protection.

And he'd worn the latex mask and hood, too, to make sure he didn't shed any of his abundant hair or slough off epidermal cells. To distort his features as well. There was the remote chance that, despite his careful selection of the secluded kill zones, he'd get spotted.

Billy Haven now examined his victim again.

Chloe.

He'd noted the name on the tag on her chest and the pretentious *Je m'appelle* preceding it. Whatever that meant. Maybe Hello. Maybe Good morning. French. He lowered his gloved hand—double-gloved—and stroked her skin, pinching, stretching, noting the elasticity, the texture, the fine resilience.

Billy noted too the faint rise between her legs, beneath the forest-green skirt. The lower line of the bra. But there was no question of misbehaving. He never touched a client anywhere he shouldn't touch.

That was flesh. This was skin. Two different things entirely, and it was skin that Billy Haven loved.

He wiped more sweat with a new tissue, carefully tucked it away again. He was hot, his own skin prickling. Though the month was November the tunnel was stifling. Long—about a hundred yards—yet sealed at both ends, which meant no ventilation. It was like many of the passages here in SoHo, south of Greenwich Village. Built in the nineteenth and twentieth centuries, these tunnels honeycombed the neighborhood and had been used for transporting goods underground to and from factories and warehouses and transfer stations.

Abandoned now, they were perfect for Billy's purposes.

The watch on his right wrist hummed again. A similar sound from a backup watch in his pocket came a few seconds later. Reminding him of the time; Billy often got lost in his work.

Just let me get God's knuckle perfect, just a minute more…

A clattering came from a bud microphone in his left

ear. He listened for a moment then ignored the noise and took up the American Eagle machine once more. It was an old-style model, with a rotary head, which moved the needle like a sewing machine's, rather than modern devices that used a vibrating coil.

He clicked it on.

Bzzzz…

Face shield down.

A millimeter at a time, he inked with a lining needle, following the bloodline he'd done quickly. Billy was a natural-born artist, brilliant at pencil and ink drawing, brilliant at pastels. Brilliant at needles. He drew freehand on paper, he drew freehand on skin. Most mod artists, however talented, used stencils, prepared ahead of time or—for the untalented—purchased and then placed on the skin for the inker to trace. Billy rarely did this. He didn't need to. From God's mind to your hand, his uncle had said.

Now time to fill. He swapped needles. Very, very carefully.

For Chloe's tat, Billy was using the famous Blackletter font, known more commonly as Gothic or Old English. It was characterized by very thick and very thin strokes. The particular family he used was Fraktur. He'd selected this font because it was the typeface of the Gutenberg Bible—and because it was challenging. He was an artist and what artist didn't like to show off his skills?

Ten minutes later he was nearly done.

And how was his client doing? He scanned her body then lifted her lids. Eyes still unfocused. Her face gave a few twitches, though. The propofol wouldn't last much longer. But of course by now one drug was replacing the other.

Suddenly pain coursed through his chest. This alarmed him. He was young and in very good shape; he dismissed the thought of a heart attack. But the big question remained: Had he inhaled something he shouldn't have?

That was a very real, and lethal, possibility.

Then he probed his own body and realized the pain was on the surface. And he understood. When he'd first grabbed her, Chloe had fought back. He'd been so charged he hadn't noticed how hard she'd struck him. But now the adrenaline had worn off and the pain was throbbing. He looked down. Hadn't caused any serious damage, except for tearing his shirt and the coveralls.

He ignored the ache and kept going.

Then Billy noted Chloe's breathing becoming deeper. The anesthetic would soon wear off. He touched her chest—Lovely Girl wouldn't have minded—and beneath his hand he could feel her heartbeat thudding more insistently.

It was then that a thought occurred to him: What would it be like to tattoo a living, beating heart? Could it be done? Billy had broken into a medical supply company a month ago in anticipation of his plans here in New York. He'd made off with thousands of dollars in equipment, drugs, chemicals and other materials. He wondered if he could learn enough to put someone under, crack open the chest, ink a design or words onto the heart itself and sew the victim back up. Living out his or her life with the altered organ.

What would the work be?

A cross.
The words: *The Rule of Skin*
Maybe:

Billy + Lovely Girl 4 Ever

Interesting idea. But thinking about Lovely Girl made him sad and he returned to Chloe, finishing the last of the letters.

Good.

A Billy Mod.

But not quite finished yet. He extracted a scalpel from a dark-green toothbrush container and reached forward, stretching out the marvelous skin once more.

CHAPTER 3

One can view death in two ways.

In the discipline of forensic science an investigator looks at death abstractly, considers it to be merely an event that gives rise to a series of tasks. Good forensic cops view that event as if through the lens of history; the best see death as fiction, and the victim as someone who never existed at all.

Detachment is a necessary tool for crime scene work, just like latex gloves and alternative light sources.

As he sat in the red-and-gray Merits wheelchair in front of the window of his Central Park West town house, Lincoln Rhyme happened to be thinking of a recent death in just this way. Last week a man had been murdered downtown, a mugging gone wrong. Just after leaving his office in the city's Department of Environmental Protection, mid-evening, he'd been pulled into a deserted construction site across the street. Rather than give up his wallet, he'd chosen to fight and, no match for the perp, he'd been stabbed to death.

The case, whose file sat in front of him now, was

mundane, and the sparse evidence typical of such a murder: a cheap weapon, a serrated-edge kitchen knife, dotted with fingerprints not on file at IAFIS or anywhere else, indistinct footprints in the slush that had coated the ground that night, and no trace or trash or cigarette butts that weren't day- or week-old trace or trash or cigarette butts. And therefore useless. To all appearances it was a random crime; there were no springboards to likely perps. The officers had interviewed the victim's fellow employees in the public works department and talked to friends and family. There'd been no drug connections, no dicey business deals, no jealous lovers, no jealous spouses of lovers.

Given the paltry evidence, the case, Rhyme knew, would be solved only one way: Someone would carelessly boast about scoring a wallet near City Hall. And the boastee, collared for drugs or domestic abuse or petty larce, would cut a deal by giving up the boaster.

This crime, a mugging gone wrong, was death observed from a distance, to Lincoln Rhyme. Historical. Fictional.

View number one.

The second way to regard death is from the heart: when a human being with whom you have a true connection is no longer of this earth. And the other death on Rhyme's mind on this blustery, grim day was affecting him as deeply as the mugging victim's killing was not.

Rhyme wasn't close to many people. This was not a function of his physical condition—he was a quadriplegic, largely paralyzed from the neck down. No, he'd never been a people person. He was a science person. A mind person.

Oh, there'd been a few friends he'd been close to, some relatives, lovers. His wife, now ex.

Thom, his aide.

Amelia Sachs, of course.

But the second man who'd died several days ago had, in one sense, been closer than all of the others, and for this reason: He'd challenged Rhyme like no one else, forced him to think beyond the expansive boundaries where his own mind roamed, forced him to anticipate and strategize and question. Forced him to fight for his life too; the man had come very close to killing him.

The Watchmaker was the most intriguing criminal Rhyme had ever encountered. A man of shifting identities, Richard Logan was primarily a professional killer, though he'd orchestrated an alpha-omega of crimes, from terrorist attacks to robbery. He would work for whoever paid his hefty fee—provided the job was, yes, challenging enough. Which was the same criterion Rhyme used when deciding to take on a case as a consulting forensic scientist.

The Watchmaker was one of the few criminals able to outthink him. Although Rhyme had eventually set the trap that landed Logan in prison he still stung from his failure to stop several plots that were successful. And even when he failed, the Watchmaker sometimes managed to wreak havoc. In a case in which Rhyme had derailed the attempted killing of a Mexican officer investigating drug cartels, Logan had still provoked an international incident (it was finally agreed to seal the records and pretend the attempted hit had never happened).

But now the Watchmaker was gone.

The man had died in prison—not murdered by a fellow inmate or a suicide, which Rhyme had first suspected upon hearing the news. No, the COD was pedestrian—cardiac arrest, though massive. The doctor, whom Rhyme had spoken to yesterday, reported that even if they'd been able to bring Logan around he would have had permanent and severe brain damage. Though medicos did not use phrases like "his death was a blessing," that was the impression Rhyme took from the doctor's tone.

A blast of temperamental November wind shook the windows of Rhyme's town house. He was in the building's front parlor—the place in which he felt more comfortable than anywhere else in the world. Created as a Victorian sitting room, it was now a fully decked-out forensic lab, with spotless tables for examining evidence, computers and high-def monitors, racks of instruments, sophisticated equipment like fume and particulate control hoods, latent fingerprint imaging chambers, microscopes—optical and scanning electron—and the centerpiece: a gas chromatograph/mass spectrometer, the workhorse of forensic labs.

Any small- or even medium-sized police department in the country might envy the setup, which had cost millions. All paid for by Rhyme himself. The settlement after the accident on a crime scene rendering him a quad had been quite substantial; so were the fees that he charged the NYPD and other law enforcement agencies that hired him. (There were occasional offers from other sources that might produce revenue, such as Hollywood's proposals for TV shows based on the cases he'd worked. *The Man in the Chair* was one suggested title. *Rhyme and Reason* another. Thom had translated his boss's response to these overtures—"Are they out of their fucking minds?"—as, "Mr. Rhyme has asked me to convey his appreciation for your interest. But he's afraid he has too many commitments at this point for a project like that.")

Rhyme now turned his chair around and stared at a delicate and beautiful pocket watch sitting in a holder on the mantelpiece. A Breguet. It happened to be a present from the Watchmaker himself.

His mourning was complex and reflected the dual views of death he'd been thinking of. Certainly there were analytical—forensic—reasons to be troubled by the loss. He'd now never be able to probe the man's mind to his satisfaction. As the nickname suggested, Logan was obsessed with time and timepieces—he actually made watches and clocks—and that was how he plotted out his crimes, with painstaking precision. Ever since their paths first crossed, Rhyme had marveled at how Logan's thought processes worked. He even hoped that the man would allow him a prison visit so that they could talk about the chess-match-like crimes he'd planned out.

Logan's death also left some other, practical concerns. The prosecutor had offered Logan a plea bargain, a reduced sentence in exchange for giving up the names of some of the people who'd hired him and whom he'd worked with; the man clearly had an extensive network of criminal colleagues whose identities the police would like to learn. There were rumors too of plots Logan had put together before he'd gone to prison.

But Logan hadn't bought the DA's deal. And, more

irritating, he'd pleaded guilty, denying Rhyme another chance to learn more about who he was and to identify his family members and associates. Rhyme had even planned to use facial recognition technology and undercover agents to identify those attending the man's trial.

Ultimately, though, Rhyme understood he was taking the man's demise hard because of the second view of death: that connection between them. We're defined and enlivened by what opposes us. And when the Watchmaker died, Lincoln Rhyme died a bit too.

He looked at the other two people in the room. One was the youngster on Rhyme's team, NYPD patrol officer Ron Pulaski, who was packing up the evidence in the City Hall mugging/homicide case.

The other was Rhyme's caregiver, Thom Reston, a handsome, slim man, dressed as immaculately as always. Today: dark-brown slacks with an enviable knife-blade crease, a pale-yellow shirt and a zoological tie in greens and browns; the cloth seemed to sport a simian face or two. Hard to tell. Rhyme himself paid little attention to clothing. His black sweats and green long-sleeve sweater were functional and good insulators. That was all he cared about.

"I want to send flowers," Rhyme now announced.

"Flowers?" Thom asked.

"Yes. Flowers. Send them. People still do that, I assume. Wreaths saying *RIP*, *Rest in Peace*, though what's the point of that? What else're the dead going to be doing? It's a better message than *Good Luck*, don't you think?"

"Send flowers to... Wait. Are you talking about Richard Logan?"

"Of course. Who else has died lately who's flower-worthy?"

Pulaski said, "Hm, Lincoln. 'Flower-worthy.' That is not an expression I would ever imagine you saying."

"Flowers," Rhyme repeated petulantly. "Why is this not registering?"

"And why're you in a bad mood?" Thom asked.

"Old married couple" was a phrase that could be used to describe caregiver and charge.

"I'm hardly in a bad mood. I simply want to send flowers to a funeral home. But nobody's doing it. We can get the name from the hospital that did the autopsy. They'll have to send the corpse to a funeral home. Hospitals don't embalm or cremate."

Pulaski said, "You know, Lincoln. One way to think about it is: There's some justice. You could say the Watchmaker got the death penalty, after all."

Blond and determined and eager, Pulaski had the makings of a fine Crime Scene officer and Rhyme had taken on the job of mentor. Which included not only instruction in forensic science but also getting the kid to use his mind. This he didn't seem to be doing presently. "And just how does a random arterial occlusion, Rookie, equal justice? If the prosecutor in New York State chose not to seek the death penalty, then you might say that a premature death *undermines* justice. Not furthers it."

"I—" the young man stammered, blushing Valentine red.

"Now, Rookie, let's move on from spurious observations. Flowers. Find out when the body's being released from Westchester Memorial and where it's going. I want the flowers there ASAP, whether there's a service or not. With a card from me."

"Saying what?"

"Nothing other than my name."

"Flowers?" Amelia Sachs's voice echoed from the hallway leading to the kitchen and the back door of the town house. She walked into the parlor, nodding greetings.

"Lincoln's going to send flowers to the funeral home. For Richard Logan. I mean, I am."

She hung her dark jacket on a hook in the hall. She was in close-fitting black jeans, a yellow sweater and a black wool sport coat. The only indication of her rank as a police detective was a Glock riding high on her hip, though the leap from weapon to law enforcer was a tentative deduction at best. To look at the tall, slim redhead—with abundant straight hair—you might guess she was a fashion model. Which she had been, before joining the NYPD.

Sachs walked closer and kissed Rhyme on the lips. She tasted of lipstick and smelled of gunshot residue; she'd been to the range that morning.

Thinking of cosmetics, Rhyme recalled that the victim of the City Hall mugging/murder had shaved just before leaving the office; nearly invisible bits of shave cream and tiny rods of beard had been found adhering to his neck and cheek. He'd also recently sprayed or rubbed on aftershave. In their analysis, while Rhyme had been noting those facts, potentially helpful for the investigation, Sachs had grown still. She'd said, "So he was going out that night, a date probably—you wouldn't shave for guy friends. You know, Rhyme, if he hadn't spent that last five minutes in the restroom, the timing would've changed. And everything would've turned out different. He'd've survived the night. And maybe gone on to live a long, full life."

Or he might've gotten into his car drunk and rammed a bus filled with schoolchildren.

Waste of time, playing the fate game.

View of Death Number One, View of Death Number Two.

"You know the funeral home?" Sachs asked.

"Not yet."

Not knowing he was about to be arrested, and believing he was minutes away from murdering Rhyme, Logan had made a promise that he would spare Sachs's life. Perhaps this clemency was another of the reasons for Rhyme's mourning the man's death.

Thom nodded to Sachs. "Coffee? Anything else?"

"Just coffee, thanks."

"Lincoln?"

The criminalist shook his head.

When the aide returned with the cup, he handed it off to Sachs, who thanked him. While the nerves throughout most of his body were insensate, Rhyme's gustatory cells, aka taste buds, worked just fine and he appreciated that Thom Reston made a very good cup of coffee. No capsules or pre-ground, and the word "instant" was not in his vocabulary.

With a wry smile the aide said to her, "So. What do you think of Lincoln's emotional side?"

She warmed her hands around the coffee. "No, Thom, I think there's method to his sentiment."

Ah, that's my Sachs. Always thinking. This was one

of the reasons he loved her. Their eyes met. Rhyme knew that his smile, minuscule though it was, probably matched hers muscle for muscle.

Sachs continued, "The Watchmaker was always an enigma. We didn't know much about him—he had California connections was about all. Some distant family we could never track down, no associates. This might be the chance to find people who knew and worked with him—legitimately or in his criminal projects. Right, Rhyme?"

One hundred percent, he reflected.

Rhyme said to Pulaski, "And when you find out the funeral home, I want you there."

"Me?"

"Your first undercover assignment."

"Not first," he corrected.

"First at a funeral."

"That's true. Who should I be?"

Rhyme said the first thing that came to his mind. "Harold Pigeon."

"Harry Pigeon?"

"I was thinking of birds." A nod toward the nest of peregrine falcons on Rhyme's window ledge, huddled down against the storm. They tended to nest lower in bad weather.

"Harry Pigeon." The patrolman was shaking his head. "No way."

Sachs laughed. Rhyme grimaced. "I don't care. Make up your own damn name."

"Stan Walesa. My mother's father."

"Perfect." An impatient look at a box in the corner of the room. "There. Get one of those."

"What's that?"

Sachs explained, "Prepaid mobiles. We keep a half dozen of them here for ops like this."

The young officer collected one. "A Nokia. Hm. Flip phone. State of the art." He said this with consummate sarcasm.

Before he dialed, Sachs said, "Just be sure to memorize the number first, so if somebody asks for it you don't fumble."

"Sure. Good." Pulaski used the prepaid to dial his personal phone and noted the number then stepped away to make the call.

Sachs and Rhyme turned to the crime scene report on the City Hall mugging case and made some edits.

A moment later Pulaski returned. "The hospital said they're waiting to hear about where to send the body. The morgue director said he's expecting a call in the next few hours."

Rhyme looked him over. "You up for this?"

"I suppose. Sure."

"If there's a service, you'll go. If not, you'll get to the funeral home at the same time as whoever's picking up the remains. The flowers from me'll be there. Now, *that'll* be a conversation starter—the man Richard Logan tried to kill and who put him in jail sends flowers to his funeral."

"Who's Walesa supposed to be?"

"An associate of Logan's. Exactly who, I'm not sure. I'll have to think it through. But it should be somebody inscrutable, dangerous." He scowled. "I wish you didn't look like an altar boy. Were you one?"

"My brother and I both."

"Well, practice looking scruffy."

"Don't forget dangerous," Sachs said, "though that's going to be tougher than inscrutable."

Thom brought Rhyme some coffee in a straw-fitted cup. Apparently the aide had noticed him glancing at Sachs's. Rhyme thanked him with a nod.

Old married couple...

Thom said, "I feel better now, Lincoln. For a minute I really did think I was seeing a soft side. It was disorienting. But knowing that you're just setting up a sting to spy on the family of a corpse? It's restored my faith in you."

Rhyme grumbled, "It's simply logical. You know, I'm really not the cold fish everyone thinks I am."

Though ironically Rhyme *did* want to send the flowers in part for a sentimental reason: to pay his respects to a worthy adversary. He suspected the Watchmaker would have done the same for him.

Views of Death Number One and Number Two were not, of course, mutually exclusive.

Rhyme then cocked his head.

"What?" Sachs asked.

"What's the temperature?"

"Right around freezing."

"So there's ice on the steps outside?" Rhyme's town house sported both stairs and a disabled-accessible ramp.

"There was in the back," she said. "Front too, I assume."

"We're about to have a visitor, I think."

Though the evidence was largely anecdotal, Rhyme had come to believe that, after the accident that deprived him of so many sensations, those that survived grew more discerning. Hearing in particular. He'd detected someone crunching up the front steps.

A moment later the buzzer sounded and Thom went to answer it.

The sound and pacing of the footsteps as the visitor entered the hallway and made for the parlor revealed who'd come a-callin'.

"Lon."

Detective First-Grade Lon Sellitto turned the corner and strode through the archway, pulling off his Burberry overcoat. It was tan and vivid with the creases that characterized most of Sellitto's garb, thanks to his portly physique and careless posture. Rhyme wondered why he didn't stick with dark clothing, which wouldn't show the rumpling so much. Though once the overcoat was off and tossed over a rattan chair, Rhyme noted that the navy-blue suit displayed its own troubled texture.

"Bad out there," Sellitto muttered. He dusted his thinning gray-black hair, and a few dots of sleet bailed. His eyes followed them down. He'd tracked in muck and ice. "Sorry about that."

Thom said not to worry and brought him a cup of coffee.

"Bad," the detective repeated, toasting his hands on the mug the way Sachs had. Eyes toward the window, on the other side of which, beyond the falcons, you could see sleet and mist and black branches. And little else of Central Park.

Rhyme didn't get out much and in any event weather meant nothing to him, unless it was a factor in a crime scene.

Or it helped his early warning system detect visitors.

"It's pretty much finished," Rhyme said, nodding at the City Hall mugging/murder crime scene report.

"Yeah, yeah, that's not why I'm here." Spoken nearly as one word.

Rhyme's attention hovered. Sellitto was a senior officer in Major Cases and if he wasn't here to pick up the report, then maybe something else, something more interesting, was on the horizon. More propitious was that Sellitto had seen a tray of pastry, homemade by Thom, and had turned away as if the crullers were invisible. His mission here had to be urgent.

And, therefore, engaging.

"We got a call, a homicide down in SoHo, Linc. Earlier today. We drew straws and you got picked. Hope you're free."

"How can I get picked if I never drew a straw?"

A sip of coffee. Ignoring Rhyme. "It's a tough one."

"I'm listening."

"Woman was abducted from the basement of the store where she worked. Some boutique. Killer dragged her through an access door and into a tunnel under the building."

Rhyme knew that beneath SoHo was a warren of tunnels, dug years ago for transporting goods from one industrial building to another. He'd always believed it was just a matter of time before somebody used the place as a killing zone.

"Sexual assault?"

"No, Amelia," Sellitto said. "The perp's a tattoo artist, seems. And from what the respondings said a pretty fucking good one. He gave her a tat. Only he didn't use ink. He used poison."

Rhyme had been a forensic scientist for many years; his mind often made accurate deductions from scant preliminary details. But inferences work only when the facts presented echo those from the past. This information was unique in Rhyme's memory and didn't become a springboard for any theories whatsoever.

"What was the toxin he used?"

"They don't know. This just happened, I was saying. We're holding the scene."

"More, Lon. The design? That he tattooed on her?"

"It was some words, they said."

The intrigue factor swelled. "Do you know what they were?"

"The respondings didn't say. But they told me it looked like only part of a sentence. And you can guess what that means."

"He's going to need more victims," Rhyme said, glancing Sachs's way. "So he can send the rest of his message."

CHAPTER 4

Sellitto was explaining:

"Her name was Chloe Moore, twenty-six. Part-time actress—had a few roles in commercials and some walk-ons in thrillers. Working in the boutique to pay the bills."

Sachs asked the standard questions: Boyfriend trouble, husband trouble, triangle troubles?

"Naw, none of the above that we could tell. I just started uniforms canvassing around the area but the prelim from the clerks in the store and her roommate is that she hung with a good crowd. Was pretty conservative. No boyfriend presently and no bad breakups."

Rhyme was curious. "Any tattoos, other than the one he killed her with?"

"I dunno. First responders scooted as soon as the ME's team declared DCDS."

Deceased, declared dead at scene. The official pronouncement by the city's medical examiner that got the crime scene clock running and started all kinds of procedures. Once DCDS was called, there was no reason for anybody to remain on the scene; Rhyme insisted that responders get the hell out to avoid contamination. "Good," he told Sellitto. He realized he was fully in View of Death Number One mode.

"All right, Sachs. Where are we with the city worker?" A glance at the City Hall report.

"I'd say it's done. Still awaiting customer records about people who bought that brand of knife. But I'm betting the perp didn't use his credit card or fill out a questionnaire about customer service. Not much else to do."

"Agreed. Okay, Lon, we'll take it. Though I can't help but note you didn't really ask. You just drew a straw on my behalf and stomped slush in here, assuming I'd get on board."

"What the fuck else'd you be doing, Linc? Cross-country skiing through Central Park?"

Rhyme liked it when people didn't shrink from his condition, when they weren't afraid to make jokes like Sellitto's. He grew furious when people treated him like a broken doll.

There, there, poor you…

Sellitto said, "I've called Crime Scene in Queens. There's an RRV en route. They'll let you take the lead, Amelia."

"On my way." She pulled on a wool scarf and gloves. She picked another leather jacket from the hook, longer, mid-thigh. In all their years together Rhyme had never seen her wear a full overcoat. Leather jackets or sport, that was about it. Rarely a windbreaker, either, unless she was undercover or on a tac op.

The wind again blasted the ancient windows, rattling

the frames, and Rhyme nearly told Sachs to drive carefully—she piloted a classic rear-wheel-drive muscle car that behaved badly on ice—but telling Sachs to be cautious was like telling Rhyme to be patient; it just wasn't going to happen.

"You want help?" Pulaski asked.

Rhyme debated. He asked Sachs, "You need him?"

"Don't know. Probably not. Single victim, confined area."

"For the time being, Rookie, you'll be our undercover mourner. Stay here. We'll think about your cover story."

"Sure, Lincoln."

"I'll call in from the scene," Sachs said, grabbing the black canvas bag that contained the com unit she used to talk with Rhyme from the field, and hurried out the door. There was a brief howl of wind, then silence after the creak and slam.

Rhyme noticed that Sellitto was rubbing his eyes. His face was gray and he radiated exhaustion.

The detective saw that Rhyme was looking his way. He said, "That fucking Met case. Not getting any sleep. Who breaks into someplace where you got a billion dollars' worth of art, pokes around and walks out empty-handed? Doesn't make sense."

Last week at least three very clever perps had broken into the Metropolitan Museum of Art on Fifth Avenue after hours. Video cameras were disabled and alarms suspended—no easy matter—but an exhaustive crime scene search had revealed that the perps had spent time in two areas. One was the antique arms hall of the museum, which was open to the public—a schoolboy's delight, filled with swords, battle-axes, armor and hundreds of other clever devices meant to excise body parts; and the museum's basement archives, storage and restoration areas. They'd left after several hours and remotely reactivated the alarms. The intrusion had been pieced together by computer analysis of the security shutdowns and physical examinations of the rooms after the alarm breaches had been discovered.

It was almost as if the burglars were like many tourists who visit the museum: They'd seen enough, grown bored and headed for a nearby restaurant or bar.

A complete inventory revealed that while some items in both areas had been moved, the intruders hadn't perped a single painting, collectible or packet of Post-it notes. Crime Scene investigators—Rhyme and Sachs hadn't worked that one—had been overwhelmed by the amount of space to search; the arms and armor displays were bad enough but the network of archives and storage rooms extended underground, far east, well past Fifth Avenue.

The case had been demanding time-wise but Sellitto had admitted that wasn't the worst of it. "Politics. Fucking politics." He'd gone on to explain, "Hizzoner thinks it looks bad his prize jewel got busted into. Which translates: My crew's working overtime and hell with everything else. We've got terror threats in the city, Linc. Code red or orange or whatever color means we're fucked. We got Tony Soprano wannabes. And what'm I doing? I'm looking through every dusty room, at every weird canvas and every naked statue in the basement. I mean, every. You wanna know my feeling about art, Linc?"

"What, Lon?" Rhyme had asked.

"Fuck art. That's my feeling."

But now the new case—the poison tat artist—had derailed the old, to the detective's apparent relief. "You got a killer like this, the papers ain't gonna be happy we're spending our time worried about paintings of water lilies and statues of Greek gods with little dicks. You see those statues, Linc? Some of those guys . . . Really, you'd think the model'd tell the sculptor to add an inch or two."

He sat heavily in a chair, sipped more coffee. Still no interest in the pastry.

Rhyme then frowned. "One thing, Lon?"

"Yeah?"

"When did this tattoo killing happen exactly?"

"TOD was about an hour ago. Ninety minutes maybe."

Rhyme was confused. "You couldn't get the tox screen back in that time."

"Naw, the ME said a couple hours."

"Then how'd they'd know she was poisoned?"

"Oh, one of the medics ran a tox case a couple years ago. He said you could tell from the rictus on the face and the posture. The pain, you know. It's one hell of a way to die. We gotta get this son of a bitch, Linc."

CHAPTER 5

Great. Just great.

Standing in the basement of the SoHo boutique where Chloe Moore had been abducted, Amelia Sachs grimaced, leaning down and peering into the utility room. She was staring at the narrow tunnel that led from that room to the crime scene itself, apparently a larger tunnel, where Chloe had been killed.

The body was just visible and brightly lit by lamps the first responders had set up.

Palms sweating, Sachs continued to peer through the tiny shaft she'd have to crawl through.

Just great.

She stepped back into the cellar and inhaled two or three times, sucking moldy, fuel-oil-scented air deep into her lungs. Years ago, Lincoln Rhyme had created a database of layouts of underground areas in New York, assembled from the Department of Buildings and other city government agencies. She'd downloaded one through a secure app on her iPhone and—with dismay—reviewed the layout before her.

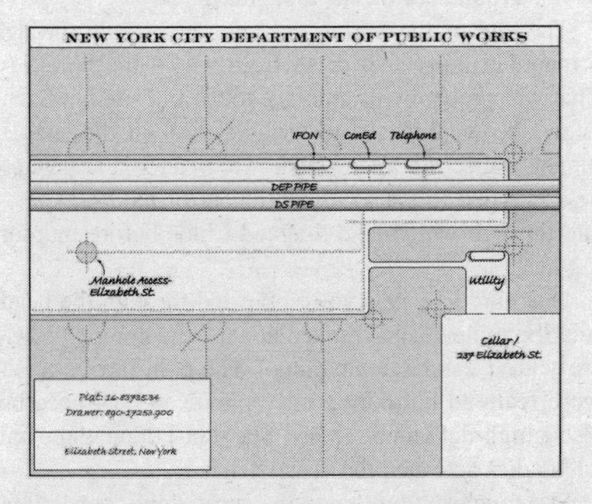

Where did phobias come from? Sachs wondered. Some childhood trauma, some genetic imprinting that discourages us from petting poisonous snakes or cavorting on mountain ledges?

Serpents and heights weren't her problem; claustrophobia was. If she believed in former lives, which she didn't, Sachs could imagine that she, in an earlier incarnation, had been buried alive. Or, if you followed the logic of karma, more likely she'd been a vindictive queen who'd slowly interred her rivals as they begged for mercy.

Sachs, close to six feet tall, looked at the chart of her nemesis: the twenty-eight- or thirty-inch-diameter tunnel from the utility room to the bigger transport tunnel, the site of the killing. The narrow passage was, according to the chart, twenty-three feet long.

It's a round coffin, she thought.

The site of the killing was also accessible through a manhole thirty feet or so from where the body lay. That was probably his entrance to the kill site but Sachs knew she would have to wriggle through the smaller tunnel, collecting trace as she went, since that's where he'd crawled to get to the basement of the boutique—and through which he'd dragged Chloe before murdering her.

"Sachs?" Rhyme's voice crackled through the headset. She jumped and cranked down the volume. "Where are you? I can't see anything." The com device Sachs wore featured not only a microphone and earpiece but also a high-def video camera. She'd just donned the unit and hadn't activated the visual yet.

She touched a button on the surprisingly small camera—about the size of a double-A battery—and heard, "Okay." Then a grumbled "It's still pretty dark."

"Because it *is* dark. I'm in a basement—and about to climb into a tunnel the size of a breadbasket."

"I've never actually seen a breadbasket," he replied. "I'm not sure they exist." Rhyme was always in good humor when approaching a new crime scene. "Well, let's get going. Scan around. Let's see what we've got."

She often wore this equipment when she searched a scene. Rhyme would offer suggestions—many fewer now than when they began working together and she was a novice. He also liked to keep an eye out for her safety, though he never admitted that. Rhyme insisted that officers search a scene solo—too much distraction otherwise. The best forensic experts bonded with the scene psychologically. They *became* the victim, *became* the perp—and accordingly located evidence they might have missed. That connection didn't happen, or it didn't happen as easily, when somebody else searched with you. But being alone was a risk. It was surprising how many times a scene turned hot: The perp returned, or remained, and attacked the officer walking the grid. It even happened that, though the perp was long gone, another, unrelated attack might occur. Sachs had once been assaulted by a homeless man, a schizophrenic who thought she'd come to steal his imaginary dog.

She looked into the utility room once more, to give Rhyme a view, and then gazed through the tunnel of hell briefly.

"Ah," he said, now understanding her concern. "Breadbasket."

Sachs made the final adjustments to her outfit. She was dressed in a white Tyvek jumpsuit, hood and booties. Because poison had been the apparent weapon, she wore an N95 respirator. The toxin had been injected, the first responders reported, via the tattoo gun, and there seemed to be no airborne chemicals to worry about that they'd noted. Still, why take the chance?

Footsteps behind her, someone approaching through the moldy, damp basement of Chez Nord.

She glanced back at an attractive Crime Scene officer who'd be helping process the boutique. Sachs had known Jean Eagleston for years; she was one of the stars of the CS operation. Eagleston had been interviewing the store manager, who'd found the body. Sachs had wanted to know if the manager had entered the scene itself—where Chloe's body lay—to check on her employee.

But Eagleston said, "No. She noticed the door was open and looked into the utility room, saw the vic lying there. That was enough for her. She didn't go any farther."

Can't blame the manager, Sachs reflected. Even if one wasn't claustrophobic, who'd go into a deserted tunnel with an apparent murder victim lying on the ground and, possibly, the killer still there?

"How could she see the victim?" Rhyme asked. He'd overheard the conversation. "I thought I could see spotlights there now, from the medics. But wasn't it dark then?"

Sachs relayed the question. But the Crime Scene officer didn't know. "All the manager said was that she could see inside."

Rhyme said, "Well, we'll find out."

Eagleston added, "The only other people at the kill site were one responding uniform and one medic. But they backed out as soon as they confirmed death. To wait for us. I've got samples of their shoes, so we can eliminate any footprints. They tell me they didn't touch anything other than the vic, to check on her condition. And the EMT was gloved."

So contamination of the scene—the introduction of evidence unrelated to the crime itself or the perp—would be minimal. That was one advantage of a murder in a hellhole like this. A crime on the street could have dozens of contaminants, from blowing dust, pouring rain and fierce sleet (like today) to passersby and even souvenir seekers. One of the worst contaminants was fellow officers, especially brass grandstanding if reporters were present and eager to grab a video bite to slap on the twenty-four-hour news cycle.

One more glance at the circular coffin.

Okay, Amelia Sachs thought: Knuckle time...

A phrase of her father's. The man had also been a cop, a beat patrolman working the Deuce—Midtown South; back then Times Square was like Deadwood in the 1800s. "Knuckle time" referred to those moments when you have to go up against your worst fears.

Breadbasket...

Sachs returned to the access door and climbed through it and down into the utility room below the cellar. Then she took the evidence collection gear bag from the other officer. Sachs said, "You search the basement, Jean?"

"I'll do it now," Eagleston said. "And then get everything into the RRV."

They'd done a fast examination of the cellar. But it was apparent that the perp had spent minimal time there. He'd grabbed Chloe, subdued her somehow and dragged her to the access door; her heel marks were visible.

Sachs set the heavy bag on the floor and opened it. She photographed and gathered evidence from the utility room, although, as with the basement, the perp and the victim would have spent little time here; he'd've wanted to get her out of sight as soon as possible. She bagged and tagged the trace and set the plastic and paper containers on the floor in the cellar for the other Crime Scene officers to cart to the RRV.

Then Sachs turned to the tiny shaft's opening, eyeing

it the way one would glance at the muzzle of a pistol in the hand of a desperate perp.

Breadbasket...

She didn't move. Heard her heart thudding.

"Sachs." Rhyme's voice sounded in her ear.

She didn't respond.

He said softly, "I understand. But."

Meaning: Get your ass going.

Fair enough.

"Got it, Rhyme. No worries."

Knuckle time...

It's not that long, she reassured herself. Twenty-three feet. That's nothing. Though, for some reason, Sachs found herself passionately resenting that extra yard past twenty. As she approached, her palms began to sweat fiercely; her scalp too, which itched more than normally. She wanted to scratch, dig her nails into her skin, her cuticles. A nervous habit. The urge rose when she was unable to move—in all senses, physically, emotionally, mentally.

Static: How she hated that state.

Her breath came in short intervals and shallow gulps.

Orienting, she touched her Glock 17, which was strapped to her hip. A slight risk of contamination from the weapon, even if she didn't blow anyone away, but there was that security issue again. And if any perp had a good scenario for hurting a Crime Scene officer, it would be here.

She hooked a nylon tie-down to her evidence collection gear bag and the other end to her weapon belt, to drag it behind her.

Moving forward. Pausing before the opening. Then

on her hands and knees. And into the shaft. Sachs wanted to leave the headlamp off—seeing the tunnel would be more troubling than concentrating on the goal at the end of it—but she was afraid she'd miss some evidence.

Click.

Under the halogen beam, the metal coffin seemed to shrink and wrap its steel shell around her.

Get. Going.

She extracted a dog hair roller from her pocket and swept the floor of the tunnel as she went forward. She knew that because of the confining space and presumably the perp's struggling with the victim, it was likely that he had shed evidence, so she concentrated on seams and rough spots that might dislodge trace.

She thought of a joke, a Steven Wright routine from years ago. "I went into the hospital for an MRI. I wanted to find out if I had claustrophobia."

But the humor and the distraction of the task didn't keep the panic away for long.

She was a third of the way through when fear stabbed her gut, a frozen blade.

Get out, get out, get out!

Teeth chattering despite the intense heat around her.

"You're doing fine, Sachs." Rhyme's voice in her ear.

She appreciated his baritone reassurance, but didn't want it. She dialed down the volume on the headset.

Another few feet. Breathe, breathe.

Concentrate on the job. Sachs tried. But her hands were unsteady and she dropped the roller, the clang of the handle on the metal skin of the tunnel nearly making her gag.

And then the madness of fear snagged her. Sachs got it into her head that the unknown subject—the unsub—was behind her. He had somehow perched on the ceiling of the utility room and dropped to the floor after her. Why didn't I look up? You always look up at crime scenes! Fuck.

Then a tug.

She gasped.

It wasn't the gear bag tethered to her. No, it was the perp's hand! He was going to tie her down here. And then fill the tunnel with dirt, slowly, starting with her feet. Or flood it. She'd heard dripping water in the utility space; there'd been pipes. He'd undo the plug, open a valve. She'd drown, screaming, as the water rose and she couldn't move forward or back.

No!

That this scenario was improbable at best didn't matter. Fear made the unlikely, even the impossible, more than plausible. Fear itself was now another occupant of the tunnel, breathing, kissing, teasing, sliding its wormy arms around her body.

She raged at herself: Don't be crazy. You're in danger of getting fucking shot when you climb out the other end of the tunnel, not getting suffocated by some nonexistent perp with a nonexistent shovel. There is no way the tunnel's going to collapse and hold you as tight as a mouse in a snake's grip. That's not. Going. To. Happen.

But then that image itself—snake and pinned mouse—screwed itself into her thoughts, and the panic notched up a level more.

Shit. I'm going to lose it. I'm going to fucking lose it.

The end of the tunnel was now about eight feet

away, and she was possessed by an urge to sprint out. But she couldn't. There wasn't enough room for her to move any more quickly than at a crawl. Anyway, Sachs knew that trying to hurry would be a disaster. For one thing, she could miss clues. And it would ratchet up the dread, which would explode within her like a chain reaction.

Also: Moving faster out of the tunnel, even if she could, would be a defeat.

Her personal mantra—which she'd also learned from her father—was: When you move they can't getcha.

But sometimes, like now, they'll getcha when you *do* move.

So, stop, she commanded.

And she did. Came to a complete halt. And felt the perverse arms of the tunnel embrace her ever more tightly.

Panic, cresting like waves. Panic, stabbing like that frosty knife.

Don't move. Be with it, she told herself. Face it. Confront it. She believed Rhyme was speaking to her, the whisper of his faraway voice perplexed or concerned or impatient. All of those, probably. Down went the headset volume to silence.

Breathe.

She did. In, out. Eyes open, looking at the disk of light ahead of her, relief a mile ahead. No, not that. *Evidence*. Look for evidence. That's your job. Her gaze took in the metal shell, inches away.

And the sting of panic began to detach. Not vanish completely. But it grew loose.

Okay. She continued through the tunnel, rolling for

trace, collecting scraps, intentionally moving more slowly than before.

And finally her head emerged. Shoulders.

Birthing, she laughed to herself, a pallid sound, and blinked sweat from her eyes.

Then she rolled quickly into the larger tunnel; it seemed like a concert hall by comparison. Rising to a crouch, drawing her Glock.

But no intruders were aiming weapons her way, not in the immediate area at least. The spotlights over the body were blinding and there might have been a threat in the blackness beyond but she immediately shone her Maglite in that direction. No threat.

Rising, Sachs tugged the gear bag out of the tunnel. She gazed around and saw that the diagram from Rhyme's database was accurate. This tunnel resembled a mine shaft, about twenty feet square. It disappeared west into the darkness. She knew it had been used, a century ago, for transporting wheeled carts of goods to and from factories and warehouses. Now the damp, moldy passageway served only as New York City infrastructure. There were large iron pipes overhead and smaller aluminum and PVC ones, perhaps for electrical cables, running through old battered junction boxes. Newer conduits sprouted from bright-yellow boxes secured with thick padlocks. These were embossed with the letters *IFON*. She didn't know what that meant. The iron pipes were stamped *NYC DS* and *NYC DEP*—Sanitation and Environmental Protection, the agencies that handled the city's sewage and water supply, respectively.

She realized it was utterly quiet and turned up the volume of the radio.

"—the hell is going on?"

"Sorry, Rhyme," Sachs said. "Had to concentrate."

He was silent for a moment. Then he seemed to get it—her wrestling with the breadbasket. "All right. Well. The scene secure, as far as you can tell?"

"The immediate scene." The tunnel was bricked off to the east but she glanced again at the darkness to the west.

"Turn one of the spotlights that way. It'll blind anybody trying to target you. And you'll be able to see him coming before he sees you."

The first responders had brought two halogen lamps on tripods, connected to large batteries. She turned one in the direction Rhyme had suggested and squinted as she examined the receding tunnel.

No indication of threats.

Sachs hoped there'd be no firefight. The big pipe overhead, newly installed, it seemed—the one stamped *DEP*—appeared to be thick iron; her rounds in the Glock, hollow-points, wouldn't break through the metal. But if the unsub returned with guns a-blazing he might be loaded with armor-piercing slugs, which could pierce the pipe. Because of the huge water pressure inside, she imagined, a rupture might create an explosion like a massive load of C-4.

And even if he had regular bullets, the ricochet off metal and the stone and brick walls could kill or wound as easily as a direct shot.

She peered up the tunnel again and saw no movement.

"Clear, Rhyme."

"Good. So. Let's get going." He'd turned impatient.

Sachs already was. Wanted to get out of here.

"Start with the vic."

She's more than a victim, Rhyme, Sachs thought. She has a name. Chloe Moore. She was a twenty-six-year-old salesclerk in a boutique that sold clothing with loose strands escaping the stitching. She was working for near minimum wage because she was intoxicated on New York. On acting. On being twenty-six. And God bless her for it.

And she didn't deserve to die. Much less like this.

Sachs slipped rubber bands on her booties, the balls of the feet, to differentiate her footfalls from those of the perp and the first responders—whose footgear she would photograph later as control samples.

She walked closer to the body. Chloe lay on her back, her blouse tugged up to below the breasts. Sachs noted that even in death her round, pretty face was distorted with an asymmetrical grimace, muscles taut. It was evidence of the obvious pain she'd experienced, pain tapering to death. She'd frothed at the mouth. And vomited copiously. The smell was vile. Sachs mentally moved past it.

Chloe's hands, under her body, were secured in cheap handcuffs. With a universal key Sachs removed these. The victim's ankles were duct-taped. With surgical scissors Sachs clipped the tape and bagged the gray, dusty strips. She scraped beneath the young woman's deep-purple fingernails, noting fibers and bits of off-white flecks. Perhaps she'd fought him and if so bits of valuable trace, even skin, might be present; if her killer was in the CODIS DNA database, they might have his identity in hours.

Rhyme said, "I want to see the tattoo, Sachs."

Sachs noted a small blue tattoo on Chloe's neck, to the right and near the shoulder, but that had been done long ago. Besides, it was easy to see which one the killer had done. She knelt down and trained her eyes, and the camera, on Chloe's abdomen.

"There it is, Rhyme."

The criminalist whispered, "His message. Well, *part* of his message. What do you think it means?"

But given the sparse letters, Sachs realized, his question had to be rhetorical.

CHAPTER 6

The two words were about six inches long and ran horizontally one inch above the woman's navel.

Although he'd presumably used poison, not ink, the inflamed wound, swollen and scarring, was easy enough to read.

the second

"All right," Rhyme said, " 'the second.' And the border, the scalloped lines. Wonder what those are about?"

Sachs commented, "They're not as swollen as the letters. Maybe there was no poison in them. They look like wounds, not tattoos. And, Rhyme, look at the characters."

"How well done they are?"

"Exactly. Calligraphy. He's good. He knows what he's doing."

"And another observation. It must've taken some time to do. He could've written them crudely. Or just injected her with the poison. Or shot her for that matter. What's his game?"

Sachs had a thought. "And if it took awhile, that means she was in pain for a long time."

"Well, yes, you can see the pain reaction but I have a feeling that was later. She couldn't have been conscious while he was writing his message. Even if she wasn't trying to get away, the involuntary movement would've ruined his handiwork. No, he subdued her somehow. Any trauma to the head?"

She examined the woman's scalp carefully and looked under her blouse, front and back. "No. And I don't see any signs of Taser barbs. No stun gun welts...Ah but, Rhyme, see that?" She pointed out a tiny red dot on her neck.

"Injection site?"

"I think so. I'm guessing sedative, not poison. There's no sign of any swelling or other irritation that toxin would cause."

"The blood work will tell us."

Sachs took pictures of the wound and then bent down and swabbed the area carefully, lifting trace. Then the rest of her body too and the ground around her. It was likely that a perp this diligent would have worn gloves—it certainly appeared that way. Yet valuable evidence from even a gloved-and-gowned perp could still easily be transferred to the victim or crime scene.

Edmond Locard, the French criminalist who lived a century before, formulated the Exchange Principle: that every time a crime occurs there is a transfer of evidence between criminal and scene, or criminal and victim. That evidence (which he referred to as "dust") might be very, very difficult to detect and collect but it exists, for the diligent and innovative forensic scientist.

"There's something odd, Rhyme."

"Odd?" A splinter of disdain for the artless word. "Go ahead, Sachs."

"I'm using only one of the first responders' spotlights—the other's pointed up the tunnel. But there're two shadows on the ground." She looked up and walked in a slow circle to get a clear view. "Ah, there's another light near the ceiling, between those two pipes. It looks like a flashlight."

"Not left by the first responders?"

"What cop or medic is going to give up his Maglite?"

The big black tubed flashlights that all cops and firemen carried around were invaluable—great sources of illumination and they doubled as bone-breaking weapons in a clutch.

But she noted it wasn't one of those expensive models. This was cheap, plastic.

"It's taped to the pipe. Duct tape. Why would he leave a light here, Rhyme?"

"That explains it."

"What?" she asked.

"How the store manager found the body. The flashlight. Our perp wanted to make sure we found the message from our sponsor."

The words seemed a little flippant to Sachs but she'd always suspected that much of Rhyme's gruff façade and sardonic delivery were defense mechanisms. Still, she wondered if he raised the barricade of protection higher than he needed to.

She preferred to leave her heart unguarded.

"I'll collect it last," Sachs told him. "Every bit of light helps."

She then walked the grid, which was Rhyme's phrase for searching a crime scene. The grid pattern was the most comprehensive approach in looking for evidence and assessing what had occurred. This technique involved walking slowly across the scene, then pivoting and moving one step to the right or left and returning to the far side. You did this over and over until you'd covered the entire space. Then you turned ninety degrees and covered the same ground again, perpendicular. Like mowing a lawn twice.

And with each step you paused to look up and down and side-to-side.

You smelled the scene too, though in this case Sachs couldn't detect more than Chloe's vomit. No methane or feces, which surprised her, considering that one of the pipes here was connected to the city's sewage system.

The search didn't reveal much. Whatever implements the perp had brought with him he'd taken—aside from the flashlight, cuffs and strips of duct tape. She did make one find, a small ball of crumpled paper, slightly yellowed.

"What's that, Sachs? I can't see very clearly."

She explained.

"Leave it as is; we'll open it back here. Might have trace inside. Wonder if it's from her."

Her. The vic.

Chloe Moore.

"Or maybe from the perp, Rhyme," Sachs added. "I found what looked like fibers of newsprint or paper under her nails."

"Ah, that could be good. Did they fight? Did she grab something of his? Or did *he* want something she had and rip it from her fingers—while she struggled to hold on to it? Questions, questions, questions."

Using additional adhesive rollers and a small handheld vacuum, Sachs continued the search. Once these samples had been bagged and tagged she used a separate vacuum and a new roller to collect trace from places as far away as possible from where Chloe lay and where the unsub had walked. These were control samples—natural trace from this area. If analysis back at the lab revealed, for example, a clay-rich earth near one of the unsub's footprints, which didn't match any control specimens, they could conclude that he possibly lived or worked in or had some other connection to a locale loaded with clay. A small step toward finding the perp . . . but a step nonetheless.

"I can't see many shoe or boot marks, Sachs."

She was looking down at where he'd stood or walked. "I can make a few out but they're not going to be much help. He wore booties."

"Brother," the criminalist muttered.

"I'll roll the footfalls for trace but there's no point in electrostaticking."

She was referring to using sheets of plastic to lift shoe prints, in much the same way that fingerprints were lifted. The resulting tread pattern not only could suggest shoe size but might show up in the massive footwear database that Rhyme had created at the NYPD years ago and that was still maintained.

"And I'd say he had his own adhesive roller with him. It looks like he swept up as much as he could."

"I hate smart perps."

No, he didn't, Sachs reflected. He hated stupid perps. Smart bad guys were challenging and a lot more fun. Sachs was smiling beneath her N95 respirator. "I'm going silent, Rhyme. Checking the entrance and exit routes. The manhole."

She withdrew her Maglite, flicked on the powerful beam and continued down the tunnel toward the ladder leading up to the manhole, noting not a bit of pain from the persistent arthritis that had plagued her for decades; recent surgery had worked its magic. Her shadow, cast by the halogen spot behind, stretched out before her, a distorted silhouette of a puppet. The ground beneath the manhole was damp. This strongly suggested it was how he'd gotten into and out of the tunnel. She noted this fact then continued on, into the darker reaches beyond.

With every step she grew more uneasy. Not because of claustrophobia this time—the tunnel was unpleasant but spacious compared with the entrance shaft. No, her discomfort was because she'd seen the perp's handiwork—the tattoo, the cutting, the poison. The combination of his cleverness, his calculation and his perverse choice of weaponry all conspired to suggest that he'd be more than happy to hang around and try to stop his pursuers.

The flashlight in her left hand, while her right hovered near the Glock, Sachs continued down the increasingly dark tunnel, listening for footsteps, an attacker's breaths, the click and snap of weapons chambering rounds or going off safety or cocking.

None of those, though she did hear a hum from one or more of the conduits or the yellow IFON boxes, whatever they were. A faint rush from the water pipe.

Then a scrape, a flash of movement.

Glock out, left hand gripping the Maglite, forearm supporting her shooting hand. The muzzle followed the beam. Sweeping, scanning.

Where?

Sweat again, a thud of heartbeat.

But very different from claustrophobia's chest-thudding panic. This wasn't sour fear. This was anticipation. This was hunt. And Amelia Sachs lived for the sensation.

She was ready, finger off the guard, onto the trigger but feather-light; it takes little more than a breath to fire a Glock.

Scanning, scanning...

Where? Where?

Snap...

She crouched.

And the rat stepped blithely out from behind a pillar, looked her way with faint concern and turned, scuttling away.

Thank you, Sachs thought, following in the creature's general direction—toward the distant end of the tunnel. If the rodent was walking so nonchalantly over the ground it was unlikely that an ambush awaited. She continued walking. In sixty or so yards she came to the bricked-up wall. There were no footprints here—normal or bootied—so their perp hadn't wandered this way. She returned to the ladder.

She lifted out her cell phone—encased in uncontaminating plastic—and called up the GPS map. She noted that she was underneath Elizabeth Street, to the east, near a curb.

Sachs turned up the volume to the headset.

"I'm below the manhole, Rhyme." She explained where it was and that this was likely how he'd gotten in, because there was significant moisture on the ground; the manhole cover had probably been removed in the past hour or so, she estimated. "It's muddy here." A sigh. "But there're no prints. Naturally. Let's have Lon canvass the stores and apartments around the neighborhood, see if anybody saw the perp."

"I'll call him. And get any security CCTVs too." Rhyme was skeptical about witnesses. He believed that in most cases they were more trouble than they were worth. They misobserved, they had bad memories—intentionally and otherwise—and they were afraid to get involved. A digital image was far more trustworthy. This was not necessarily Sachs's opinion.

She swabbed the rungs as she climbed the ladder, depositing the adhesive cloth in plastic evidence collection bags.

At the top she rolled the underside of the manhole cover, then lifted a small alternative light source unit to check for fingerprints on the surface. ALS's are lamps that use colors of the spectrum of visible light (like blue or green) combined with filters to make apparent evidence that's impossible to see under regular bulbs or in daylight. ALS sources also include invisible light, like ultraviolet, which makes certain substances glow.

The scan, of course, revealed no prints or other evidence from their unsub. She tested the manhole cover's weight; she could budge it but just barely. She supposed it weighed close to a hundred pounds. Hard to push open but not impossible for a strong individual.

She heard traffic overhead, the *shushhh* sound of tires cutting through the wet sleet. She was shining the light straight up, looking into the hole through which a worker would feed the hook to remove the cover. Wondering about marks that might lead them to a particular brand of tool the perp had used. Nothing.

It was then that an eye appeared through the hole.

Jesus . . . Sachs gasped.

Inches away, on the street above her, someone was crouching and looking through the pry hole, down at her. For a moment nothing happened; then the eye narrowed, as if the person—a man, she sensed—squinted slightly. Maybe smiling, maybe troubled, maybe curious about why a flashlight beam was firing out of a manhole cover in SoHo.

She spun away, thinking he'd seat a pistol muzzle in the hole and start shooting. The Maglite plummeted as she grabbed the top rung with both hands to keep from falling.

"Rhyme!"

"What? What's going on? You're moving fast."

"There's somebody on top of the manhole. Did you call Lon?"

"Just. You think it's the perp?"

"Could be. Call Dispatch! Get somebody to Elizabeth Street now!"

"I'm calling, Sachs."

She pressed her hand against the bottom of the manhole and pushed. Once. Twice. All her strength.

The slab of iron rose a fraction of an inch. But no more.

Rhyme said, "I got Lon. He's sending uniforms. Some ESU too. They're on their way, getting close."

"I think he's gone. I tried to open the cover, Rhyme. I couldn't. Goddamn it. I couldn't. I was looking right at him. Had to be the perp. Who else'd kneel down in the middle of the street on a day like this and look through a manhole cover?"

She tried once more, thinking maybe he'd been squatting on it and that's what had prevented her from pushing it up. But, no, it was impossible to move with her one free hand.

Shit.

"Sachs?"

"Go ahead."

Rhyme said, "An officer saw somebody at the manhole in a short dark-gray coat, stocking cap. He took off running. Disappeared into the crowd on Broadway. White male. Slim or medium build."

"Damn it!" she muttered. "It was him! Why run otherwise? Have somebody pop the cover, Rhyme!"

"Look, there're plenty of people after him. Keep walking the grid. That's our priority."

Heart racing, she shoved a palm into the manhole cover once more. Convinced, unreasonably, that if she could get to the surface she could find him, even if the others couldn't.

She pictured his eye. She saw the narrowing lid.

She believed the perp was laughing at her, taunting her because she hadn't been able to open the cover.

What color was the iris? she wondered. Green, gray,

hazel? She hadn't thought to register the color. This lapse infuriated her.

"One thing occurs to me." Rhyme brought her back to earth.

"What's that?"

"We know that's how he got into the tunnel—through the manhole. And that means he'd've rigged a work zone. He'd have cones and tape or a barricade of some kind. And that might show up on video."

"Or a witness might've seen."

"Well. Yes, maybe. For what *that's* worth."

Sachs climbed back down the ladder and returned to the victim. She had done a fast sex-crime exam of Chloe's body but now wanded it with the ALS to look for traces of the three S's present in most sexual assault cases—semen, sweat and saliva.

Negative on that but it was clear he'd probed her skin with his gloved fingers—or at least the abdomen, arms, neck and face. No other parts of the body appeared to have been touched.

She used the light on the rest of the scene—from the manhole to the breadbasket—and found nothing.

All that remained for her was removing the flashlight that the unsub had left as a beacon.

"Sachs," Rhyme called.

"Yeah?"

"Why don't we have city workers pop the manhole and you come out that way? You'll have to search that area on the street anyway. We know that's how he got in—and he was there about five minutes ago. Could have some trace."

But she knew he was suggesting this so she could avoid the smaller of the two tunnels.

The circular coffin...

Sachs glanced at the black maw. It seemed even smaller now. "It's a thought, Rhyme. But I think I'll go out the way I came in."

She'd beaten the fear once; she wasn't going to let it win now.

Using a rough ledge on the brick wall to support her weight, she stepped up and boosted herself to within reach of the unsub's flashlight. She took the surgical scissors from her pocket and cut the tape.

Pulling it down, she dislodged a handful of grayish powder, which she suddenly realized the perp had set as a trap for the Crime Scene officers. *That's* why he'd left the light! The material poured straight into her eyes and, desperately brushing it away, she dislodged the N95 respirator and inhaled a good amount of the toxin.

"No!"

Choking, choking, drowning on the stinging powder. Instantly the fierce burn began. She fell to the ground and stumbled back, nearly tripping over Chloe's body.

Rhyme's voice was in her ear. "Sachs! What was that? I couldn't see."

She struggled to inhale, to clear the poison from her lungs. The barbed hooks scorched her windpipe and eyes and nose. She ripped off the face mask, spitting, aware that she was contaminating the scene but she was unable to stop.

Rhyme was shouting. It was hard for her to hear but she believed he was calling, probably into his phone, "Medics down there! Now!" And "I don't care." And "Poison control. Fast."

But then she heard nothing more than the choking that consumed her.

CHAPTER 7

Making his way back to his workshop off Canal Street, west of Chinatown, Billy Haven was thinking of Lovely Girl again, after the memories of her face, her voice, her touch had arisen so persistently during the modding session with Little Miss Pretentious, Chloe.

He was thinking of the letters he'd done: *the second.* The borders too.

Yes, a good work.

A Billy Mod.

He'd changed out of his coveralls, which had possibly been contaminated with poison (why take chances?), and had slipped them into a garbage bag. Then into a Dumpster a long way from the boutique. He was wearing street clothes underneath: black jeans, leather gloves, also black. His dark-gray wool coat. It was short—to mid-thigh. Warm enough and not so long that it might interfere if he had to sprint to escape from someone, which as Billy was well aware was a very real possibility at some point over the next few days.

On his head was the ski mask scrunched up as a stocking cap, also wool. He looked like any other young man in Manhattan heading to his apartment through the freezing rain, hunched over, cold.

Lovely Girl…

Billy remembered seeing her for the first time, years ago. It was a photograph, actually, not even the girl herself. But he'd fallen in love—yes, yes, at first sight. Not long after that his aunt had commented, "Oh, she's a lovely girl. You could do much worse than her."

Billy immediately took that as the pet name for his beloved.

The girl with the beautiful ivory skin.

Squinting against the crappy weather—the wind firing BBs of ice and freezing rain into his face—Billy pulled his coat tighter around him. Concentrated on avoiding icy patches. This was difficult.

It was now some hours after he'd finished with Chloe in the tunnel beneath the boutique. He'd stayed around the area, sticking to the shadows, to see about the police. Somebody had dialed 911 about five minutes after Billy had climbed from the manhole on Elizabeth Street. The cops had arrived en masse and Billy'd checked out their procedures. He'd observed and taken mental notes and would later transcribe his thoughts. The Modification Commandments weren't phrased like the biblical ones, of course. But if they had been, one would be: *Know thy enemy as thyself.*

Trudging along, walking carefully. He was young and in good shape, agile, but he could hardly afford a fall. A broken arm would be disastrous.

Billy's workshop wasn't far from the site of the attack but he was walking a complicated route back home, making sure no one had seen him near the manhole and followed.

He went around the block once, then twice, just to be safe, and returned to the ugly, squat four-story former warehouse, now a quasi-residential structure. That is, quasi-*legal*. Or maybe completely illegal. We're talking New York City real estate, after all. He'd paid cash for the short-term rental, a lot of cash. The agent had taken the money with a smile and made a point of not asking a single question.

Not that it mattered. He'd been prepared to spin a credible tale, forged documents included.

Thou shalt have thy cover story memorized.

Then, confirming that the sidewalk was deserted, Billy walked down a short flight of stairs to his front door. Three clicks of three locks and he was inside, exchanging as a soundtrack the horns of irritated drivers stuck in Chinatown by the bad weather for the rumble and brake squeals of the subway cars running directly beneath his place.

Sounds from underground. Comforting.

Billy pressed a switch and anemic lights filled the twenty-by-twenty-five-foot space—a combination living room/bedroom/kitchen/everything else. The room had a certain dungeon feel to it. One wall was exposed brick, the others halfhearted Sheetrock. He had a second rental, farther north, a safe house, which he'd planned to stay in more frequently than here on his mission for the Modification, but the workshop had turned out to be more comfortable than the safe house, which was smack on a busy street populated with the sort of people he despised.

The workbench was filled with glassware, books, syringes, tattooing machine parts, plastic bags, tools. Dozens of books on toxins and thousands of downloaded Internet documents, some more helpful than others. The *Field Guide to Poisonous Plants* was sumptuously illustrated but didn't have quite the same level of useful information as the underground blog called *Knock 'Em Off: A Dozen Deadly Recipes for When the Revolution Comes and We Have to Fight Back!!*

All arranged neatly on the workspace, just like in his tattoo parlor back home. The far corner of the room was pooled in the cool glow of ultraviolet lights that illuminated eight terrariums. He walked to these now and examined the plants inside. The leaves and flowers comforted him, they were so reminiscent of home. Pinks and whites and purples and greens in a thousand shades. The colors fought against the dull mud tone of the city, whose hateful spirit lapped every minute at Billy Haven's heart. Suitcases contained changes of clothes and toiletries. A gym bag held several thousand dollars, sorted by denomination but wrinkled and old and very untraceable.

He watered the plants and spent just a few minutes finishing a sketch of one of them, an interesting configuration of leaves and twigs. Even as someone who'd drawn all his life, Billy sometimes wondered where the urge came from. Sometimes he just *had* to take out a pencil or crayon and transfer something from life, which would fade, into something that would not. That would last forever.

He'd sketched Lovely Girl a thousand times.

The pencil now drooped in his hand and he left a sketch of a branch half-finished, tossing the pad aside.

Lovely Girl...

He couldn't think of her without hearing his uncle's somber voice, the deep baritone: "Billy. There's something I have to tell you." His uncle had gripped him by the shoulders and looked down into his eyes. "Something's happened."

And, with those simple, horrific words, he'd learned she was gone.

Billy's parents too were gone—though their deaths had been years ago and he'd come to some terms with the loss.

Lovely Girl's? No, never.

She was going to be his companion forever. She was going to be his wife, the mother of his children. She was going to be the one to save him from the past, from all the bad, from the Oleander Room.

Gone, just like that.

But today he wasn't thinking so much of the terrible news, wasn't thinking of the unfairness of what had happened, though what had happened was unfair.

And he wasn't thinking of the cruelty, though what had happened was cruel.

No, at the moment, having just finished inking Chloe, Billy was thinking that he was on the road to the end of pain.

The Modification was under way.

Billy sat at the rickety table in the kitchen area of the basement apartment and removed from his shirt pocket the pages of the book he'd found that morning.

He'd found out about the volume weeks ago and knew he needed a copy to complete his planning for the Modification. It was out of print, though he'd found a few copies he could buy online through secondhand-book sellers. But he couldn't very well order one with a credit card and have it shipped to his home. So Billy had been searching through used-book shops and libraries. There were two copies in the New York Public Library but they weren't where they should have been in the stacks, in either the Mid-Manhattan branch or a satellite branch in Queens.

He'd tried once more, though, earlier today, returning on a whim to the library on Fifth Avenue.

And there it was, reshelved and Dewey Decimaled into place. He'd pulled the book down from the shelf and stood in the shadows, skimming.

Badly written, he'd noted from his brief read in the stacks. An absurdly sensational cover in black, white, red. Both the style and the graphics helped explain the out-of-print status. But what the book contained? Just what he needed, filling in portions of the plan the way flats or round shader needles filled in the space between the outlines of a tattoo.

Billy had worried about getting the book out of the library—he couldn't check it out, of course. And there'd been security cameras near the photocopiers. In the end he'd decided to slice out the chapter he wanted with a razor blade. He'd cut deep and carefully before hiding the book away so no one else could find it. He knew that the book itself probably contained a chip in the spine that would have set off the alarm at the front doors if he'd tried to walk out with the entire thing. Still, he'd flipped through all the pages he'd stolen, one by one, to search for a second chip. There'd been none and he'd walked out of the library without a blare of alarms.

Now he was eager to study the pages in depth, to help with the rest of the plans for the Modification. But as he spread them out before him, he frowned. What was this? The first page was damaged, the corner torn off. He was sure that he'd extracted all of them intact from the spine without any tearing. Then he glanced at his shirt breast pocket and noted it too was torn. He remembered that Chloe'd ripped his coveralls when she'd fought back. That's what had happened. She'd torn both the clothing and the page.

The damage wasn't too bad though and only a small portion was missing. He now read carefully. Once, twice. The third time he took notes and tucked them into the Commandments.

Helpful. Good. Real helpful.

Setting the pages aside, he answered some texts, received some. Staying in touch with the outside world.

Now it was cleaning time.

No one appreciates germs, bacteria and viruses more than a skin artist. Billy wasn't the least concerned about infecting his victims—that was, really, the whole point of the Modification—but he was very concerned about infecting *himself*, with whatever tainted the blood of his clients and, in particular, with the wonderful substances he was using in place of ink.

He walked to the sink and unzipped his backpack. Pulling on thick gloves, he took the American Eagle tattoo machine to the sink and dismantled it. He drained the tubes of liquid and washed them in two separate gallon buckets of water, rinsing them several times and drying them with a Conair. The water he poured into a hole he'd cut in the floor, letting it soak into the earth beneath the building. He didn't want to flush or pour the water down the drain. That little matter of evidence, once again.

This bath was just the start, however. He cleaned each piece of the machine with alcohol (which sanitizes only; it doesn't sterilize). He placed the parts in an ultrasonic bath of disinfectants. After that he sealed them in bags and popped them into the autoclave—a sterilization oven. Normally needles are disposed of but these were very special ones and hard to come by. He autoclaved these too.

Of course, only part of this was to protect himself from poisons and infection. There was a second reason as well: What better way to sever any link between you and your victims than to burn it away at 130 degrees Celsius?

Might even make hash of your "dust" theory, don't you think, Monsieur Locard?

CHAPTER 8

Lincoln Rhyme was waiting impatiently.

He asked Thom, "And Amelia?"

The aide hung up the landline. "I can't get through."

"Goddamn it. What do you mean you can't get through? Which hospital?"

"Manhattan General."

"Call them again."

"I just did. I can't get through to the main line. There're some problems."

"That's ridiculous. It's a hospital. Call nine one one."

"You can't call emergency to find out the status of a patient."

"I'll call."

But just then the front door buzzer sounded. Rhyme bluntly ordered Thom to "answer the damn bell" and a moment later he heard footsteps in the front hall.

Two Crime Scene officers, the ones who'd assisted Sachs at the Chez Nord boutique homicide, entered the parlor, carrying large milk crates, filled with evidence bags—both plastic and paper. Rhyme knew the woman, Detective Jean Eagleston, who nodded a greeting, which he acknowledged with a nod. The other officer, a large bodybuilder of a cop, said, "Captain Rhyme, an honor to work with you."

"Decommissioned," Rhyme muttered. He was noting that the weather must have been worse—the officers' jackets were dusted with ice and snow. He saw that they'd wrapped the evidence cartons in cellophane. Good.

"How is Amelia?" asked Eagleston.

"We don't know anything yet," Rhyme said.

"Anything else we can do," said her burly male partner, "just give us a call. Where do you want them?" A nod at the crates.

"Give them to Mel."

Rhyme was referring to the latest member of the team, who'd just arrived.

Slim and with a retiring demeanor, NYPD Detective Mel Cooper was a renowned forensic lab man. Rhyme would bully anybody, all the way up to and including the mayor, to get Cooper assigned to him, especially for a case like this, in which toxin seemed to be the murder weapon of choice. With degrees in math, physics and organic chemistry, Cooper was perfect for the investigation.

The CS tech cop nodded greetings to Eagleston and her partner, who like him were based in the massive NYPD Crime Scene operation in Queens. Despite the ornery weather and a chill in the parlor, Cooper wore a short-sleeve white shirt along with baggy black slacks, giving him the appearance of a crusading Mormon elder or high school science professor. His shoes were Hush Puppies. People usually weren't surprised to learn that he lived with his mother; the astonishment came when they met his towering and beautiful Scandinavian girlfriend, a professor at Columbia. The two were champion ballroom dancers.

Cooper, in a lab coat, latex gloves, goggles and mask, gestured to an empty evidence examination table. His colleagues set the cartons on it and nodded goodbye, then went out once more into the storm.

"You too, Rookie. Let's see what we've got."

Ron Pulaski pulled on similar protective gear and stepped up to the table to help.

"Careful," Rhyme said unnecessarily, since Pulaski had done this a hundred times and no one was more careful than he with evidence.

But the criminalist was distracted; his thoughts returned to Amelia Sachs. Why wasn't she calling? He remembered seeing the powder pour into the video camera lens at the same time it hit her face. Remembered her choking.

And then: a key in the door.

A moment later. Wind. A cough. A throat clearing.

"Well?" Rhyme called.

Amelia Sachs turned the corner of the parlor, pulling her jacket off. A pause. More coughing.

"Well?" he repeated. "Are you all right?"

Her response was to guzzle a bottle of water that Thom handed to her.

"Thanks," she said to the young man. Then to Rhyme: "Fine," her low sultry voice lower and sultrier than normal. "More or less."

Rhyme had known that she hadn't been poisoned. He'd spoken to the EMT who specialized in toxins as she'd been shepherded to Manhattan General Medical Center. Her symptoms were atypical for poisoning, the med tech had reported, and by the time the ambulance got to Emergency, her only symptoms were a racking cough and teary eyes, which had been flushed several times with water. The unsub had created a less-than-lethal trap—but the irritant might have blinded her or played havoc with the lungs.

"What was it, Sachs?"

She now explained that swabs of mucous membranes and a lightning-fast blood workup had revealed that the "poison" was dust composed mostly of ferric oxide.

"Rust."

"That's what they said."

Pulling the duct tape off an old metal armature to which the unsub had attached the flashlight had dislodged a handful of the stuff, which had poured into Sachs's face.

As a criminalist, Rhyme was familiar with Fe_2O_3, more commonly known as iron (III) oxide. Rust is a wonderful trace element since it has adhesive properties and transfers readily from perp to victim and vice versa. It can be toxic but only in massive quantities—more than 2500 mg/m^3. Its presence didn't seem weaponized to Rhyme. He instructed Pulaski to call the city works department to find out if ferric oxide dust was common in the tunnels.

"Yep," the young officer reported after he'd hung up. "The city's been installing pipes throughout Manhattan—because of the new water tunnel. Some of the fixtures they're cutting away are a hundred and fifty years old. End up with a lot of dust. All their workers're wearing face masks, it's so bad."

So the unsub had just happened to pick one of those fixtures to mount the flashlight to.

Sachs coughed some more, drank another gulp or two of water. "I'm pissed off I got careless."

"And, Sachs, we *were* waiting for a phone call."

"I tried. The lines were out. One of the EMS techs said it was an Internet problem that's also screwing up the phone switches. Been happening for the past couple of days. Some dispute between the hardwire cable companies and the new fiber-optic ones. Turf wars. Even talking sabotage."

Rhyme's look said, Who cares?

With another faint, alto cough Sachs suited up for the lab and walked to the evidence cartons.

"Let's get our charts going." Rhyme nodded at the cluster of large whiteboards, standing about like herons on their stalky legs. They used these to list the evidence in a case. Only one was filled: the case of the recent mugging turned homicide near City Hall. The man who'd shaved so carefully for his date before stepping out into the street to be robbed and killed.

Sachs moved that board to the corner and pulled a clean one front and center. She took an erasable marker and asked, "What do we call him?"

"November fifth's today's date. Let's stick with our tradition. Unknown Subject Eleven-Five."

Sachs coughed once, nodded, then wrote in her precise script:

237 ELIZABETH STREET

— Victim: Chloe Moore

Rhyme glanced at the white space. "Now let's start filling it in."

CHAPTER 9

Before they could get to the evidence, though, the doorbell hummed once more.

With the familiar howl of wind and Gatling gun of falling ice, the door opened and closed. Lon Sellitto walked into the parlor, stomping his feet and missing the rug.

"Getting worse. Man. What a mess."

Rhyme ignored the AccuWeather. "The security videos?"

Referring to any surveillance cameras on Elizabeth Street, near the manhole that the perp had used to gain access to the murder site. And where he had apparently been spying on Sachs.

"Zip."

Rhyme grimaced.

"But there was a witness."

Another sour look from Rhyme.

"I don't blame you, Linc. But it's all we got. Guy coming home from his shift saw somebody beside the manhole about ten minutes before nine one one got the call."

"Home from his shift," Rhyme said cynically. "So your wit was tired."

"Yeah, and a fucking tired witness who sees the perp is better than a fresh one who doesn't."

"In which case he wouldn't be a witness," Rhyme replied. A glance at the evidence board. Then: "The manhole was open?"

"Right. Orange cones and warning tape around it."

Rhyme said, "Like I thought. So he pops the cover with a hook, sets up the cones, climbs down, kills the vic and leaves." He turned to Sachs. "Moisture at the bottom of the ladder, you said. So he kept it open the whole time. What happened to the cones and tape?"

"None there," Sachs said. "Not when I came out."

"He's not going to be leaving them lying around nearby. Too smart for that. Lon, what'd your wit say about him, the perp?"

"White male, stocking cap, thigh-length dark coat. Black or dark backpack. Didn't see a lot of the face. Pretty much the same descrip of the guy by the manhole when Amelia was running the scene underneath."

The one peering at Sachs. Who'd escaped into the crowds on Broadway.

"What about the evidence on the street?"

"In that storm?" Sachs replied.

Weather was one of the classic contaminators of evidence and one of the most pernicious. And at the scene near the manhole, there'd been another problem: The emergency workers' footprints and gear would have destroyed any remaining evidence as they raced to get Sachs into the ambulance after the apparent poisoning from the trap that wasn't.

"So we'll write off that portion of the scene and concentrate on underground. First, the basement of the boutique?"

Jean Eagleston and her partner had photographed and searched the basement and the small utility room that opened onto it but they'd found very little. Mel Cooper examined the trace they'd collected. He reported, "Matches the samples from the cellar. Nothing helpful there."

"All right. The big question: What's the tox screen result? COD?"

They were starting with the assumption that the cause of death was poison but that wouldn't be known until the medical examiner completed the analysis. Sachs had called and harangued the chief examiner to send over a preliminary report ASAP. They needed both the toxin and whatever sedative, as seemed likely, the perp had injected into Chloe to subdue her. Sachs had sealed the urgency by pointing out that they believed this murder was the start of a serial killing spree. The ME, she reported, had sounded as burdened as doctors generally do, especially city employee doctors, but he'd promised to move the Chloe Moore case to the front of the queue.

Again piqued by impatience, Rhyme said, "Sachs, you swabbed the site of the tattoo?"

"Sure."

"Run that, Mel, and let's see if we can get a head start on the poison."

"Will do." The tool Cooper used for this analysis was the gas chromatograph/mass spectrometer—two large, joined instruments sitting in the corner of the parlor. The gas chromatography portion of the equipment analyzes an unknown sample of trace by separating out each chemical it contains based on its volatility—that is, how long it takes to evaporate. The GC separates the component parts; the second device, the mass spectrometer, *identifies* the substances by comparing their unique structure with a database of known chemicals.

Running the noisy, hot machine—the samples are, in effect, burned—Cooper soon got results.

"Cicutoxin."

The NYPD had an extensive toxin database, which Rhyme had used occasionally when he'd been head of Investigation Resources—the old name for Crime Scene—though murder by poison was uncommon then and even less so now. Cooper scrolled through the entry for this substance. He paraphrased: "Comes from the water hemlock plant. Attacks the central nervous system. She'd have experienced severe nausea, vomiting, we can see frothing too. Muscle twitching." He looked up. "It's one of the most deadly plants in North America."

He nodded at the machine. "And it's been distilled. No instances of that level of concentration ever recorded. Usually takes some time to die after it's been administered. At these levels? She'd be dead in a half hour, little longer, maybe."

"What some famous Greek killed himself with, right?" Pulaski asked.

Cooper said, "Not quite. Different strain of hemlock. Both in the carrot family, though."

"Who cares about Socrates?" Rhyme snapped. "Let's focus here. Does anyone *else*, aside from me, notice anything troubling about the source?"

Sachs said, "He could've found it in any field or swamp in the country."

"Exactly."

A *commercial* substance that was toxic, like those used in industrial processes and easily purchased on the open market, might be traced to a manufacturer and onward to a buyer. Some even had chemical tags that might lead investigators to receipts with the perp's name on them. But that wasn't going to happen if he dug his weapon out of the ground.

Impossible to narrow down beyond regions of the country. And presumably, the month being November, he'd picked the plant long ago. Or might even have grown it in a hothouse in his basement.

Equally troubling was the fact that he'd somehow reduced it to create a particularly virulent form of the toxin.

Ron Pulaski happened to be standing beside the whiteboard. Rhyme said to him, "Add that to the list in your concise handwriting, Rookie, which the Sisters of the Skeptical Heart Church would be exceedingly proud of."

Rhyme's mood had improved considerably now that there were challenges to confront, mysteries to unravel... and they had some evidence to work with.

Sachs continued, "Now, there were no friction ridges."

Rhyme hadn't expected fingerprints. No, the perp was too smart for that.

"As far as hairs—I found some from rats and some from Chloe but no others, so I'm guessing headgear beyond the stocking cap."

Close-fitting hats tended to dislodge hair more than keep it from falling out, especially wool or nylon, since the wearer would tend to scratch or rub itches. Rhyme guessed the perp had known this and taken other, more careful precautions to keep his fiber and DNA evidence to himself.

She continued, "The prelim for sexual assault was negative—though the ME might find something else. But genitals and secondary sexual locations don't seem to have been touched. Aside from her abdomen"—she nodded at the photographs—"she was fully clothed. But when I wanded her with the ALS, I found something interesting: dozens of places where he touched her skin, stroked it. More than just to pull it taut to do the tattoo. And she had a small tat on her neck. A flower." Sachs displayed the picture on Rhyme's high-def monitor. "He rubbed that a few times, the wand showed."

"But not sexual touching?" Sellitto muttered.

"Not traditionally sexual," Sachs pointed out. "He may have a fetish or paraphilia. My impression was that he was fascinated with her skin. He wanted to touch it. Or was driven to, maybe."

Rhyme said, "Driven? That's getting a little fishy for me, Sachs. A little soft. Noted but let's move on."

They began on the trace, analyzing substances that Sachs had found near the body and comparing them with control samples from the tunnel, trying to isolate those that were unique to the unsub.

Cooper kept the GC/MS humming.

"Okay, clustered together we have nitric oxide, ozone, iron, manganese, nickel, silver, beryllium, chlorinated hydrocarbon, acetylene."

Rhyme nodded. "Those were near the body?"

"Right." Sachs looked over her detailed chain-of-custody card, which noted the exact location of each sample.

"Hm." He grunted.

"What, Linc?" Sellitto asked.

"Those're materials used in welding. Oxy-fuel welding primarily. Maybe it came from our unsub but I'd think it's more likely from the workers who installed the pipe. But we'll put it on the chart anyway."

Cooper selected another sample. It was from the floor near the ladder that led to the manhole. When this analysis was finished the tech frowned. "Well, may have something here."

Rhyme sighed. Then share it, please and thank you, his burdened smile said.

But Cooper wasn't going to be rushed. He carefully read the mass spectrum—the computer analysis from the instruments.

"It's tetrodotoxin."

Rhyme was intrigued. "Ah, yes, we *do* have something here. Another possible murder weapon."

"Poison, Linc?" Sellitto asked.

Mel Cooper said, "Oh, indeed. A good one. It's from the ovaries of the puffer fish, the fugu. It's a neurotoxin with no known antidote. Sixty or so people a year die in Japan—from eating it intentionally. In low dosages you can get a high . . . and survive to pay the check. And for what it's worth, tetrodotoxin's the zombie drug."

"The what?" Sellitto asked, barking a laugh.

"Really." Cooper added, "Like out of a movie. In the Caribbean people take it to lower their heart rate and respiration to the point where they appear dead. Then they come back to life. Either for religious rituals or as scams. Anthropologists think it might've been the source for the zombie myth."

"*Just* the diversion for a slow Saturday night in Haiti," Rhyme muttered. "Could we stay on point here? On focus? On message?"

Cooper pushed his glasses higher up on his nose. "Very small trace amounts."

"Unless the ME finds some in Chloe's blood, he's probably planning to use it for a future attack." Rhyme grimaced. "And where the hell did he get it? Probably caught a puffer fish himself. Like he grew the hemlock. Keep going, Mel."

Cooper was reading from Sachs's chain-of-custody card. "Here's something from a footprint—one of his, I'm assuming, since it was near the ladder. And obscured."

Booties...

"That's right," Sachs confirmed. Cooper showed her the mass spectrum and she nodded, then transcribed the computer analysis to the whiteboard.

— Stercobilin, urea 9.3 g/L, chloride 1.87 g/L, sodium 1.17 g/L, potassium 0.750 g/L, creatinine 0.670 g/L

"Crap," Rhyme muttered.

"What's wrong?" Pulaski asked.

"No," Rhyme replied. "Literally. Fecal material. Why that? Why there? Any deductions, boys and girls?"

"There were DS—Sanitation—pipes overhead, but I

couldn't see any sewage on the ground or walls. Probably didn't come from there."

"Dog-walking park?" Sellitto suggested. "Or he owns a dog."

"Please," Rhyme said, refraining from rolling his eyes. "Those chemicals suggest human shit. We could run DNA but that would be a waste of time. Excuse the choice of words."

"Bathroom just before he came to the scene?"

"Possibly, Rookie, but I'd guess he picked it up from the sewage system somewhere. I think it tells us he's been spending a lot of time in underground New York. That's his killing zone. He's comfortable there. And if there wasn't any effluence at the Chloe Moore scene, that means he's already got a few other sites selected. And it also tells us he's scoping out his targets ahead of time."

The parlor phone rang. Sachs answered. Had a brief conversation and then hung up. "The ME. Yep, COD was cicutoxin—and no tetrodotoxin. You were right, Mel: This was eight times more concentrated than what you'd find in a natural plant. And he sedated her with propofol. Neck and arm. Two injection sites."

"Prescription drug," Rhyme noted. "You can't grow *that* in your backyard. How did he have access to that? Well, put it on the chart and let's keep going. The tattoo itself. That's what I'm really curious about."

the second

Rhyme gazed at the picture Sachs had taken: inkless but easy to see from the red, inflamed skin. A much clearer image than what he'd viewed through the video camera at the dim crime scene.

"Man," Ron Pulaski said, "it's good."

"I don't know the tattoo world," Rhyme said. "But I wonder if there're only a limited number of artists who could do that in a short period of time."

"I'll hit some of the bigger parlors in town," Sellitto said. "See what I can find."

Rhyme mused, "Those lines." He pointed to the border, scallops above and below the words. "You were right, Sachs. They look cut, not tattooed. Like he used a razor blade or scalpel."

Sellitto muttered, "Just fucking decorations. What a prick."

"On the chart. Don't know what to make of that. Now, the words: 'the second.' Meaning? Thoughts?"

"The second victim?" Pulaski offered.

Sellitto laughed. "This guy ain't really covering up his tracks. We probably woulda heard if there was a number one, don'tcha think? Bet CNN would've caught on."

"Sure, true. Wasn't thinking."

Rhyme regarded the picture. "Not enough to draw conclusions at this point. And what's the rest of the message? My impression is that somebody who knows calligraphy that well also knows spelling and grammar. Lowercase 't' on the article 'the.' So something preceded it. There's no period so something comes after the phrase."

Sachs said, "I wonder if it's a line he made up. Or is it a quotation? A puzzle?"

"No clue...Lon, get some bodies at HQ to search the databases."

"Good idea. Efficient: a task force to find 'the second' in a book or something? You think that's ever appeared before, Linc?"

"First, Lon, aren't air quotes a bit overused? More to the point: How's this? Have them search for the words in famous quotes about crimes, killers, tattoos, underground New York. Tell them to be creative!"

Sellitto muttered, "All right. 'The second.' And for the number—the numeral two—with 'nd' as a suffix."

"Hm," Rhyme muttered, nodding. He hadn't thought of that.

The bulky detective placed a call, rising and walking to the corner of the parlor, and a moment later began barking orders. He disconnected and wandered back.

"Let's keep going," Rhyme said to the others.

After more trace analysis Mel Cooper announced, "We've got several instances of benzalkonium chloride."

"Ah," Rhyme said. "It's a quat. Quaternary ammonium. A basic institutional sanitizer, used mostly where there's particular concern about exposure to bacteria and a vulnerable clientele. School cafeterias, for instance. On the board."

Cooper continued, "Adhesive latex."

Rhyme announced that the product was used in everything from bandages to construction work. "Generic?"

"Yep."

"Naturally," Rhyme grumbled. Forensic scientists vastly preferred brand-name trace—it was more easily sourced.

The tech ran additional tests. After a few minutes he regarded the computer screen. "Good, good. Strong results for a type of stone. Marble. Specifically Inwood marble."

"What form?" Rhyme asked. "Put it up on the screen."

Cooper did and Rhyme found they were looking at dust and grains of various sizes, white, off-white and beige. The tech said, "Fractured. See the edge on that piece in the upper left-hand corner?"

"Sure is," Rhyme offered. "Bake it!"

The tech ran a sample through the GC/MS. He announced, "We're positive for Tovex residue."

Sellitto said, "Tovex? Commercial explosive."

Rhyme was nodding. "Had a feeling we'd find something like that. Used in blasting foundations out of rock. Given the trauma to the marble grains, our unsub picked up that trace at or near a construction site. Someplace where there's a lot of Inwood marble. Call the city for blasting permits, Rookie. And then cross-reference with the geological database of the area. Now, what else?"

The scrapings beneath Chloe Moore's fingernails revealed no skin, only off-white cotton cloth and paper fibers.

Rhyme explained to Sellitto: "Chloe may've fought him and picked those up in the struggle. A shame she didn't get a chunk of his skin. Where's the DNA when you need it? On the board, and let's keep at it."

The duct tape that the unsub had used to bind Chloe's feet was generic; the handcuffs too. And the flashlight—the beacon to reveal his handiwork—was a cheap, plastic variety. Neither that nor the D batteries inside bore fingerprints, and no hairs or other trace adhered, except a bit of adhesive similar to that used on sticky rollers—exactly what Crime Scene officers employed to pick up trace. As Sachs had speculated, he'd probably rolled himself before leaving for the crime scene.

"This boy's even better than I thought," Rhyme said. Dismay mixing with a certain reluctant admiration. "Now, any electrical outlets down there, Sachs? I don't recall."

"No. The spotlights that the first responders set up were battery-powered."

"So his tattoo gun would be battery-operated too. Rookie—when you take a break from your marble quest, find out who makes battery tattoo guns."

Pulaski went back online, saying, "Hopefully, they'll be pretty rare."

"Now, that's going to be interesting."

"What?"

"Finding a tattoo gun that's filled with hope."

"That's filled with... what?"

Sellitto was smiling sourly. He knew what was coming.

Rhyme continued, "That's what 'hopefully' means. Your sentence didn't say 'I hope that portable tattoo guns're rare.' Using 'hopefully' as a disjunct—an opinion by the speaker—is non-standard. English teachers and journalists disapprove."

The young officer's head bobbed. "Lincoln, sometimes I think I've walked into a Quentin Tarantino movie when I'm talking to you."

Rhyme's eyebrows arched. Continue.

Pulaski grumbled, "You know, that scene where two

hit men are going to blow somebody away but they talk and talk and talk for ten minutes about how 'eager' and 'anxious' aren't the same, or how 'disinterested' doesn't mean 'uninterested.' You just want to slap 'em."

Sachs coughed a laugh.

"Those two misuses bother me just as much," Rhyme muttered. "And good job knowing the distinction. Now, that last bit of evidence. That's the one I'm most interested in."

He turned back to the collection bag, thinking he'd have to find out who this Tarantino was.

CHAPTER 10

Mel Cooper carefully opened the sole remaining evidence bag over an examination table. Using tweezers, he extracted the crumpled ball of paper. He began to unwrap it. Slowly.

"Where was it, Amelia?" he asked.

"About three feet from the body. Below one of those yellow boxes."

"I saw those," Rhyme said. "IFON. Electric grid, telephone, I'd guess."

The paper was from the upper corner of a publication, torn out. It was about three inches long, two high. The words on the front, the right-hand page, were these:

ies
that his greatest skill was his ability to anticipate

On the reverse page:

the body was found.

Rhyme looked at Cooper, who was using a Bausch + Lomb microscope to compare the paper fibers from this sample with those found under the victim's fingernails.

"We can associate them. Probably from the same source. And there were no other samples of the cloth fibers under her nails from the scene."

"So the presumption is that she tore the scrap in a struggle with him."

Sellitto asked, "Why'd he have it with him? What was it?"

Rhyme noted that the stock was uncoated, so the scrap was likely not from a magazine. Nor was the paper newsprint, so the source probably wasn't a daily or weekly paper or tabloid.

"It's probably from a book," he announced, staring at the triangular scrap.

"But what'd the scenario be?" Pulaski asked.

"Good question: You mean if the scrap was from the pocket of our unsub and she tore it off while grappling with him, how can the pages be from a book?"

"Right."

"Because I would think he sliced important pages *out of* the book and kept them with him. I want to know what that scrap is from."

"The easy way?" Cooper suggested.

"Oh, Google Books? Right. Or whatever that thing is called, that online service that has ninety percent or however many of the world's books in a database. Sure, give it a shot."

But, unsurprisingly, the search returned no hits. Rhyme didn't know much about how the copyright laws worked but he suspected that there were more than a few authors of books still protected by the U.S. Code that didn't want to share their creative sweat labor royalty-free.

"So, it's the hard way," Rhyme announced. "What do they call that in computer hacking? Brute-force attack?" He reflected for a moment then added, "But we can maybe narrow down the search. Let's see if we can find out *when* it was printed and look for books published around then that deal with—to start—crimes. The word 'bodies' is a hint there. Now let's get a date."

"Carbon dating?" Ron Pulaski asked, drawing a smile from Mel Cooper. "What?" the young officer asked.

"Haven't read my chapter on radiocarbon, Rookie?" Referring to Rhyme's textbook on forensic science.

"Actually I have, Lincoln."

"And?"

Pulaski recited, "Carbon dating is the comparison of non-degrading carbon-12 with degrading carbon-14, which will give an idea of the age of the object being tested. I said 'idea'; I think you said 'approximation.' "

"Ah, well quoted. Just a shame you missed the footnote."

"Oh. There were footnotes?"

"The error factor for carbon dating is thirty to forty years. And that's with recent samples. If our perp had carried around a chapter printed on papyrus or dinosaur hide, the deviation would be greater." Rhyme gestured toward the scrap. "So, no, carbon dating isn't for us."

"At least it would tell us if it was printed in the last thirty or forty years."

"Well, we know *that*," Rhyme snapped. "It was

printed in the nineties, I'm almost certain. I want something more specific."

Now Sellitto was frowning. "How do you know the decade, Linc?"

"The typeface. It's called Myriad. Created by Robert Slimbach and Carol Twombly for Adobe Systems. It became Apple's font."

"It looks like any other sans serif font to me," Sachs said.

"Look at the 'y' descender and the slanting 'e.'"

"You studied that?" asked Pulaski, as if a huge gap in his forensic education threatened to swallow him whole.

Years ago Rhyme had run a kidnapping case in which the perp had crafted a ransom note by cutting letters from a magazine. He'd used characters from editorial headlines as well as from a number of advertisements. Correlating the typefaces from dozens of magazines and advertisers' logos, Rhyme had concluded it was from a particular issue of the *Atlantic Monthly*. A warrant for subscriber lists—and some other evidence—led to the perp's door and the rescue of the victim. He explained this to Pulaski.

"But how do we date it more specifically?" Sellitto asked.

"The ink," Rhyme said.

"Tags?" Cooper asked.

"Doubt it." In the 1960s ink manufacturers began adding tags—chemical markers, in the same way that explosives manufacturers did—so that, in the event of a crime, the ink sample would be easy to trace to a single source or at least to a brand name of ink or pen. (The primary purpose of tagging was to track down forgers, though the markers also nailed a number of kidnappers and psychopathic killers, who left messages at the scenes of their crimes.) But the ink used for book printing, as in this sample, was sold in large batches, which were rarely if ever tagged.

So, Rhyme explained, they needed to compare the composition of this particular ink with those in the NYPD ink database.

"Extract the ink, Mel. Let's find out what it's made out of."

From a rack of tools above the evidence examination tables, Cooper selected a modified hypodermic syringe, the point partially filed down. He poked this through the paper seven times. The resulting tiny disks, all of which contained samples of the ink, he soaked in pyridine to extract the ink itself. He dried the solution to a powdery residue, which he then analyzed.

Cooper and Rhyme looked over the resulting chromatogram—a bar chart of peaks and valleys representing the ink used in the printing of the mysterious book.

By itself, the analysis meant nothing, but running the results through the database revealed that the ink was similar to those used in the production of adult trade books from 1996 through 2000.

"Adult?" Pulaski asked.

"No, not *your* kind of adult books," Sellitto said, laughing.

"My—" The officer was blushing furiously. "Wait."

Rhyme continued, "It means as opposed to juvenile publishing. *Legitimate* books for adults. And the paper? Check acidity."

Cooper ran a basic pH analysis, using a small corner of the paper.

"It's very acidic."

"That means it's from a mass-produced commercial hardcover—not paperback because they're printed on newsprint. And it's commercial because more expensive, limited-edition books are printed on low-acid or acid-free paper.

"Add that to your team's to-do list, Lon. Find the book. I'm leaning toward nonfiction, the aforementioned years. Possibly true crime. And each chapter devoted to a different subject, since he sliced out only what he needed. Have your people start talking to editors, bookstores, crime book collectors . . . and true crime writers themselves. How many could there be?"

"Yeah, yeah, in all the free time they have when they're not browsing for the trillion quotations featuring the words 'the second.' "

"Oh, and by the way, make it a priority. If our unsub went to enough trouble to find a copy of the book, cut out the pages and carry them around with him, I *really* want to know what's in it."

The big detective was looking at the picture of the tattoo once more. He said to Cooper, "Print out a picture of that, willya, Mel? I'll start hitting those tattoo parlors—is that what they still call 'em? Probably 'studio' now. And get me a list of the big ones."

Rhyme watched Cooper print out the picture then go online with the NYC business licensing agency. He downloaded a list of what seemed to be about thirty tattoo businesses. Cooper handed it to the detective.

"That many?" Sellitto grumbled. "Wonderful. I just

can't really get outside enough on these fine fall days." He tossed the list and the photo of the tattoo into his briefcase. Then pulled on his Burberry and dug his wadded gloves from the pocket. Without a farewell he stalked out of the room. Rhyme once again heard the wind briefly as the door opened and slammed shut.

"And, Rookie, how're we coming on the marble?"

The young officer turned to a nearby computer. He read through the screen. "Still going through blasting permits. They're blowing up a lot of stuff in the city at the moment."

"Keep at it."

"You bet. I'll have some answers soon." He turned his gaze to Rhyme. "Hopefully."

"Hopefully?" Rhyme frowned.

"Yep. I'm filled with hope that I don't get any more damn grammar lessons from you, Lincoln."

237 ELIZABETH STREET CRIME SCENE

- Victim: Chloe Moore, 26
  - Probably no connection to Unsub
  - No sexual assault, but touching of skin
- Unsub 11-5
  - White male
  - Slim to medium build
  - Stocking cap
  - Thigh-length dark coat
  - Dark backpack
  - Wore booties
  - No friction ridges

— COD: Poisoning with cicutoxin, introduced into system by tattooing
    — From water hemlock plant
    — No known source
    — Concentrated, eight times normal
— Sedated with propofol
    — How obtained? Access to medical supplies?
— Tattooed with "the second" Old English typeface, surrounded by scallops
    — Part of message?
    — Task force at police HQ checking this out
— Portable tattoo gun used as weapon
    — Model unknown
— Cotton fiber
    — Off-white
    — Probably from Unsub's shirt, torn in struggle
— Page from book, true crime?
    — Probably torn from Unsub's pocket in struggle
    — Probably mass produced hardcover 1996–2000
        ies
        that his greatest skill was his ability to anticipate
      On next page:
        the body was found.
— Possibly used adhesive rollers to remove trace from clothing prior to attack
— Handcuffs
    — Generic, cannot be sourced
— Flashlight
    — Generic, cannot be sourced
— Duct tape
    — Generic, cannot be sourced

- Trace evidence
  - Nitric oxide, ozone, iron manganese, nickel, silver beryllium, chlorinated
    hydrocarbon, acetylene
    - Possibly oxy-fuel welding supplies
  - Tetrodotoxin
    - Fugu fish poison
    - Zombie drug
    - Minute amounts
    - Not used on victim here
  - Stercobilin, urea 9.3 g/L, chloride 1.87 g/L, sodium 1.17 g/L, potassium 0.750 g/L, creatinine 0.670 g/L
    - Fecal material
    - Possibly suggesting interest/obsession in underground
    - From future kill sites underground?
  - Benzalkonium chloride
    - Quaternary ammonium (quat), institutional sanitizer
  - Adhesive latex
    - Used in bandages and construction, other uses too
  - Inwood marble
    - Dust and fine grains
  - Tovex explosive
    - Probably from blast site

CHAPTER 11

"Hey, dude. Take a seat. I'll get to you in a few. You want to check out the booklet there? Find something fun, something to impress the ladies. You're never too old for ink."

The man's eyes alighted on Lon Sellitto's unadorned ring finger and turned back to the young blonde he was speaking to.

The tattoo artist—and owner of the parlor (yeah, *parlor*, not studio)—was early thirties, scrawny as a crab leg. He was wearing well-cut and pressed black jeans and a sleeveless T-shirt, white, immaculate. His dark-blond hair was pulled back in a long ponytail. He had a dandy beard, an elaborate affair that descended from his upper lip in four thin lines of dark silky hair that circled his mouth and reunited on his chin in a spiral. His cheeks were shaved smooth but his sideburns, sharp as hooks, swept forward from his ears. A steel rod descended from his upper ear down to the lobe. Another, smaller, pierced each eyebrow vertically. After the facial hair and the metalwork, the full-color tattoos of Superman on one forearm and Batman on the other were pretty tame.

Sellitto stepped forward.

"A minute, dude, I was saying." He studied the cop for a moment. "You know, for an older guy, a bigger guy—I don't mean any offense—you're a good candidate. Your skin isn't going to sag." His voice faded. "Oh, hey. Look at that."

Sellitto had grown tired of the ramble. He'd thrust his gold shield toward the hipster in a way that was both aggressive and lethargic.

"Okay. Police. You're police?"

The tat artist was sitting on a stool next to a comfortable-looking but well-worn reclining chair of black leather, occupied by the girl he'd been speaking with when Sellitto walked in. She wore excessively tight jeans and a gray tank top over what seemed to be three bras or spaghetti-strap camisoles, or whatever they were called. Pink, green and blue. Her strikingly golden hair was long on the left and crew cut on the right. Pretty face if you could get past the skewed hair and nervous eyes.

"You want to talk to me?" the tattoo artist asked.

"I want to talk to TT Gordon?"

"I'm TT."

"Then I want to talk to you."

Nearby another artist, a chubby thirty-something in cargo pants and T, was working away on another client—a massive bodybuilder—who was lying facedown on a leather bed, the kind a masseur would use. The man was getting an elaborate motorcycle inked on his back.

Both employee and customer looked at Sellitto, who stared back.

They returned to inking and being inked.

The detective shot a glance at Gordon and the girl with the unbalanced hair. She was upset, really bothered. Gordon, though, didn't seem fazed by the cop's presence. The owner of the Sonic Hum-Drum Tattoo Parlor had all his permits in a row and his tax bills paid, the detective knew. He'd checked.

"Let me just finish up here."

Sellitto said, "It's important."

"This's important too," Gordon said, "dude."

"No, dude," Sellitto said. "What you're going to do is sit down over there and answer my questions. Because *my* important is more important than *your* important. And, Miss Gaga, you're gonna have to leave."

She was nodding. Breathless.

"But—" Gordon began.

Sellitto asked bluntly, "You ever hear about section two sixty point twenty-one, New York State Penal Code?"

"I. Uhm. Sure." Gordon nodded matter-of-factly.

"It's a crime to tattoo minors under the age of eighteen and the crime is defined as unlawfully dealing with a child in the second degree." Turning to the client. "How old're you really?" Sellitto barked.

She was crying. "Seventeen. I'm sorry. I just, I didn't, I really, I mean..."

"You want to finish that sentence sometime soon?"

"Please, I just, I mean..."

"Lemme put it this way: Get outta here."

She fled, leaving behind her vinyl leather jacket. As

both Sellitto and Gordon watched, she stopped, debated then snuck back fast, grabbed the garment and vanished again, permanently this time.

Turning to the owner of the store, Sellitto was enjoying himself, though he was also noting that Gordon still wasn't cringing with guilt. Or fear. The detective pushed harder. "That happens to be a class B misdemeanor. Punishable by three months in jail."

Gordon said, "Punishable by *up to* three months in jail but production of an apparently valid identification card is an affirmative defense. Her license? It was really, really good. Top-notch. I believed it was valid. The jury'd believe it was valid."

Sellitto tried not to blink but wasn't very successful.

Gordon continued, "Not that it mattered. I wasn't going to ink her. I was in my Sigmund mode."

Sellitto cocked his head.

"Freud. The doctor is in, kind of thing. She wanted a work, real badly, but I was *counseling* her out of it. She's some kid from Queens or Brooklyn who got dumped by a guy for a slut and was inked with quinto death heads."

"What?"

"Five. Quinto. Death heads, you know. She wanted seven. Septo."

"And how was the therapy going, Doc?"

The man pulled a face. "It was going great—I was talking her out of it. When you walked in. Discouragus interruptus. But I think she's scared off for the time being."

"Talking her out of it?"

"Right. I was making some shit up about inking would ruin her skin. In a few months she'd look ten years older. Which is funny because women in the South

Pacific used to get tattooed because it made them look *younger*. Lips and eyelids. Ouch, yeah. I figured she wouldn't know Samoan customs."

"But you thought she was legal. Then why talk her out of it?"

"Dude. First, I had my doubts about the license. But that wasn't the point. She came in here for all the wrong reasons. You get inked to make a positive statement about yourself. Not for revenge, not to shove it in somebody's face. Not because you want to be that stupid girl with a dragon tattoo. Ink's about who *you* are, not being anybody else. Get it?"

Not really, Sellitto's expression said.

But Gordon continued, "You saw her hair, the goth makeup? Well, despite all that, she was *not* a candidate for inking. She had a Hello Kitty purse, for Christ's sake. And a Saint Timothy's cross around her neck. In your day, you would've called her the girl next door, you know, going to the malt shop."

My day? Malt? Still, Sellitto found himself leaning reluctantly toward the veracity of his story.

"Besides, I didn't have a big enough pussy ball for her," the young man said, grinning. Pushing Sellitto some.

"A...?"

He explained: a tennis ball you gave to customers you didn't think could handle the pain of the tattooing process. "That kid couldn't take it. But, you gonna get inked, you gotta have the pain. Them's the rules: pain and blood. The commitment, dude. Get it? So what can I do you for, now that I know there's no, you know, midlife crisis involved."

The detective grumbled. "You ever say 'Dig it' instead of 'Get it'?"

" 'Dig it.' From your day."

"From my day," Sellitto said. "Me and the beatniks."

TT Gordon laughed.

"There's a case we're working on. I need some help."

"I guess. Gimme one minute." Gordon stepped to a third workstation. This fellow tat artist, arms blue-and-red sleeves of elaborate inking, was working on a man in his late twenties. He was getting a flying hawk on his biceps. Sellitto thought of the falcons on Rhyme's window ledges.

The customer looked like he'd just subwayed it up here from Wall Street and would head back to his law firm afterward for an all-nighter.

Gordon looked over the job. Gave some suggestions.

Sellitto examined the shop. It seemed to belong to a different era: specifically, the 1960s. The walls were covered with hundreds of bright samples of tats: faces, religious symbols, cartoon characters, slogans, maps, landscapes, skulls...many of them psychedelic. Also, several dozen photos of piercings available for purchase. Some frames were covered by curtains. Sellitto could guess in what body parts those studs and pins resided.

The inking stations reminded Sellitto of those in a hair salon with the reclining chairs for customers and stools for the artists. Equipment and bottles and rags sat on a counter. On the wall was a mirror, on which were pasted some bumper stickers and taped certificates from the Board of Health. Despite the fact that the place existed for the purpose of spattering body fluids about, it looked immaculate. The smell of disinfectant was strong and there were warning signs everywhere about cleaning equipment, sterilizing.

130 Degrees Celsius Is Your Friend.

Gordon finished his suggestions and gestured Sellitto to the back room. They pushed through a plastic bead curtain into the office part of the shop. It too was well ordered and clean.

Gordon took a bottle of water from a mini fridge and offered it to Sellitto, who wasn't putting in his mouth anything from this shop. Shook his head.

The owner of the store unscrewed the top and drank. He nodded to the doorway, where the beads still pendulumed. "That's what we've become." As if Sellitto was his new best dude.

"How's that?"

"The guy in the business suit," he said softly. The hawk man. "You see where his tat is?"

"His biceps."

"Right. High. Easy to hide. Guy's got two point three children, or will have in the next couple years. Went to Columbia or NYU. Lawyer or accountant." A shake of the head. The ponytail swung. "Tats used to be insidious. The inked were bad boys and girls. Now getting a work's like putting on a charm bracelet or a tie. There's a joke somebody's going to open a tattoo franchise in strip malls. Call it Tat-bucks."

"That's why the rods?" Sellitto nodded at the bars in Gordon's head.

"You have to go to greater lengths to make a statement. That sounded effete. Sorry. So. What can I do for you, Officer?"

"I'm making the rounds of the big parlors in the city. None of 'em could help so far but they all said I had to come see you. This's the oldest parlor in the city, they said. And you know everybody in the community."

"Hard to say about the oldest. Inking—I mean modern inking in the U.S., not tribal—pretty much began in New York. The Bowery, late eighteen hundreds. But it was banned in 'sixty-one after some hepatitis outbreaks. Only legalized again in 'ninety-seven. I found some records that this shop dated back to the twenties—man, those must've been the days. You got a tat, you were Mr. Alternative. Or Miss, though women rarely got works done then. Not unheard of. Winston Churchill's mother had a snake eating its tail." He noted that Sellitto was not much interested in the history lesson. A shrug. *My* enthusiasm isn't *your* enthusiasm. Got it.

"This is, what I'm about to tell you, this's confidential."

"No worries there, dude. People tell me all sorts of shit when they're under the machine. They're nervous and so they start rambling away. I forget everything I hear. Amnesia, you know." A frown. "You here about somebody might be a customer of mine?"

"Don't have any reason to think so but could be." Sellitto added, "If we showed you a tat, you think you could tell us something about the guy who did it?"

"Maybe. Everybody's got their own style. Even two artists working from the same stencil're going to be different. It's how you learned to ink, the machine you use, the needles you hack together. A thousand things. Anyway, I can't guarantee it but I've worked with artists from all over the country, been to conventions in almost every state. I might be able to help you out."

"Okay, here."

Sellitto dug into his briefcase and extracted the photo Mel Cooper had printed out.

Gordon bent low and, frowning, studied the picture carefully. "The guy drew this knows what he's doing—definitely a pro. But I don't get the inflammation. There's no ink. The skin's all swollen and rough. Real badly infected. And there's no color. Did he use invisible ink?"

Sellitto thought Gordon was joking and said so. Gordon explained that some people didn't want to make a commitment, so they were inked with special solutions that appeared invisible but showed up under blacklight.

"The pussy-ball crowd."

"You got it, dude." A fist poked in Sellitto's direction. The detective declined to bump. Then the artist frowned. "I got a feeling something else is going on, right?"

Sellitto nodded. They'd kept the poison out of the press; this was the sort of MO that might lead to copycatting. And if there were informants, or the perp himself decided to ring up City Hall and gloat, they'd need to know that the caller had access to the actual details of the killing.

Besides, as a general rule, Sellitto preferred to explain as little as possible when canvassing for witnesses or asking advice. In this case, though, he had no option. He needed Gordon's help. And Sellitto decided he kind of liked the guy.

Dude...

"The suspect we're looking for, he used poison instead of ink."

The artist's eyes widened, the metal pins lifting dramatically. "Jesus. No! Jesus."

"Yeah."

"Ever hear about anybody doing that?"

"No way." Gordon brushed the backs of his fingers across the complicated facial hair. "That's just wrong. Man. See, we're...what we do is we're sort of this hybrid of artist and cosmetic surgeon—people put their trust in us. We've got a special relationship with people." Gordon's voice grew taut. "Using inking to kill somebody. Oh, man."

The parlor phone rang and Gordon ignored it. But a few moments later the heavyset tat artist—working on the motorcycle—stuck his head through the curtain of beads.

"Hey, TT." A nod to Sellitto.

"What?"

"Got a call. Can we ink a hundred-dollar bill on a guy's neck?" The accent was Southern. Sellitto couldn't place where.

"A hundred? Yeah, why not?"

"I mean, ain't it illegal to reproduce money?"

Gordon rolled his eyes. "He's not going to feed himself into any slots in Atlantic City."

"I'm just asking."

"It's okay."

The artist said into his phone, "Yessir, we'll do it." Then disconnected. He started to turn but Gordon said, "Hold on a sec." To Sellitto he added, "Eddie's been around. You might want to talk to him too."

The detective nodded, and Gordon introduced them. "Eddie Beaufort, Detective Sellitto."

"Nice to meet you." A Mid-Atlantic Southern lilt, Sellitto decided. The man had a genial face, which didn't fit with the elaborate sleeves—mostly of wild animals, it seemed. "Detective. Police. Hm."

"Tell Eddie what you were telling me."

Sellitto explained the situation to Beaufort, whose look of astonishment and dismay matched Gordon's. The detective now asked, "You ever heard of anybody using ink or tattoo guns as a weapon? Poison or otherwise? Either of you?"

"No," Beaufort whispered. "Never."

Gordon said to his colleague, "Good inking."

"Yep. Man knows what he's about. That's poison, hm?"

"That's right."

Gordon asked, "How'd he get her, I mean, how'd she stay still for that long?"

"Knocked her out with drugs. But it didn't take him very long. We think he did that tat in about fifteen minutes."

"*Fifteen?*" Gordon asked, astonished.

"That's unusual?"

Beaufort said, "Unusual? Church, man. I don't know anybody could lay a work like that in fifteen. It'd take an hour, at least."

"Yep," Gordon offered.

Beaufort nodded to the front of the shop. "Got a half-nekkid man. Better git."

Sellitto nodded thanks. He asked Gordon, "Well, looking at that, is there *anything* you can tell me about the guy did it?"

Gordon leaned forward and examined the photos of the inking on Chloe Moore's body. His brows V'ed together. "It's not all that clear. Do you have anything closer up? Or in better definition?"

"We can get it."

"I could come to the station. Heh. Always wanted to do that."

"We're working out of a consultant's office. We—Hold on." Sellitto's phone was humming. He looked at the screen, read the text. Interesting. Responded briefly.

He turned to Gordon. "I've gotta be someplace but get over here." Sellitto wrote down Rhyme's name and address. "That's the consultant's place. I've gotta stop by headquarters then I'll meet you there."

"Okay. Like when?"

"Like ASAP."

"Sure. Hey, you want a Glock or something?"

"What?" Sellitto screwed up his face.

"I'll ink you for free. A gun, a skull. Hey, how about an NYPD badge?"

"No skulls, no badges." He jabbed his finger at the card, containing the Central Park address. "All I need is you to show up."

"ASAP."

"You got it, dude."

CHAPTER 12

"How're we doing, Rookie?"

Sitting on a stool in Rhyme's parlor, Ron Pulaski was hunched over the computer keyboard. He was narrowing down the locations in the city from which the Inwood marble trace might have come. "Moving slow. It's not just blasting for foundations. There's a lot of demolition going on in the city too. And it's November. In this weather. Who would've thought? I—"

A mobile phone buzzed. The young officer fished into his pocket and removed the unit. It was the prepaid.

The Watchmaker undercover assignment was heating up. Rhyme was encouraged that somebody had called the officer so quickly.

And what would the substance of the conversation be?

He heard some pleasantries. Then: "Yes, about the remains. Richard Logan. Right." He wandered off to the corner. Rhyme could hear no more.

But he noted Pulaski's grave expression—a pun that

Rhyme decided not to share, given that this assignment seemed to be weighing on the man.

After two or three minutes Pulaski disconnected and jotted notes.

"And?" Rhyme asked.

Pulaski said, "They transferred Logan's body to the Berkowitz Funeral Home."

"Where?" Rhyme asked. It sounded familiar.

"Not far from here. Upper Broadway."

"A memorial service?"

"No, just somebody's coming to pick up his ashes on Thursday."

Without looking up from the large computer monitor, Rhyme muttered, "Nothing from the FBI on sources for the poisons and not a goddamn thing about 'the second.' Though I suppose we can't be too optimistic about that. Who?"

Neither Pulaski nor Cooper responded. Sachs too was silent.

"Well?" Rhyme called.

"Well what?" From Cooper.

"I'm asking Pulaski. Who'll be where? To pick up Logan's ashes? Did you ask the funeral director who'd be there?"

"No."

"Well, why not?"

"Because," the patrol officer replied, "it'd seem suspicious, don't you think, Lincoln? What if it's the Watchmaker's silent partner coming to pay his last respects and the director casually mentions that somebody was curious who's going to be there—which isn't really a question you'd ask—"

"All right. Made your point."

"A good point," Cooper said.

A *fair* point.

Then Rhyme was thinking again about the message of the tattoo on Chloe Moore's body. He doubted that "the second" was part of a findable quotation at all. Maybe it was something that the unsub had spontaneously chosen and couldn't be tracked down. And maybe there was no meaning at all behind it.

A distraction, a misdirection.

Smoke and mirrors...

But if you *do* mean something, what could it be? Why are you playing your thoughts out like fishing line?

"I don't know," Cooper said.

Apparently Rhyme had spoken the query to the cryptic perp aloud.

"Damn message," he muttered.

Everyone in the room looked at it once more.

"...the second, the second..."

"Anagram?" the tech suggested.

Rhyme scanned the letters. Nothing significant appeared by rearranging them. "Anyway, I have a feeling the message is mysterious enough. He doesn't need to play Scrabble with us. So, Rookie, you'll be going undercover to the funeral home. You okay with that?"

"Sure."

Spoken too quickly, Rhyme reflected. He knew this reluctance about the job had nothing to do with physical risk. Even if the late Watchmaker's mantle had been inherited by an associate, and he was the one collecting the ashes, he wasn't going to pull out a gun in a funeral parlor and start a shootout with an undercover cop. No, it was a fear of inadequacy that plagued the young officer, all thanks to the head injury he'd suffered some years ago. Pulaski was great in searching crime scenes. He was good, for a non-scientist, in the lab. But when he had to deal with people and make fast decisions, uncertainties and hesitations arose. "We'll talk about what to wear, how to act, who to be, later."

Pulaski nodded, slipped away the phone, which he'd been kneading nervously in his hand, and returned to the Inwood marble job.

Rhyme now eased his Merits wheelchair close to the examination table on which rested evidence from the Chloe Moore murder in SoHo. Then he lifted his gaze to the monitor above it, the one displaying the photos Sachs had taken at the scene, glowing in difficult, high-definition glory. He studied the dead woman's face, the flecks of spittle, the rictus, the vomit, the wide, glazed eyes. The expression reflected her last moments on earth. The deadly toxin extracted from a water hemlock would have induced fierce seizures and excruciating abdominal pain.

Why poison? Rhyme wondered again.

And why a tattoo gun as a means of slipping it into her body?

"Hell," Sachs muttered, leaning away from her own workstation. She was helping Pulaski trace commercial blasting permits. "The computer's down again. Happened twice in the past twenty minutes. Just like the phones earlier."

"Not just here," Thom said. "Outages all over the city. Slow download times. A real pain. About a dozen neighborhoods've been affected."

Rhyme snapped, "Great. Just what we need." You couldn't run a criminal investigation now without computers, from DMV to encrypted police and national security agency databases to Google. If the stream was choked off, cases ground to a halt. And you never thought about how dependent you were on those invisible bits and bytes until the flow of data choked to a stop.

Sachs announced, "Okay, it's back now."

But the concerns about the World Wide Web were sidelined when Lon Sellitto, tugging off his coat, burst into Rhyme's parlor. He tossed the Burberry onto a chair, piled his gloves atop the garment and pulled something out of his briefcase.

Rhyme looked at him, frowning.

Sellitto said defensively, "I'll mop the fucking floor, Linc."

"I don't care about the floor. Why would I care about the floor? I want to know what you have in your hand."

Sellitto wiped sweat. His internal thermometer was unaffected, apparently, by the coldest, nastiest November in the past twenty-five years. "First off, I found a tattoo artist who's going to help and he's on his way. Or he better be. TT Gordon. You should see the mustache."

"Lon."

"Now this." He held up a book. "Those guys at HQ? They tracked down where that scrap of paper came from."

Rhyme's heart beat faster—a sensation that most people would feel in their chest but that for him, of course, registered simply as an upped pulsing in his neck and head, the only sensate parts of his body.

ies
that his greatest skill was his ability to anticipate

"How'd they do it, Lon?" Sachs asked.

Sellitto continued, "You know Marty Belson, Major Cases."

"Oh, the brainiac."

"Right. Loves his puzzles. Does Sudoku in his sleep." Sellitto explained to Rhyme: "Works financial crimes mostly. Anyway, he figured out the top letters were part of the title, you know how books have the author's name at the top of one side and the title at the top of the facing page?"

"We know. Keep going."

"He was playing with what words end in 'ies'?"

Rhyme said, "A word on the reverse page was 'body,' so that's an option, pluralized. We speculated it was a crime book. Or given the corpse theme, maybe *Enemies*."

"Nope. *Cities*. The full title is *Serial Cities*. That was on the short list of about six that Marty came up with. He called all the major book publishers in town—there aren't as many as there used to be—and read them the passages. One editor recognized it. He said his company'd published it a long time ago. *Serial Cities*. It's out of print now but he even knew the chapter that the passage was from. Number Seven. Had a copy messengered to us."

Excellent! Rhyme asked, "And what's this special chapter about?"

Sellitto wiped more sweat. "You, Linc. It's all about you."

CHAPTER 13

And you too, Amelia."

Sellitto was opening the book. Rhyme noted the full title: *Serial Cities: Famous Killers from Coast to Coast.*

"Let me guess: The theme is that every major city's had a serial killer."

"Boston Strangler, Charles Manson in LA, the I-5 Killer in Seattle."

"Sloppy journalism. Manson wasn't a serial killer."

"I don't think the public cares."

"And we made it into the book?" Sachs asked.

"Chapter Seven's titled 'The Bone Collector.' "

That was the popular name, courtesy of the press and an overblown novelization, of a serial kidnapper who taunted Rhyme and the NYPD some years ago by stashing his victims in places where they would die if he couldn't figure out in time where they'd been hidden.

Some of the victims had been saved, some had not. The case had been significant for several reasons: It had brought Rhyme back from the dead—almost literally.

He'd been planning to take his own life, so depressed had he been about his quadriplegia, but he'd decided to stick around for a while after the exhilaration of mentally wrestling with the brilliant killer.

The case had also brought Rhyme and Sachs together.

Rhyme now muttered, "And we're not the *first* chapter?"

Sellitto shrugged. "Oh, sorry, Linc."

"But it's New York."

And it *is* me, Rhyme couldn't help thinking.

"Can I see it?" Sachs asked. She opened the book to the chapter and began to read quickly.

"Short," Rhyme observed, even more irritated. Did the Boston Strangler investigation get more pages?

"You know," Sachs said, "I seem to remember talking to a writer awhile ago. He said he was working on a book and took me out for coffee to find out some details that weren't in the press or the official record." She smiled. "I think he said he called you too, Rhyme, and you chewed his head off and hung up on him."

"I don't recall," he grumbled. "Journalism. What's the point of it anyway?"

"You wrote *that*," Pulaski pointed out, nodding toward a bookshelf on which sat Rhyme's own nonfiction account of famous crime scenes in New York City.

"It was a lark. I don't devote my life to regurgitating lurid stories to a bloodsucking audience."

Though perhaps he *should* have been more lurid, he reflected; *The Scenes of the Crime* had been remaindered years ago.

"The important question is, what's Unsub Eleven-

Five's interest in the Bone Collector case?" He nodded at the book. "What's the nature of my chapter? Does it have a theme? Does the author have an ax to grind?"

How long *was* it, for God's sake? Only ten pages? Rhyme grew even more offended.

Sachs continued skimming. "Don't worry. You come off well. I do too, I have to say...It's mostly a description of the kidnapping incidents and the investigation techniques."

She flipped more pages. "A lot of procedural details about the crime scene work. Some footnotes. There's a long one about your condition."

"Oh, that must be some truly compelling reading."

"Another one about the politics of the case."

Sachs had gotten into hot water by closing down a train line to preserve evidence—which resulted in a rift all the way up to Albany.

"And one more footnote—about Pam's mother," Sachs said.

A young girl named Pam Willoughby and her mother had been kidnapped by the Bone Collector. Rhyme and Sachs had saved them—only to have the mom turn out to be someone other than an innocent victim. After learning this, Sachs and Rhyme had tried desperately to find the child. A few years ago they'd managed to rescue her. Pam was now nineteen, in college and working in New York. She'd become Sachs's de facto younger sister.

Sachs read to the end. "The author's mostly concerned with the perp's psychological makeup: Why was he so interested in bones?"

The kidnapper had stolen human bones and carved,

sanded and polished them. His obsession, it seemed, stemmed from the fact that he had suffered a loss in the past, loved ones killed, and he found subconscious comfort in the permanence of bones.

His crimes were revenge for that loss.

Rhyme said, "First, I think we need to see if our unsub's got any connection to the Bone Collector himself. Look up the files. Track down any family members of the perp, where they lived, what they're up to."

It took some time to unearth the files—the official reports and evidence were at the NYPD, in the archives. The case was quite old. Rhyme had some material on his computer but the word processing files weren't compatible with his new system. Some of the info was on three-and-a-half-inch disks, which Thom unearthed from the basement—the verb appropriate since the boxes were so dust-covered.

"What're those?" asked Pulaski, a representative of the generation that measured data storage in gigabytes.

"Floppy disks," Sellitto said.

"Heard of them. Never seen one."

"No kidding? And you know, Ron, they used to have big round black vinyl things you listened to music on. Oh, and we roasted our mastodon steaks over real fire, Rookie. Before microwaves."

"Ha."

The disks proved useless but Thom also managed to find hard copies of the files in the basement. Rhyme and the others were able to piece together a bio of the Bone Collector and use the Internet (now working at a fine clip) to determine that the perp from back then had no living relatives, none close at least.

Rhyme was quiet for a moment as he thought: And I know why he doesn't have any family.

Sachs caught his troubled gaze. She gave a reassuring nod, which Rhyme didn't respond to.

"How about the survivors?"

More online research, more phone calls.

It turned out that aside from Pam none of the victims saved from the Bone Collector were still alive or living in the city.

Rhyme said brusquely, "All right, doesn't sound like there's any direct connection to the Bone Collector case. Revenge might be a dish best served cold but too much time has elapsed for somebody to come after us for that."

"Let's talk to Terry," Sachs suggested.

The NYPD's chief psychologist, Terry Dobyns. He was the one who'd formulated the theory that the Bone Collector's obsession with bones was rooted in their permanence and reflected some loss in the perp's past.

Dobyns was also the doctor who'd been a pit bull after Rhyme's accident some years ago. He'd refused to accept Rhyme's withdrawal from life and his flirtation with suicide. He'd helped the criminalist adjust to the world of the disabled. And no "How does that make you feel" crap. Dobyns *knew* how you felt and he guided the conversation in directions that took the hard edges off what you were going through while not shying from the truth that, yeah, sometimes life fucks with you.

The doctor was smart, no question. And a talented shrink. But Sachs's suggestion for enlisting him now was another matter altogether; she wanted a psychological profile of Unsub 11-5 and profiling was an art—not a science, mind you—that Rhyme found dubious at best.

"Why bother?" he asked.

"Cross our t's and—"

"No clichés, please, Sachs."

"—dot our j's."

Sellitto took sides. "What can it hurt, Linc?"

"It'll take time away from doing something valuable—analyzing the evidence. It'll be distracting. *That's* what will hurt, Lon."

"You analyze away," Sellitto shot back. "Amelia and I'll give Terry a call. You don't even have to listen. Look, our unsub went to a lot of trouble to get his hands on a book that's about the Bone Collector. I want to know why."

"All right," Rhyme said, surrendering.

Sellitto placed a call and when Dobyns answered, the detective hit a button on his mobile.

"You're on speaker, Terry. 'S Lon Sellitto. I'm here with Lincoln and a couple of others. We've got a case we'd like to ask you about."

"Been awhile," the doctor said in his smooth baritone. "How are you doing, Lon?"

"Okay, okay."

"And Lincoln?"

"Fine," Rhyme muttered and began looking over the evidence chart once more. Inwood marble. Being blown up. *That*, he was far more interested in than spongy psychological guesswork.

Alchemy…

"It's Amelia too," she said. "And Ron Pulaski and Mel Cooper."

"I'm deducing this's about the tattoo case. I saw it on the wire."

Though the press hadn't been informed about the nuances of the Unsub 11-5 case, all law enforcement agencies in the area had been contacted, with a request for matching MOs (none had answered in the affirmative).

"That's right. There's a development and we'd like your thoughts."

"I'm all ears."

Rhyme had to admit that he found the man's intonation calming. He could picture the sinewy, gray-haired doctor, whose smile was as easy as his voice. When he was listening to you, he truly listened. You were the center of the universe.

Sachs explained about the perp's theft of the chapter about the Bone Collector—and the fact that he'd been carrying it around with him during the crime. She added too that there was no direct connection with the Bone Collector case but that he'd probably gone to some trouble to obtain a copy of the book.

Lon Sellitto added, "And he left a message." He explained about the tattooed phrase "the second" in Old English type.

The doctor was silent for a moment. Then: "Well, the first thing that I thought of, which you obviously have too, is that he's a serial doer. A partial message means there're more to come. And then his interest in the Bone Collector, who was a serial kidnapper."

"We assume he's going to keep hunting," Sellitto said.

"Do you have any leads at all?"

Sachs said, "Description—white male, slim. Some details on the poisons he used and one that he probably intends to."

"And the victim's white female?"

"Yes."

"Fits the serial killer model." Most such killers hunted in the same racial pool as their own.

Sachs continued, "He subdued her with propofol. So maybe he's got a medical background."

"Like the Bone Collector," Dobyns said.

"Right," Rhyme said, eyes shifting from the evidence to the speakerphone. "I hadn't thought about that." His attention to the psychiatrist now edged over the 50 percent mark.

"Sexual component?"

"No," Sellitto said.

Sachs added, "It took her some time to die. Presumably he was there, watching. And possibly enjoying it."

"Sadistic," Ron Pulaski said.

"Who's that?" Dobyns asked.

"It's Ron Pulaski, Patrol. I work with Lincoln and Amelia."

"Hello, Officer. Well, no, actually I don't see sadism. That occurs only in a sexual context. If he enjoys inflicting pain for its own sake his condition would probably be diagnosed as anti-social personality disorder."

"Yessir." Pulaski was blushing, not from the correction but, it seemed, because of Rhyme's glare at the interruption.

Dobyns said, "Off the top of my head, he's an organized offender and he'll be planning out the attacks carefully. I'd also say there're two possible reasons for your unsub's interest in the Bone Collector and in you, Lincoln. Amelia too, don't forget. One, he might have been affected by the Bone Collector's crimes a decade ago. Emotionally moved by them, I mean."

"Even if he had no direct connection?" Rhyme asked, forgetting he was trying to ignore the doctor's input.

"Yes. You don't know his age exactly but it's possible he was in early adolescence then—just the time when a news story about a serial doer might've spoken to him. As for that message? Well, the Bone Collector was, if I remember, all about revenge."

"That's right."

Sellitto asked, "What kind of revenge would our unsub be after, Doc? Family members who'd died? Some other personal loss?"

"Really, it could be anything. Maybe he suffered a loss, a tragedy that he blames someone for—or some *thing*, a company, organization, institution. The loss might've happened when the Bone Collector story hit the press and he embraced the idea of getting retribution the same way the Bone Collector did. He's been carrying that thought around with him. That's one explanation for why this murder echoes the attacks from a decade ago—some of those crimes were underground too, weren't they?"

"That's right," Rhyme confirmed.

"And your unsub has a morbid interest in the morphology of the human body. Skin, in his case."

Sachs added, "Yes, I found evidence that he touched the victim in a number of places—not sexually. There was no reason related to the tattooing for that that I could see. It gave him some satisfaction, I was thinking. My impression."

The doctor continued, "So, the first reason he might be interested in the Bone Collector: a psychological bonding with him." He chuckled. "An insight that, I suspect, is rather low in your estimation, Lincoln." He knew of Rhyme's distrust of what the criminalist called "woo-woo" policing. "But that might hint he too is out for revenge," Dobyns added.

Rhyme said, "Noted, Doctor. We'll put it on our evidence chart."

"I think you'll be more interested in the second reason he was interested in the chapter of this book. Whatever his motive—revenge or joy killing or distracting you so he could rob the Federal Reserve—he knows you'll be after him and he'll want to learn as much as he can about you, your tactics, how you think. How specifically you tracked down a serial criminal. So he doesn't make the same mistakes. He wants to know where your weaknesses are. You and Amelia."

This made more sense to Rhyme. He nodded at Sachs, who told the doctor, "The book is practically a how-to guide on using forensics to stop a serial criminal. And it's clear from running the scenes that he's been paying attention to scrubbing the evidence."

Pulaski asked, "Doctor, any idea why *this* victim? There was no, you know, prior contact between them that we could find." He gave a brief bio of Chloe Moore.

Sachs said, "Seems to be random."

"With the Bone Collector, remember, his true victims were somebody else: the city of New York, the police, you, Lincoln. I'd guess that the choice of victim by your unsub is mostly accessibility and convenience—to have a place and the time to do the tattoo undisturbed... Then I think there's the fear factor."

"What'sat?" Sellitto asked.

"He's got another agenda beyond murdering individuals—clearly it's not to rob them, it's not sexual. It may serve his purposes to put the whole city on edge. Everybody in New York's going to be thinking twice about heading into basements and garages and laundry rooms and using back doors to their offices and apartments. Now, a few other points. First, if he's truly been influenced by the Bone Collector, then he may think about targeting you personally, Lincoln. And Amelia. In fact, you all might be in danger. Second, he's clearly an organized offender, as I said. And that means he's been checking out his victims, or at least the kill sites, ahead of time."

Rhyme said, "We're going on that assumption."

"Good. And finally—if he were really a copycat he would have concentrated on the victim's bones. But he's obsessed with skin. It's central to his goal. He could just as easily be injecting them with poison or making them drink it. Or for that matter stabbing people or shooting them. But he's not. He's obviously a professional artist—so every time he puts one of his designs on a body, he claims somebody else's skin as his own."

"A skin collector," Pulaski said.

"Exactly. If you can find out why he's so fascinated with skin, that's key to understanding the case." Rhyme heard another voice, indistinct, from the doctor's office. "Ah, you'll have to excuse me now. I'm afraid I have a session to get to."

"Thanks, Doctor," Sachs said.

After he disconnected, Rhyme told Pulaski to put Dobyns's observations up on the chart.

Quasi-babble... but, Rhyme reluctantly admitted, it might be helpful.

He said, "We should talk to Pam. See if anybody's contacted her about the Bone Collector."

Sachs nodded. "Not a bad idea."

Pam was now out of the foster system and living on her own in Brooklyn, not far from where Sachs kept her apartment. It seemed unlikely that the unsub would even know about her. Because Pam was a child at the time of the Bone Collector kidnapping, her name had never come up in the press. And *Serial Cities* hadn't mentioned her either.

Sachs gave the young woman a call and left a message asking her to come over to Rhyme's. There was something she wanted to discuss.

"Pulaski. Get back to marble detail. I want to find where that stone dust came from."

The doorbell buzzed. And Thom disappeared to answer it.

He returned to the parlor a moment later beside a sinewy man in his thirties, with a weathered, creased face and long blond ponytail. He also had the most extravagant beard Rhyme had ever seen. He was amused at the difference between the two standing before him. Thom was in dark dress slacks, a pastel-yellow shirt and a rust-colored tie. The visitor wore a spotless tuxedo jacket, way too thin for the raging weather, ironed black jeans and a black long-sleeve pullover emblazoned with a red spider. His brown boots were polished like a mahogany table. The only attribute this man and the aide shared was a slender build, though Thom was a half foot taller.

"You must be TT Gordon," Rhyme said.

"Yeah. And, hey, you're the dude in the wheelchair."

CHAPTER 14

Rhyme took in the bizarre beard, the steel rods in the ears and eyebrows.

Parts of tats were visible on the backs of Gordon's hands; the rest of the inking vanished under his pullover. Rhyme believed he could make out *POW!* on the right wrist.

He drew no conclusions about the man's appearance. He'd long ago given up on the spurious practice of equating the essence of a person with his or her physical incarnation. His own condition was the prototype for this way of thinking.

His main reaction was: How badly had the piercings hurt? This was something Rhyme could relate to; his ears and brows were places in which he could feel pain. And the other thought: If TT Gordon ever got busted he'd be picked out of a lineup in an instant.

A nod to Sellitto, who reciprocated.

"Hey. The wheelchair thing I said? It wasn't as stupid as it sounded," Gordon said, smiling and looking at everyone in the room. His eyes returned to

Rhyme's. "Obviously you're in a wheelchair. I meant, hey, you're the *famous* dude in the wheelchair. I didn't make the connection before. When he"—a nod at Sellitto—"came to my shop, he said 'consultant.' You're in the papers. I've seen you on TV. Why don't you do that Nancy Grace show? That'd be very cool. Do you watch it?"

This was just natural rambling, Rhyme deduced, not awkward, I-don't-want-to-be-with-a-gimp rambling. The disability seemed to Gordon merely another aspect of Rhyme, like his dark hair and fleshy nose and intense eyes and trim fingernails.

An identifying marker, not a political one.

Gordon greeted the others, Sachs, Cooper and Pulaski. Then he gazed around the room, whose decor Rhyme had once described as Hewlett-Packard Victorian. "Hm. Well. Cool."

Sachs said, "We appreciate your coming here to help us."

"Like, no problem. I want this guy taken down. This dude, what he's doing? It's bad for everybody who mods for a living."

"What does that mean? 'Mods'?" Sachs asked.

"Modifying bodies, you know. Inking people, piercing, cutting." He tapped his ear bars. "Everything. 'Modding' covers the gamut." He frowned. "Whatever a gamut is. I don't really know."

Rhyme said, "Lon says you're pretty well connected in the tattoo community here and that you don't have any specific idea who it might be."

Gordon confirmed this.

Sellitto added that Gordon had looked over a picture

of the victim's tattoo but wanted a better image; the printout hadn't been that clear.

Cooper said, "I'll call up the raw .nef files and save them as enhanced .tiffs."

Rhyme had no clue what he was talking about. In the days when he worked crime scenes himself he used actual thirty-five-millimeter film that had to be developed in chemicals and printed in a darkroom. Back then you made every frame count. Now? You shot the hell out of a crime scene and culled.

Cooper said, "I'll send them to the Nvidia computer—the big screen there."

"Whatever, dude. As long as it's clear."

Pulaski asked, "You seen *The Big Lebowski*?"

"Oh, man." Gordon grinned and punched a fist Pulaski's way. The rookie reciprocated.

Rhyme wondered: Maybe Tarantino.

The pictures appeared on the largest monitor in the room. They were extremely high-definition images of the tattoo on Chloe Moore's abdomen. TT Gordon gave one blink of shock at the worried skin, the welts, the discoloration. "Worse than I thought, the poisoning and everything. Like he created his own hot zone."

"What's that?"

Gordon explained that tattoo parlors were divided into zones, hot and cold. The cold zone was where there was no risk of contamination by one customer's blood getting into another's. No unsterilized needles or machine parts or chairs, for instance. Hot, obviously, was the opposite, where the tattoo machine and needles were tainted by customers' blood and body fluids. "We do everything we can to keep the two separate. But here, this dude did the opposite—intentionally infected, well, poisoned her. Man. Fucked up."

But then the artist settled into an analytic mode that Rhyme found encouraging. Gordon eyed a computer. "Can I?"

"Sure," Cooper said.

The artist hit keys and scrolled through the images, enlarging some.

Rhyme asked, "TT, are the words 'the second' significant in any way in the tattoo world?"

"No. Has no meaning that I know about and I've been inking for nearly twenty years. Guess it's something significant to the dude who killed her. Or maybe the victim."

"Probably the perp," Amelia Sachs explained to Gordon. "There's no evidence that he knew Chloe before he killed her."

"Oh. She was Chloe." Gordon said this softly. He touched his beard. Then scrolled once more. "Well, it's weird for a client to make up a phrase or a passage for a modding. Sometimes I'll ink a poem they've written. I'll tell you, mostly they suck, big time. Usually, though, if somebody wants text, it's a passage from something like their favorite book. The Bible. Or a famous quote. Or a saying, you know. 'Live Free or Die.' 'Born to Ride.' Things like that." Then he frowned. "Hm. Okay."

"What?"

"Could be a splitter."

"And that is?" Rhyme asked.

"Some clients split their mods. They get half a word on one arm, the other half on another. Sometimes they'll get part of the tat inked on their body, and their girlfriend or boyfriend gets the other part on theirs."

"Why?" Pulaski asked.

"Why?" Gordon seemed perplexed by the question. "Tats connect people. That's one of the whole points of getting inked. Even if you've got unique works, you're still part of the ink world. You got something in common, you know. That connects you, see, dude?"

Sachs said, "You seem to've done some thinking about all this."

Gordon laughed. "Oh, I could be a shrink, I tell you."

"Freud," Sellitto said.

"Dude," Gordon responded with a grin. That fist again. Sellitto didn't take the offer.

Sachs asked, "And can you tell us anything concrete about him?"

Sellitto added, "We're not going to quote you. Or get you on the witness stand. We just want to know who this guy is. Get into his head."

Gordon was looking at the equipment, hesitating.

"Well, okay. First, he's a natural, a total talent as an artist, not just a technician. A lot of inkers are paint-by-numbers guys. They slap on a stencil somebody else did and fill it in. But"—a nod at the picture—"there's no evidence of a stencil there. He used a bloodline."

"Which is what?" Rhyme asked.

"If they're not using a stencil, most artists draw an outline of the work on the skin first. Some draw freehand with a pen—water-soluble ink. But there's no sign of that here. Your guy didn't do that. He just turned on his tattoo machine and used a lining needle for the outline, so instead of ink you have a line of blood that's the outer perimeter of your design. So, bloodline. Only the best tat artists do that."

Pulaski asked, "A pro then?"

"Oh, yeah, dude'd have to be a pro. Like I told him." A nod at Sellitto. "Or was at some point. That level of skill? He could open his own shop in a blind second. And probably he's a real artist too—I mean like with paint and pen and ink and everything. And I don't think he's from here. For one thing, I probably would've heard. Not from the tristate area, either. Doing this in fifteen minutes? Man, that's lightning. His name'd get around. Then, look at the typeface."

Rhyme's, and everyone else's, eyes slipped to the screen.

"It's Old English, or some Gothic variation. You don't see that much now around here. I'd guess he's got rural roots: redneck, shit kicker, biker, meth cooker. On the other hand, maybe born-again, righteous, upstanding. But definitely a country boy."

"The typeface tells you that?" Sachs asked.

"Oh, yeah. Here, if somebody wants words, they'll go for some kind of flowery script or thick sans serif. At least that's current now. Man, for a few years everybody wanted this Elvish crap."

"Elvis Presley?" Sellitto asked.

"No, Elvish. *Lord of the Rings*."

"So country," Rhyme said. "Any particular region?"

"Not really. There's city inking and country inking. All I can say is this smells like country. Now, look at the border. The scallops. The technique is scarification. Or cicatrization is the official name for it. That's important."

He looked up and tapped the scallops surrounding the words "the second."

"What's significant is that usually people scar to draw attention to an image. It's important for this dude to make that design more prominent. It would've been easier just to ink a border. But, no, he wanted cicatrization. There's a reason for it, I'm guessing. No clue what. But there it is.

"Now, there's one other thing. I was thinking about it. I brought show-and-tell." Gordon reached into his canvas shoulder bag and lifted out a plastic sack containing a number of metal parts. Rhyme recognized the transparent container as the sort in which surgical and forensic instruments are sterilized in an autoclave. "These are part of a tattoo machine—you don't call them guns, by the way." Gordon smiled. "Whatever you hear on TV."

He took a small Swiss Army knife from his pocket and cut open the bag. In a moment he'd assembled a tattoo gun—well, machine. "Here's what it looks like put together and ready to ink." The tattoo artist walked closer to the others. "These're the coils that move the needle up and down. This's the tube for the ink and here's the needle itself, coming out the end."

Rhyme could see it, very small.

"Needles have to go into the dermis—the layer of skin just below the outermost layer."

"Which is the epidermis," Rhyme said.

Nodding, Gordon disassembled the device and lifted out the needle, displaying it to everyone. Resembling a thin shish kebab skewer, about three inches long, it had a ring on one end. The other end contained a cluster of tiny metal rods soldered or welded together. They ended in sharp points.

"See how they're joined together, in a star-shaped pattern? I make 'em myself. Most serious artists do. But we have to buy blanks and combine 'em. There're two types of needles: those for lining—outlining the image—and then those for filling or shading. The dude needed to get a lot of poison into her body fast. That means he had to use filling needles after he was done with the bloodline. But these wouldn't work, I don't think. They wouldn't go deep enough. This kind of needle would, though." He reached into his bag once more and extracted a small plastic jar. He shook out two rods of metal, similar to his needles but longer. "They're from an old-time rotary machine—the new ones, like mine, are two-coil, oscillation models. Was it a portable machine?"

"Had to be. There was no electric source," Sachs told him.

Pulaski said, "I've been looking for portable guns... machines. But there're a lot of them."

Gordon thought for a moment. Then said, "I'm guessing it would have to be an American Eagle model. Goes way back. One of the first to run off battery power. It comes from the days when tattooing wasn't very scientific. The artist could adjust the stroke of the needles. He could make them go real deep. I'd look for somebody who's got an Eagle."

Sellitto asked, "Are they sold here? In supply stores?"

"I've never seen any. They're not made anymore. You could get them online, I'd guess. That'd be the only way to find them."

"No, he's not going to be buying anything that way, too traceable," Rhyme pointed out. "He probably picked it up where he lives. Or maybe he's had it for years or inherited it."

"Needles're a different story. You might be able to find somebody who's sold needles for American Eagles. Anybody who bought those recently could be he."

"What'd you say?" Rhyme asked.

"What did I say?" The slim man frowned. "When, now? Whoever's buying needles for an American Eagle machine, it could be your perp. Don't you say that? They do on *NCIS*."

The criminalist laughed. "No. I was noting the proper use of the pronoun. Nominative case."

Rhyme noted Pulaski roll his eyes.

"Oh, *that*? The 'he'?" Gordon shrugged. "I never did very...*well* in school. Thought I was going to say 'good,' didn't you? Couple years at Hunter but got bored, you know. But when I started inking, I'd do a lot of text. Bible verses, passages from books, poems. So I learned writing from famous authors. Spelling, grammar. I mean, dude, it was pretty interesting. Typography too. The same passage in one font has a whole different impact when it's printed in another.

"Sometimes a couple'd come in and they'd want to ink wedding vows on their arms or ankles. Or crappy love poems they'd written, like I mentioned. I'd say, okay, dudes, you sure you want to go through life with 'Jimmy I love you you're heart and mine for ever' on your biceps. That's *Jimmy* no comma, *you* no period or semicolon, *Y-O-U* apostrophe *R-E*, and *for ever* two words. They'd say, 'Huh.' I'd edit anyway when I inked them. They'll have kids and have to go to a PTA meeting, meet the English teacher. After all, not like you can use White-Out, right?"

"And cut and paste would be really bad," Pulaski joked, drawing smiles.

But not from Gordon. "Oh, there's a version of scarification where people actually cut strips of skin out of their body."

Rhyme then heard a click in the front door latch and the door open—or, more accurately, the wind howl and the sleet clatter from the sky.

The door closed.

After that footsteps and a light, airy laugh.

He knew who had come to visit and shot a glance to Sachs, who quickly rose and turned around the whiteboard that contained the crime scene pictures of Chloe Moore and switched the high-def screens away from the images TT Gordon had been examining.

A moment later Pam Willoughby stepped into the room. The pretty, slim nineteen-year-old was enwrapped in a brown overcoat trimmed in faux fur. Her long, dark hair was tucked up under a burgundy stocking cap, and her outer garments were dusted with dots of sleet or snow, melting fast. She waved hello to everyone.

Accompanying her was her boyfriend, Seth McGuinn, a handsome, dark-haired man of about twenty-five. She introduced him to Pulaski and Mel Cooper, neither of whom he'd met.

Seth's dark-brown eyes, which matched Pam's, blinked when they turned to TT Gordon, who greeted the couple pleasantly. Pam had a similar reaction.

Rhyme had seen athletic Seth in a T-shirt and jogging shorts, when he and Pam had been going to the park several weeks ago, and noted he'd sported no tattoos. Pam had none either, visible at least. The young couple now tried, unsuccessfully, to hide their surprise at Rhyme's quirky visitor.

Pam detached herself from Seth's arm, kissed Rhyme on the cheek and hugged Thom. Seth shook everyone's hand.

TT Gordon asked if they needed any more help with the case. Sellitto glanced around the room at the others and when Rhyme shook his head, said, "Thanks for coming in. Appreciate it."

"I'll keep an eye out for anything weird. In the community, you know what I mean? So long, dudes."

Gordon stashed his gear, pulled on his pitifully thin jacket and headed out the door.

Seth and Pam shared a smile, looking after Gordon's exit.

Sachs said, "Hey, Pam. I think Seth needs a 'stache."

The clean-cut young man nodded, frowning. "Hell, I can outdo him. I'd go with braids."

Pam said, "Naw, get pierced. That way we can swap earrings."

Seth said he had to be going; a deadline for his ad agency loomed. He kissed Pam, chastely, as if Rhyme and Sachs were the girl's real parents. Then he nodded a farewell to the others. At the archway he turned and reminded Sachs and Rhyme that his parents would like to have lunch or dinner with them soon. Rhyme generally disliked such socializing but since Pam was, in effect, family, he'd agreed to go. And reminded himself to endure the pleasantries and mundane conversation with a smile.

"Next week?" Rhyme asked.

"Perfect. Dad's back from Hong Kong." He added that his father had found a copy of Rhyme's book about New York crime scenes. "Any chance of an autograph?"

Recent surgery had improved Rhyme's muscle control to the point that he actually could write his name—not as clearly as before the accident but as good as any doctor writing a prescription. "Delighted to."

When he'd left, Pam pulled off her jacket and hat, set them on a chair, asked Sachs, "So, your message? What's up?"

The detective nodded toward the sitting room, across the hall from Rhyme's lab/parlor, and said, "How 'bout we go in there."

CHAPTER 15

Now," Sachs said, "listen. I don't think there's anything to worry about."

In her charming lilt of an alto voice Pam said, "Okay, *there's* a way to start a conversation." She tossed her hair, which she wore like Sachs's, beyond shoulder length, no bangs.

Sachs smiled. "No, really." She was looking the girl over closely and decided that she had a glow about her. Maybe it was her job, "costuming," Pam called it, for a theater production company. She loved behind-the-scenes Broadway. College too she enjoyed.

But, no. Sachs asked herself: What'm I thinking? Of course. The answer was Seth.

Thom appeared in the doorway with a tray. Hot chocolate. The smell was both bitter and sweet. "Don't you just love the winter?" he asked. "When the temperature's below thirty-five hot chocolate doesn't have any calories. Lincoln could come up with the chemical formula for that."

They thanked the aide. He then asked Pam, "When's the premiere?"

Pam was attending NYU but she had a light class load this semester and—as a talented seamstress—was working part-time as an assistant to the assistant costumer for a Broadway revival of *Sweeney Todd*—the musical adaptation, by Stephen Sondheim and Hugh Wheeler, of an older play detailing the life of the homicidal barber in London. Todd would slice his customers' throats and a conspirator would bake the victims into pies. Rhyme had reported to Sachs and Pam that the perp reminded him of a criminal he'd once pursued, though he added that Todd was purely fictional. Pam had seemed playfully disappointed at that factoid.

Cutting throats, cannibalism, Sachs reflected. Talk about body modification.

"We open in a week," Pam said. "And I'll have tickets for everybody. Even Lincoln."

Thom said, "He's actually looking forward to going."

Sachs said, "No!"

"Gospel."

"Heart be still."

Pam said, "I've got a disabled slot reserved. And you know the theater has a bar."

Sachs laughed. "He'll be there for sure."

Thom left, closing the door behind him, and Sachs continued, "So, here's what's happened. The man who kidnapped you and your mother? Years ago?"

"Oh, yeah. The Bone Collector?"

Sachs nodded. "It looks like there's somebody who's

copying him. In a way. He's not obsessed with bones, though. But skin."

"God. What does he . . . ? I mean, does he skin people?"

"No, he killed his victim by tattooing her with poison."

Pam closed her eyes and shivered. "Sick. Oh, wait. That guy on the news. He killed the girl in SoHo?"

"Right. Now, there's no evidence he has any interest in the surviving victims from back then. He's using the tattoos to send a message, so he'll pick targets in out-of-the-way places, we think—if we don't stop him first. We checked but none of the other survivors of the Bone Collector are in the area. You're the only one. Now, has anybody asked you anything about being kidnapped, about what happened?"

"No, nobody."

"Well, we're ninety-nine percent sure he has no interest in you at all. The killer—"

"The unsub," Pam said, offering a knowing smile.

"The unsub won't know about you—your name wasn't in the press because you were so young. And your mother used a pseudonym back then anyway. But I wanted you to know. Keep an eye out. And at night we're going to have an officer parked outside your apartment."

"Okay." Pam didn't seem fazed by this information. In fact, Sachs now realized something: The news that there might be a connection, however tenuous, with Unsub 11-5, whom the press had dubbed the Underground Man, was greeted with what seemed to Sachs to be such lack of concern that she realized the girl had another topic in mind.

And it was soon placed—no, dumped—on the table.

Pam sipped some cocoa and her eyes looked everywhere but at Sachs's. "So, here's the thing, Amelia. Something *I* wanted to talk about with *you.*" Smiling. Smiling too much. Sachs grew nervous. She too took a sip. Didn't taste a bit of the rich brew. She thought immediately: Pregnant?

Of course. That was it.

Sachs stifled her anger. Why hadn't they been careful? Why—?

"I'm not going to have a baby. Relax."

Sachs did. Coughed a brief laugh. She wondered if her body language was that readable.

"But Seth and me? We're moving in together."

This soon? Still, Sachs kept the smile on her face. Was it just as fake as the teenager's?

"Are you now? Well. That's exciting news."

Pam laughed, apparently at the disconnect between the modifier and Sachs's less-than-excited expression. "Look, Amelia. We're not getting married. Just, it's time for this to happen. I feel it. He feels it. It's just right. We're like totally compatible. He knows me, really knows me. There're times I don't even have to say anything and he knows what I'm thinking. And he's just so nice, you know?"

"It's kind of fast, don't you think, honey?"

Pam's enthusiasm, the sparkle, dimmed. Sachs recalled that her mother, who'd beaten the girl and locked her in a closet for hours on end, had called her "honey," and Pam had grown to hate the endearment. Sachs regretted using it but she'd been flustered and forgotten the word was tainted.

She tried again. "Pam, he's a great guy. Lincoln and I both think so."

This was true.

But Sachs couldn't stop herself. "It's just, I mean, don't you really think it'd be better to wait? What's the hurry? Just hang out, date. Spend the night... Go away on a trip."

Coward, Sachs told herself, having given the last two suggestions, since her goal was to wedge some distance between Pam and Seth. She was negotiating against herself.

"Well, interesting you say that."

Interesting? Sachs reflected. If she's not pregnant... Oh, no. Her jaw tightened and the next words confirmed her fear.

"What we're going to do is take a year off. We're going to travel."

"Oh. Okay. A year." Sachs was simply buying time at this point. She might've said, "How 'bout them Yankees?" Or "I hear the sleet's going to break in a day or so."

Pam pressed forward. "He's sick of copywriting freelance. He's totally talented. But nobody appreciates him in New York. He doesn't complain but I can see he's upset. The ad agencies he works for, they have budget problems. So they can't hire him full-time. He wants to go places. He's ambitious. It's so hard here."

"Well, sure. New York is always a tough place to get ahead."

Pam's voice hardened as she said, "He's tried. It's not like he hasn't tried."

"I didn't mean—"

"He's going to write travel articles. I'm going to help him. I've always wanted to travel; we've talked about that."

They had, yes. Except Sachs had always imagined that she and Pam would explore Europe or Asia. Big sister and kid sister. She had a fantasy of touring the parts of Germany her ancestors had come from.

"But school...The statistics show it's so hard to come back after dropping out."

"Why? What statistics? That doesn't make sense."

Okay, Sachs didn't have any numbers. She was making that up. "Hon—Pam, I'm happy for you, both of you. Just, well, you have to understand. This's a pretty big surprise. Fast, like I was saying. You haven't known him that long."

"A year."

True. In a way. They'd met last December and dated briefly. Then Seth had gone to England for training with an ad agency planning to open a New York office, and he and Pam had joined the ranks of those keeping a relationship afloat via text, Twitter and email. The company had decided not to venture into the U.S. market, though, and Seth had come back a month ago and returned to freelance copywriting. Normal dating had resumed.

"And so what if it's fast?" An edge to Pam's voice again. She'd always had a temper—you couldn't have her upbringing and not find anger near the surface. But she pulled back. "Look, Amelia. Now's the time to do this. When we're this age. Later? If we get married and if we have kids?"

Please. Don't go there.

"You can't backpack around Europe then."

"What about money? You can't work over there."

"That's not a problem. He'll sell his articles. And Seth's been saving for a while and his parents're totally rich. They can help us out."

His mother was a lawyer and father an investment banker, Sachs recalled.

"And we have the blog. I'll keep doing that from the road."

Seth had created a website a few years ago where people could post their support for various social and political issues, mostly left-leaning. Women's right to choose, support for the arts, gun control. Pam was now more involved than he was in running the site. Yes, it seemed popular, though Sachs estimated that the donations they received totaled about a thousand dollars a year.

"But . . . where? What countries? Is it safe?"

"We don't know yet. That's part of the adventure."

Desperate to buy time, Sachs asked, "What do the Olivettis say?"

After Sachs had rescued her the girl had gone into a foster home (which Sachs had checked out as if vetting the president's personal bodyguard). The temporary parents had been wonderful but at eighteen, last year, Pam had wanted to be on her own and—with Rhyme's and Sachs's help—she enrolled in college and got a part-time job. Pam had remained close to her foster mom and dad, though.

"They're okay with it."

But, of course, the Olivettis were professional parents; they'd had no connection with Pam before she'd been placed with them. They hadn't kicked in a door and saved her from the Bone Collector and a wild dog eager to shake her to death. They hadn't leapt into a firefight with Pam's stepfather, who was trying to suffocate her.

And, those traumas aside, it had been Sachs who'd spent a lot more time than the busy foster parents schlepping Pam to and from after-school activities, doctors' appointments and counseling sessions. And it was the detective who'd used some of the few existing connections from her former fashion model career to get Pam the wardrobe department job on Broadway.

Sachs couldn't help but note too that the girl had told the Olivettis first about her travel plans.

Come on, I deserve a hearing, Sachs thought.

Which was not, however, Pam's opinion. She said brusquely, "Anyway, we've decided."

Then Pam grew suddenly giddy, though Sachs could see the emotions were fake. That was clear. "It'll be a year. Two, tops."

Now *two*?

"Pam," Sachs began. "I don't know what to say."

Yes, you do. So say it.

As a cop, Sachs never held back. She couldn't as a big sister either. Or surrogate mother. Or whatever her role in the girl's life might be.

"Knuckle time, Pam."

The girl knew of Sachs's father's expression. She gauged Sachs with narrowed eyes, which were both cautious and flinty.

"A year on the road with somebody you don't really *know*?" Sachs said this evenly, trying to keep some tenderness in the tone.

But the woman responded as if Sachs had thrown open the parlor window and let in a flood of sleety wind. "We *do* know each other," Pam said defiantly. "That's the whole point. Didn't you hear me?"

"I mean *really* know each other. That takes years."

Pam shot back, "We're right for each other. It's simple."

"Have you met his family?"

"I've talked to his mother. She's totally sweet."

"Talked to?"

"Yes," the girl snapped. "Talked to. And his father knows all about me."

"But you haven't met them?"

A cool chill. "This's about me and Seth. Not his parents. And this cross-examination is pissing me off."

"Pam." Sachs leaned forward. She reached for the girl's hand. It was, of course, eased out of reach. "Pam, have you told him about what happened to you?"

"I have. And he doesn't care."

"Everything? Have you told him everything?"

Pam fell silent and looked down. Then she said defensively, "There's no need to... No, not everything. I told him my mother was crazy and did some bad things. He knows she's in jail and will be there forever. He's totally fine with it."

Then he was from *The Walking Dead*, Sachs reflected. "And *where* you grew up? *How* you grew up? Did you tell him any of that?"

"Not really. But that's in the past. That's over with."

"I don't think you can ignore it, Pam. He has to know. Your mother did a lot of damage—"

"Oh, I'm crazy too? Like my mother? That's how you look at me?"

Sachs was stung by this comment but she tried to keep a light tone. "Come on, you're saner than any politician in Washington." She smiled. It wasn't reciprocated.

"There's nothing wrong with me!" Pam's voice rose.

"Of course not, no! I'm just concerned about you."

"No. You're saying I'm too fucked up, I'm too immature to make decisions on my own."

Sachs was growing angry herself. The defensive didn't suit her. "Then make smart ones. If you really love him and it's going to work out, a year or so of dating won't mean anything."

"We're going away, Amelia. And then we're moving in when we get back. I mean, get over it."

"Don't talk that way to me," Sachs snapped back. She knew she was losing it but couldn't stop herself.

The young woman rose abruptly, knocking over her cup and spilling cocoa onto the silver tray.

"Shit."

She bent forward and angrily mopped it up. Sachs leaned in to help but Pam pulled the tray away and continued cleaning by herself, then tossed down the brown, saturated napkin. She glared at Sachs with shockingly feral eyes. "I know exactly what's going on. You want to break us up. You're looking for any excuse." A cold grin. "It's all about you, isn't it, Amelia? You want to break us up just so you can have the daughter you were too busy being a cop to have."

Sachs nearly gasped at the searing accusation—perhaps, she admitted silently, because there was a splinter of truth in it.

Pam stormed to the door, paused and said, "You're not my mother, Amelia. Remember that. You're the woman who put my mother in prison."

Then she was gone.

CHAPTER 16

Near midnight, Billy Haven cleared away his supper dishes, washing everything that wasn't disposable in bleach to remove DNA.

Which was as dangerous—to him—as some of the poisons he'd extracted and refined.

He sat back down at the rickety table in the kitchen area of his workshop, off Canal Street, and opened the dog-eared, battered notebook, the Commandments.

Delivered, in a way, by the hand of God.

Those stone tablets to Moses.

The notebook, with its dozen or so pages of tightly packed sentences—in Billy's beautiful, flowing cursive writing—described in detail how the Modification should unfold, who should die, when to do what, the risks to avoid, the risks to take, what advantages to seize, how to cope with unexpected reversals. An exact timetable. If Genesis were a how-to guide like the Modification Commandments, the first book of the Bible would read:

Day Three, 11:20 a.m.: Create deciduous trees.

Okay, now You have seven minutes to create evergreens…

Day Six, 6:42 a.m.: Time for salmon and trout. Get a move on!

Day Six, noon: Let's do the Adam and Eve thing.

Which naturally brought to mind Lovely Girl. He pictured her for a moment, face, hair, pure-white skin, then eased away the distracting image the way you'd set aside a precious snapshot of a departed loved one—carefully, out of a superstitious fear of harming your love if you dropped the frame.

Flipping through the pages, he studied what was coming next. Pausing once again to reflect that the Modification was certainly complicated. At various points in the process he'd wondered if it was too much so. But he thought back to the pages of the chapter he'd stolen from the library earlier that day, *Serial Cities*, recalling all the surprising—no, shocking—information it had revealed.

Experts in law enforcement universally voice the opinion of Lincoln Rhyme that his greatest skill is his ability to anticipate what the criminals he's pursuing will do next.

He believed that was the quotation; he wasn't sure, since Chloe Moore, no longer of this earth, had inconsiderately ripped a portion of that passage from the book.

Anticipate…

So, yes, the plan for the Modification *had* to be this precise. The people he was up against were too good for him to be careless, to miss a cue in any way.

He reviewed plans for the next attack, tomorrow. He

memorized locations, he memorized timing. Everything seemed in order. In his mind he rehearsed the attack; he'd already been to the site. He now pictured it, he smelled it.

Good. He was ready.

Then he glanced at his right wrist, the watch. He was tired.

And what, he wondered, was going on with the investigation into the demise of Ms. Chloe?

He turned on the radio, hoping for news.

The earlier reports had been that a young resident of Queens, a woman clerk in a stylish boutique in SoHo, had been found dead in an access tunnel off the cellar. Well, Billy had thought, perplexed, it was hardly very stylish. Chinese crap, overpriced and meant for frothy-hair sluts from Jersey and mothers seared by the approach of middle age.

Initially Chloe's name had not been released, pending notification of next of kin.

Hearing that, Billy had reflected: How sadistic can one cop be? To release the news that a young woman from Queens has been killed and not divulge the name? How many parents of kids living in that area had started making desperate phone calls?

Now, waiting for an update, all he got were commercials. Didn't anyone care about poor Chloe Moore?

Chloe Moore, Chloe the whore...

He paced back and forth in front of his terrariums. White leaves, green leaves, red leaves, blue...

Then, as often happened when he looked over the plants who were his companions, he thought of Oleander.

And the Oleander Room.

Billy resented that that thought intruded but there was nothing to do about it. He could—

Ah, now the news. Finally.

A city council scandal, a minor train derailment, an economic report. Then, at last, a follow-up on Chloe Moore's demise. Additional details were coughed up now, a bit of history. The facts suggested the attack was not sexual in nature. (Of course not; Billy was offended that the subject had even come up. The media. Despicable.) A rough description. So someone had spotted him near the manhole.

He listened as the story wound down.

Still nothing about tattooing. Nothing about poison.

That was typical, Billy knew. He'd read about police procedures in verifying confessions. The cops ask people taking credit for a crime certain unique details and, if they can't answer, the supposed perpetrators are dismissed as crackpots (a surprising number of people confessed to crimes they hadn't committed).

Nor had the story mentioned anything about the phrase "the second."

But *that* would be a thorn in their sides, of course.

What on earth could the message be that their mysterious perp was sending?

The Modification Commandments required, however, that it be impossible for the police to decipher his message from the first several victims.

He shut the radio off.

Billy yawned. Sleep soon. He checked email, sent some texts, received some, then two hums of the watches told him it was time to get some rest.

When he was through in the bathroom, where he cleaned the basin and toothbrush with bleach—banishing the DNA once more—he returned to his bed, flopping down in it. He tugged his Bible from under the pillow and propped it on his chest.

Billy had had a crisis of faith a few years ago. A serious one. He believed in Jesus and the power of Christ. But he also believed he was meant to put his talents to use as a tattoo artist.

The problem was this: The book of Leviticus warned, *You shall not make any cuttings in your flesh for the dead, nor tattoo any marks upon you: I am the LORD.*

He'd been depressed for weeks upon learning this. He wrestled with how to reconcile the conflict.

One argument was that the Bible was full of such dissonance: In the same chapter, for instance, it was written: "Nor shall a garment of mixed linen and wool come upon you." Yet God surely had other priorities than sending to hell people wearing blended cloth suits.

Billy had wondered if He intended future generations to reinterpret the Bible, to bring it into line with contemporary society. But that seemed suspect; it was like those Supreme Court justices who said that the Constitution was a living thing and should change to suit the times.

Dangerous, thinking like that.

Finally the answer to this apparent contradiction appeared. Billy had reasoned: The Bible also says, *Thou shalt not kill.* But the Good Book was filled with instances of outright murder—including a fair amount of carnage by the Almighty Himself. So, it was okay to kill in certain instances. Such as to further the glory of God, eliminate infidels and threats, further the values of truth and justice. Dozens of reasons.

So in Leviticus, it was clear, God had to mean that tattooing too was acceptable under *certain circumstances*, just like taking lives.

And what better circumstances could there be than the mission Billy was on at the moment?

The Modification.

He opened his Bible. He settled on a verse in Exodus, a well-read page.

> And if men strive together, and hurt a woman with child, so that her fruit depart, and yet no harm follow; he shall be surely fined, according as the woman's husband shall lay upon him; and he shall pay as the judges determine. But if any harm follow, then thou shalt give life for life, eye for eye, tooth for tooth, hand for hand, foot for foot, burning for burning, wound for wound, stripe for stripe.

WEDNESDAY, NOVEMBER 6 II

THE UNDERGROUND MAN

CHAPTER 17

NOON

The morning had been a flurry of activity, trying to correlate the evidence Sachs had come up with to pinpoint a place where the unsub might be living or had decided to make his stalking ground.

Rhyme wheeled back and forth in front of the chart, feeling in his neck and jaw the thump as the Merits chair rolled over one of the power cables bisecting the floor of his parlor.

237 ELIZABETH STREET CRIME SCENE

- Victim: Chloe Moore, 26
    - Probably no connection to Unsub
    - No sexual assault, but touching of skin
- Unsub 11-5
    - White male
    - Slim to medium build
    - Stocking cap
    - Thigh-length dark coat
    - Dark backpack

    - Wore booties
    - No friction ridges
    - Professional tattoo artist or has been
    - May be using a "splitter" for the tattoos
    - Uses bloodline to outline the tattoos
    - Not from area; more rural probably
    - Using book to learn techniques and outthink Rhyme and police?
    - Obsessed with skin
    - Will possibly be targeting the police
    - Organized offender; will be planning attacks ahead of time
    - Probably returned to the scene
- COD: Poisoning with cicutoxin, introduced into system by tattooing
    - From water hemlock plant
    - No known source
    - Concentrated, eight times normal
- Sedated with propofol
    - How obtained, access to medical supplies?
- Tattooed with "the second" Old English typeface, surrounded by scallops
    - Part of message?
    - Task force at police HQ checking this out
    - Scallops are cicatrization—scarring—and probably significant
- Portable tattoo machine used as weapon
    - Probably American Eagle
- Cotton fiber
    - Off-white
    - Probably from Unsub's shirt, torn in struggle
- Page from book

    — Probably torn from Unsub's pocket in struggle
    — Probably mass produced hardcover 1996–2000
    — Book is *Serial Cities.* He was interested in Chapter 7, about Bone Collector.
    — Psychological connection with Bone Collector? Revenge?
— Possibly used adhesive rollers to remove trace from clothing prior to attack
— Handcuffs
    — Generic, cannot be sourced
— Flashlight
    — Generic, cannot be sourced
— Duct tape
    — Generic, cannot be sourced
— Trace evidence
    — Nitric oxide, ozone, iron manganese, nickel, silver beryllium, chlorinated
    hydrocarbon, acetylene
        — Possibly oxy-fuel welding supplies
    — Tetrodotoxin
        — Fugu fish poison
        — Zombie drug
        — Minute amounts
        — Not used on victim here
    — Stercobilin, urea 9.3 g/L, chloride 1.87 g/L, sodium 1.17 g/L, potassium 0.750 g/L, creatinine 0.670 g/L
        — Fecal material
        — Possibly suggesting interest/obsession in underground
        — From future kill sites underground?
    — Benzalkonium chloride

  - Quaternary ammonium (quat), institutional sanitizer
- Adhesive latex
  - Used in bandages and construction, other uses too
- Inwood marble
  - Dust and fine grains
- Tovex explosive
  - Probably from blast site

Rhyme turned from the chart to Amelia Sachs, whom he caught staring out the window into the sleety morning. She was still obviously troubled by the news she'd received yesterday—that Pam was going on a 'round-the-world tour with her boyfriend, then moving in with him when they returned.

Seth was a nice young man, she'd explained as they'd lain in his sumptuous bed last night, lights out, the wind battering the windows. "To date. Not hole up in a hostel in Morocco or Goa. Maybe he's Mr. Perfect, maybe he's not. Who can tell?"

"Think it'll blow over?"

"No. She's determined."

"Like you. Remember your mother didn't like you going out with a gimp in a wheelchair?"

"You could've been a marathon runner and she wouldn't've liked you. Nobody could meet my mother's standards. She likes you now, though."

"My point exactly."

"I like Seth. I'll like him better in a year."

Rhyme had smiled.

She had asked, "Any thoughts?"

"Afraid not." Rhyme had been married for a few years. He'd gotten divorced not long after his accident (his call; not his wife's), but the marriage had been doomed for some time. He was sure he'd been in love at some point but the relationship had soured for reasons he could never isolate, quantify and analyze. As for what he had with Sachs? It worked because it worked. That was the best he could say. Lincoln Rhyme was admittedly in no position to offer romantic advice.

But then who, ultimately, was? Love is an occurrence for which there are no expert witnesses.

Sachs had added, "And I didn't handle it well. I got protective. Too motherly. It turned ugly. I should've been objective, rational. But, no, I let things get out of control."

Now, this morning, Rhyme could see that Sachs was still deeply troubled. He was thinking he should say something reassuring when, to his relief, the professional deflected the personal.

"Have something here," Pulaski called from across the lab, where he'd been staring at a monitor. "I think..." He fell silent, glowering. "Damn Internet. Just when I had some hits."

Rhyme could see that his screen was frozen.

"Okay, okay, up again."

He was tapping more keys. Maps and schematics and what appeared to be lists of compounds and elemental materials popped up on the big screen.

"You're getting to be quite the scientist, Rookie," Rhyme said, regarding the notes.

"What do you have, Ron?" Mel Cooper asked.

"Some good news for a change. Maybe."

CHAPTER 18

Harriet Stanton's family trip to New York, which she'd been looking forward to for years, had not turned out as planned.

It had been derailed by a chance incident that could have changed her life forever.

Harriet now stood before the mirror of the hotel suite she'd spent a restless night in and looked over her suit. Dark. Not black but navy blue.

How close she'd come to selecting the former color. Bad luck, making that choice.

She plucked a few pieces of random lint off the wool, brushed at some dust—the hotel was not as nice as advertised online (but it was affordable and frugality was important in the Stanton family, which hailed from a town where accommodation standards were set by a Holiday Inn).

Fifty-three years old, with slim shoulders and a pear-shaped build (but a slim pear), Harriet had a staunch face that was ruddy and weathered—from gardening, from marshaling children after class in the backyard, from picnics and barbecues. Yet she was the least vain woman on earth, and the only creases that troubled her were not in her face but in the skirt of the suit—one set of wrinkles that she could control.

Given her destination, a grim place, she might easily have ignored the imperfection. But that wasn't Harriet's way. There was a right approach and a wrong, a lazy, a misguided approach. She unzipped and sloughed off the skirt, which slid easily over the beige slip.

She deftly ratcheted open the cheap ironing board with one hand (oh, Harriet knew her laundry implements) and plugged in the inadequate iron, which was secured to the board with a wire; were handheld appliance thefts such a terrible problem in New York? And didn't the hotel have the guests' credit cards anyway?

Oh, well. It was a different world here, so different from home.

As she waited for the heat to gather she kept replaying her husband's words from yesterday as they'd walked through the chill streets of New York.

"Hey, Harriet, hey." He'd stopped on the street, halfway between FAO Schwarz and Madison Avenue, hand on a lamppost.

"Honey?" she'd asked, circling.

"Sorry. I'm sorry." The man, ten years older than his wife, had seemed embarrassed. "I'm not feeling so good. Something." He'd touched his chest. "Something here, you know."

Cab or call? she'd wondered, debating furiously.

Nine one one, of course. Don't fool around.

In twenty minutes they were at a nearby hospital emergency room.

And the diagnosis: a mild myocardial infarction.

"A what?" she'd asked.

Oh, it seemed: heart attack.

This was curious. Outfitted with low cholesterol, the man had never smoked cigarettes in his life, only occasional cigars, and his six-foot-two frame was as narrow and strong as the pole he'd gripped to steady himself when the heart attack had struck. He trekked through the woods after deer and boar every weekend during hunting season when he could find the time. He helped friends frame rec rooms and garages. Every weekend he muscled onto his shoulder forty-pounders of mulch and potting soil and carried them from pickup truck to shed.

"Unfair," Matthew had muttered, upon hearing the diagnosis. "Our dream trip to the city, and look what happens. Damn unfair."

As a precaution, the doctors had transferred him to a hospital about a half hour north of their hotel, which was apparently the best cardiac facility in the city. His prognosis was excellent and he'd be released tomorrow. No surgery was called for. There would be some medication to lower his blood pressure and he'd carry around nitroglycerine tablets. And he should take an aspirin a day. But the doctors seemed to treat the attack as minor.

To test the iron she flicked a dot of spit onto the Teflon plate. It sizzled and leapt off. She spritzed a bit of water onto the skirt from the Dannon bottle and ironed the wrinkles into oblivion.

Slipping the skirt back on, she reexamined herself in the mirror. Good. But she decided she needed some color and tied a red-and-white silk scarf around her neck. Perfect. Bright but not flamboyant. She collected her handbag and left the room, descending to the lobby in an elevator car outside which a chain jangled at every passing floor.

Once outside, Harriet oriented herself and flagged down a cab. She told the driver the name of the hospital and climbed into the backseat. The air inside was funky and she believed the driver, some foreigner, hadn't bathed recently. A cliché but true.

Despite the sleet, she rolled down the window, prepared to argue if he objected. But he didn't. He seemed oblivious to her—well, to everything. He punched the button on the meter and sped off.

As they clattered north in the old taxi, Harriet was thinking about the facilities at the hospital. The staff seemed nice and the doctors professional, even if their English was awkward. The one thing she didn't like, though, was that Matthew's room in Upper Manhattan Medical Center was in the basement at the end of a long, dim corridor.

Shabby and creepy. And when she'd visited last night it had been deserted.

Looking at the elegant town houses to the left and Central Park to the right, Harriet tried to cast off any concerns about visiting the unpleasant place. She was thinking that maybe the bad luck of the heart attack was an omen, hinting at worse to come.

But then she put those feelings down to superstition, pulled out her phone and sent a cheerful text that she was on her way.

CHAPTER 19

With his backpack over his shoulder—the pack containing the American Eagle machine and some particularly virulent poison—Billy Haven turned down a side street, past a large construction area, avoiding pedestrians.

That is, avoiding witnesses.

He stepped into the doctors' office building annex, next to the Upper Manhattan Medical Center complex. In the lobby he kept his head down and walked purposefully toward a stairwell. He'd scoped the place out and knew exactly where he was going and how to get there invisibly.

No one paid any attention to the slim young man, like so many slim young men in New York, an artist, a musician, a wishful actor.

Just like them.

Though their backpacks didn't contain what his did.

Billy pushed through the fire door and started down the stairs. He descended to the basement level and followed the signs to the hospital proper, through a long, dim corridor. It was deserted, as if not many workers knew about it. More likely, they were aware of the dingy route but preferred to walk from office building to hospital on the surface, where you could not only find a Starbucks or buy a slice of Ray's original pizza but not get dragged into a closet and raped.

The tunnel leading to the hospital was long—several hundred feet—and painted a gray that you associated with warships. Pipes ran overhead. It was dark because the hospital, perhaps in a move to save money, had placed a bulb in every third socket. There were no security cameras.

Billy knew time was critical but he, of course, had to make one stop. He'd noted the detour yesterday, when he'd checked to see if this would be a suitably private route into the hospital.

The sign on the door had intrigued him.

He'd simply *had* to go inside.

And he did so now, aware of the time pressure. But feeling like a kid playing hooky to hang out in a toy store.

The large room, labeled by the sign *Specimens*, was dim but lit well enough by the emergency exit lights, which cast an eerie rosy glow on the contents: a thousand jars filled with body parts floating in a jaundiced liquid, presumably formaldehyde.

Eyes, hands, livers, hearts, lungs, sexual organs, breasts, feet. Whole fetuses too. Billy noted that most of the samples dated to the early twentieth century. Maybe back then medical students used the real thing to learn anatomy, while today's generation went for high-def computer images.

Against the wall were shelves of bones, hundreds of them. He thought back to the infamous case Lincoln Rhyme had worked years ago, the Bone Collector crimes. Yet bones held little interest for Billy Haven.

The Rule of Bone?

No, didn't resonate like the Rule of Skin. No comparison.

He now walked up and down the aisles, examining the jars, which ranged from a few inches to three feet in height. He paused and stared, eye-to-eye with a severed head. The features seemed of South Pacific heritage to Billy, or so he wanted to believe—because, to his delight, the head sported a tattoo: a cross just below where the hairline would have been.

Billy took this as a good sign. The word "tattoo" comes from the Polynesian or Samoan *tatau*, the process of inking the lower male torso with an elaborate geometric design, called a *pe'a* (and a woman's with a similar inking, called a *malu*). The process takes weeks and is extremely painful. Those who finish the inking get a special title and are respected for their courage. Those who don't even try are called "naked" in Samoan and marginalized. The worst stigma, though, was awarded to the men and women who started the procedure but didn't finish it because they couldn't stand the pain. The shame remained with them forever.

Billy liked the fact that they defined themselves according to their relationship to inking.

He decided to believe that the man he was staring at

had endured getting his *pe'a* and had gone on to be a force in his tribe. Heathen though he might have been, he was brave, a good warrior (even if not clever enough to avoid having his head end up on a steel shelf in the New World).

Billy held the jar in one hand and leaned forward until he was only a few inches from the severed head, separated by thick glass and thin liquid.

He thought about one of his favorite books. *The Island of Doctor Moreau.* The H. G. Wells novel was about an Englishman shipwrecked on an island, on which the doctor of the title surgically combined humans and animals. Hyena-men, Leopard-men... Billy had read and reread the book the way other kids would read *Harry Potter* or *Twilight*.

Vivisection and recombination were the ultimate modding, of course. And *Doctor Moreau* was the perfect example of the application of the Rule of Skin.

All right. Time to get back to reality, he chided himself.

Billy now stepped to the door and looked up and down the corridor. Still deserted. He continued his way to the hospital and knew when he'd crossed into the building. The neutral scent of cleanser and mold from the office building was overrun by a mélange of smells. Sweet disinfectants, alcohol, Lysol, Betadine.

And the others, repulsive to some, but not to Billy: the aromas of skin in decay, skin melting under infection and bacteria, skin burning to ash... perhaps from lasers in operating rooms.

Or maybe hospital workers were disposing of discarded tissue and organs in an oven somewhere. He couldn't think of this without recalling the Nazis, who had used the skin of Holocaust victims for practical purposes, like lamp shades and books. And who had devised a system of tattooing that was the simplest—and most significant—in history.

The Rule of Skin . . .

Billy inhaled deeply.

He sensed some other aroma: extremely offensive. What, what?

Oh, he understood. With so many foreign workers in the medical fields, the foods the hospital prepared included those aromatic with curry and garlic.

Disgusting.

Billy finally entered the heart of the hospital, the third sub-basement. It was completely deserted here. A perfect place to bring a victim for some deadly modding, he reflected.

The elevator would have surveillance cameras so he found the stairwell, entered it and started to climb. At the next sub-basement, number two, he paused and peeked out. It was the morgue, presently unstaffed. Apparently the medicos had not managed to kill anyone yet today.

Up another flight to the basement level, a floor with patient rooms. Peering out through the fire door's greasy glass, crosshatched with fine metal mesh, he could see a flash of color, then motion: a woman walking down the corridor, her back to him.

Ah, he thought, noting that while her skirt and jacket were navy blue, the scarf around her neck was red-and-white shimmery silk. It stood out like a flag in the drab setting. She was alone. He eased through the door and followed. He noted her muscular legs—revealed clearly by the knee-length skirt—noted the slim waist, noted the hips. The hair, in a tight bun, was brown with a bit of gray. Although the sheer pantyhose revealed a few purplish veins near the ankle, her skin was superb for an older woman's.

Billy found himself aroused, heart pounding, the blood throbbing in his temples. And elsewhere.

Blood. The Oleander Room... blood on the carpet, blood on the floor.

Put those thoughts away. Now! Think of Lovely Girl.

He did and the urges dimmed. But dimming isn't vanishing.

Sometimes you just gave in. Whatever the consequences might be.

Oleander...

He moved more quickly now, coming up behind her.

Thirty feet away, twenty-five...

Billy closed the distance to about fifteen feet, ten, three, his eyes staring at her legs. It was then that he heard a woman's no-nonsense voice behind him.

"You, in the cap. Police! Drop the backpack. Put your hands on your head!"

CHAPTER 20

About thirty feet away from the man, Amelia Sachs steadied her Glock and repeated, more harshly, "Backpack on the ground. Hands on your head! Now!"

The woman he'd been about to assault, only a few feet from him, turned. The confusion in her face became horror as she stared at her would-be assailant and understood what was happening. "No, please, no!"

The attacker was in a jacket, not the longer thigh-length coat that the witness reported their unsub wore, but he had the same telltale stocking cap and black backpack. If she was wrong, she'd apologize. "Now!" Sachs called again.

With his back to her still, he slowly lifted his hands. As his sleeve rode up she got a glimpse of a red tattoo of some kind on his left arm, starting at the back of his hand and disappearing under his coat. A snake, a dragon?

He was raising his hands, yes, but not dropping the backpack.

Shit. He's going to rabbit.

And, sure enough, in an instant he tugged his hat down into a ski mask and leapt forward, grabbing the woman, spinning her around. He got his arm around her neck. She cried out and struggled. Her dark eyes were wide with fear.

Okay. He's Unsub 11-5.

Sachs eased forward slowly, the blade sights of the Glock searching for a clear target.

Couldn't find one. Thanks largely to the panicked hostage, who was struggling to get away, kicking and twisting. He pressed his face close to her ear, apparently whispered something and, with wide eyes, she stopped struggling.

"I have a gun!" he shouted. "I'll kill her. Drop your gun. Now."

Sachs called back, "No."

Because you never dropped your weapon, you never went off target. Period. She doubted he had a gun—because he would've pulled it out and started firing by now—but even if he did, you never lowered your aim.

Sachs rested the sights on the new moon of his head. It was an easy shot with a static target but he was walking backward and sideways and kept ducking behind the hostage.

"No, please don't hurt me! Please!" the woman cried in a low voice.

"Shut up!" the unsub muttered.

Reasonably, Sachs said, "Listen, there's no way you're getting out of here. Raise your hands and—"

A door nearby opened and a slim man in blue scrubs

stepped into the corridor. It was just enough of a distraction to draw Sachs's eye for an instant.

And *that* was enough for the unsub to seize his chance. He shoved his hostage directly toward Sachs and, before she could sidestep and draw a target, he crashed through another doorway and vanished.

Sachs was sprinting past the woman in the navy suit. Terrified, she stared with wide eyes, backing up against the wall.

"What was he—?"

No time for back-and-forth. Sachs flung the door open and peered in fast. No threat, no target. She shouted over her shoulder to the woman and the medico, "Get back to the lobby. Now! Wait there! Call nine one one."

"Who—?" the hostage called.

"Go!" Sachs turned and eased through the doorway the unsub had just disappeared into. She listened. A faint click—from below. Made sense; he wasn't going to escape from the upper floors. Unsub 11-5 was their Underground Man.

Sachs hadn't come here on a tactical mission so she didn't have a radio but she pulled her iPhone out and called 911. It was easier than going roundabout to Central Dispatch. She reported a 10-13, officer needing assistance. She supposed the hostage and the hospital worker might be calling too but they could also simply have vanished, not wanting to get involved.

Down another flight of stairs. Steady but slow. Who's

to say the guy hadn't clicked the ground-floor door latch to fool her and then returned to snipe away with the pistol he did, in fact, have in his pocket?

Sachs had never thought this trip would actually end up in a sighting of the unsub. She'd come here simply to see if any staffers had spotted anyone fitting the perp's description. Rhyme had speculated that there might be an attack at this hospital. Terry Dobyns's profile was that, as an organized offender, the unsub would plan the attacks ahead of time. That meant some of the trace they'd found at the Chloe Moore scene might have come from the sites of future poisonings.

Ron Pulaski's find forty minutes ago was that the Inwood marble trace Sachs had collected was unique to this portion of Manhattan and that explosives permits had been issued to the general contractor building a new wing of the Upper Manhattan Medical Center. Other trace—the industrial cleanser quats and the adhesive that could be used in bandages—also suggested that he'd been inside the hospital to plan his attack on victim number two.

Sachs had hardly expected to actually interrupt him.

Breathing deeply, she paused at the fire door, pushed it open, dropping into a combat shooting pose. Swiveling back and forth. This was the morgue level; there were four employees in scrubs chatting and sipping coffee, standing beside two covered gurneys.

They turned, saw the gun, then Sachs, and went wide-eyed, frozen.

She held up her shield. "White male in dark coat. About six feet, stocking cap or mask. Slim build. Come by here?"

"No."

"How long you been here?"

"Ten, fifteen min—"

"Get inside and lock the door."

One attendant started to push the gurney through the door. Sachs called, "Only the live ones."

Back to the dim stairwell. Down more stairs. She hit the lowest sub-basement. He had to've come here.

Go.

Fast.

When you move, they can't getcha...

She pushed through the door, swinging the muzzle right and left.

This floor was deserted, devoted mostly to infrastructure and storerooms, it seemed.

She kept swiveling, right, left. Because in the back of her mind was the persistent thought that maybe this wasn't an escape at all. Maybe it was a trap. Maybe he was hiding here to kill a pursuer.

She remembered the line from the book *Serial Cities*, about Rhyme: *Experts in law enforcement universally voice the opinion of Lincoln Rhyme that his greatest skill was his ability to anticipate what the criminals he's pursuing will do next.*

Maybe Unsub 11-5 was anticipating too.

Terry Dobyns had also suggested that he might target the police.

As her eyes oriented to the dimness, she examined the corridor. He couldn't go to the left—that was a dead end. To the right, a sign announced, was the tunnel that led to the doctors' office building.

He could either escape that way...or lie in wait for her.

But nothing to do other than go for it.

Knuckle time...

She started in that direction.

Suddenly a figure appeared in front of her, coming down the tunnel. She paused, plastered herself against the wall, aiming her weapon high but in the general direction of the man.

"Hey," he called. "I can see you there. You police?"

A large African American dressed in a black rent-a-cop security outfit—more intimidating than an NYPD uniform—walked closer. "I can see you! Officer."

She whispered harshly, "Come here! Get under cover. We've got a perp somewhere."

He joined her and they both pressed against the wall.

"Amelia."

"I'm Leron." The man had quick eyes and he took in the hallway. "I heard a ten-thirteen."

"Heard?"

"Got a scanner."

"Backup's on their way?"

"Right."

She noted he had a Beretta Nano on his hip, a small gun, 9mm, and accurate enough under good conditions if you mastered the long trigger pull. Unusual for a hospital guard to be armed. She noted that he hadn't drawn it. No need, no target. This explained him.

"You were in?" she asked.

"Nineteenth."

One of the Upper East Side precincts.

"Patrol. Retired, medical. Diabetes. That sucks. Keep your weight down." He was breathing hard. "Not that you—"

"You came from the doctors' office building?"

"Yep. Drew that detail today. Security in the hospital called me." He looked behind her and snickered. "None of the brothers I work with decided to come take a look-see. Ha."

"So he couldn't've gotten out that way."

"Nope. Not past me. " Leron scanned again, behind them, to the left, then to the right.

So 11-5 was here somewhere near, then. But there weren't many places to hide. There were only a few doors and most of them, storage or electrical and infrastructure, were padlocked.

Leron whispered, "Backpack."

"Right."

"Bomb?"

"Not his MO. Serial doer, we're thinking."

"Weapon?"

"Said so but I didn't see it."

"If they say and don't show they usually don't have."

This was true.

"But, Leron, time for you to get upstairs." Nodding toward the stairwell. "I'll take over." She was supposed to keep civilians—which Leron was, even in his storm trooper uniform and with an American-made Italian gun—out of tactical situations.

"Sorry, Detective," the man said firmly. "The hospital, 's my 'hood here. Nobody fucks with it. You tell me to stay put, I'll follow you anyway. An' I don't suppose you want to hear footsteps behind you in a spooky place like this."

Backup, she guessed, was still ten, fifteen minutes away.

She debated. But not very long. "Deal. Just don't fire

that sissy gun of yours unless the perp's about to park one in me. Or you. And you get yourself shot, I'll be writing up reports till kingdom come. That'll piss me off."

"Got it."

"We'll go together, Leron. Now let's move."

CHAPTER 21

As they eased along the wall, she asked the guard, "Where would *you* hide?"

"He can't've gone that way." Leron nodded toward a corridor to the right. "Dead end and no doorways to get through. Gotta be somewhere off this hallway." He gestured forward. She took the lead and they moved about twenty feet farther down the tunnel connecting the hospital proper to the office building.

He whispered, "There?" The men's and women's restrooms were across from each other.

A nod from Sachs.

Leron continued, "You ladies got all those stalls for cover. I'll take that one first. And—"

"I take it and you wait here."

"I can back you up."

"No, if he sees we're both inside and he's someplace else, he'll rabbit." She was speaking near his ear. He wore a pleasant aftershave. "If you fire, remember the tile."

"Got it. Amplifies the sound. One shot, we're both

deaf for five minutes. I've been there. That happens, we have to scan visually. We can't hear him coming... That is, if I don't hit him. I am not, by any stretch, Amelia, a bad shot."

She liked him. "You've done this before."

"Way, way too many times."

"Draw," she said.

The Nano was in his hand, dwarfed and nearly invisible in the dark flesh. He had two rings: wedding and a police academy signet. "Gotcha covered. Go."

She breached the women's room.

No drama. There were only two stalls and the doors were open.

Then she was outside. Scanning. He nodded his all-clear.

The one-stall men's room was even faster.

Outside once more, Sachs gazed at the dozen storerooms opening onto the corridor. Then noted that Leron's head was cocked. He touched his ear and pointed to a doorway, about twenty feet away. He'd heard something. The door was marked with the word *Specimens.*

Leron whispered, "A scrape. In there. I'm sure."

"Any windows?"

"No. We're way underground here."

"Locked?"

"Yeah, but that doesn't mean anything. Anybody can get through these doors, you got a bobby pin. Women still use bobby pins?"

"Sure, to pick locks," she replied.

She and Leron moved close. There was a rippled glass window in the door, and the guard ducked under to the other side as they flanked it.

You've done this before...

Amelia Sachs debated.

On the other side was most likely a perp they had to assume was armed—and at the very least in possession of deadly toxins.

Wait for full backup from Emergency Service? With bio-chem gear?

Debating...

Yes, no?

She decided. She was going in. Every minute the unsub could fortify himself behind barricades and rig traps.

But mostly, she was going in because she wanted to go in.

Had to go in. Thinking: Can't explain it, Rhyme. Just the way it is.

When you move...

"You back me up," she mouthed. "From the hall."

"No, I..." But Leron fell silent, looking at her eyes. He nodded.

She gripped the knob, which turned. Unlocked.

Then pushing forward... The door plowed open, revealing nothing on the other side except blackness. Sachs jogged left and dropped into a crouch, so she wouldn't be silhouetted by the open doorway.

Then, a huge crash from the back left corner of the room.

Leron surged forward as Sachs gave a whisper-shout, "No!"

But the guard pressed through the door anyway, gallantly coming to a rescue she didn't need, a rescue that was purely a diversion.

For what was coming next.

"Look out!" Sachs cried. Seeing something flying out of the blackness toward Leron. It glinted in the light from the doorway as it arched overhead. She knew the bottle contained toxin, more cicutoxin or maybe that zombie fish crap.

No known antidote...

"It's poison!" she called and ducked instinctively. Leron leapt to the left but stumbled and fell on his back, hard. He grunted in pain.

But it seemed the unsub hadn't been aiming for her or the guard directly. Of course not. Their flesh wouldn't shatter the poison container; he'd tossed it high, at the ceiling.

Leron was directly under the bottle when it hit a pipe and burst. The poison rained down on him. He dropped his Nano and began screaming.

By the time Sachs rolled to her feet, the unsub had pushed through a second door to the specimens room, thirty feet up the corridor. She heard his footfalls fading as he sprinted toward the doctors' office building.

She turned back to Leron, who was moaning and wiping desperately at his face. "Water, wash it off...I can't see."

What the hell was it? She smelled a noxious odor, astringent.

Acid! It looked like parts of his flesh were melting off.

Jesus!

Sachs debated. Go after the unsub...or do what she could for Leron?

Hell. She grabbed her phone and called 911 again,

reporting that the perp was escaping through the connecting tunnel to the doctors' office building next to the hospital.

She then ran to a nearby fire station and yanked the hose off the rack, turning on the stream of water and spraying Leron's face and chest, though this didn't seem to offer much relief, to judge from his screams, which were far louder than the fiercely loud rush of water.

"Nuh, nuh, nuh..."

Then the heavyset man was sitting up, waving his hands fiercely. "Enough, enough, enough!"

He started choking and Sachs realized she was firing the water directly into his face, half drowning him. She shut off the stream.

Leron rose to his knees, spitting.

His eyes were red, but he seemed otherwise all right—aside from the choking.

"How are you feeling?" she asked. "Are you burned? Was it acid? Poison?"

"'S okay, 's okay... I'm all right."

Sachs squinted at the floor, the broken glass. She walked over to a shard that held a yellowing label.

Oh.

Leron nodded, squinting. "He threw one of them samples at me, a specimen. One of the jars, right?"

"Looks that way. Probably formaldehyde."

"Stings, but not bad. You washed most of it off me."

Sachs then scanned the floor and noted the tissue sample on the floor, near where Leron sat. She'd thought the unsub had thrown acid, which had melted off the guard's skin. In reality, the flesh was what had been in the bottle.

Leron looked down too, prodded the lumpy tube of flesh with his foot. "Shit. That what I think it is?"

"I'd say so."

"He threw a dick and balls at me? Motherfucker. After you collar his ass, Amelia, I wanna piece of him."

CHAPTER 22

In the doctors' office building, Billy Haven emerged from the connecting tunnel, where his pursuers—cop and security guard—were, he hoped, writhing in pain and clutching their inflamed eyes.

He hadn't seen exactly how much formaldehyde spattered them—hadn't, of course, been able to watch, however appealing that sight might have been.

Now he spotted a men's room down a deserted corridor, entered and stepped into a stall. He dug through his backpack for a change of clothing. Not many options. He slipped on worker's coveralls and replaced the stocking cap with a Mets hat. Pulled on dark-rimmed reading glasses too. Finally, he extracted a canvas gear bag, like a contractor would use, and shoved the backpack and his coat into it. He carried the bag around for this very purpose—to change his identity in case of escape.

Thou shalt be prepared to become someone else…

He eased out of the restroom and made his way to the front door. He was about to step out onto the street through the double-door entry when a police car showed up, followed by two others, the tires squealing in brief skids. Officers leapt out and began speaking to every white male between fifteen and fifty near the building, asking for IDs, looking through bags.

Hell.

Soon other officers arrived, along with a large, blue-and-white NYPD Emergency Service truck. They formed a perimeter in the front—and presumably they were ganging at the back door and loading dock too.

Billy turned back. He shivered in anger. The policewoman's presence, so unexpected, had ruined everything. He'd been shocked to see that it was Amelia Sachs herself, ironically looking just as steely-eyed as in the photo in Chapter Seven of *Serial Cities*. Wearing pretty much the same unsexy outfit too. Oh, he wanted so badly to get her on her back and give her one of his special mods. Angel's trumpet. *Brugmansia*. Lethal quickly, but not so fast that Officer Sachs wouldn't die in excruciating pain.

But before that he had to get out of here. The police, it seemed, were getting ready to search the building.

And he knew they'd search carefully.

The first wave of officers was moving toward the door.

Billy casually pivoted and headed to the elevator bank, where he paused and, as nonchalantly as he could, carefully regarded the building directory as if he didn't have a care in the world—other than finding his doctor for a mole removal or colonoscopy appointment.

He was thinking furiously. The building was ten or eleven stories tall. Did it have external fire escapes? Probably not. You didn't see those much anymore.

There were probably fireproof stairwells, leading to unmarked doors opening onto alleyways. The cops would be stationed there, of course. Guns out, waiting for the perp.

Then he noticed a sign for a doctor's office on the sixth floor.

Billy Haven thought for a moment.

Good, he concluded, and turned away from the directory as the first cops stepped into the lobby.

Thou shalt always be ready to improvise…

CHAPTER 23

Lon Sellitto jogged into the main hallway of Upper Manhattan Medical Center. The elevator seemed sluggish—four people waited. Impatient patients, he joked to himself—and so he descended the stairs to the basement level, where Amelia Sachs had stopped the unsub from another attack. Stopped him with seconds to spare, it seemed. If Rhyme and Pulaski hadn't figured out the target location the perp had been checking out earlier, they'd be running a homicide now, not conducting a manhunt.

His gold shield, on a lanyard, bounced on his substantial belly. His Burberry over his arm, Sellitto was moving fast and he was out of breath.

Fucking diets. Was there *any* one that worked?

Also, gotta work out more.

Think about it later.

Downstairs he entered the cardiac care unit and walked a good fifty yards before he found the room he sought. Outside were two uniforms, male, one Latino, one black. In the room, he observed a white-haired man in bed, lean, with a wrinkled—and unhappy—face. Sitting in the chair beside him was a handsome woman in her early fifties, he guessed. She was in a conservative navy suit and nearly opaque stockings, a bright scarf. Her long face was hollow and her green eyes zipped around the room uneasily. Then she glanced at Sellitto in the corridor and went back to perusing the patient. Her ruddy hands were kneading a tissue to shreds. A young blond man—resembling her slightly, son probably—sat on the other side of the bed.

Sellitto nodded to the uniforms and they stepped away from the door.

The detective asked in a low voice, "So. Detective Sachs?"

"She stayed with the guard, the hospital guard, till the emergency room guys got there. Now? She's sweeping the hallway and room where the perp attacked them, her and the guard, I mean. She already ran the scene where he was going after the vic, the woman." A nod toward the hospital room. Name badge: *Juarez.*

"It was poison?"

"Naw."

"*Naw*?" Sellitto mocked.

The kid didn't get he was being challenged and continued, "Naw. The perp threw this jar from a storeroom or something at her and the guard. Broke. He's the one got hit with whatever crap was inside. He'd been on the force. Retired from the Nineteenth."

"Detective Sachs wasn't hurt," his partner added. *Williams.*

"What kind of crap?"

Juarez: "They don't know. But the first report was that it coulda been acid or something like that."

"Fucker. Acid?"

"Naw, it wasn't. Just preservative."

Sellitto asked, "Hospital's secure?"

"Lockdown, yeah."

The final word of that sentence prompted a glare at Juarez. He got it this time. "Yessir. That's right. But they're pretty sure he's in the building next door. Detective Sachs saw him get out through the access tunnel. Only one place to end up. There, the doctors' office building."

"And ESU thinks he's still there?"

Juarez said, "He'd have to be fast, real fast, to get out. Detective Sachs called it in right away. Had the place sealed two minutes after the attack. Possible he got out, Detective, but real unlikely."

"Two minutes." Sellitto brushed at his wrinkled tie, as if that would iron the cloth flat as steel, then forgot about it. Pulling out a battered notebook, he stepped into the hospital room.

He identified himself.

The man in bed said, "I'm Matthew Stanton. Don't they have security here?" His dark eyes bored into Sellitto as if the detective had held the door open for the psycho.

Sellitto could understand but he had a job. "We're looking into that." Which didn't really answer the question. Then he turned to the woman. "And you're—"

The man said stiffly, "My wife. Harriet. That's my son, Josh."

The young man rose and shook Sellitto's hand.

"Could you tell me what happened?" the detective asked Harriet.

Matthew rasped, "She was just walking down the corridor, coming to visit me. And this—"

"Sir, please. Could I hear from your wife?"

"All right. But I'm talking to my lawyer. When we get home. I'm going to sue."

"Yessir." An eyebrow raised to Harriet.

"I'm, I'm kind of flustered," she said.

Sellitto didn't feel like smiling but he did anyway. "It's fine. Take your time."

Harriet seemed numb as she explained that the family had come to town several days ago with their son and his cousin. It was a toss-up between the Big Apple and Disney. But New York, closing in on Christmas, had won. Yesterday, on the way to toy shop at FAO Schwarz, her husband had suffered what turned out to be a minor heart attack. She'd come to visit this morning and was here, on this floor, when she'd heard the policewoman calling out stop or something like that.

"I didn't know anybody was there. He came up real quiet. I turned around and, goodness, there was this man. Do you think he was going to, Detective? I mean, going to attack me?"

"We don't know, Mrs. Stanton. The individual fits the description of a suspect in a prior attack—"

"And," the husband said, "you didn't warn people about him?"

"Matthew, please. You can also look at it the other way. The police saved me, you know."

The man fell silent but seemed even more furious. Sellitto was hoping he didn't have another coronary.

"What was this earlier assault?" Harriet asked hesitantly. Her voice left no doubt what she was asking.

"Not sexual assault. Homicide."

She was breathing rapidly now and under the heavy makeup her face seemed to grow paler. "A, like a serial killer?" What was left of the tissue disintegrated further.

"Again, we don't know. Could you describe him?"

"I'll try. I only saw him for a few seconds before he pulled a mask down, grabbed me and turned me around."

Sellitto had been interviewing witnesses for decades and knew that even the best-intentioned remembered little or accidentally supplemented accurate observations with mistaken ones. Still, Harriet was pretty specific. She described a white man around thirty wearing a dark jacket, probably leather, gloves, a black or navy-blue wool cap, dark slacks or jeans. He was slim of build but had a round face—it struck her as Russian in appearance.

"My husband and I went to Saint Petersburg a few years ago and we noticed that was typical of how young men look. Round heads, round faces."

Matthew pointed out in a sneering tone, "Crime there too but only pickpockets. They don't sneak up on you in hospitals."

"Higher standards, yeah," Sellitto replied. Then: "Or the guy's appearance: maybe Slavic in general? Eastern European?"

"I don't know. I suppose so. We've only been to Russia. Oh, and his eyes were light blue. Very light."

"Scars?"

"I didn't see any. I think he had a tattoo. One of his arms. Red. But I couldn't see much of it. He had the coat on."

"Hair?"

Harriet's eyes scanned the floor. "He pulled that hat down pretty quick. I just couldn't tell you for sure."

"Did he say anything to you?"

"Just whispered to stop struggling or he'd hurt me. I didn't hear an accent."

And that was it.

Age, build, eye color and a round head. Russian or Slavic. Clothing.

Sellitto radioed to Bo Haumann, the head of NYPD Emergency Service and the officer in charge of the manhunt. He gave the description and the latest information.

"Roger that, Lon. We've sealed the office building. Don't think he got out but I've got some teams canvassing the streets nearby. K."

"I'll get back to you, Bo." Sellitto didn't bother with radio code propriety. Never did. It wasn't that rank had privilege; tenure did.

He turned back to Harriet Stanton and her husband, who was still glowering. Heart attack? He looked pretty spare. And had an outdoor-weathered face, so he probably got a fair amount of exercise. Maybe being in a bad mood was a risk factor for coronaries. Sellitto felt bad for Harriet, who seemed like a nice enough lady.

Since there didn't seem to be any connection between the unsub and the first victim, the same was probably true now; he was hunting randomly. Still, Sellitto asked if she'd ever seen him before, or had any awareness of being followed prior to her visit to the hospital. Or if she and her husband were wealthy or involved in anything that might make them a target of criminals.

The last query seemed to amuse Harriet. No, she explained, they were just working-class tourists—whose vacation to New York had been ruined.

Sellitto took her number and the name of the hotel where they were staying and wished her husband a fast recovery.

Harriet thanked him. Matthew nodded gruffly, grabbed the TV's remote control and upped the volume on the History Channel.

Then the would-be victim vanished from Sellitto's thoughts as his radio crackled to life.

"All units, report of assault on sixth floor of physicians' office building, where search operation for unsub is under way. Next to Upper Manhattan Medical Center. There's been chemical weapon release, substance unknown. Only personnel with bio-chem masks are to remain in the building."

Sellitto's thoughts tumbled. "Son of a bitch."

Gasping, he ran up the hallway and out of the hospital, into the circular drive. He looked up at the office building, which was to his left. He began jogging toward it, pulling his radio from his belt. He made a call.

"Bo?" He was breathless. "Bo?" he tried again.

"That you, Lon? Over."

"Yeah, yeah, yeah. I just heard. The assault. What happened?"

The former drill sergeant said crisply, "I'm getting secondhand reports. Looks like the perp tried to steal some scrubs in a doctor's office on the sixth floor. An orderly spotted him and he ran. But not before he opened a bottle and spilled something on the floor."

"Maybe formaldehyde, like with Amelia."

"No, he said it was bad. People puking, passing out. Fumes everywhere. Definitely toxic."

Sellitto considered this. Finally he asked, "Do you know what office? That he dumped the poison in?"

"I can find out. I'm on the first floor, near the directory. I'll see." A moment later he came back on. "There's only one doctor on six. He has the whole floor."

Sellitto asked, "Is he a plastic surgeon?"

"Wait. You're right. How'd you know?"

"Because our boy wrapped his face in bandages and is strolling down the fire stairs right now with all the other patients you're evacuating."

A pause. Haumann said, "Hell. Okay, we'll marshal 'em in the lobby, get IDs. Nobody with a Band-Aid on is getting out the front door. Good call, Lon. We're lucky, we'll have him in ten minutes."

CHAPTER 24

Rhyme was wheeling back and forth, back and forth, in front of the high-definition monitor. It was around forty minutes after the report had come in about the perp releasing the poison gas in the sixth-floor suite in the doctors' office building.

On the screen was an image of the front of the building and, beyond that, the hospital itself.

Courtesy of an Emergency Service Unit video cam.

The buzzer sounded and Thom went to answer. The door clicked, the wind howled.

Then a familiar clomp of footsteps, which told Rhyme that Lon Sellitto had arrived.

Ah...

The detective turned the corner. Stopped. His face was a grimace.

"Now," Rhyme said, his voice infused with sharp humor. "I'm just curious—"

"All right, Linc," Sellitto said, stripping off the wet Burberry. "It was—"

"Curious, I was saying. Did it occur to *anyone*? Any

single one? Did it occur to any person on the face of the earth that it wasn't an orderly reporting the poison gas? That it was the unsub *himself* who called in a fake report? So that everyone would start checking out patients with bandages on their faces?"

"Linc—"

"And no one would start checking out anyone in a dental face guard, like tattoo artists would wear, and coveralls, strolling casually out the front door like an emergency worker."

"I know that now, Linc."

"So I guess it didn't occur to anyone at the time. It's only—"

"You made your fucking point."

"—now that we can figure out—"

"You can be a real prick sometimes, Linc. You know that."

Rhyme did know that and he didn't care. "And the manhunt around Marble Hill?"

"Checkpoints at main streets, officers at every bus stop and subway station in the area."

"Looking for... ?" Rhyme asked.

"Any white male around thirty with a pulse."

Rhyme's computer dinged, and he called up the email. It was Jean Eagleston again, the Crime Scene officer. She was the one who'd done an Identi-Kit composite rendering of the man, based on Harriet Stanton's observation. It depicted an unsmiling young man with Slavic features, a prominent forehead and brows close together. The unsub's pale eyes gave him a startling, eerie visage.

Rhyme didn't believe that good or evil could be objectively reflected in appearance. But his gut told him this was the face of a truly dangerous person.

A second high-def monitor nearby fluttered to life and there was Amelia Sachs, peering his way.

"You there, Rhyme?"

"Yes, yes, Sachs. Go ahead." This was the computer they used for face-to-face videoconferencing with law enforcers in other cities, for occasional interrogation of suspects and for Skyping with the children of Rhyme's closest relative—his cousin who lived in New Jersey—well, Sachs primarily, who read them stories and told jokes. Sachs and Pam would also Skype, sometimes spending hours, chatting away.

He wondered if now, after their fight, that wouldn't be happening anymore.

She asked, "What's the story? Is it true, the get-away?"

Rhyme grimaced and glanced at Sellitto, who rolled his eyes and said, "He's gone, yeah. But we got a good description from the hostage."

"What's the prognosis, Sachs? The guard?"

"Eyes're going to need some treatment is all. He got hit by formaldehyde and severed male genitals. That's what was in the jar. Which he's not happy about." She gave a faint laugh. "It was dark, I saw some flesh on the ground. I thought the unsub had used acid and it was melting the guard's flesh off. But he'll be okay. Now, Lon, how's the manhunt going?"

The detective explained to her, "We've got under-cover at all the bus and subway stations in Marble Hill and north and south—the Number One train. He could get a cab but I'm thinking he won't want to be seen one-on-one by the driver. According to our tat expert, he's not from around here so he probably doesn't know about gypsy cabs. We're betting he'll stick to public transportation."

Rhyme could see Sachs nodding, then the image was breaking up, freezing. The unreliable Internet.

The picture came in clear again.

She said, "He might try for a train farther east."

"Yeah, I suppose he could."

Rhyme said, "Good point." He told Sellitto, "Get some of your people to the Number Four train and the D and B lines. That's central Bronx. He's not going to get farther east than that."

"Hm. I'll do it." The detective stepped away to make the call.

Sachs said, "One thing occurred to me, Rhyme?"

"And?"

"There were dozens of storerooms he could've hidden in. Why did he pick that one?"

"Your thought?"

"He'd spent time there before. I think that's where he was going to take Harriet Stanton to tattoo her."

"Why?"

"It was like a skin museum." She described the preserved tissue samples in jars.

"Skin. Sure. His obsession."

"Exactly. Internal organs, brains. But easily half the jars contained external flesh."

"You working up some kind of dark psychology here, Sachs? I'm not sure that's helpful. We know he's interested in skin."

"I'm just figuring he'd spent more time there than

just checking it out as a possible murder site. Like a tourist at MoMA, you know. It drew him. So I walked the grid three times there."

"Now, *that's* a valid use for psychobabble," Rhyme said.

CHAPTER 25

Head down, Billy strode quickly toward the subway in the Bronx that would take him south to Manhattan, to his workshop, to his terrariums, to safety and comfort.

He reflected back to the hospital corridor, picturing Amelia Sachs... He couldn't help but think of her with some familiarity, having learned everything he could about the woman—and Lincoln Rhyme.

How had she found him? Well, that wasn't quite the question. How had *Rhyme* found him? She was good, sure. But Rhyme was better.

Okay, how? How *exactly*?

Well, he'd been to the hospital earlier. Maybe he'd picked up some trace there and, despite his diligence, had unwittingly deposited a bit near Chloe Moore's body.

Were the police thinking they'd avert another attack by sending Amelia Sachs to stop him?

But, no, Billy decided, they couldn't predict that he'd return when he had. The policewoman had come to the hospital just to ask if any staffers had seen a man fitting his description.

His thoughts strayed to Amelia Sachs...She reminded him in some ways of Lovely Girl, her beautiful face, her hair, her keen and determined eyes. Some women, he knew, you had to control by reasoning with them, some by dominating. Others you couldn't control, and that was a problem.

Picturing her pale skin.

The Oleander Room...

He imagined Amelia there, lying on the couch, the settee, the love seat, the lounger.

Breath growing faster, he pictured blood on her skin, he tasted blood on her skin. He smelled blood.

But forget that now.

Another word came to mind: anticipate.

If Rhyme had figured out about the hospital, he might have figured out Billy would come this way to escape. So he picked up his pace. It was a busy street. Discount shops, diners, and mobile phone and calling card stores. The clientele, working class. *Payroll Advances. Best Rates in Town.*

And people everywhere: parents with little kids, bundled up like sock puppets against the cutting chill and endless sleet. Teenagers ignoring the cold or genuinely not feeling it. Thin jackets, jeans, short skirts and fake-fur collars on loud jackets. High heels, no stockings. Constant motion. Billy dodged a skateboarder a moment before collision.

He wanted to grab the kid, fling him off the board. But he was past in a flash. Besides, Billy wouldn't have made a scene. Bad idea, under the circumstances.

Back to his eastward escape. He noted here too a lot of skin art—Billy's preferred term for tats. Here, lower class, mixed race, he noticed a lot of writing on skin. In script primarily. Bible passages maybe or poems or manifestos. Martin Luther King Jr. was represented, Billy speculated. But the lines might have been from Shaq or the Koran. Some writings were prominent—seventy-two-point type. Most, though, were so tiny you needed a magnifier to read them.

Crosses in all designs—inked on men who looked like gangbangers and drug dealers and on girls who looked like whores.

A young man, around twenty, approached from the opposite direction, very dark-skinned, broad, a bit shorter than Billy, who stared at the keloids on his cheeks and temples—an intricate pattern of cross-hatched lines.

He noticed Billy's attention and slowed, then stopped, nodded. "Hey." Just stood there, smiling. Maybe he sensed that Billy was appreciating the scarification. Which he was.

Billy stopped too. "You've got some righteous marking."

"Yo. Thanks."

In sub-Saharan African tradition this form of modification was done by cutting flaps in the skin and packing in irritating plant juices to raise welts, which hardened into permanent designs. Keloids serve several purposes: They identify the bearers as members of a particular family or tribe, they indicate fixed social or political positions, they mark milestones in life's transit, like puberty and readiness for marriage. In some African cultures, scarification indicates sexual prowess and appetite—and the scars themselves can become erogenous zones. The more extensive a woman's scarring, the more appealing she is as a partner because it implies she's better able to withstand the pain of childbirth and produce many offspring.

Billy had always appreciated keloids; he'd never done any. The ones on the young man's face were impressive, linked chains and vines. African skin art is largely geometric; rarely are animals, plants or people depicted. Never words. Billy was nearly overcome by an urge to touch the pattern. With effort, he resisted.

The local, in turn, regarded Billy with an odd gaze that embraced both curiosity and camaraderie. Finally he looked around and seemed to come to a decision. A whisper: "Yo, you want brown? Moonrock? Sugar? Whatchu want?"

"I..."

"How much you got to spend? I hook you up."

Drugs.

Disgusting.

In an instant the admiration of the scarification turned to hatred. It felt like the young man had betrayed him. The skin art was ruined. Billy wanted to stick his neck with a needle, get him into an alley and ink a message on his gut with snakeroot or hemlock.

But then Billy realized this was just another incident that proved the Rule of Skin true. No surprise here. He could be no more upset at this than at a law of physics.

He gave a disappointed smile, walked around the man and kept moving.

"Yo, I hook you up!"

A block east, Billy glanced behind him—he saw no one that was a threat—and stepped into a clothing store. He paid cash for a Yankees baseball cap and a pair of cheap sneakers. He tugged the hat on and swapped shoes. His old ones he didn't throw out—concerned that the police might search the trash cans and find a pair of Bass with his prints on them—but when the clerk wasn't looking he left one in a bin of discount shoes and the other on a rack, behind a row of similar footwear. He then stepped outside, striding fast toward his goal: the subway that would take him back to Canal Street, back to safety. Head down, once more, examining the congested sidewalks, filthy, marred with ovals of dog pee and dark dots of chewing gum, bordered with tired slush.

Yet no one looked at the coveralls, at the gear bag, no one glanced his way as if wondering: Is he the man who killed that girl in SoHo? The man who was nearly cornered and gunned down at the hospital in Marble Hill?

Walking fast once more, inhaling cold air rich with noxious exhaust. Of course he wouldn't take the Number One train, which had a Marble Hill stop, because it was so close to the hospital. He'd spent days studying the New York City transit system. He was making for a station farther east, even if it meant a fast walk through unpleasant weather and amid more unpleasant people.

Yo, I hook you up…

And there were lots of them. The crowds were thicker now, more shoppers—taking advantage of the pre-Christmas season to stock up on presents, he guessed. Dressed in dark clothing, worn and shabby.

Doctor Moreau's Swine-men, Dog-men…

Some police cars sped past, heading toward Marble Hill. None of them paused.

Breathing hard, chest hurting again, he finally approached the metro entrance. Here the trains were not underground but elevated. He swiped his MetroCard and walked nonchalantly up the steep stairs and onto the platform, where he huddled as the damp wind sliced around him.

He pulled his cap lower, swapped the reading glasses for some with different frames, then pulled his gray scarf up around his mouth; the air was frigid enough so that this camo didn't look odd.

Scanning for police. No flashing lights on the streets below, no uniformed officers in the crowds or on the platform. Maybe—

But wait.

He noted two men in overcoats about thirty feet away on the platform. One looked his way then turned back to his companion. They stood out here, being white and dressed in conservative clothing, white shirts and ties, under the bulky coats; most of the other passengers on the platform were black or Latino or mixed, and dressed much more casually.

Undercover cops? He had a feeling they were. They might not have been part of the actual manhunt—were here investigating a drug deal, maybe—but they'd heard the alert, and now believed they had the Underground Man.

One made a brief call and Billy had a feeling that it had been placed to Lincoln Rhyme. No basis for this, but instinct told him the cop was a friend and colleague of Rhyme.

A train was approaching but was still two hundred

yards away. The men whispered something to each other and then walked his way, steadying themselves in the wind.

He'd been so careful, so smart in escaping from the doctors' office building. Was he about to get caught because of a coincidence? Two cops who happened to be nearby.

Billy was nowhere near the exit. If he ran, he'd never make it in time. Could he jump?

No, twenty feet to the traffic-filled street below. He'd break bones.

Billy decided he'd just have to bluff. He had a city employee ID, which would pass fast examination, but one call to downtown and they'd find out it was fake. He also had legitimate ID, which was, technically, a breach of the Commandments.

Thou shalt remain unidentifiable.

But, of course, that wouldn't work. One radio or phone call and they'd find out who he really was.

He'd have to go on the offense. He'd pretend to ignore the men until they were right next to him and turn, smiling. Then he would shove one, or both, onto the tracks. He could escape in the chaos afterward.

A messy plan. Clumsy and dangerous. But, he decided, there was little choice.

The men were getting closer now. Smiling but Billy didn't trust that expression for a second.

The train was near now. A hundred feet away, eighty, thirty . . .

He looked for guns on the men's hips, but they hadn't unbuttoned their coats. He glanced toward the exit, judged timing and distance.

Get ready. The big one. Push him first. Lincoln Rhyme's buddy.

The train was almost to the platform.

The taller of the two men, the one who was about to die first, nodded as he caught Billy's eye.

Wait, wait. Give it ten seconds more. Eight, seven, six...

Billy tensed.

Four, three...

The man then smiled. "Eric?"

"I'm, uhm, I'm sorry?"

"Are you Eric Wilson?"

The train rushed into the station and squealed to a stop.

"Me? No."

"Oh, hey, you look just like the son of a guy I work with. Sorry to bother you."

"No problem." Billy's hands were trembling, his jaw too, and only partly from the cold.

The men turned and walked away, toward the train, which was now discharging passengers.

Billy walked onto the subway car, choosing a spot to stand that was close enough to the men to hear their conversation. Yes, he realized, they were just as they seemed to be—businessmen who'd finished some meeting uptown and were heading back to their office on Madison Avenue to write up some reports about how the meeting had gone.

Brakes released, and with a grind the train started south, rocking, squealing through the switches.

Soon they were in Manhattan, and diving beneath the surface. The Underground Man was in his world once again.

It had been a risk, taking the subway, but at least he'd minimized the danger. And apparently won. Rather than take the Number One train or the Number Four—the next one east—or even the B and D, he'd sped the several miles to the Allerton Avenue station, to catch the Number Two train. He'd assumed that someone—well, Lincoln Rhyme of course—might have ordered officers to the closer stations. But even the NYPD didn't have the resources to search everywhere. He'd hoped his brisk pace would put him beyond the reach of a manhunt.

Apparently this was so.

As they sped south, Billy reflected: You're not the only one who can anticipate, Captain Rhyme.

CHAPTER 26

Mr. 11-5 knows what he's doing, Lincoln Rhyme reflected yet again, as he guided his Merits to the table where Mel Cooper and Sachs were examining the evidence from the hospital.

Despite her exhaustive search of the corridors, the doctors' office building and the "skin museum," the evidentiary findings from the abortive assault on Harriet Stanton were minimal.

There were no friction ridges; he'd been clever enough not to actually touch Harriet with his fingers (prints can be lifted off skin). He'd either gripped only her clothing or touched her flesh with his sleeves. And somewhere between fleeing the site of the attack in the basement and his slipping into the specimens room, he'd pulled on latex gloves (not vinyl, which display distinctive wrinkle patterns that can be introduced at trial).

But unlike the earlier scenes, he'd been taken by surprise, so he didn't have the chance to don booties. Sachs got some good electrostatic footprints.

Size eleven Bass shoe, though that meant only that

he was wearing a size eleven Bass shoe, not that he had size eleven feet.

The wear pattern of the tread marks, which sometimes could give details about weight and posture, didn't reveal much but, Rhyme reflected, who cared? They knew his weight and posture.

Sachs rolled the floor around the footprints for trace, just in case. But Mel Cooper reported that the analysis revealed "a lot of Inwood marble and more of the medical materials that led us to the hospital in the first place. Some of the cleanser again. Nothing else."

She had found some unique trace in the specimens room, identified by the chromatograph/spectrometer as dimethicone, which was used in cosmetics and industrial lubricants and processed foods to prevent caking. Interestingly it was also the primary ingredient in Silly Putty. Rhyme didn't dismiss this fact immediately but after some consideration decided that the novelty toy didn't figure in the unsub's plan.

"I think he picked dimethicone up when he grabbed Mrs. Stanton." Sachs explained that, as a woman in her fifties, she had worn a fair amount of makeup. Sachs dug out her mobile and called the number Harriet had given her. She answered and, after Sachs gave her an update of the case, got the brand name of the woman's preferred makeup products. Running the manufacturer's website, Sachs learned that dimethicone was in fact one of the ingredients in her foundation.

Dead end there.

And no other trace or fibers.

As she wrote the details up on the whiteboard chart Sachs said, "One other thing. I saw he had a tattoo on his—" She frowned. "Yes, his left arm. An animal or some kind of creature. Maybe a dragon. From that thriller book. The *Dragon Tattoo*. In red."

"Right," Sellitto added, looking at his notebook. "Harriet Stanton said he had one. She didn't see what it was, though."

"Any trace of the poison he intended to use on the vic?" Pulaski asked Cooper.

"Nothing. No toxins on anything that Amelia collected."

"I think we can assume he keeps his love potions sealed up until he's ready to start using them." Rhyme was wondering again: Why *that* MO? Poison was a rare murder weapon now. The technique of killing with toxins, popular through the ages, began to fall out of fashion long ago, in the mid-1800s, after the famed English chemist James Marsh invented a test that could detect arsenic in tissue postmortem. Tests for other toxins soon followed. Homicidal husbands and greedy heirs, who'd believed that doctors would rule cause of death coronary or stroke or illness, began ending up in prison or on the gallows after early forensic detectives presented their cases in court.

Some substances like ethylene glycol—automotive coolant—were still fed to husbands by unhappy wives, and Homeland Security worried about all sorts of toxins as terrorist weapons, ranging from castor beans turned into ricin, to cyanide, to botulinum, which was the deadliest substance in existence (a very mild form of which was used in cosmetic Botox injections); a few kilograms of botulinum could kill every person on earth.

Yet poisons were cumbersome and detectable and hard to administer, not to mention potentially lethal to the poisoners. Why do you love them so much? Rhyme silently asked the unsub.

Mel Cooper interrupted his musings. "It was a close call at the hospital. Do you think he'll go away?"

Rhyme grunted.

"That means no?"

Sachs interpreted. "That means no."

"The only question," Rhyme said, "is where's he going to strike next?" He wheeled to the board. "The answer's there. Maybe."

UPPER MANHATTAN MEDICAL CENTER

- Victim: Harriet Stanton, 53
    - Tourist
    - Not hurt
- Unsub 11-5
    - See details, prior scene
    - Red tattoo on left arm
    - Russian or Slavic in appearance
    - Light-blue eyes
    - No accent
    - Size 11 Bass shoes
    - No friction ridges
    - Spent time in Specimens Room at hospital ("skin museum")
- Trace
    - No toxin found
    - Dimethicone
        - But probably from makeup worn by Harriet Stanton

CHAPTER 27

Provence[2] was crowded.

As soon as the *Times* had bestowed its stars, this hole-in-the-wall in Hell's Kitchen had been inundated with folks desperate to cram into the loud, frantic rooms and to sample dishes that were a fusion of two southern cuisines, American and French.

Fried chicken with capers and ratatouille.

Les escargots *avec* grits.

Improbable. But the dish works…

Straddled by a warehouse to the south and a chic steel-and-glass office building to the north, the restaurant was housed in a structure typical of those on the west side of Midtown: a century old, angled floors that snapped and creaked underfoot, and ceilings of hammered tin. Low archways led from one cramped dining room to the next and the walls were sandblasted brick, which did nothing to dim the din.

Lighting was low, courtesy of yellow bulbs in what seemed to be lamp fixtures as old as the structure itself (though they'd come not from a Victorian-era ironworks on the Hudson but a factory outside Seoul).

At one of the tables in the back, the conversation ricocheted like an air-hockey puck.

"He doesn't have a chance. It's ridiculous."

"Did you hear about his girlfriend?"

"She's not his girlfriend."

"She *is* his girlfriend, it was on Facebook."

"Anyway I don't even think she's a girl."

"Ooo. That's sweet."

"When the press finds out, he's toast. Let's get another bottle. The Chablis."

Samantha Levine listened to her companions' banter but not with her full attention. For one thing, she wasn't much concerned about local politics. The candidate they were speaking of probably wouldn't win the next election but not because of girlfriends who might or might not pass the physical but because he was bland and petty and you needed the quality of *more* to be mayor of the city of New York.

You needed that *je ne sais quoi*, y'all.

Apart from that, though, Samantha's thoughts kept returning to her job. Major trouble lately. She'd worked late—close to eight p.m., a half hour ago—then hurried here from her office in the glitzy building next door to join her friends. She tried a memory dump of the concerns she'd lugged with her but in the high-tech world you couldn't really escape from the puzzle and problems you faced every day. Sure, there were advantages: You could wear—as she did now—jeans and sweaters (tank tops in the summer), you made six figures, you could be inked or studded, you could work flex hours, you could bring a pillow couch to your office and use that for your desk.

Only you had to produce.

And be one step ahead of the competition.

And, fuck, there was a lot of competition out there.

The capital-I Internet. What a place. So much money, so many chances for breathtaking success. And for bottomless fuckups.

The thirty-two-year-old, with a voluptuous figure, ornery brown-and-purple hair and big doey Japanese anime dark eyes, sipped more white wine and tried to focus past a particularly difficult meeting with her boss not long ago, a meeting that had floated in her thoughts ever since.

Put. It. Away.

Finally, she managed to. Spearing and eating a wedge of fried green tomato topped with ground anchovies, she turned her attention back to her friends. Smiling, all of them (except Text Girl), as Raoul—her roommate, yes, just a roommate—was telling a story about her. He was an assistant to a fashion photog who shot for *Vogue*-wannabe mags, all online. The slim, bearded boss had come to pick up Raoul in the apartment they shared in Chelsea and he'd looked over Samantha's T-shirt and PJ bottoms, sprouting hair tamed with mismatched rubber bands and very, very serious glasses. "Hmmmm. Can I shoot you?"

"Oh, you're the one got the contract for the Geek Girl calendar?" Samantha had offered. Raoul now gave his delivery a little extra oomph and the table roared.

This was a good group. Raoul and James—his best bud—and Louise from Samantha's office and Some

Other Woman, who'd arrived on James's arm. Was her name Katrina or Katharine or Karina? And James's blonde of the week. Samantha had dubbed her Text Girl.

The men continued their discussion of politics, as if they had money on the outcome of the election, Louise was now trying to discuss something serious with Samantha and the K woman texted some more.

"Be back," Samantha said.

She rose and started along the antique floor, which was—after the three glasses of anti-stress wine—not as even as it had been when she'd arrived. Easy, girl. You can drink-fall in the Hamptons, you can drink-fall in Cape May. You don't drink-fall in Manhattan.

Two flirts from the tiny bar. She ignored them, though she ignored one less stridently than the other. It was the fellow sitting by himself at the end. He was a slim guy, pale—only-goes-out-at-night kind of skin. Painter or sculptor or some other artist, she guessed. Handsome, though there might be a weak-chin factor if he looked down. Piercing eyes. They offered one of *those* glances. Samantha called them "laps," as in a dog lapping up food.

She got a chill. Because the look went on a little too long and then got scary.

He was undressing her, looking over her body.

She regretted tapping his eyes with hers. And continued quickly to the most challenging route the restaurant offered: the narrow stairway down to the restrooms in the basement.

Clunk, clunk...

She made it.

Dark and quiet down here, clean, which had surprised her the first time she'd come to the place. The people who'd renovated had spent plenty of time making the dining rooms rough-edged rustic (yeah, we get it: French and American *countryside*), but the bathrooms were pure SoHo. Slate, recessed lighting, ornamental grasses for decoration. Mapplethorpe on the walls but nothing too weird. No whips, no butts.

Samantha walked to the *W*, tried the door.

Locked. She grimaced. Provence^2 wasn't big but no fucking restaurant in the world should have a single-occupancy women's room. Were the owners crazy?

Creaks overhead, from footsteps on the sprung wood flooring. Muted voices.

Thinking of the man at the bar.

What *was* I doing, looking back at him like that? Jesus. Be a little smarter. Okay? Why flirt? You've got Elliott from work. He isn't a dream boy but he's decent and dependable and watches PBS. Next time he asks, say yes. He has those sweet eyes and he's probably even pretty decent in bed.

Come on, I've gotta pee. One damn restroom?

Then, with a different pitch of creak, footsteps were coming down the stairs.

Clunk, clunk...

Samantha's heart thudded. She knew it was the flirter, the dangerous one.

She saw boots appearing on the steps. Men's ankle boots. Out of the '70s. Weird.

Her head swiveled. She was at the far end of the corridor. Nowhere to go from here. No exits. What do I do if he rushes me? The decibel level in the restaurant itself was piercing; nobody would hear. I left my cell phone upstairs, I—

Then: Relax. You're not alone. There was the bimbo in the restroom. She'd hear a scream.

Besides, nobody, however horny, would risk a rape in a restaurant corridor.

More likely it would be just an Awkward Incident. The slim guy coming on too strong, pushing the flirt, growing angry, but ultimately backing off. How many dozens of times had that happened? The worst injury would be branding her a cocktease.

Which was what happened when women glanced at a guy. Different rules. When men did the glancing, oh, it was all right. With men, oh, that's what they do.

Would things ever change?

But then: What if he was a real psycho? With a knife? A slasher. The man's piercing eyes had suggested maybe he was. And there was that murder just the other day—some girl in SoHo killed in the basement.

Just like here. Hell, I'll hold it—

Then Samantha barked a laugh.

The boot-wearer appeared. A fat old guy in a suit and string tie. A tourist from Dallas or Houston. He glanced at her once, nodded a vague greeting and walked into the men's room.

Then she was turning back to the door of the *W*.

Come on, honey. Jesus. You got your slutty makeup on just right? Or are you puking up your fourth Cosmo? Samantha gripped the knob again to remind the inconsiderate occupant that there was a queue.

The handle turned.

Hell, she thought. It'd been unlocked all along. She'd probably turned it the wrong way a moment ago.

How stupid can you be? She pushed inside and swept the light on, letting the door swing shut.

And saw the man standing behind it. He wore coveralls and a stocking cap. In a flash he locked the door.

Oh, Jesusjesusjesus...

His face was burned! No, distorted, mushed under a latex hood, transparent but yellow. And rubber gloves, the same color, on his hands. On his left arm, a sliver of a red tattoo was visible between the end of the glove and the start of the sleeve. An insect, with pincers, spiny legs, but human eyes.

"Ahhhh, no, no, no..."

She spun about fast, grabbing at the door, but he got to her first, arm around her chest. And she felt a sharp pain as he punched her neck.

Kicking, starting to scream, but he clapped a thick cloth over her mouth. The sounds were absorbed.

And then she noticed a small door across from the toilet, two by three feet or so, open onto a blackness—a tunnel or passage to an even deeper basement, below the restaurant.

"Please!" she muttered but the word was swallowed by the gag.

Growing limp, growing tired. Hardly afraid anymore. And she realized: the neck punch. He'd injected her with something. Before sleep took her completely Samantha felt herself being eased to the floor then dragged across it, closer and closer to the black doorway.

She sensed warmth, felt the trickle down her leg—

fear and the lack of control as whatever drug he'd stuck her with took effect.

"No," she whispered.

And heard a voice in her ear. "Yes." The word was drawn out for a very long time, as if it weren't the assailant who was speaking but the insect on his arm, hissing, hissing, hissing.

CHAPTER 28

The Rule of Skin…

As he labored away on his new victim's very nice belly with the American Eagle, Billy reflected on his fascination with the substance, God's own canvas.

Skin.

It was Billy's canvas too and he'd become as fixated on it as the Bone Collector had been on the skeletal system of the body—which Billy had found interesting reading in *Serial Cities*. He appreciated the Bone Collector's obsession but frankly he couldn't understand his fascination with bones. Skin was far and away the more revealing aspect of the human body. Far more central. More important.

What insights did bones give? Nothing. Not like skin.

Of the integumentary organs, which protect the body, skin is the most evolved, far more than hooves, nails, scales, feathers, and the clever, creepy arthropod exoskeletons. In mammals, skin is the largest organ. Even if organs and vessels might be maintained by some alternative Dr. Seuss contraption, skin does so much more. It prevents infection and is an early warning system against and protection from excessive cold and heat, from disease or invasion, from ticks to teeth to clubs and, under certain circumstances, even spears and bullets. Skin retains that vitally precious substance, water. It absorbs the light we need and even manufactures vitamin D. How about that?

Skin.

Delicate or tough as, yes, leather. (Around the eyes it's only a half millimeter thick; on the soles of the feet, five millimeters.)

The epidermis is the top layer, the beige or black or brown sheath we can see, and the dermis, into which a tattoo machine's needles must penetrate, is below. Skin is a master at regeneration, which means that the most beautiful tattoo in the world will vanish if the needles don't go deep enough, which would be like painting the Mona Lisa on sand.

But these basic facts about skin, as interesting as they were to Billy Haven, didn't touch on its true value. Skin reveals, skin explains. Wrinkles report age and childbearing, calluses hint at vocation and hobby, color suggests health. And then there's pigmentation. A whole other story.

Now Billy Haven sat back and surveyed his work on the parchment of his victim's skin. Yes, good.

A Billy Mod…

The watch on his right wrist hummed. Five seconds later the second watch, in his pocket, did so too. Sort of a snooze alarm, prescribed by the Modification Commandments.

And not a bad idea. Like most artists, Billy tended to get caught up in his work.

He rose and, with illumination provided by the halogen headlamp strapped to his forehead, walked around the dim space underneath Provence^2.

This area was an octagonal chamber, about thirty feet across. Three arches led to three darkened tunnels. In a different century, Billy had learned in research, these corridors had been used to direct cattle to two different underground abattoirs here on the West Side of Manhattan.

Healthy cows were directed to one doorway, sickly to another. Both were slaughtered for meat but the tainted ones were sold locally to the poor in Hell's Kitchen or shipped down to Five Points or the city of Brooklyn, for the filthy markets there. The more robust cattle ended up in the kitchens of the Upper East- and Westsiders and the better restaurants in town.

Billy didn't know which of the exits was for the healthy beef, which for the sickly. He'd been down both until they ended, one in brick, one in rubble, but he couldn't deduce which was which. He wished he knew because he wanted to tattoo the young lady in the tainted beef corridor—it just seemed appropriate. But he'd decided to do his mod in the place where the livestock cull had been made: the octagon itself.

He looked her over carefully. The tattoo was good. The cicatrized border too. He was pleased. When he did a work for clients in his shop back home, Billy never worried about their reaction. He had his own standards. A job they seemed indifferent to might fill him with ecstasy. Or a girl could tearfully look over her wedding cake tattoo (yes, pretty popular) and cry at how beautiful it was but he'd see one flaw, a tiny stroke out of place, and Billy would be furious with himself for days.

This art was good, though. He was satisfied.

He wondered if they'd catch on to the message now. But, no, not even Lincoln Rhyme was that good.

Thinking about the difficulty he'd had earlier—at the hospital and the doctors' office building—he'd decided it was time to start slowing down those pursuing him.

One of the passages in the Commandments, written in Billy's flowing script, was this: "Continually reassess the strengths of the officers investigating you. It may be necessary to throw up roadblocks to their investigation. Aim for the lower-level officers only; too senior, and the authorities will bring more effort to bear on finding you."

Or, in Billy's terms: *Thou shalt smite all those who are trying to mess with the Modification.*

His idea for slowing them down was simple. People who've never been inked think that machines use a hollow needle. But that's not the case. Tattoo needles are solid, usually several soldered together, allowing the ink to run down the shaft and into the skin.

But Billy had some hypodermics, to sedate his victims. He now reached into his gear bag and withdrew a plastic medicine bottle with a locking cap. He opened the lid carefully and set the brown cylinder on the ground. He selected a surgeon's hemostat, long tweezers, from his stash of stolen medical equipment. With this instrument he reached into the plastic bottle and picked up the three-quarter-inch tip of a thirty-gauge hypodermic—one of the smallest diameters. He'd carefully fatigued this tip off the syringe and packed it with poison.

He now picked up the woman's purse and worked the dull end of the needle into the leather under the clasp so that when the crime scene cop opened the bag, the business end of the nearly microscopic needle would pierce the glove and the skin. The tip was so thin, it was unlikely that the person pricked would feel a thing.

Until, of course, about an hour later, when the symptoms hit them like a fireball. And those symptoms were delicious: Strychnine produces some of the most extreme and painful reactions of any toxin. You can count on nausea, convulsion of muscles, hypertension, grotesque flexing of the body, raw sensitivity and finally asphyxiation.

Strychnine, in effect, spasms you to death.

Though in this case, the dosage would, in an adult, lead to severe brain damage rather than death.

Visit pestilence upon your pursuers.

A moan from behind him.

She was swimming to consciousness.

Billy turned toward her, the beam of the halogen whipsawing around the room, fast, leveraged by the motion of his head.

He carefully set the purse on the ground in a spot that looked as if he'd tossed it aside casually—they'd think it contained all sorts of good trace evidence and fingerprints. He hoped it would be Amelia Sachs who picked it up. He was angry at her for finding him at the hospital, even if Lincoln Rhyme was the one responsible. He'd hoped someday to go back to the specimens room but, thanks to her, he never could.

Of course, even if she didn't get jabbed, maybe one of Lincoln Rhyme's assistants would.

And Rhyme himself? He supposed it was possible; he'd learned that the man had regained some use of his arm and hand. Maybe he'd don a glove and pick up the purse. He *definitely* wouldn't feel the sting.

"Oh..."

He turned to look at the art gallery of beautiful skin stretched out before him. Ivory. He taped a flashlight in place over his canvas, flicked it on. Looked at her eyes, squinting first in confusion, then in pain.

His wristwatch hummed.

Then the other.

And it was time to leave.

CHAPTER 29

Lights flashed off the falling sleet, off the encrusted piles of old snow, off the wet asphalt.

Blue glows, white, red. Pulsing. Urgent.

Amelia Sachs was climbing out of her maroon Torino, parked beside several ambulances, though several ambulances weren't necessary. None were. The only required medical vehicle was the city morgue van. The first responders to this scene reported that Samantha Levine, the unsub's second victim, was deceased, declared dead at the scene.

Poison again, of course. That was the preliminary, from the first responders, but there was no doubt this was Unsub 11-5's work.

When she hadn't returned to the table of the chic restaurant Provence^2, her friends had become concerned. A search of the restroom revealed an access door, which was slightly askew. A waiter had pulled it open, stuck his head in, gasped and vomited.

Sachs stood on the street, looking over the restaurant

and the assembling vehicles. Lon Sellitto walked up. "Amelia."

She shook her head. "We stopped him at the hospital this morning and he got somebody else. Right away. Telling us basically: 'Fuck you.'"

Diners were settling checks and leaving and the staff was looking about as thrilled as you could imagine, upon learning that a patron had been abducted in the restroom and dragged into a tunnel beneath their establishment and murdered.

It was only a matter of time, Sachs guessed, before Provence^2 would be shuttered. It was as if the restaurant itself were a second victim. She supposed the boutique on Elizabeth Street too would be out of business soon.

"I'll start canvassing," the big detective muttered and ambled off, digging a notebook from his pocket.

The Crime Scene bus arrived and nosed up to the curb. Sachs waved to the CS techs who were climbing out. Jean Eagleston was the lead, the woman who'd worked the Chloe Moore scene in SoHo—only yesterday though it seemed like last month. She had a new partner, a slim Latino who had calm but probing eyes—hinting that he was perfect for crime scene work. Sachs walked up to them. "Same procedure. I'll go in first, process the body, walk the grid. You can handle the restroom where he snatched her, any exit routes."

Eagleston said, "Will do, Amelia." She nodded and Sachs went to the back of the CS vehicle to suit up in the Tyvek, booties, hood and gloves. The N95 respirator too. Remembering that, whatever happened, she should leave it in place.

Rust...

Goggles this time.

As she was stepping into the legs of the coveralls, she happened to glance up the street. On the corner, the same side of the street as the restaurant, was a man in a dark jacket that was similar to what the unsub had worn at the hospital, the attempted assault on Harriet Stanton, though he was in a baseball cap, not a stocking. He was on a phone and paying only moderate attention to the scene. Still, there was something artificial about his pose.

Could it be the unsub, back again, as he'd done in SoHo?

She looked away quickly and continued to gown herself, trying to act casual.

It wasn't common for a perp to return to the scene of the crime—that was a cliché helpful only in bad murder mysteries and made-for-TV movies—but it did happen sometimes. Particularly perps who weren't professional criminals but psychopaths, whose motives for murder were rooted in mental or emotional disturbance, which pretty much described Unsub 11-5.

On the pretext of getting a new pair of gloves from the far side of the bus, Sachs eased up to a detective she knew, a sharp, streetwise officer who'd recently been assigned to Midtown North. Nancy Simpson was handling crowd control detail and directing diners out of the immediate scene as they exited the restaurant.

"Hey," she said, "Nancy."

"This guy again?" the woman muttered. She was in an NYPD windbreaker, collar pulled high against the weather. Sachs liked the stylish beret, in dark green.

"Looks like it."

"Got people scared all over town," Simpson told her. "Reports of intruders in basements're up a hundred percent. None of 'em pan out, but we send Patrol anyway. Tying up everything." She added with a wink, "And nobody's washing their clothes. Afraid of the laundry room."

"We may have a situation, Nancy."

"Go ahead."

"Don't look behind you."

"I won't. Why?"

"We've got a fish I'm interested in. A guy on the corner. This block. He's in a jacket, baseball cap. I want you to get close but don't see him. You know what I mean?"

"Sure. I saw somebody. Peripheral. Wondered."

"Get close. And then stop him. Keep your weapon ready. There's an off-chance it might be the perp."

"Who did *this*?"

"Who did this. Not likely, I'm saying. But maybe."

"How should I get close?"

"You're checking traffic, you're on your phone, pretending you're on your phone, I mean."

"Arrest?"

"Just ID at this point. I'll come up behind. I'll have my weapon drawn."

"Fish. I'm bait."

Sachs glanced to the side. "Oh, hell. He's gone."

The unsub, or whoever he was, had disappeared around the corner of a glass-and-chrome building, about ten stories high, next to the restaurant where Samantha Levine had been dining—before the fateful trip to the restroom.

"I'm on it," Simpson said. She sprinted in the direction the man had gone.

Sachs ran to the command post and told Bo Haumann there was a possible suspect. Instantly he marshaled a half dozen ESU and other officers. She glanced toward Simpson. From the way she paused and looked around, Sachs deduced the suspect had vanished.

The detective turned and trotted back to Sachs and Haumann.

"Sorry, Amelia. He's gone. Maybe ducked into that building—the fancy one on the corner—or took off in a car."

Haumann said, "We'll follow up. We have a picture of your unsub from the homicide yesterday, the Identi-Kit image."

She pictured the surly, Slavic-looking face, the weirdly light eyes.

The ESU leader said to the men he'd called around him, "Deploy. Go find him. And somebody call it in to Midtown South. I want a team moving west down Fifty-Two Street. We'll hem him in, if we can."

"Yessir."

They trotted off.

As much as she wanted to go with them—she considered handing off the crime scene—Sachs finished dressing for the grid.

When she was gowned, bootied and hooded, she grabbed the collection kit and, with a glance back at the street down which the fish had swum away, Sachs started for the door of the restaurant.

CHAPTER 30

Sachs was grateful that, as at the previous scene, she didn't have to lug the heavy halogen spots down to the murder site; they were already set up and burning brightly.

Thank you, first responders.

She glanced at the diagram from Rhyme's database of underground New York to orient herself.

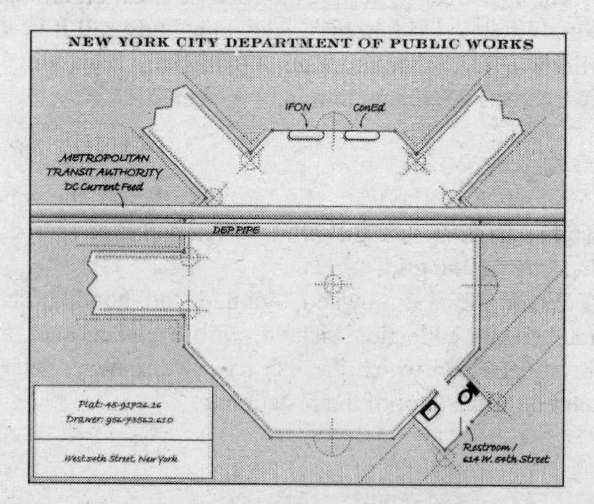

There were some similarities to the prior scene: the water and pipe, the utility conduits, the yellow boxes marked *IFON*. But there was a major difference too. This space was much bigger. And she could climb directly into it through the access doorway in the bathroom. No circular coffin breadbaskets.

Thank you…

From the ancient wooden pens surrounding the dirt floor, she deduced that it had been part of a passageway to move animals to and from one of the stockyards that used to operate near here, in Hell's Kitchen. She remembered that the perp seemed to be influenced by the Bone Collector; that killer too had used a former slaughterhouse as a place to stash one of his victims—and staked her down, bloody, so she would be devoured alive by rats.

Unsub 11-5 certainly had learned at the feet of a master.

The access door in the restroom opened into a large octagon, from which three tunnels disappeared into the darkness.

Sachs clicked on the video and audio feed. "Rhyme? You there?"

"Ah, Sachs. I was wondering."

"He might've come back again. Like on Elizabeth Street."

"Returned to the scene?"

"Or never left. I saw someone on the street, matching. Bo Haumann's got officers checking it out."

"Anything?"

"Not yet."

"Why's he coming back?" Rhyme mused. Not expecting an answer.

The camera was pointed in the direction she was looking—toward the dimness of a tunnel's end. Before turning to the body, though, she slipped rubber bands over her booties and tracked along the unsub's footprints, also muted by protective plastic, which led down one of the tunnels.

"That's how he got in? I can't see clearly."

"Looks that way, Rhyme. I see some lights up ahead."

The perp hadn't used a manhole to gain access. This tunnel, one of three, opened onto a train track—the line running north from Penn Station. The opening was largely obscured by a pile of debris but there was plenty of room for a person to climb over it. The unsub had simply walked up or down the tracks, from a spot near the West Side Highway, and then scaled the rubble and made his way to the octagon-shaped space where Samantha had died. She radioed Jean Eagleston and told her about the secondary crime scene—the entrance/exit route.

Then Sachs returned to the center of the octagon, where the victim lay. She looked up and shielded her eyes from the brilliant halogens the medics had set up. "Another flashlight, Rhyme. He sure wants to be certain nobody misses the vic."

Messages from our sponsor...

Like Chloe, Samantha was handcuffed and her ankles duct-taped. She'd also been partially disrobed—but only to expose her abdomen, where the unsub had inked her. A fast examination revealed no apparent sexual contact here either. Indeed, there was something oddly chaste about the way he'd left both victims. This was, she reflected, eerier than a straight-up sex crime—since it suggested the underlying mystery of the case: Why was he doing this? Rape, at least, was categorical. This?

She gazed down at the tattoo.

forty

Rhyme's voice intruded on the quiet. "'forty.' Lowercase again. Part of the phrase. Cardinal number this time, not the ordinal 'fortieth.' Why?" Testily he added, "Well, no time to speculate. Let's get going."

She processed the body, scraping nails (nothing obvious this time, as with Chloe), taking samples of the blood, the body fluids and presumably the poison oozing from the wounds. Then scanning her for prints, though he'd worn gloves again, of course.

Sachs walked the grid, collecting trace near the body and distant samples of dirt and trace too, for control. She studied the ground. "Booties again. No tread marks."

"He's wearing new shoes," Rhyme said. "He'll've pitched the others, the famous Bass size elevens. They're in the sewer in the Bronx by now."

As she walked the grid, she noticed something against one of the far walls. At first she thought it was a rat lying on its side. The lump wasn't moving so she speculated that the creature had chewed a bit of Samantha's flesh, ingested the poison and crawled away to die.

But as she got closer she noted that, no, it was a purse.

"Got her handbag."

"Good. Maybe there'll be trace on that."

She collected it and dropped the leather purse into an evidence bag.

This and all of the other samples of trace, also bagged in plastic or paper, she added to a milk crate.

Sachs wanded with the alternative light source—Samantha's body, the ground of the octagon, the tunnels. Again, 11-5 had pinched and probed her flesh. She noted from the bootie prints that the unsub had walked up and down the tunnel several times to and from the debris pile, which seemed curious, and she told Rhyme. Maybe because he'd heard intruders, he suggested. Or maybe he'd left some of his gear at the mouth. She took pictures and finally returned to the access door, muttering thanks once more to no one in particular that there was nothing claustrophobic about this search.

Once on the outside again, she handed off to the other CS techs, who had finished with the secondary scenes. Detective Jean Eagleston reported the not-surprising news that any of the perp's movements around the train tracks and the entrance to the tunnel from the outside were obliterated by the rain and sleet.

Aside from what presumably had been a brief struggle in the women's room, there were no signs that he'd touched anything. There were no tool marks in the screws he'd removed to gain access to the bathroom. And no footprints either, except those of dozens of street shoes—from the people who'd used the toilet.

The sleet beat an irritating drum tap on the hood she wore and she told Rhyme she was disconnecting the video camera for fear the moisture would short out the expensive, high-def system.

She returned to her car, where she filled out chain-of-custody cards for each item collected, working under the trunk lid to keep the cards and evidence bags dry. Stripping off the Tyvek suit, she slipped it into a burn bag in the Crime Scene van and returned to the street, pulling on her leather jacket.

Sachs noticed Nancy Simpson, the detective, speaking to Bo Haumann. The other officers who'd gone off in pursuit of the fish were straggling back.

Haumann rubbed his grizzled crew cut as Sachs walked up. "Nothing. Nobody saw him. But—" He glanced up at the inhospitable skies. "Not a lot of people out tonight."

She nodded then headed over to Lon Sellitto, who was talking to a group of people about Samantha's age. She told him about the pursuit—of the unsub or an innocent voyeur—the unsuccessful pursuit. He took the news with a grunt, and then they both turned to the others, who were, the detective reported, Samantha's fellow diners. She'd deduced this earlier from their expressions.

"I'm sorry for your loss," Sachs said. One woman's face was streaked with tears—a co-worker. The other woman, a blonde, looked put out and uneasy. Sachs guessed she had coke in her purse. Let it go.

The two men were angry and resolute. None of these had been Samantha's lover, it seemed. But one was her roommate; the greatest sorrow within the four resided in his eyes.

She and Sellitto both asked questions, learning the

unsurprising news that Samantha Levine had no enemies that they'd ever heard of. She was a businesswoman and had never been in trouble with the law. No problems with former boyfriends.

Another random death. In some ways this was the most tragic of all crimes: the happenstance victim.

And in many ways the most difficult to solve.

It was then that a man in an expensive suit—no overcoat—came hurrying up to them, oblivious to the sleet and cold. He was in his fifties, tanned, hair carefully cut. He wasn't tall but was quite handsome and well proportioned.

"Mr. Clevenger!" one of the women cried and hugged him. Samantha's co-worker. He gripped her hard and greeted the others in Samantha's party with a somber nod.

"Louise! Is it true? I just heard. I just got a call. Is she, Samantha? Is she gone?" He stepped back and the woman he'd been embracing said, "Yes, I can't believe it. She's...I mean, she's dead."

The newcomer turned to Sachs, who asked, "So you knew Ms. Levine?"

"Yes, yes. She works for me. She was...I was talking to her a few hours ago. We had a meeting...just a few hours ago." He nodded at the glossy building beside the restaurant. "There. I'm Todd Clevenger." He handed her a card. International Fiber Optic Networks. He was the company's president and CEO.

Sellitto asked, "Was there any reason anybody would want to hurt her? Anything about her job that was sensitive? That might've exposed her to threats?"

"Can't imagine it. All we do is lay fiber optic for

broadband Internet…just communications. Anyway, she never said anything, like she was in danger. I can't imagine. She was the sweetest person in the world. Smart. Really smart."

The woman named Louise said to Sachs, "I was thinking about something. There was that woman killed the other day. In SoHo. Is this the same psycho?"

"I can't really comment. It's an ongoing investigation."

"But that woman was killed underground too. Right? In a tunnel. It was on the news."

The scrawny young artistic-looking man, who'd identified himself as Raoul, Samantha's roommate, said, "That's right. It was the same thing. The, you know, MO."

Sachs again demurred. She and Sellitto asked a few more questions but it was soon clear there was nothing more these people could help them with.

Wrong place, wrong time.

A happenstance victim…

Ultimately, in cases where the victim had been alone with the perpetrator, no witnesses, the truth would have to be revealed through the evidence.

And this was what Sachs and the other Crime Scene officers now packed carefully into the trunk of her Torino.

In five minutes she was racing up the West Side Highway, blue light on the dash pulsing madly, as she skidded around cars and trucks—the slaloming more a function of her powerful engine and her comfort in high revs than the inclement weather.

CHAPTER 31

At close to 11 p.m. Rhyme heard Sachs enter the hallway, her arrival announced by the modulating hiss of sleet-filled wind.

"Ah, finally."

She stepped into the parlor a moment later, holding a large milk crate containing a dozen plastic and paper bags. She nodded a greeting to Mel Cooper, who sagged with fatigue but seemed game to start on the analysis.

Rhyme asked quickly, "Sachs, you said you thought he might be around the scene?"

"That's right."

"What came of that?"

"Nothing. Bo sent a half dozen ESU boys and girls after him. But he was gone. And I didn't get a good look at him. It was maybe nothing. But my gut told me it was him." She called up a map of Hell's Kitchen on the main computer monitor and pointed out the restaurant, Provence[2], and on the corner an office building. "He went down there but, see? It's only a few blocks from Times Square. He got lost in the crowd. Not sure it was him but it's too much of a coincidence to ignore completely. He seems curious about the investigation; after all, the perp did come back to Elizabeth Street and spy on me through the manhole cover."

Eye-to-eye…

"Well, let's get to the evidence. What do we have, Sachs?"

Thom Reston said firmly, "Find out—what she has, that is—but find out *quickly*. You're going to bed soon, Lincoln. It's been a long day."

Rhyme scowled. But he also accepted that the caregiver's job was to keep him healthy and alive. Quadriplegics were susceptible to a number of troublesome conditions, the most dangerous of which was autonomic dysreflexia—a spike in blood pressure brought on by physical stress. It wasn't clear that exhaustion was a precipitating factor but Thom had never been one to take anything for granted.

"Yes, yes, yes. Just a few minutes."

"Nothing spectacular," Sachs said, nodding at the evidence.

But then, Rhyme reflected, there rarely were any smoking guns. Crime scene work was incremental. And obvious finds, he felt, were automatically suspect; they might be planted evidence. Which happened more than one might suspect.

First, Sachs displayed the photographs of the tattoo.

forty

Surrounded by the scalloped border that, according to TT Gordon, was in some way significant.

Which made its cryptic nature all the more infuriating.

"First 'the second' and now 'forty.' No article preceding this one but, again, no punctuation."

What the hell was he saying? A gap of thirty-eight from two to forty. And why the switch from ordinal to cardinal? Rhyme mused, "Smells like a place to me, an address. GPS or longitude and latitude coordinates. But not enough to go on yet."

He gave up speculating and turned back to the evidence she'd collected. Sachs selected a bag and gave it to Cooper. He extracted the cotton ball inside.

"The poison," Sachs said. "One sample's gone to the ME's Office but I want a head start. Burn it, Mel."

He ran the materials through the chromatograph and a few minutes later had the mass spectrum. "It's a combination of atropine, hyoscyamine and scopolamine."

Rhyme was staring at the ceiling. "That comes from some plant... yes, yes... Hell, I can't remember what."

Cooper typed the cocktail of ingredients into the toxin database and reported a moment later, "Angel's trumpet: *Brugmansia*."

"Yes," Rhyme called. "Of course that's it. But I don't know the details."

Cooper explained that it was a South American plant, particularly popular among criminals in Colombia, who called it devil's breath. They blew it into the faces of their victims and the paralyzing, amnesiac drug rendered them unconscious or, if they remained awake, unable to fight their assailants.

And with the right dose, as with Samantha Levine, the drug could induce death in a matter of minutes.

Coincidentally, at that moment, the parlor landline rang: the Medical Examiner's Office.

Cooper lifted an eyebrow, looking toward Sachs. "Must be a slow night. Or you scared them into prioritizing us, Amelia."

Rhyme knew which.

The ME official on call confirmed that devil's breath was the poison that had been used on Samantha Levine's abdomen in the tattooed message. He added that it was a highly concentrated version of the toxin. And there was residue of propofol in her bloodstream. Cooper thanked him.

Sachs and the tech continued to examine the trace she'd collected. This time, though, they found no variation from the control samples, which meant the residues found on her body and where the unsub had walked in the crime scene had not been tracked in by him; they were all indigenous to the underground stockyard pen.

That, in turn, meant the substances wouldn't lead to anywhere the perp might have been.

"*Ergo*," Rhyme muttered, "fucking useless."

Finally, Sachs used tongs to pick up a plastic bag containing what seemed to Rhyme to be a purse. "Thought it was a rat at first. Brown, you know. And the strap seemed to be the tail. Be careful. There's a booby trap inside." A glance at Cooper.

"What?" Rhyme asked.

She explained, "It was sitting by itself about ten feet from Samantha's body. It just felt wrong being there. I looked at it closely and saw a needle sticking up. Very small. I used forceps to collect the bag." Sachs added that she'd been on the lookout for traps because the NYPD psychologist, Terry Dobyns, had told them the perp might start targeting his pursuers.

"That's sneaky," Cooper said, donning an eye loupe to examine the needle. "Hypodermic. I'd say thirty-gauge. Very small. White substance inside."

Rhyme wheeled close and looked; his keen eyes could make out a tiny glint near the clasp.

Cooper selected a hemostat and then cautiously lifted the purse from the bag.

"Check for explosives," Rhyme said. This wasn't the unsub's MO but you could never be too careful.

The scan came back negative. Still, Cooper decided to put the purse in a containment vessel and use remote arms to open it, given the possibility that it was also rigged with some trap that might spray with toxin whoever opened it.

But, no, the needle was the only trap. The contents were mundane, if wrenching, clues to a life now abruptly ended: a health club membership card, a breast cancer donation thank-you note, a discount certificate to a Midtown restaurant. Pictures of children—nieces and nephews, it seemed.

As for the booby trap, Cooper extracted the needle carefully.

"It's small," Rhyme said. "What do we make of that?"

Cooper said, "Can be used for insulin but this type is mostly used by plastic surgeons."

Rhyme reminded, "He's got propofol too. A general anesthetic. Could be that he's planning some cosmetic surgery as part of his escape plan. Though maybe he just broke into a medical supply house and stole what he wanted. Sachs, check if there've been any reports of that in the past month or so in the area." She stepped away to make a call downtown, requesting an NCIC search. Rhyme continued, "But more to the point—excuse the expression—that needle in particular: What's inside his little present to us? Is it more of the angel's trumpet?"

Cooper ran the sample. And a moment later he read the results. "Nope. It's worse. Well, I shouldn't say worse. That's a qualitative judgment. I'll just say it's more efficient."

"Meaning deadlier?" Rhyme asked.

"A lot. Strychnine." Cooper explained: The toxin came from *Strychnos*, a genus of trees and climbing shrubs. The substance was popular as a rodenticide. It had been a common murder weapon a century ago though it was less so now since it was easily traced. Strychnine was the most pain-inducing of any toxin.

"Not enough to kill an adult," Cooper said. "But it would keep the victim out of commission for weeks and might cause brain damage."

On the positive side, though, from the investigators' perspective, the poison was still sold commercially as a pesticide. Rhyme mentioned this to Sachs and Cooper.

"I'll see if we can find any commercial suppliers," the tech said. "They have to keep records of poison sales."

Cooper was looking at his computer, though, and frowning. "Dozens of sources. Brick-and-mortar stores. And all he'd need is a fake ID to buy some. Pay cash. No trace."

In the world of forensic science too many options were as bad as too few.

Sachs got a phone call and listened for a moment, then thanked the person on the other end and disconnected. "No reported thefts of drugs or other medical equipment or supplies in the area, the last thirty days, except a few stoners or crackheads knocking over pharmacies; they all got busted. No propofol missing."

Thom appeared in the doorway.

"Ah, my, what a stern expression."

"Close to midnight, Lincoln. You're going to bed."

"Yes, dear, yes, dear." Then Rhyme said to Cooper, "Be careful, Mel. No reason for him to know you're working this case but still, be careful. Sachs, text Lon and Pulaski and tell them the same thing." A glance at the mass spectrum of the strychnine. "We're targets now. He's declared war."

She sent messages to the two officers, then stepped to a clean whiteboard and wrote down the evidence, as well as the information she and Lon Sellitto had learned about the victim.

614 W. 54TH STREET

- Victim: Samantha Levine, 32
    - Worked for International Fiber Optic Networks
    - Probably no connection to Unsub
    - No sexual assault, but touching of skin
- Unsub 11-5
    - See details from prior scene
    - Might have returned to the scene
        - No sightings
    - No friction ridges
    - No footprints

- COD: Poisoning with Brugmansia, introduced via tattooing
    - Angel's trumpet, devil's breath
    - Atropine, hyoscyamine, scopolamine
- Tattoo
    - "forty" surrounded by scarring scallops
    - Why cardinal number?
- Sedated with propofol
    - How obtained? Access to medical supplies? (No local thefts)
- Location
    - Abducted from restroom of Provence[2] restaurant, basement
    - Kill site was underneath restroom, in 19th-century slaughterhouse culling area underground
    - Similar infrastructure to earlier scene:
        - IFON
        - ConEd router
        - Metropolitan Transit Authority DC current feed
        - Department of Environmental Protection pipe
- Flashlight
    - Generic, cannot be sourced
- Handcuffs
    - Generic, cannot be sourced
- Duct tape
    - Generic, cannot be sourced
- No trace
- Purse left as booby trap
    - Plastic surgeon's hypodermic needle
    - Strychnine loaded into needle

— Can't locate source

— Probably not enough to kill

Rhyme gazed at the entries and then shrugged. "It's as mysterious as the message he's trying to send."

Thom said, "Witching hour."

"Okay, you win."

Cooper pulled his jacket on and said good night.

"Sachs?" Rhyme asked. "You coming upstairs?"

She'd turned from the board and was staring out the window at the stark, ice-coated branches bending in the persistent wind.

"What?" She hadn't heard, it seemed.

"You coming to bed?"

"I'll be a few more minutes."

Thom climbed the stairs and Rhyme wheeled to the elevator that would take him to the second floor. Once there, he rolled toward the bedroom. He paused, though, cocked his head, listening. Sachs was on the phone, speaking softly, but he could still make out the words.

"Pam, hey, it's me...Hope you're checking messages. Really like to talk. Give me a call. Okay, love you. 'Night."

That was, Rhyme believed, the third such call today.

He heard her footfalls on the stairs and immediately veered into the bedroom and struck up a conversation with Thom—which must have bordered on the surreal to the aide, given that Rhyme was concentrating on his words not one bit; he simply wanted to keep Sachs from knowing he'd overheard her plea to Pam Willoughby.

Sachs crested the top stair and walked into the bedroom. Rhyme was thinking how unsettling it is when the people who are the hubs of our lives are suddenly vulnerable. And worse yet when they mask it with stoic smiles, as Sachs did now.

She saw his glance and asked, "What?"

Rhyme vamped. "Just thinking. I have a feeling we're going to get him tomorrow."

He expected her to look incredulous and say something like, "*You?* Have a *feeling*."

But instead she glanced subtly at her phone's screen, pocketed the unit and said, eyes out the window, "Could be, Rhyme. Could be."

THURSDAY, NOVEMBER 7 III

THE RED CENTIPEDE

CHAPTER 32

9:00 A.M.

Sweating, groaning loudly, Billy Haven awoke from a difficult dream.

Involving the Oleander Room.

Though all dreams set there—and there were lots of them—were, by definition, difficult.

This one was particularly horrifying because his parents were present, even though they'd died some years before he'd ever stepped into the Oleander Room for the first time. Maybe they were ghosts but they looked real. The odd reality of the unreality of dreams.

His mother was gazing at what he was doing and she was screaming, "No, no, no! Stop, stop!"

But Billy was smiling reassuringly and saying, "It's okay," even though he knew it wasn't. It was anything but okay. Then he realized the reassurance didn't mean anything because his mother couldn't hear him. Which wiped the smile away and he felt miserable.

His father merely shook his head, disappointed at what he was seeing. Vastly disappointed. This upset Billy too.

But their part in the dream made sense, now that he thought about it: His parents had died and died bloody.

Perfectly, horrifically logical.

Billy was smelling blood, seeing blood, tasting blood. Inking his skin temporarily with blood. Which happened both in the dream and in real life in the Oleander Room. Painting his skin the way people in some cultures do when piercing is forbidden.

Billy flung off the sheet and sat up, swinging his feet to the cold floor. Using a pillow, he wiped his forehead of sweat, picturing all of them: Lovely Girl and his parents.

He glanced down at the works on his thighs. On the left:

ELA

On the other:

LIAM

Two names that he was proud to carry with him. That he'd carry forever. They represented a huge gap in his life. But a gap soon to be closed. A wrong soon to be righted.

The Modification...

He looked at the rest of his body.

Billy Haven was largely tat-free, which was odd for

someone who made much of his income as a tattoo artist. Most inkers were drawn to the profession because they enjoyed body mods, were even obsessed with the needles, the lure of the machine. More. Give me more. And they'd often grow depressed at the dwindling inches of uninked skin on their bodies to fill with more works.

But not Billy. Maybe it was like Michelangelo. The master had liked painting but did not particularly like being painted.

Finger skin to finger skin...

The truth was that Billy hadn't wanted to be a tat artist at all. It had been a temporary job to put himself through college. But he'd found that he enjoyed the practice and in an area where a pen-and-paintbrush artist would have trouble making a living, a skin artist could do okay for himself. So he'd tucked aside his somewhat worthless college degree, set up shop in a strip mall and proceeded to make pretty good ducats with his Billy Mods.

He looked again at his thighs.

ELA

LIAM

Then he glanced at his left arm. The red centipede. The creature was about eighteen inches long. Its posterior was at the middle of his biceps and the design moved in a lazy S pattern to the back of his hand, where the insect's head rested—the head with a human face, full lips, knowing eyes, a nose, a mouth encircling the fangs.

Traditionally, people tattooed themselves with animals for two reasons: to assume attributes of the creature, like courage from a lion or stealth from a panther. Or to serve as an emblem to immunize them from the dangers of a particular predator.

Billy didn't know much about psychology but knew that, between the two, it was the first reason that had made him pick this creature with which to decorate his arm.

All he really knew, though, was that it gave him comfort.

He dressed and assembled his gear, then ran a pet roller over his clothing, hair and body several times.

His wristwatch hummed. Then the other, in his pocket, made a similar noise a few seconds later.

It was time to go hunting once more.

Okay. This is a pain.

Billy was in a quiet, dim tunnel beneath the East Side of Midtown, making his way toward where he was going to ink a new victim to hell.

But his route had been blocked off.

In the nineteenth century, he'd learned, this tunnel housed a connector for a narrow-gauge spur line linking a factory with a rail depot around 44th Street. It was a glorious construction of smooth brick and elegant arches, surprisingly free of vermin and mold. The ties and rails were gone but the passageway's transportation heritage was still evident: Several blocks away, Billy could hear, trains moved north and south out of Grand Central Station. You could hear subways too. Overhead and under. Some so close that dust fell.

The tunnel would have led him very close to his next victim—if not for some inconsiderate laborers who'd bricked off the doorway in the past twenty-four hours, some construction work Billy hadn't planned on.

A pain...

He surveyed the murky passageway, illuminated by light filtering in from runoff gratings and ill-matched manhole covers. From cracks in some of the nearby buildings too. How to get around the wall, without having to climb to the surface? The Underground Man should stay, well, underground.

Walking another fifty yards, Billy noted a ladder of U-shaped iron bars set into the brick wall. The rungs led, ten feet up, to a smaller passage that looked like it would bypass the obstruction. He shucked the backpack and walked to the ladder. He climbed up and peered inside. Yes, it seemed to lead to another, larger tunnel that would take him where he wanted to go.

He returned to the floor to collect his backpack and continue his journey.

Which was when the man came out of nowhere.

The shadowy form charged him, enwrapped Billy in a bear's grip and pressed him against the tunnel wall.

Lord, Billy prayed. Save me, Lord...

His hands shook, heart pounded at the shock.

The man looked him up and down. He was about Billy's size and age but very strong. Surprisingly strong. He stank, that complex aroma of unwashed human skin and hair and street oils. Jeans, two Housing Works shirts, white and pale blue. A tattered plaid sport coat, originally nice quality, stolen or plucked out of a Dumpster in this fancy neighborhood. The man sported wild hair but was clean-shaven, curiously. His dark eyes were beady and narrow and feral. Billy thought immediately of Doctor Moreau.

Bear-man...

"My block. Here, it's my block. You're in my block. Why are you in my block?" His predator's eyes dancing around.

Billy tried to pull away but stopped fast when Bear-man flicked open a straight razor expertly and touched the gleaming edge to Billy's throat.

CHAPTER 33

"Careful there. Please." Billy was whispering these words. Maybe others too. He wasn't sure.

"My block," Bear-man was repeating, apparently not the least inclined to be careful. The razor scraped, scraped on the one-day growth of beard on his throat. It sounded like a car transmission to Billy.

"You," the man growled.

Thinking of his parents again, his aunt and uncle, other relatives.

Lovely Girl, of course.

He was going to die, and like this? Wasteful, tragic.

The massive vise grip tightened. "Are you the one. I'll bet you are. Who else would you be, of course. Of course."

What was the response supposed to be to that?

Not to move, for one thing. Billy sensed that if he did, he'd feel a tickling pain beneath his jaw and, after the stroke, giddiness, as blood sprayed and sprayed. And then he'd feel nothing at all.

Billy said, "Look, I'm with the city. I work for the

city." He nodded at his coveralls. "I'm not here to hassle you. I'm just doing my job."

"You're not a reporter?"

"With the city," he repeated, tapping the coveralls—very carefully and with a cautious finger. Then he gambled. "I hate reporters."

This seemed to be reassuring to Bear-man, though he didn't relax much. The razor was still held firmly in one massive, filthy paw. The other continued to press Billy painfully into the wall of the tunnel.

"Julian?" Bear-man asked.

"What?"

"Julian?"

As if the name was a code and Billy was supposed to respond with the counter-password. If he got it wrong he'd be decapitated. His palms sweated. He rolled the dice. "No, I'm not Julian."

"No, no, no. Do you *know* Julian Savitch?" Irritated that Billy wasn't catching on.

"No."

Bear-man said skeptically, "No, no? He wrote that book."

"Well, I don't know him. Really."

A close examination of Billy's face. "It was about me. Not just me. All of us. I have a copy. I got a copy that was signed. Somebody from the city—" He poked the logo on the coveralls. "*Somebody* from the city brought him down here. Brought him into our block. Here. *My* block. Did you do that?"

"I didn't... No, I don't even know—"

"The law says I can cut you if I feel I'm in danger and the jury believes I really felt I was in danger. Not that I *was* actually in danger. But if I *felt* I was in danger. See the difference? That's all I need. And you're dead, buddy."

The sentences ran into each other, clattering, like cars on a fast-braking freight train.

Billy asked calmly, "What's your name?"

"Nathan."

"Please, Nathan." Then he shut up as the razor scraped his throat once more.

Rasp, rasp...

"You live down here?" he asked Bear-man.

"Julian said bad things about us. He called us that name."

"Name?"

"That we don't *like*! Are you the one who sent him down here? Somebody from the city did. When I find him I'm going to kill him. He called us that name."

"What name?" Billy was thinking this was a logical question to ask and he wouldn't incur the wrath of Bear-man by at least raising the issue, an apparently sensitive one.

The answer, spat out, was "'Mole People.' In his book. About us who live down here. Thousands of us. We're homeless most of us. We live in the tunnels and subways. He called us Mole People. We don't like that."

"Who would?" Billy asked. "No, I didn't lead anybody down here. And I don't know a Julian."

The razor gleamed, even in the dim light, lovingly kept. It was Bear-man's treasure, and Billy understood the value of a clean shave—not very common among the homeless, he guessed.

"We don't like that, being called that, moles," Bear-man repeated, as if he'd forgotten he'd just said it. "I'm a person like you and me."

Well, that sentence hardly worked. But Billy nodded in agreement, thinking he was close to vomiting. "Sure you are. Well, I don't know Julian, Nathan. I'm just here checking on the tunnels. For safety, you know."

Bear-man stared. "Sure you say that but why should I believe you why why why?" Words running together in a growl.

"You don't have to believe me. But it's true."

Billy thought he was actually about to die. He thought of the people he'd loved.

ELA

LIAM

He said a prayer.

Bear- not Mole-man gripped Billy harder. The razor stayed in place. "You know, some of us don't *choose* to live here. We don't *want* to live here. Don't you think that? We'd rather have a home in Westchester. Some of us would rather fuck a wife every Thursday night and take her to see the in-laws on nice spring days. But things don't always work out as planned now, do they?"

"No, they don't, Nathan. They sure don't." And Billy, desperate to forge some connection between them, came seconds away from telling Bear-man about the tragedies of his parents and Lovely Girl. But, no. You didn't need a Modification Commandment to remind you not to do stupid things. "I'm not helping authors write about you. I'm here to make sure the tunnels don't collapse and there are no water or gas leaks." He pointed up to an array of pipes running along the tunnel's ceiling.

"What's that?" Nathan was tugging up Billy's sleeve.

He was staring at the centipede with a child-like fascination.

"A tattoo."

"Well, now. That's pretty nice. Pretty good." The razor drooped. But didn't fold away. God, Nathan's hand was huge.

"It's my hobby."

"You did that? You did that on yourself?"

"I did, yeah. It's not that hard. You like it?"

Nathan admitted, "I guess I do."

"I could give you a tattoo, Nathan. If I do that would you move that razor away from my throat?"

"What kind of tattoo?"

"Anything you like."

"I'm not going up top." He said this as if Billy had suggested strolling through a nuclear reactor core that was melting down.

"No, I can do it here. I can give you a tattoo here. Would you like one?"

"I guess I might."

A nod at the backpack. "I've got my machine with me." He repeated, "It's a hobby. I'll give you a tattoo. And how 'bout some money? I've got some clothes too. I'll give you all that if you move that razor and let me go."

My Lord, he's strong. How could he be that strong, living down here? Nathan could kill him with his hands; he hardly needed the shining blade.

Eyebrows flexing closer.

Nathan was kneading the razor, then gripping it harder, Billy thought. The blade moved as twitchy and train-clattery as Bear-man's sentences.

"Nathan?" Billy asked.

The man didn't answer.

"Nathan. I didn't know this was your block. I just was doing my work, checking the pipes and valves and things. I want people to be safe down here."

The razor hovered.

And Bear-man's breathing seemed harder now as he stared at the centipede. The red ink. The face, the fangs, the segments of the body.

The indecipherable eyes.

"Nathan?" Billy whispered. "A tattoo. You want that tattoo?"

Because what utility worker doesn't cart around an American Eagle tattoo machine to ink people on a whim?

"I'll give you my best tattoo. Would you like that? It'll be a present. And the clothes and money I told you about? A hundred dollars."

"It won't hurt?"

"It'll sting a little. But not bad. I'm going to get my backpack now. That's where the money and clothes are, and my tattoo machine. Is it all right if I reach into my backpack?"

"I guess you can," Nathan whispered.

Billy slid the backpack closer and extracted the parts to his machine. "You can sit down there. Is that all right?" The razor was still not far away and was still open. God or Satan or the ghost of Abraham Lincoln might tell Nathan to kill this interloper at any moment. Billy moved very slowly.

Hmm. It seemed that Nathan *was* receiving transmission from on high.

He laughed and whispered an indecipherable string of syllables.

Finally he dropped into a cross-legged position and grinned. "Okay. I'll sit here. Give me a tattoo."

It wasn't until Billy too squatted on the packed-dirt ground that his breathing steadied and his thudding heart began to tap more slowly.

As Nathan watched carefully, Billy finished assembling his American Eagle. He extracted several vials and set them on the ground. He tested the unit. It hummed.

"One thing," the man said ominously, the razor rising slightly.

"What's that?"

"Not a mole. Don't tattoo me with a mole."

"I won't do a mole, Nathan. I promise."

Nathan folded the razor and put it away.

CHAPTER 34

"We don't call them guns."

"Yeah, yeah, I know. I forgot. I meant 'machine.' Tattoo *machine*," Lon Sellitto was saying.

"And we prefer 'skin art' or 'work.' 'Tattoo' has a cultural connotation I'm not happy with." The petite woman, highly tattooed (*skin arted*?), gazed at Sellitto from over an immaculate glass counter, inside which were neatly arranged packets of needles, machine not gun parts, books, stacks of tattoo stencils, washable pens in all colors. *Draw first, ink later*, a sign warned.

The parlor was as clean as TT Gordon's. Apparently legit skin artists took the disease stuff pretty seriously. You even got the impression that this woman would step out of the room to sneeze.

Her name was Anne Thomson and she was the owner of Femme Fatale Modification and Supplies. Mid-thirties, with short dark hair and only one tasteful nose piercing, she was really pretty. And part of that was the four-color tats, okay, artwork, on her chest and neck and arms. One—on the chest—was a combination of a snake and a bird. It vaguely reminded Sellitto of a picture he'd seen a few times on vacation in Mexico, some religious symbol. On her neck were some of the constellations, not only the stars but the animals they were inspired by. Crab, scorpion, bull. And when she turned once, he saw two sparkling red shoes on her shoulder. They looked real. Dorothy, my pretty...

Fuck art, Linc. That's how I feel about art.

But not this. Sellitto liked the images. He really liked them. The pictures seemed to move, to expand and contract. Almost three-dimensional. How the hell did that work? It was as if he were looking at living paintings. Or at some entirely different creature, something not human but *more* than human. It took him back to some of the computer games his son had played a few years ago as a teenager. Sellitto remembered looking over the boy's shoulder. "What's that?" Pointing at one of the creatures in the game. It looked like a snake with legs and sported a fish's tail and a human head.

"You know, a *nyrad*." Like, obviously.

Oh. Sure. Nyrad.

Sellitto now looked up and realized he'd been caught staring at the woman's chest.

"I—"

"It's okay. They're there to be looked at. Plural. Works, I mean. Not boobs."

"I—"

"You just said that. I'm not thinking you're a dirty old man. And you're about to ask if they hurt."

"Naw, I figure they hurt."

"They did. But what in life doesn't, if it's important?"

Sex, dinner and collaring a prick of a criminal, Sellitto thought. Most of the time those didn't hurt. But he shrugged. "What I was going to ask was, you draw them yourself? Design them, I mean."

"No. I went to an artist in Boston. The best on the East Coast. I just wanted Quetzalcoatl. Mexican god." Her finger touched the snake on her chest. "And we talked for a couple of days and she got to know me. She did the plumed serpent and recommended the constellations. I got Dorothy's shoes too." She smiled. Sellitto smiled. "I don't mean to be overly political, except I do. See, that's how *women* artists handle an inking. A man goes into a male artist and says I want a chain, a death's-head, a flag. And out he comes with a chain, a death's-head or a flag. Women take a different approach. Less impulsive, less instant, more thoughtful."

Sellitto muttered, "Kinda like life in general. Men and women, I mean." The questions about Unsub 11-5 still needed to be answered. But he now asked, "Hey, just curious, you know. How'd you get into this business?"

"You mean, aside from the skin art, I seem like a schoolteacher?"

"Yeah."

"I was a schoolteacher." Thomson let the pause linger. Timing. "Middle school. Now, *there's* a DMZ for you. You know, a no-man's-land between the hormones to the south and the attitudes to the north."

"I got a kid. A boy. He's outta college now. But he had to get to that age, you know."

She nodded. "It wasn't flying for me. I went to get a work at a parlor in town and, hard to explain, it set me free. I quit the school and opened a shop. Now I do skin art *and* canvas painting too. Shows in SoHo, uptown too. Couldn't've done it, though, if I hadn't gotten inked in the first place."

"Impressive."

"Thanks. Now you were asking about the American Eagle machine."

Thomson's was the one shop in the tristate area that sold parts and needles for that model. She also had a used model for sale. To Sellitto it looked gnarly, dangerous. Like a ray gun from some weird science-fiction flick.

"Can I ask? Why're you interested?"

The detective debated. He decided he owed it to her to tell all. Maybe it was that she was so devoted to the art. Or that she had a really incredible chest. He told her what 11-5 was doing.

"No, my God, no." Her eyes were as wide as the Mexican snake-bird's were narrow. "Somebody's actually doing that, killing people with a machine?" She shuddered and for a moment Thomson, for all her imposing creatures and *Wizard of Oz* shoes, didn't seem mysterious or more than human at all. She seemed vulnerable and small. TT Gordon had had the same reaction—a sense of betrayal that somebody in their close-knit profession would use his talent to kill and do so in a particularly horrific way.

"Afraid so."

"The American Eagles," she said. "Old machines, not as reliable as the new ones. One of the first portables."

"That's what TT said."

Thomson nodded. "He's a good guy. You're lucky

he's helping you. And I think I can help you too. Nobody's ever bought a machine here but about a week ago a man came in and bought some needles for an American Eagle." She leaned forward, resting her hands on the counter. The shiny black ring on her right index finger turned out to be ink.

"I didn't pay much attention. Late twenties, thirties. White. Had a cap on, dark, and a scarf around his neck. It came up high, almost covering his chin. Sunglasses too. Which he didn't need because the weather was as bad as now. That, the glasses, seemed hipster and uncool. But we get imagistas in here a lot. It's a fine line between posing with ink and being real with ink."

Imagistas. Clever.

Sellitto showed her the Identi-Kit pic.

Thomson shrugged. "Could be. Again, not paying much attention. Oh, but one thing I remember. He wasn't inked that I could see. Wasn't pierced either. Most skin artists're pretty modded."

"He has one on his arm. Maybe a dragon, some creature. In red. Does that mean anything?"

The snake-and-bird woman shook her head. "No—after that book, that thriller, a lot of people wanted dragons. Copycats. No significance that I know."

He then asked, "You know anything significant about a tattoo of the words 'the second'? Or 'forty'? They mean anything in the skin art world?"

"No, not that I've ever heard."

He displayed pictures of the tattoos.

"Well," she said. "Old English font. That's hard to do. And the lesions, the raised part? That was because of the poison?"

"Yeah."

"Well, whatever else, he's good. Real good."

"And he worked fast. Probably did that in ten, fifteen minutes."

"Really?" She seemed astonished. "And the scarification too? The scalloped border?"

"All in ten or fifteen. Does that, or the style, give you any idea who this guy might be?"

"Not really . . . But I don't see the outlines."

"No, TT said he used a bloodline. Freehand."

"Then nobody I know could do a work like that in fifteen minutes. And I know all the talented people in town. That's one hell of an artist you're dealing with."

"TT said he was from out of town but didn't know where."

"Well, you don't see that font much in the area. But I couldn't tell you what's hot now in Albany—or Norwalk or Trenton. My clientele's pretty much downtown Manhattan."

"He paid cash for the needles, right?"

Why bother to ask?

"Right."

"Any chance you'd still have the money? For prints."

"No. But it wouldn't matter. He wore gloves."

Natch . . .

"I thought that was a little weird too. But not suspicious weird, you know?"

Imagistas.

"Did he say anything?"

"To me? No. Other than to ask for the needles."

Sellitto, paying attention to that first sentence. "But?"

"When he was leaving he got a call on his mobile.

After I'd rung him up I stepped into the back room. When he was walking out the door he said, 'Yeah, the Belvedere.' And then I think he said 'address.' Anyway, that's what I thought. But it might've been 'bella dear' or something else."

Sellitto wrote this down. Asked the standard: "Anything else you can think of?"

"No, I'm afraid not."

It was usually afraid not or no or don't think so. But at least Thomson had thought about the question and was being honest.

He thanked her and, with a last glance at Quetzawhatever on her chest, headed back into the sleet, speed-dialing Rhyme to tell him he might don't get your fucking hopes up but he *might* have a lead.

CHAPTER 35

A good workout.

As he walked from his health club back to his apartment on East 52nd Street to collect his car, Braden Alexander was counting the crunches he'd done. He'd given up after a hundred.

Counting them, that is. The crunches themselves? Plenty. He'd forgotten how many.

Alexander had a sedentary job—writing code for one of the big investment firms (one that actually had *not* been the subject of an investigation)—and the thirty-seven-year-old was determined to stay in good shape, despite the eight-hour days at his workstation—and the one-hour reverse commute to Jersey, where his company's IT headquarters building was located.

And the curls? With the thirty-pound bells? Maybe two hundred. Damn, he sure felt it. He decided he'd take it a bit easier tomorrow. No need to push *too* far. It was more important to be consistent, Alexander knew. Every day he made the trek from his apartment west to the health club on Sixth Avenue. Every day, the stationary bike and curls and squats and, yeah, crunches, crunches, crunches... What do we think, 150?

Probably.

He glanced at himself in a window and thought: The weight's okay. His skin seemed a little pale. Not so good, that. He and his family would get to an island soon. Maybe after Thanksgiving. Anyway, who wouldn't look sickly on a day like this? The sleet had let up but the light was gray and anemic. He was actually looking forward to getting into his cubicle. He found it cozy, a word he wouldn't use with anybody but his wife.

Today there was something else to look forward to. He'd be picking up a bicycle at his brother's house in Paramus. Joey'd gotten a new mountain bike and was giving his old one to Alexander's son. The boy was ecstatic and had texted twice from school, just to see how "everything was going?"

The impatience of youth.

He looked south and caught sight of the new Trade Tower, or whatever it was going to be called. He'd been working at his first job, crunching code for a bank, when the attack had happened, 2001. The new structure was impressive, architecturally more interesting than the simple rectangles of its predecessors. Still, nothing could ever match their grandeur, their style.

What a time that was. His first son had been born the day after the attack. Alexander and his wife had abandoned plans to name him after her father and had picked instead Emery, after the architectural firm Emery Roth & Sons, which along with Minoru Yamasaki had designed the original Trade Towers.

Alexander continued east back toward his apartment,

where he'd collect his car and head to work. As he paused for a red light he happened to look back and caught a glimpse of someone behind him, head down. Some guy, young, in dark clothes and stocking cap. A bag or backpack on his shoulder. Was he the same one who'd been sitting in a coffee shop across the street from the health club?

He following me?

Alexander had lived in the city for fifteen years. He considered New York the safest urban area on earth. But he wasn't a fool, either. He made his living because of bad guys. When he'd started as a programmer some years ago most of his work had been to hack together code that made the servers run more smoothly, expanded web traffic and allowed the various operating systems to talk to each other without stuttering. Over the years, though, he'd developed the specialty of security. Commercial hackers, terrorists and punks with too much time on their hands and too many cells in their brains now preyed on banking institutions like his employer with increasingly bold and brilliant attacks.

That had become Alexander's specialty, throwing nails in the path of some pretty smart and pretty nasty hackers.

He'd heard of some computer security pros who'd been physically attacked. He sometimes wondered if he was at personal risk. He had no specific knowledge that any hackers knew his name but he also was aware that it was impossible to keep all information about yourself hidden from someone with enough drive to track you down.

Near his apartment building Alexander paused and,

on the pretext of making a phone call, glanced back once more. The man in the cap and coat continued following, head down. He didn't seem to be paying any attention to Alexander. Then without a pause the supposed hit hacker walked into a building across the street, an old one, now a commercial space, with a *For Rent* sign pasted across a dirty window. Maybe he was a Realtor or new tenant. Or a janitor examining a temperamental boiler—it was supposed to be another bone-chilling evening.

Amused at his own wasted concern, Alexander continued on to his building and to the entrance to the parking garage, where they kept the Subaru. The parking space was a luxury—it alone cost more than his first apartment. But a guaranteed slot in the city that brought the world alternate-side-of-the-street parking? Didn't get any better than that—except it did: The space was enclosed, so he never had to shovel snow or scrape ice. Extremely enclosed, in fact. The space was in the third sub-basement.

He now waved to the cashier, who called, "Hey, Mr. Alexander. When's it gonna let up? You know what I mean?" The skinny, gray-complexioned man gazed up at the sky.

He'd said virtually the same thing every day for the past week.

Alexander grinned and shrugged. He descended the spiral ramp of the dim place.

On the bottom floor, the Subie's floor, as his wife had dubbed the vehicle, Alexander walked under the low ceiling toward where the front of his green car peeked out. The garage—this floor at least—seemed completely deserted. But he wasn't feeling uneasy anymore, now that the imaginary killer shadowing him had disappeared into the building across the street. Besides, no mugger—or hacker intent on breaking Alexander's typing fingers—would dare risk an attack here. The only way in was past the watchful attendant.

You know what I mean?...

As he approached the Subaru he pulled his keys out and hit the unlock button on the fob. The lights flashed. He continued on to the car, thinking of the bike for his son. He was looking forward to riding his own ten-speed with Emery through Central Park this weekend.

He was smiling at the prospective pleasure when a man stepped casually out from behind a wall to Alexander's right and punched him in the neck.

"The hell—?" Alexander gasped and spun around.

Oh, Christ, Christ... The guy wore gray coveralls like a repairman or utility worker but his face looked like an alien's—encased in a tight yellowish mask, latex.

Then he saw the hypodermic needle in the gloved, yellow hand.

Alexander touched his neck, which stung.

He'd poked him with something! The first thing he thought was: AIDS.

Some kind of psycho. No, no, no...

Then he thought: Nobody's going to get away with this crap. Alexander had taken several self-defense courses and a kickboxing class at the gym. Not to mention being racked from the thousands of crunches and curls. He turned to face the guy and planted his feet firmly on the ground, drawing back his right arm, recalling how to hit fast and follow up.

One, two, feint, hit.

One, two...

But his arm wasn't behaving. It was heavy. Too heavy even to lift. And he noted the terrible panic, the shock, fading. He didn't even feel scared anymore.

And when the dim light grew dimmer he understood:

No, not tainted blood. Of course not. It was a sedative of some kind the asshole had injected him with. Sure, sure, this *was* the guy who'd been following him. He'd slipped down here from the building across the street. But how...? Oh, there. There was a small metal access door open. Behind it darkness, like a tunnel or a basement. And the guy's mission? To kidnap Alexander. To get him to reveal codes or security flaws in his clients' programs.

"Ahhhl talll you...whah..." Alexander was speaking. *Trying* to speak.

Say it! Come on! I'll tell you what you want. Just let me go.

"Lllll. Tllll. You waaaaa..."

The syllables were falling apart.

Then the words were just gurgling from his throat.

He was surprised to find he wasn't standing any longer but sitting down, paralyzed, staring up at the masked freak. Looking around at his surroundings. The Subie's tire. A Hershey bar wrapper. An oval of dried dog pee.

The attacker bent down over a backpack.

As the darkness grew, serious darkness now, Alexander squinted, looking at a weird tattoo on the man's left arm. A snake...no, a centipede. With a human face.

Then he was lying on his back, too weak even to sit

up any longer. The attacker roughly tugged Alexander's wrists behind his back and cuffed them. Rolled him over on his back once more.

But just because this guy had the melted skin mask and a macabre tattoo didn't mean he was a psychotic killer. No, he just wanted to get the codes to the Livingston Associates main server. Or the password to crack the Bank of Eastern Nassau's security lock-out system.

Sure.

Not a wacko.

This was business was all. Only business. They didn't want to hurt him. They were after data? Fine, he'd give them data. Passcodes? They'd get passcodes.

Only business, right?

But then why was he lifting Alexander's jacket and shirt and staring at his abdomen intently? And reaching forward and stroking the skin with a rigid, probing finger?

Has to be . . . only . . .

Blackness enwrapped him completely.

CHAPTER 36

"Where are you, Sachs?"

"Almost there." Her voice was echoing through the speaker in Rhyme's parlor. The criminalist was here with Pulaski and Cooper, while Amelia Sachs was presently streaking across Central Park, one of the traverses, headed east. "Hanging up. Gotta drive."

It turned out there were forty-eight places in Manhattan in which "Belvedere" figured in the name. This had been the conclusion of yet another team that Lon Sellitto had assembled at One Police Plaza. There'd been the Find-the-Out-of-Print-Book team, now disbanded. Then the current What-the-Fuck-Do-the-Words-the-Second-and-Forty-Mean team, still active.

Now the Which-Belvedere-Is-It team, assembled thanks to skin artist Anne Thomson's fortuitous eavesdropping.

Four dozen instances of Belvedere in Manhattan (which seemed to be 11-5's preferred hunting borough; besides, you can't search everywhere).

Delis, apartment buildings, transport companies, boutiques, a cab company, a ferry.

An escort service.

A half hour ago, in Rhyme's parlor, he and Sachs, along with Sellitto, Cooper and Pulaski, had debated which of the Belvederes were the most likely to be connected to the unsub. Of course, the name might have nothing to do with the next or a future target. It could be where he lived, or near where he lived, or his dry cleaner or where he boarded his cat. Or a business he was curious about. But, being cautious, they assumed it was a kill site and wanted to get tac teams to the most likely ones ASAP.

They'd decided three were good candidates for an attack. One was a deserted warehouse in the Chelsea area of Manhattan—north of Greenwich Village. It featured an extensive labyrinth of underground passages and storerooms. Perfect for their unsub's purposes, though Cooper had made the point that it might be a little too deserted. "He needs to get a victim from somewhere."

Rhyme considered this but tapped into some CCTV images there and noted that it had more pedestrian traffic than you'd think—including even some joggers out on this blustery day.

"He only needs one," Rhyme pointed out.

Sellitto'd called ESU to have a team sent there.

The second Belvedere was an old movie theater on the Upper West Side, the sort of grande dame you used to see on Broadway, the ornate venues where Clark Gable or Marilyn Monroe would open films. It was closed at this hour and, according to one of Rhyme's underground diagrams, had a number of basements, just the place for Unsub 11-5 to take his victims. Another ESU team was sent there.

The final possibility was an apartment building on Midtown's East Side named the Belvedere. A grimy old structure, like the gothic Dakota. It featured both a large basement and an underground parking garage. The detective arranged for a third team to speed there.

Sachs had said, "Smells like that's the one. I'll go too."

Rhyme had noted her eyes, that huntress look, the undeterred focus. Which he found so appealing, and so unnerving, at the same time. Sachs was one of the best crime scene cops Rhyme had ever known. But she was never more alive than when leading a dynamic entry in a tactical scenario.

She'd sprinted out the door, pulling her jacket on as she went. Sellitto had followed shortly after.

Now Rhyme got a message from Sellitto, also mobile, reporting that a tac team had hit the Belvedere warehouse in Chelsea and found nothing. ESU commander Bo Haumann had left a small surveillance team and divided up the others; one group was heading to the Belvedere Apartments and one to the theater, which was massive; the search would take some time.

Just after he disconnected, his phone line rang again. "Rhyme?" Sachs's voice came through the speakers.

"Just heard from Lon," he told her. He explained that the warehouse was a bust. "But that means you're getting some reinforcements. An ESU team's headed to the apartment building where you are."

"Not are, Rhyme," she muttered. "*Will be.* Traffic's

lousy. And nobody knows how to drive in this weather. I'm on the sidewalk. Hold on." Rhyme heard a crash as presumably her Torino reseated itself on New York City asphalt. He wondered about debilitating damage to the drive train or the axles. "At this rate, ten minutes. And it's just cross town. Jesus."

Rhyme noted another incoming call on his phone.

"I'll call you back, Sachs. ESU's on the other line."

"Lincoln, you there?" It was Haumann.

"Yes, Bo. What's the status?"

"Tac Team Two's almost to the Belvedere Apartments. We'll hit the basement in the building and the garage too. Any more evidence that he's armed?" Haumann would be remembering the earlier incident, at the hospital in Marble Hill, where Unsub 11-5 had threatened to shoot Harriet Stanton and Sachs.

"Nothing further. But assume he is."

"I'll pass it along." A pause as Haumann spoke to someone else in his car or ESU van. Rhyme couldn't hear the exchange. "Okay, we're rolling up silent."

"I'll tell Amelia you're there. She'll want to be included in any tactical op. I wouldn't take any chances. You can't wait. Go in, dynamic, ASAP."

"Sure, Lincoln, we'll do it."

Rhyme said, "Tell your folks to look out for traps. That's his new game. Gloves and respirators."

"Roger that. Hold on... Okay, Lincoln?"

"I'm here."

"We've got a chopper in place. You want to log in and watch?"

"Sure."

The ESU commander gave him the code and a moment later Rhyme, Pulaski and Cooper were staring at the screen. It was a high-def image of two boxy ESU tactical trucks, designation numbers clearly visible on their roofs. Rhyme could see two dozen troops deploy through the front door of the apartment building and down the exit ramp of the garage. The parking attendant was being led away to safety by one of the officers.

The audio was up too. Rhyme could hear the ESU troops as they made their way through the facilities. "*...Southwest corridor, level one, clear...Access door here...no, it's sealed...*"

Haumann disconnected and Rhyme called Sachs back. Told her about the conversation.

She sighed. "I'm ETA five minutes." He could hear the disappointment about missing the entry.

Rhyme's attention swiveled to the radio feed from the tactical operation.

"*Tac Two A is going in, heading down the stairs to the lower level. Two B is heading down the garage ramp. Hold on...So far, no resistance, no innocents. We're green. K.*"

"Rhyme, I'm almost there. I—"

But he missed what she said next. An officer's voice blared out of the radio. "*Tac Two B...we have a situation. Lower level, parking garage...Jesus...Call it in, call it in!...Fire department...Move, move, move! We need fire now! K.*"

Fire? Rhyme wondered.

Another officer echoed his question. "*What's burning? I don't see anything burning. K?*"

"*Tac Two B. Negative on fire. The perp opened a standpipe to cover his getaway. We've got a flood. We can't get through. Already six inches of water. And it's rising. Need a fireman with a wrench to close the fucker. K."*

Rhyme heard a chuckle from the ether—apparently relief that they had to contend only with water, not an arson blaze.

He, however, was not amused. He knew exactly what their nimble unsub had done: unleashed the flood not only to slow down his pursuers, but to destroy whatever evidence he'd left behind.

CHAPTER 37

Running now, sprinting.

Billy Haven was underground, in the old train tunnel once more, heading back past the spot where Bear-man Nathan had come close to performing his straight-razor modification.

His backpack light as a leaf on his shoulder—that's what adrenaline does—he sprinted fast. The latex mask was off but not the gloves or coveralls. He carried his shoes. He was in his stocking feet. There wasn't, he'd learned in his research, any database for cloth footwear that might allow them to trace him. The booties were too slippery for sprinting.

Move, move, move...

The warning that had precipitated his rapid escape from the Belvedere parking garage had not been the squeal of brakes from the Emergency Service trucks or the quiet footfalls of the cops. He'd known a few moments before that that he was in danger. The police dispatcher had reported the address and mentioned the name Belvedere, as Billy had heard through the earbud, connected to his police scanner.

He'd then taken some measures to make sure the location—and the victim—would be useless to the police.

Thou shalt cleanse the crime scene of all that can incriminate.

Then he was back through the utility access port in the Belvedere parking garage's wall.

And underground once more.

Finally it was safe, Billy figured, to get to the surface. Chest aching, coughing shallowly, he climbed through another access door into the basement of a Midtown office building. It was one of those scuffed limestone functionaries of architecture, three-quarters of a century old, possibly more. Ten, twelve stories high, with dimly lit, jerky elevators that prompted you to bless yourself before you stepped inside.

Billy, though, took the stairs from the basement and, after checking, eased into the first-floor hallway, the professional home of ambulance chasers, accountants and some import-export operations whose names in English appeared under Cyrillic letters or Asian pictograms. He stripped off the coveralls, stuffed them into a trash bin and pulled on a different stocking cap, beige for a change. Shoes back on.

At the greasy glass door leading onto the street Billy paused and looked for police. None. This made sense; he was far enough away from the site of the attack at the Belvedere. The officers would have their hands full for some time there. It amused him to think of what was going on in the garage.

Stepping out onto the street he moved quickly east.

How had the great anticipator anticipated this? Yes, he'd been to the Belvedere several times to scope out the place. Maybe he'd picked up some trace there that had been discovered. That seemed unlikely but, with Rhyme, anything was possible.

Walking through the sleet, he kept his head down and thought back to any mistakes he might've made. Then: Yes, yes…he remembered. A week or so ago he'd called directory assistance to get the number for the Belvedere to check on the hours of the parking garage. He'd been in the tattoo supply store, buying extra needles for the American Eagle machine. That's how they'd found him.

This raised a question: The only reason the owner would have mentioned the Belvedere was because the police wanted to know who'd bought an American Eagle or needles for it. But how had they learned that this was his murder weapon?

He'd have to do some more thinking about that.

A subway station loomed and he descended the slushy stairs then caught a train south. In twenty minutes Billy was back at his workshop, in the shower, letting the hot water blast his skin as he scrubbed and scrubbed.

Then toweling off, dressing again.

He clicked on the radio. A short time later the news reported another attack by the "Underground Man," which had struck him as a rather pathetic nickname. Couldn't they come up with anything better?

Still no mention of Amelia Sachs or anybody else falling victim to a strychnine attack. Which meant that by either diligence or luck the Crime Scene people had missed getting stuck by the needle in Samantha's purse.

Billy had known all along the Modification would be like a battle, with wins and losses on both sides. He'd succeeded with two victims. The police had had some victories too. This was to be expected—in fact, it had been anticipated. Now, he reflected, he had to be a bit more serious about protecting himself.

An idea occurred to him.

Surprisingly simple, surprisingly good.

The applicable Commandment for this situation would be: *Know thine enemy. But know the friends and family of thine enemy too.*

CHAPTER 38

"Hell, Amelia, how bad is it?" Sellitto asked.

He and Sachs were standing in parallel positions—hands on hips—looking down into the dusky parking garage beneath the Belvedere Apartments.

"Bad," she muttered. She looked over the city schematic of this scene. She ran her finger over the parking area and the abandoned New York Central train tunnel. "Ruined. Gone. All of the evidence."

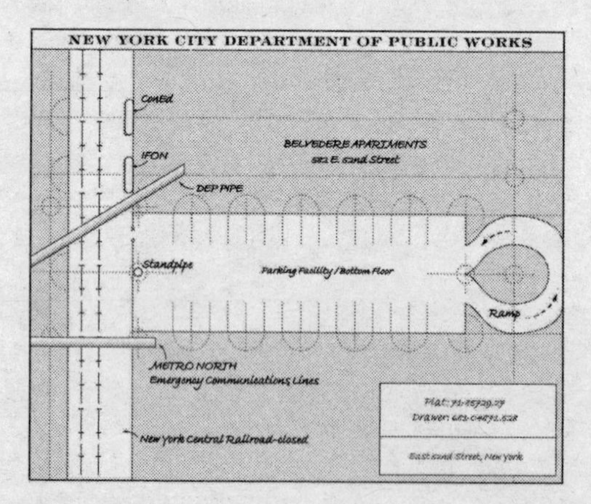

Sellitto stamped his feet, presumably to warm them against the stabbing chill of the icy muck they stood in. Sachs had stamped too; it didn't work. Just made her toes sting more.

She noted Bo Haumann nearby, on his mobile. The ESU commander disconnected and strode over to them. Nodded.

Sellitto asked, "Anything?"

The wiry, compact man, wearing a turtleneck under his shirt, strode forward. He rubbed a hand over his gray crew-cut hair. His eyebrows were frosty but he seemed completely unfazed by the cold. "He's gone. Rabbited. Got a team into the tunnel from a manhole up the street. But even that's useless. All they could say is 'No trace of him.' "

Sachs gave a grim laugh. "No trace. In both senses of the word."

Rhyme's concern had proved warranted. By opening the fire department standpipe, Unsub 11-5 had managed to obliterate the crime scene with calculated efficiency. The perp had then slipped out through the doorway by which he'd gained access to the parking garage, leaving it open. Within minutes, the geyser of water had flooded the ground floor of the garage and cascaded through the door into the tunnel below—which was to have been the killing zone.

When it comes to crime scene contaminants, water can be worse than fire. Much trace can survive flames and, while walls may collapse, the position of objects and architectural elements and even human bodies at the scene remains largely unchanged. A flood, though, is like a big mixing bowl, not only diluting and destroying and blending, but also moving items far from their original positions.

Water is, Rhyme had frequently pointed out, the universal solvent.

Emergency Service officers had cleared the scene and gotten the victim to the street level. He was doped up but conscious and his only injuries appeared to be bruises from where the water had slammed him into a wall. The unsub hadn't had time to start on the mod. The vic was bordering on hypothermia but the medical technicians got him out of his drenched clothing and into thermal blankets.

After extracting him, and clearing the scene, the police retreated while two firemen in full biohazard outfits waded through the torrent to shut the flow off. They took water samples too. Rhyme had been concerned that the unsub might have spilled into the water some toxin that, even if diluted, could injure or kill.

An ESU officer came up to them. "Detectives. Captain."

"Go ahead," Haumann said.

"It's draining and the fire department's hooked up a pumper. But it's still a flood. Oh, and they've done a preliminary test of the water and there's no biohazard or chemicals, nothing significant, at any rate. So they're pumping to the sewer drains. Should be pretty clear in about an hour."

The officer said to Sachs, "They said they found something you'll want to see, Detective. One of the firemen's bringing it out now."

"What?" she asked.

"Just a plastic bag. All I know."

She nodded, not holding out much hope it had anything to do with the case. It might hold a banana peel, a joint, coins for parking meters.

Though there was always the chance it was the perp's wallet or Social Security card.

Nothing more to do here. Sachs and Sellitto walked to the ambulance. They stepped inside, through the back, closed the door. Braden Alexander was sitting in a blue robe, shivering. The ambulance was heated but the man had just gone for a serious dunking in near-freezing water.

"How're you doing?" Sellitto asked.

His jaw trembling. "Cold, hazy from whatever the son of a bitch gave me. They said it's propofol." He stuttered as he spoke. His words were slurred too. "And seeing him, what he was wearing, it freaked me out."

"Could you describe him?"

"Not real well. He was about six feet, pretty good shape. White. But he wore this yellow latex mask. Jesus. I freaked. I mean, I totally freaked. I said that, didn't I? Eyeholes and nose and mouth. That was it."

Sellitto showed him the Identi-Kit image.

"Could be. Probably. But the mask, you know."

"Sure. Clothes?"

"When he came at me in the garage, he was in coveralls, I think. I was freaked." More shivering. "But I'd seen him earlier and he was wearing something else. If it was him. He went into that building there."

Ah, maybe they had an intact crime scene after all. Sachs sent a CS officer to take a look, with an Emergency Service backup.

"Did he say anything?" Sellitto asked.

"No. Just jabbed me with a needle. Then I started to

pass out. But I saw him..." His voice faded. "I saw him get a scalpel out of his backpack."

"A scalpel, not just a knife?"

"Definitely a scalpel. And he looked like he knew what to do with it. Oh, and he was touching my skin. On my stomach. Touching and pinching it. Jesus. What was that all about?"

"He's done that before," Sachs said. "We don't know exactly why."

"Oh, but I remember that as he reached down, his sleeve went up, you know. And I saw he had this tattoo. It was weird. A centipede, I'm pretty sure. Yeah. But, you know, with a face."

"What color was it?" Sellitto asked.

"Red. Now, next I know I came to and was choking and the cops, the police were dragging me out of the water. I was so cold, cold. Man. It was like I was spinning around in the ocean. Is this the guy who's been killing those people in town?"

Sometimes you withheld, sometimes you told.

"It's likely."

"Why me?"

"We aren't sure what his motive is. Do you have any enemies, anybody who might want to do this?" Sachs and Rhyme had not completely dismissed the theory that the unsub was using the apparent serial killings to cover up the murder of a specific victim, lost in the general carnage of Unsub 11-5.

But Alexander said, "I do computer security work and I was thinking I jammed the wrong hacker, and he wanted to nail me. I thought the guy who went into the building, the one maybe following me, might've been a strong-arm, whatever you'd call it. But I don't know of anybody specific."

"That's probably unlikely," Sellitto said. "We think the people he's picking are random."

Happenstance victims...

They took Alexander's contact information.

Sachs donned gloves and collected the cuffs, which had been removed by a responding, put them into a collection bag and filled out the chain-of-custody card. She made a note to get the fingerprints of the medic who'd removed the cuffs. But she had no doubt that their diligent unsub wasn't going to get careless now.

They stepped out of the ambulance and were blasted by the chill wind.

A Crime Scene officer approached, the one she'd sent to check on the building nearby—where Alexander had said he'd seen a man following him. The CS cop, a sinewy young man in round glasses, said, "Nobody in the building. And we went through the basement real careful. No exit from down there, no way to get to the parking garage."

"Okay, thanks."

Two firemen approached, their gear dripping. One held a small plastic bag by the corner. Ah, the maybe evidence. She wasn't concerned about contamination; the fireman wore neoprene biohazard gloves.

He greeted them. "Heard you were the Crime Scene officer in charge."

"Right." Sachs nodded. "How is it down there?"

"Mess. It's still under eight inches of water. And covers the whole ground floor. Then the tunnel underneath the lower level? That's a lake too."

"What'd you find?" Nodding at the bag.

"Was against the wall near where the victim was. Might be from your boy, might not. There was nothing else, though."

Banana peel, pot, coins…

She took the bag in her gloved hand. Inside were small metal fixtures, about an inch high, in various shapes. Hardware of some kind, Sachs guessed. She showed the bag to Sellitto, who shrugged. She slipped this into an evidence bag and took the fireman's name and badge number for the chain-of-custody card. Wrote the details down and had him sign. She did the same.

"I want to go down there," Sachs said to one of the firemen. "Borrow some boots?"

"Sure. We'll suit you up."

Another fireman came by with a cardboard tray, passing around coffee. Sellitto took one but Sachs declined. She had no taste for anything at the moment except finding a lead, any lead, to Unsub 11-5.

CHAPTER 39

"They're implants."

TT Gordon, the tat artist decorated with superheroes and an excessively stylish chin, was back in Rhyme's parlor.

Standing at the examination table beside Mel Cooper, he peered at what the fireman had collected at the crime scene in the Belvedere Apartments parking garage: loose metal bits in a plastic bag. They weren't hardware, as Sachs had originally thought, but were in the shape of numbers and letters. Grooves had been filed in them and some off-white substance smeared into the notches.

1 h 7 t

About an inch high each, they sat on a sterile pad of Teflon.

"And what are implants?" Rhyme asked, wheeling closer.

The skinny man rubbed at Batman's face on his lean arm. Rhyme could see a portion of another superhero on the other. Why those particular two comic characters? he wondered.

But then: Why not?

"Implants're, they're sort of an extreme form of modding. You cut slits into the skin and feed them in. Eventually the skin shrinks and you can see the shape or the letters raised. You don't find 'em much. But inkings're a dime a dozen nowadays—like I was saying yesterday. Every clerk, public relations assistant and lawyer has a tat now. You need implants and scars to be different. Who knows what it'll be in ten years. Actually, I don't think I want to know."

Sachs asked, "Does it tell us anything about the unsub?"

"Confirms what I was saying before. They're rare here. I don't know any artists who do them in the area. It's technically, you know, a surgical procedure and you need good training. You see them mostly in the Midwest and Appalachia, West Virginia, mountains of North Carolina. People who want to lead a more alternative life. I mean, more alternative than I," said TT Gordon, the grammarian tattoo artist.

"You'd think implants were a macho thing but, fact is, women go for them more. They're pretty dangerous. They're made out of materials where there's not much chance of rejection but there's the infection issue. And, worse, they'll migrate. And then you're in trouble."

"And," Mel Cooper said, regarding a computer, attached to the gas chromatograph/mass spectrometer, "you're also in trouble if the implants happen to contain extremely concentrated doses of nicotine. Which these do."

"Nicotine," Rhyme mused.

"That's poison?" Ron Pulaski asked.

"Oh, yes," Cooper said. "I worked a case a few years ago. Nicotine used to be applied as an insecticide. You could buy it raw, concentrated. The perp in that case got his hands on some. He wanted to dispatch his mother for the inheritance and, since she smoked, he thought it'd be a good idea to lace her food with it. She was dead in about a half hour. If he'd done small doses instead of a single large one he might've gotten away with it. We found out that it was as if she'd smoked eight hundred cigarettes in an hour and covered her arm with patches."

"What's the formula?" Rhyme asked.

"A parasympathomimetic alkaloid. Comes from the nightshade family of plants."

Sachs said, "The implants don't look that big. How concentrated was the dosage?"

Regarding the mass spectrum, Cooper said, "Huge. If he'd implanted these in the dermis, the victim would have been dead within twenty minutes, I'm estimating."

"God almighty." From superhero man.

"A painful death?" Sachs asked.

"Would be," Rhyme said, uninterested in that. He cared more about origins: "Where would he've gotten the implants?"

Gordon shrugged. "I don't know any sources here. Mostly you want them, you go online."

"No," Rhyme countered, "he'd buy them in a brick-and-mortar store, again. And pay cash."

He gazed at the bits of metal again. What they represented, Rhyme reflected, was obvious. A simple rearrangement resulted in yet another number. The ordinal "17th."

Sachs had donned a face mask and double gloves. She was examining one metal character. The number 7. "We've got tool marks. Distinctive filing. That's something."

It might be possible to link the poisoned implants to a metal file in the suspect's possession—provided that they found the file, of course; there was no national registry of tool marks, as there was for fingerprints, DNA and rifle slugs.

"Source of the poison?" Rhyme inquired.

Sachs went online and reported, "Well, this's interesting. You know e-cigarettes?"

"No."

"Smokeless cigarettes. They have batteries and a flavor capsule. There's sort of a vapor you inhale. You can buy commercial nicotine, unflavored and in flavors, to add to the capsules. It's in liquid form. They call it 'juice.'"

What people do to their bodies, Rhyme reflected. "How many sources?"

"Several dozen." Mel Cooper looked over the computer. "What's for sale on the market is toxic, yeah, but nothing like this. The unsub either distilled that or made his own."

"Okay. What else do we have?"

Sachs had explained that wading through the ground floor of the parking garage and the tunnel had yielded nothing; the flood had been massive. Still, they had found some evidence on and inside the bag containing the implants.

The bag was a typical (and untraceable) food storage bag. At the top was a strip of matte-finish plastic so a cook could write down what the bag contained or the date it went into the freezer. Though the water had washed away much of the unsub's writing, faint pink lettering remained. The message was *No. 3*—for the third attack, Rhyme assumed.

"Don't know how helpful that is," Rhyme grumbled. "But put it on the board."

Cooper ran several other samples. "Here's a combination of human albumin and sodium chloride—the percentages are consistent with drugs used in plastic surgery procedures."

"Ah, that again," Rhyme said. "Our perp's got in mind changing appearance. But can't see him going under the knife quite yet. He's too busy. Afterward, though, that's part of his plan."

Lon Sellitto called in. He had remained at the Belvedere to run the canvassing for witnesses. "Linc, nobody saw anything. You know what's happening, don't you?"

"Enlighten me."

"People know this guy is using the underground to get close to his victims. They're afraid that if they say they saw anything, he'll get them in their bathroom or laundry room or garage."

Rhyme couldn't argue with that attitude. What could be more frightening than to think you were alone and safe in the lower levels of your home or office or a public building and learn that you weren't alone at all; you had lethal company. Like a moist, venomous centipede uncurling under the blankets of your bed as you slept.

Sachs had brought Braden Alexander's clothing too. Cooper went through each item carefully but the water had eradicated all trace—if there'd been any in the first place, which was unlikely, Sachs said, because the contact between the two men had been minimal. The handcuffs revealed no trace and, like the others, were generic.

Cooper ran other samples of swabs from the implant bag. Most were negative. But finally he had a hit. Reading from the computer screen, he said, "Hypochlorous acid."

Rhyme looked over the mass spectrum. "Curious. It's pure. Not diluted."

"Right." Cooper reached under the face shield and shoved his glasses higher on his nose. Rhyme wondered, as he often did, why he didn't get frames that fit.

Hypochlorous acid—a form of chlorine—was added to New York City drinking water, as in most cities, for purification. But because this sample was undiluted, it had not come from the flood that had destroyed the Belvedere parking garage crime scene. This was the form of the chemical in its pure state, before it was added to the water system.

Rhyme said, musing, "It's a weak acid. At higher levels, I suppose, it could be deadly, though. Or maybe he just picked it up because he was near one of the boxes that dispense it into the water supply. Sachs, at the first or second scenes, in the tunnels? There were water pipes, right?"

"Water and, in one, sewage."

"Incoming and outgoing," joked Pulaski. Drawing laughs. From everyone except Rhyme.

"Any other pipes—maybe some feeding chlorine into the mains?"

"I don't remember."

"I want to find out. If this chlorine is from tap-water purification it's not helpful. If it's from a poison he's planning to use, then we can start checking sources." Rhyme called up the pictures from the first two crime scenes. "Let's get somebody back to the scenes and find out if there's a feeder line for the chemical."

Sachs asked, "Do you want Crime Scene to search?"

"No, just a uniform'll be fine," Rhyme said. "Anybody. But soon. *Now*."

Sachs called Dispatch and had patrol cars sent to each of the two previous crime scenes, with instructions on what to look for.

Twenty minutes later Sachs's phone rang. She answered, then hit speaker.

"Okay, Officer, you're on with me and Lincoln Rhyme."

"I'm at the Elizabeth Street scene, Detective. The Chloe Moore homicide."

"Where are you exactly?" Rhyme asked.

"In the tunnel, next to the crime scene lamps and battery packs."

Rhyme told him, "I need you to look for any pipes or reservoirs marked *hypochlorous acid*, *chlorine* or the letters *Cl*. They'd have a hazard diamond on them and probably a skin and eye irritant warning."

"Yes, sir. I'll do that."

The patrolman kept up a narrative as he walked from the place where the body'd been found, near the claustrophobia tunnel, to the bricked-off wall a hundred yards away.

Finally: "Nothing, sir. Only markings are *DS* and *DEP* stamped on the pipes." Department of Sanitation and Department of Environmental Protection, which was the agency overseeing the New York City water supply.

"And some kind of boxes marked *IFON*—don't know what that is. But nothing about chemicals."

Sachs thanked him and disconnected.

Soon a member of the other team called in, from underneath the Provence^2 crime scene—the slaughterhouse octagon, where Samantha Levine had died.

This officer reported the same. No DEP systems for introducing hypochlorous acid into the water system.

After disconnecting, Rhyme said, "So, it's probably got some connection with the unsub. Let's find out where somebody would buy it, or how it's made. Ron?"

But a search revealed what Rhyme suspected: There were dozens of chemical supply companies in the tristate area. And the unsub would have bought a small amount, so he'd use cash. He might even have stolen a can or two. A useless lead.

Rhyme wheeled forward to the examination table, staring at the implants, his mind considering the implications of the numbers.

17th

"We have 'the second,' 'forty' and 'seventeenth.' What the hell is he saying?" Rhyme shook his head.

"I still like the idea he's sending us someplace. But where?"

Sachs said, "No scalloped border, like the others."

But TT Gordon pointed out, "That was scarification, remember? If he was going to include them he would have used the same scalpel that he used to cut the incisions for the implants. He would've done that later, after he'd placed the implant. From what I heard, sounds like you interrupted him before he could get very far."

"Well, he *escaped* before he got very far," Sachs muttered.

Pulaski added, "No 'the' with the seventeenth."

"Maybe that's exactly how the quote goes, whatever that quote is."

"Implants take time, too," Gordon noted.

"Good point. He'd want to move fast." Rhyme nodded toward the tattoo artist. " 'The' might have been too much."

Everyone's eyes were on the numbers.

What the hell was the unsub's message? What could he possibly be wanting to say to us, to the city, to the world?

If his model was the Bone Collector, as it seemed to be, that message was about revenge most likely. But for what? What did "the second," "forty," and now "17th" say about a wrong he wanted vindicated?

That you could also dub Unsub 11-5 the Skin Collector wasn't enough for Rhyme. There was more to his purpose, he sensed, than being a legacy of a psychotic killer stalking the streets of New York more than a decade ago.

TT Gordon broke the silence, "Anything else you need me for?"

"No," Rhyme said. "Thanks for your help. Appreciate it."

Drawing a raised eyebrow from Amelia Sachs. Civility was not a Lincoln Rhyme quality. But he found he was enjoying the company of this man with elaborate facial hair and a command of Strunk and White's *The Elements of Style*.

Gordon pulled his tuxedo jacket on. Again, Rhyme thought, it seemed too thin for such a slight frame on a foul, gray day like this one. "Good luck." He paused in front of Rhyme, looking him over. "Hey, looks like you're one of us, dude."

Rhyme looked up. "One of who?"

"You're modded."

"How's that?"

He pointed to Rhyme's arm, where scars were prominent, from the surgery to restore motion to his right arm and hand. "Looks like Mount Everest, those scars there. Upside down to you."

True, curiously, the triangular pattern did look like the famous mountain.

"You want me to fill it in, just let me know. Or I could do something else. Oh, dude, I know. I could add a bird." He nodded toward the window. "One of those hawks or whatever they are. Flying over the mountains."

Rhyme laughed. What a crazy thought. Then his eyes strayed to the peregrine falcons. There *was* something intriguing about the idea.

"Trauma to the skin is contraindicated for someone in his condition." Thom was in the doorway, arms crossed.

Gordon nodded. "Guess that means no."

"No."

He looked around the room. "Well, anybody else?"

"My mother would kill me," near-middle-aged Mel Cooper said.

"My wife," Pulaski said.

Amelia Sachs only shook her head.

Thom said, "I'll stick with the one I have."

"What?" Sachs asked, laughing. But the aide said nothing more.

"Okay, but you've got my number. Good luck, dudes."

Then the man was gone.

The team was looking at the images of the tattoos once more. Lon Sellitto wasn't picking up so Sachs called Major Cases and had the team at headquarters add "17th" to the list of numbers they were searching for.

Just after she'd disconnected, her phone hummed again and she answered. Rhyme saw immediately that she stiffened. She asked breathlessly, "What? You have somebody on the way?"

She slammed the disconnect button and looked at Rhyme, eyes wide. "That was a sergeant at the Eight-Four. A neighbor just called in a nine one one, intruder outside Pam's apartment. White male in a stocking cap and short gray coat. Seemed to be wearing a mask. Yellow. Jesus."

Sachs flipped open her phone and hit a speed-dial button.

CHAPTER 40

Answer!

Please answer! Sachs gripped her mobile hard and shivered in hopeless rage when Pam's voice mail came on.

"If you're at home, Pam, get out of your house! Now! Go to the Eighty-Fourth Precinct. Gold Street. I think the perp in our case is at your place."

Her eyes met Rhyme's, his face equally troubled, and she jammed her finger onto the redial button.

Rhyme asked, "Is she working? Or at school?"

"I don't know. She works odd hours. And's in school part-time this semester."

Ron Pulaski called, "There should be a unit there in seven, eight minutes."

But the question: Is it too late?

The hollow buzzing of the phone filled the speaker.

Goddamn it. Voice mail once more.

No, no...

"Sachs—"

She ignored Rhyme and hit the redial button again.

Why the hell hadn't they put protection on Pam full-time? True, their unsub's targets—like the Bone Collector's—were random and the Skin Collector surely didn't even know she existed, they'd assumed. But now, of course, he'd decided to target not only those tracking him down, but their friends and family too. It wouldn't be impossible to discover Pam's relationship to Rhyme and Sachs. Why hadn't—

Click. "Amelia," Pam said, breathless. "I got your message. But I'm not home. I'm at work."

Sachs lowered her head. Thank you, thank you...

"But Seth's there! He's there now. He's waiting for me. We're going out later. Amelia, what...what should we do?"

Sachs got his mobile and spun to Pulaski. "Call Seth!" She shouted the number across the room. The young officer dialed fast.

"The doors are locked, Pam?"

"Yes, but...Oh, Amelia. Are police there?"

"They're on their way. Stay where you are. And—"

"Stay where I am? I'm going home. I'm going there now."

"No. Don't do that."

Pam's voice was ragged, accusatory. "Why's he doing this? Why is he at *my* apartment?"

"Stay where—"

The girl hung up.

"It's ringing." Pulaski's expression changed instantly.

"Speaker," Rhyme snapped.

The young officer hit the button. Seth's voice came from the line. "Hello?"

"Seth, it's Lincoln Rhyme."

"Hey, how—"

"Listen to me carefully. Get out. Somebody's breaking into the apartment. Get out now!"

"Here? What do you mean? Is Pam all right?"

"She's okay. Police are coming but you have to get out. Drop whatever you're doing and leave. Go out the front door and get to the Eighty-Fourth Precinct. It's on Gold Street. Or at least some populated place. Call Amelia or me as soon as—"

Seth's next words were muted, as if he was turning and the phone was no longer next to his mouth. "Hey!"

A sound like breaking glass could be heard and another voice, a man's: "You. Put the phone down."

"The hell're you—"

Then several thuds. Seth screamed.

And the line went dead.

CHAPTER 41

The squad cars beat Amelia Sachs to Pam's apartment.

But not by much.

Sachs had kept the gears low in her Torino, the RPMs high, and her foot largely off the brake as she sped to Brooklyn Heights. Sidney Place, a narrow street ending at State, runs north, one way, but that didn't stop Sachs from pounding the Ford the opposite way, sending several oncoming cars up on the sidewalk, squeezing for protection between the many trees here. One rattled elderly driver scraped a fender on the stairs of St. Charles Borromeo church, tall and red as a fire truck.

Sachs's fierce eyes, more than the blue dashboard flasher, cleared the way with little resistance.

Pam's apartment building was shabbier than most here, a three-story walk-up, one of the few gray buildings in a neighborhood of crimson stone. Sachs aimed for the semicircle of police vehicles and an ambulance. She laid on the horn—no siren in the Torino—and parted the craning-neck crowd then gave up and parked.

She sprinted to the door, noting that the ambulance door was open but there were no EMS techs nearby. Bad sign. Were they working away desperately on Seth?

Or was he dead?

In Pam's apartment hallway, a stocky uniform glanced at the shield on her belt and nodded her in. She asked, "How is he?"

"Dunno. It's a mess."

Her phone buzzed. She glanced at caller ID. Pam. Sachs debated but let it ring. She didn't have anything to tell her yet.

I will in a few minutes, she thought. Then wondered what exactly the message would be.

A mess...

Pam lived on the ground floor, a small dark space of about six hundred square feet, whose resemblance to a jail cell was enhanced by the exposed brick walls and tiny windows. Such was the price of living in a posh neighborhood like the Heights, the center of town when Brooklyn was a city unto itself.

She stepped inside and saw two officers.

"Detective Sachs," one said, though she didn't recognize him. "You running the scene? We've cleared it. Had to make sure—"

"Where is he?" She looked past the uniform but then she realized that, of course, the Underground Man would have taken Seth to the basement.

The officer confirmed that he was in the cellar. "The medics, coupla detectives from the Eight Four." He shook his head. "They're doing the best they can. But."

Sachs tossed her hair off her shoulder. Wished she'd banded it up outside. No time then, no time now. She turned and headed back into the corridor, which smelled of onion and mold and some powerful cleaner. It turned her stomach. She found herself walking slowly. The sight of death or gore didn't bother her; you don't sign on to crime scene work if that troubles you. But the looming thought of a somber call to Pam was a sea anchor.

Or given that the perp's weapon of choice was toxins, even a non-fatal injury could be devastating: blindness, nerve or brain damage, kidney failure.

She found the door to the cellar and started down the rickety stairs. Overhead bulbs lit the way, bare and glaring. The basement was well underground, with slits of greasy windows at ceiling level. The large expanse, which smelled astringently of furnace fuel and mildew, was mostly open but there were several smaller areas with doorless entryways, maybe storerooms at one time. It was into one of these that the perp had dragged Seth. She could see the backs of one detective and one uniform in the room, both looking down.

Her heart thudded as she also noted a medical tech standing with crossed arms outside the doorway, peering in. His face a mask.

He looked at her blankly and nodded, then glanced back into the storeroom.

Alarmed, Sachs stepped forward, peered in and stopped.

Seth McGuinn, shirtless, lay on the damp floor, hands under him—probably cuffed like the other victims. His eyes were closed and his face was as gray as the ancient paint on the troubled cellar walls.

CHAPTER 42

Amelia. They don't know," said one of the uniformed officers, standing near Seth. His name was Flaherty and she knew the big, redheaded officer from the Eight Four.

Two other medics were working on Seth, clearing an airway, checking vitals. She could see on the portable monitor that, at least, his heart was beating, if weakly.

"Did the perp tattoo him?" She couldn't see his abdomen from here.

Flaherty said, "No."

Sachs said to the medics, "Might be propofol. That's what he's been using. To knock them out."

"A sedative's consistent with this condition. He's not convulsing and there are no gastrointestinal reactions and his vitals are stable so I'd guess it's not a toxin."

Sachs moved to the side and noted a red spot on Seth's neck—where 11-5 had used the hypodermic. "There. See the injection site?"

"Right."

"He's done that in all the prior cases. Is he—"

A moan. Shivering suddenly, Seth opened his eyes. Blinked in confusion. Then alarm flooded his face; he would be first wondering, then recalling, how he'd ended up here.

"I... What's going—"

"It's okay, sir," one of the medics said.

"You're all right; you're safe," Flaherty said.

"Amelia!" Urgent, though groggy.

"How're you feeling?"

"Did he poison me?"

"Doesn't look like it."

One of the medics asked a series of questions about possible symptoms. They jotted the young man's responses. The EMT said, "All right, sir. We'll have the lab run your blood but it's looking like he just got some sedative into you. We'll get you into the ER and run a few more tests, but I think you're good."

Sachs: "Can I ask him a few questions?"

"Sure."

Sachs donned gloves, helped him sit up and removed the handcuffs. Wincing, Seth lowered his arms and rubbed his wrists. "Man, that hurts."

"Can you walk?" The scene down here was already badly contaminated, but she wanted to preserve as much as she could. "I'd like to get you upstairs into the hallway."

"I guess. Maybe with some help."

She eased him up. With her arm around his waist, he staggered through the basement and up the stairs. In the front hallway they sat on the stairs leading to the second story.

The front door opened once more and Sachs greeted the Crime Scene team from Queens. The detective running the detail was an attractive young officer named Cheyenne Edwards, one of the stars of the department. Her specialty was chemical analysis. If a perp had a molecule of controlled substance or gunshot residue on his body, Edwards could find it. She also had a rep, as in reputation, as in gold.

As in don't fuck with her.

Once, she and her partner had been confronted by a perp who'd returned to a scene to collect the loot he'd left behind. The killer, surprised by the cops, had turned his weapon first on the older, broad-shouldered CS officer, assuming the pretty young woman would be less of a threat—only to find out the hard way that this wasn't quite the case. Edwards had reached into her pocket, where her Taurus .38 backup rested, and fired through the cloth, parking three slugs in his chest. ("Looks like, we just solved the case," she'd noted but continued to search the scene expertly, because that was just what you did.)

"Chey, you run the scene, okay?" Sachs asked.

"You got it."

Then to Seth: "So, tell me what happened."

The man told Sachs about the initial assault, which they'd heard part of on the phone. A man in mask and gloves had broken the patio door and lunged as Seth stood in the living room. They'd fought but, gripping Seth around the chest with one arm, the perp had jabbed a needle into his neck. He passed out and came to in the basement. The man was getting a portable tattoo gun from a backpack.

Sachs displayed a picture of an American Eagle tattoo machine.

"Yeah, that looks like what he had. He was pissed off I'd come to and gave me another shot. But then he suddenly stopped. He kind of cocked his head. I saw he had an earbud in. It was like somebody warned him."

Sachs grimaced. "There's no evidence he's working with anybody. It was probably a police scanner."

Costing all of $59.99. And if you act now, you get a list of frequencies of your favorite police department.

"He just shoved his stuff into his backpack and ran. I passed out again."

She asked for a description and learned what she expected: "White male around thirty, I'd guess. What I could see of his hair it was dark, round face. Light eyes. Blue or gray. Kind of weird, that color. But I really couldn't see much. He had this yellowish see-through mask on." His voice was soft. "Scared the hell out of me. And this tattoo. On his . . . yeah, his left arm. Red. A snake with legs."

"A centipede?"

"Could be. A human face. Way creepy." He closed his eyes for a minute, actually shivered.

Sachs showed him the Identi-Kit picture that the near-victim Harriet Stanton had done at the hospital. Seth looked at it but just shook his head. "Could be—the face was round like that. The eyes're the same. But I just can't be sure. I'm trying to think about what he was wearing. I really can't remember. Something dark, I think. But it could've been orange tie-dye, for all I know. Seeing that mask and the tattoo, I was really freaked out."

"Wonder why?" Sachs offered with a droll smile.

"I better call my parents. They might hear about this. I want to tell them I'm okay."

"Sure."

While Seth did this, dialing with shaking hands, Sachs called Rhyme. She gave him the details. "Cheyenne's running the scene."

"Good."

"She'll get everything over to you in a half hour."

He disconnected.

Seth winced as he pressed his bandaged left wrist, the one that had taken the bulk of his weight and been cut by the handcuffs. "What does he want, Amelia? Why's he doing this?"

"We aren't sure. It seems he was inspired by a perp Lincoln and I investigated years go. The first case we worked together."

"Oh, Pam told me about that. The Bone Collector, right?"

"That's the one."

"Serial killer?"

"Not technically. Serial killing's a sado-sexual crime—if the perp's male. The criminal a decade ago had another agenda and so does this one. The first killer was obsessed with bones; our unsub's obsessed with skin. 'Cause we stopped him a few times, he's turned on us. He must've found out Pam and I are close and he went after her. You had the bad luck to be here at the wrong time."

"Better me than Pam. I—"

"Seth!"

The front door to the building flew open and Pam, breathless after her run from the subway, burst into the hall. She threw herself into his arms before he had even risen to his feet. He wobbled and nearly fell.

"Are you all right?"

"Fine, I guess," he muttered. "Bumped and scraped a little." Seth glanced at her with hollow eyes, wary eyes. It was as if he was struggling to keep from blaming her for the attack. Pam noticed, frowned. She wiped tears, then swiped away strands of hair plastered to her pink cheeks.

Sachs put her arm around the girl, sensed the tension and let go. She stepped back.

"What happened?" Pam asked.

The detective explained, not sparing any details. Given the difficult life that Pam had experienced, she wasn't a person you had to hand-feed hard news to.

Still, her taut face seemed to take on an accusatory gaze as she listened to the story, as if it was Sachs's fault the killer had come here. Sachs dug a fingernail into her thumb, hard.

Cheyenne Edwards appeared in the doorway, still in coveralls but without the face mask or surgeon's cap. She carted a milk crate containing a dozen plastic and paper bags.

"Chey, how's it look?"

The officer grimaced and said to Sachs, "Had to save his life, did you? I mean, could you get any more outsiders into that storeroom? One of the most contaminated scenes I've ever run." She laughed and then winked at the young man. "Can I roll you?"

"Can you—?"

"The perp touched you, right?"

"Yeah, grabbed me around the chest when he injected me with that crap."

Edwards took a dog hair roller and collected trace everywhere on his shirt that Seth indicated. She bagged the adhesive strips and headed to the CSU rapid response van, calling, "I'll get this stuff to Lincoln."

Sachs said to Pam, "You can't stay here. I think you should move into your bedroom at Lincoln's. We'll have officers here until you pack what you need."

The young woman looked at Seth, and the implicit question that fluttered between them was: I could stay with you, right?

He said nothing.

Sachs said, "And, Seth, you should probably stay with some friends or your family. He could've gotten your address. You're a witness and that means you're at risk." This was purely practical, not a ploy to separate Romeo and Juliet. Pam, though, shot Sachs an expression that said, I know what you're up to.

Seth wasn't looking at Pam as he said, "There're a couple guys I know from the ad agency. Have a place in Chelsea. I can crash there." Sachs could see he wasn't concealing his blame for Pam very well.

"I hope it won't have to be long. And?" she asked Pam. "You coming to Lincoln's?"

Her eyes looked over Seth with dismay. She said softly, "Think I'll stay with my family."

Referring to the foster family who'd raised her, the Olivettis.

A good choice. But Sachs was nonetheless stabbed by jealousy. By the subtle reproach. And the blatant choice of words.

My family.

Which doesn't include you.

"I'll drive you there," Sachs said.

"Or we could take the train," Pam said, glancing at Seth.

"They want me to go to the hospital," he said. "For tests, I guess. After that I think I'll just go hang with the guys downtown."

"Well, I could go with you. To the hospital at least."

"Naw, just after this...kind of want to chill. Get some alone time, you know?"

"Sure. I guess. If you want."

He staggered to his feet and walked into her apartment, collected his jacket and computer bag, then returned. He hugged Pam once, in a brotherly way, and pulled on his jacket and snagged his bag, then joined the EMTs outside, who helped him into the ambulance.

"Pam—"

"Not a word. Don't say a word," the young woman growled. She pulled out her cell phone and placed a call to her "family," asking for a ride. She walked inside. Sachs asked a patrolman to keep an eye on her until the Olivettis showed up. He said he would.

Then her phone hummed. She glanced at caller ID and answered, saying to Lincoln Rhyme, "I'm finished here. I'll—"

The criminalist's grim voice interrupted. "He got another vic, Sachs."

Oh, no. "Who?"

"Lon Sellitto."

CHAPTER 43

Lincoln Rhyme observed that he'd have no problems getting into the critical care unit of Hunter University Medical Center, where Lon Sellitto had been admitted not long before. The place was, of course, fully disabled-accessible. Houses of healing are made for wheels as much as feet.

"Oh, Lincoln, Amelia." Rachel Parker, Sellitto's partner of many years, rose and gripped Rhyme's hand and then hugged Sachs. She turned to Thom and threw her arms around him too.

The handsome, solid woman, whose face was red from crying, sat back down in one of the orange fiberglass chairs in the scuffed room. Two vending machines, one of soda, the other full of sugary or salty treats in crisp cellophane bags, were the only decorations.

"How is he?" Sachs asked.

"They don't know yet. They don't know anything." Rachel wiped more tears. "He came home. He said he had the flu and just wanted to lie down for a bit. When

I was leaving for my shift he didn't look good. I left but then I thought, no, no, he doesn't have the flu. It's something else." Rachel was a nurse and had worked trauma rooms for some years. "I came back and found him convulsing and vomiting. I cleared an airway and called nine one one. The medic said it seemed to be poisoning. What had he eaten or had to drink recently? They thought it was food poisoning. But no way. You should've seen him."

"Sachs, show your shield. Tell somebody that Lon was running a case involving water hemlock, tetrodotoxin, concentrated nicotine and a plant that contains atropine, hyoscyamine and scopolamine. Oh, and hypochlorous acid. That might help them."

She scribbled this down and walked to the nurses' station, relayed the information and then returned.

"Was he attacked? Tattooed?" Rhyme asked. Then explained about the unsub's MO.

"No. He must've ingested it," said Rachel. She straightened her mass of brown hair, laced with gray strands. "On the way to the hospital he came to briefly. He was pretty disoriented but he looked at me and seemed to recognize me. His eyes, they kept flipping into and out of focus. The pain was terrible! I think he broke a tooth, his jaw was pressed so tight together." A sigh. "He said a couple of things. First, that he'd had a bagel with some salmon, cream cheese. At a deli in Manhattan, downtown."

"Unlikely to get any poison into his food in a public facility," Rhyme said.

"I thought that too. But he said something else."

"What was that?" Sachs asked.

"He said your name, Amelia. And then 'coffee.' Or 'the coffee.' Does that mean anything?"

"Coffee." Sachs grimaced. "It sure does. At the Belvedere scene there was a fireman walking around with cartons of coffee. He offered some to both of us. Lon took one. I didn't."

"Fireman?" Rhyme asked.

"No," Sachs said grimly. "It was Eleven-Five, wearing a fireman's uniform. Goddamn it! He was right in front of us. Of course that's who it was. I remember he was wearing gloves when he passed out the coffee. Jesus. He was two feet away from me. And he had a bio mask on. Naturally."

"Excuse me." A voice behind them.

The doctor was a slight East Indian with a powdery complexion and busy fingers. He blinked when he noted the pistol on Sachs's right hip then relaxed, seeing the gold shield on the left. Rhyme's wheelchair received a fast, uninterested glance.

"Mrs. Sellitto?"

Rachel stepped forward. "It's Parker. Ms. I'm Lon's partner."

"I'm Shree Harandi. The chief toxicologist here."

"How is he? Please?"

"Yes, well, he is stable. But his condition is not good, I must tell you. The substance he ingested was arsenic."

Rachel's face filled with dismay. Sachs put her arm around the woman.

Arsenic was an element, a metalloid, which meant it had characteristics of metals and non-metals, like antimony and boron. And it was, of course, extremely toxic. Rhyme reflected that the unsub had moved beyond plant-based toxins to a different category altogether—elemental poisons were no more dangerous but they were easier to come by since they had commercial uses and could simply be purchased in lethal strengths; you didn't need to extract and concentrate them.

"I see there are police here." Now he glanced at the wheelchair with more understanding. "Ah, I've heard about you. You are Mr. Rhymes."

"Rhyme."

"And I know Mr. Sellitto is a police officer too. You gave me the information about the possible poisons?"

"That's right," Sachs said.

"Thank you for that but we determined arsenic quickly. Now, I must tell you. His condition is critical. The dose of the substance was high. The organs affected are the lungs, kidneys, liver and skin and he's already had changes in fingernail pigmentation known as leukonychia striata. That is not a good sign."

"Inorganic arsenite?" Rhyme asked.

"Yes."

Arsenic (III) is the most dangerous of all varieties of the toxin. Rhyme was quite familiar with it. He'd run two cases in which it had been used as a murder weapon—in both cases spouses (one husband, one wife) had dispatched their partners with the substance.

Three other cases he'd run of suspected arsenic poisoning had turned out to be accidental. The toxin occurs naturally in groundwater, particularly where fracking—high-pressure geologic fracturing to extract oil and gas—has occurred.

In fact, throughout history, for every intentional victim of arsenic poisoning—like Francesco I de'Medici,

Grand Duke of Tuscany—there were many more accidental victims: Napoléon Bonaparte, possibly done in by the wallpaper of the rooms to which he'd been exiled on St. Helena; Simón Bolívar (the water in South America); and the American ambassador to Italy in the 1950s (flaking paint in her residence). It was also possible that the madness of King George was due to the metalloid.

"Can we see him?" Sachs asked.

"I'm afraid not. He's unconscious. But a nurse will call you when he comes to."

Rhyme noted and, for Rachel's sake, appreciated the conjunction.

When, not if.

The doctor shook hands. "You believe someone actually did this intentionally?"

"That's right."

"Oh, my."

His mobile rang and without a word he turned away to answer.

CHAPTER 44

In October 1818 an attractive woman with an angular face and piercing eyes died at the age of thirty-four in Spencer County, Indiana.

There is some debate as to what was the cause of Nancy Lincoln's death—possibly tuberculosis or cancer but the general consensus is that she was a victim of milk sickness, which claimed thousands of lives in the nineteenth century. Although the actual cause can't be pinpointed, one fact about Nancy's death is well documented: Her nine-year-old son, Abraham, the future president of the United States, helped his father build the woman's coffin.

Milk sickness perplexed medical professionals for years, until it was finally discovered that the cause was tremetol, a highly toxic alcohol, which made its way into a cow's milk after the animal had grazed on white snakeroot.

This plant is a nondescript, workaday herb that is hardly an aesthetic contribution to any garden, and accordingly Billy Haven didn't enjoy the plant as a subject to sketch. But he loved its toxic properties.

When ingested, tremetol causes the victim to suffer excruciating abdominal pain, intense nausea and thirst, uncontrollable tremors and explosive vomiting.

Even a small dosage can result in death.

Head down, wearing a short-brimmed brown fedora—very hipster—and long black raincoat, Billy was making his way through Central Park, the west side. In his gloved hand was a briefcase. He was walking south and had made a serious trek from Harlem, but he wanted to avoid the CCTV cameras in the subway, even if his appearance was different from what the Underground Man had worn during the prior attacks.

Yes, tremetol was his weapon but the pending attack wouldn't involve tattooing, so he'd left his machine back at his workshop near Canal. Today the circumstances dictated a different means of poisoning. But one that could be just as satisfying.

Billy was enjoying a good mood. Oh, with the earlier attacks, he'd had felt satisfaction, sure, buzzing the poison into the victims, getting the bloodline just right, angling the careful serifs of the Old English letters.

A Billy Mod...

But that was good in the same way you felt good doing your job or completing chores around the house.

What he was about to do now was a whole different level of good.

Billy slipped out of the park and examined the streets carefully, uptown and cross, noting no one looking at him with suspicion. No police on patrol. He continued his journey south toward his target.

Yes, this attack would be different.

For one thing, there was no message to send. He'd simply deliver the tremetol. No scars, no tats, no mods.

Also, he was not interested in killing the victim. That death would ultimately be detrimental to the Modification. No, he was going to wield the poison to debilitate.

Though it would be a very different life that his target would live in the future; perhaps the most disturbing symptoms of non-lethal white snakeroot poisoning were delirium and dementia. The man he was going to poison in a few moments would stay alive but become a raving madman for a long, long time.

Billy nonetheless had one regret: that his victim would be incapable of feeling the searing, unbearable nausea and gut pain that white snakeroot's toxin caused. Lincoln Rhyme was numb to sensation below his neck. The vomiting, tremors and other symptoms would be unpleasant but not as horrific as in a person who had a fully functioning nervous system.

Billy now turned west down a cross street and entered a brightly lit Chinese restaurant, which was filled with the smells of garlic and hot oil. He made his way to the restroom, where, in a stall, he lost the hat and overcoat and dressed in coveralls.

Outside once more—unnoticed by diners or staff, he observed—Billy walked across the street and into the service alley that would lead to the back of Rhyme's apartment.

The cul-de-sac was pungent—smelled a bit like the Chinese restaurant, now that he thought about it—but relatively clean. The ground was ancient cobblestones and patches of asphalt, dotted with slush and ice. Several Dumpsters sat well ordered against brick walls. It seemed that several town houses, including Rhyme's, and a larger apartment building backed onto this area.

Noting a video camera at the rear of Rhyme's town house, he went about his faux business of checking electrical lines.

Ducking behind a Dumpster, as if searching for a troublesome bit of electrical wire conduit, Billy circumvented the camera and approached the door. He extracted the hypodermic that contained the snakeroot toxin from his toothbrush holder and slipped the syringe into his pocket.

Tremetol, a clear liquid, is an alcohol and would blend instantly with what Billy's research had revealed was Rhyme's favorite beverage—single-malt scotch. It would also be tasteless.

Billy's palms sweated. His heart thudded.

For all he knew there might be ten armed officers inside, meeting with Rhyme at the moment. The alarm wouldn't be on, not during the day, but he could easily be spotted lacing the bottle.

And possibly shot on the spot.

But the Modification, naturally, involved risk. What important missions didn't? So, get on with it. Billy pulled out his phone, a prepaid model, untraceable, and pressed in a number.

Almost immediately he heard, "Police and fire. What's your emergency?"

"A man with a gun in Central Park! He's attacking a woman."

"Where are you, sir?"

"He's got a gun! I think he's going to rape her!"

"Yes, sir. Where are you? Where exactly?"

"Central Park West, about . . . I don't know. It's . . . uhm, okay, in front of Three Fifty Central Park West."

"Is anyone hurt?"

"I think so! Jesus! Please. Send somebody."

"Describe him."

"Dark-skinned. Thirties."

"What's your name—?"

Click.

It was sixty seconds later that he heard the sirens. He knew the 20th Precinct, located in Central Park, was nearby.

More sirens.

Dozens of squad cars, he guessed.

He waited until the sirens grew louder; they'd have to be drawing the attention of everyone in the town house. Gambling that no one could see the security monitor, Billy walked matter-of-factly to Rhyme's back door. Paused again. He looked around. Nobody. He turned to the lock.

Later, the police might look at the security tape—if it was recorded at all—and see the intruder. But all they'd see would be a vague form, head down.

And by then it would be too late.

CHAPTER 45

The hell is going on?" Rhyme barked.

The criminalist and Mel Cooper were in the front hallway of the town house, the door open. Ron Pulaski joined them. They were peering out into the street, which was filled with police cars, two ESU vans and two ambulances.

Blue lights, white, red. Flashing urgently.

Cooper's and Pulaski's hands were near their sidearms.

Thom was upstairs, probably observing from a bedroom window.

Five minutes ago Rhyme had heard frantic wails grow loud as emergency vehicles streaked along the street outside. He'd expected them to continue on Central Park West, but they didn't. The vehicles braked to a stop just one door north. The piercing howls remained at peak pitch for a moment then one by one shut off.

Peering outside, Rhyme said, "Call downtown, Mel. Find out."

He'd assumed at first that the incident had something

to do with him—maybe the unsub had been making a frontal assault on the town house—but then he noted that the attention was focused on the park itself and that none of the officers who were part of the operation approached his place.

Cooper had a conversation with someone at Dispatch and then disconnected.

"Assault in the park. Dark-skinned male, thirties. Maybe attempted rape."

"Ah." They continued to watch for another three or four minutes. Rhyme examined the park. It was hard to see anything through the mist and reinvigorated sleet. A rape? The urge for sex is more impulsive than that for money and more intense, he knew, but in this weather?

He wondered if he'd draw the crime scene side of the case and was thinking that given the icy rain the evidence would be a challenge.

But that put in mind Lon Sellitto, who would normally be the NYPD representative who'd contact him about potential jobs. The detective was still in the most intensive of intensive care wards, nowhere near consciousness.

Rhyme put the rape, or attempted rape, out of his mind. He, Pulaski and Cooper returned to the parlor laboratory, where they'd been analyzing the evidence Detective Cheyenne Edwards had delivered—the finds from the crime scene at Pam Willoughby's.

There hadn't been much, though the unsub had left in such a hurry that he'd neglected to pick up the hypodermic needle he'd stabbed Seth with and a vial of the poison he'd presumably been about to use on the young man. The substance was from the white baneberry plant—also called doll's eyes, because the berries resemble eyeballs. Eerie. The toxin, Cooper explained, was cardiogenic; it basically stopped the heart. Of all the poisons their unsub was using this was the most humane, killing without the pain of toxins that attacked the GI and renal systems.

Rhyme noticed Ron Pulaski looking down at his phone. His face was lit with a faint blue glow.

Checking messages or the time? Rhyme wondered. Mobiles were used as watches more and more frequently nowadays.

Pulaski hung up and said to Rhyme, "I should go."

So, time. Not texts.

Ron Pulaski's undercover assignment at the funeral home was about to begin: to see who was collecting the Watchmaker's remains and maybe, just maybe learn a bit more about the enigmatic criminal.

"You all set, you ready to be Serpico, you ready to be Gielgud?"

"Was he a cop? And, wait, didn't Serpico get shot in the face?"

Rhyme and Pulaski had spent some time that morning on a cover story that would seem credible to the funeral home director and whoever was coming to collect the man's remains.

Rhyme had never done undercover work but he knew the rules: Less is more and more is less. Meaning you research the hell out of your role, learn every possible fact, but when you present yourself to the perp, you offer up only the minimal. Inundating the bad guys with details is a sure giveaway.

So he and Pulaski had come up with a bio for

Stan Walesa, a bio that would have made credible some connection with the Watchmaker. Rhyme had noted him walking around the lab all day, reciting facts they'd made up. "Born in Brooklyn, has an import-export company, investigated for insider trading, questioned in connection with a banking scam, divorced, knows weapons, was hired by an associate of the Watchmaker to transport some containers overseas, no, I can't give his name away, no, I don't know what was in the containers. Again: Born in Brooklyn, has an import-export..."

Now, as Pulaski pulled on his coat, Rhyme said, "Look, Rookie, don't think about the fact that this is our only chance to fill in gaps on the late Watchmaker's biography."

"Um, okay."

"And if you mess up, we'll never have this opportunity again. Don't think about that. Put it out of your mind."

"I..." The patrolman's face relaxed. "You're fucking with me, aren't you, Lincoln?"

Rhyme smiled. "You'll do great."

Pulaski chuckled and disappeared into the hallway. His exit was announced a moment later by a blast of wind through the open door. The latch clicked; then silence.

Rhyme turned to look at the containers of evidence that Detective Edwards had collected at Pam's apartment, following the unsub's attack on Seth. But he focused past the bags.

Well, what was this?

A miracle had occurred.

He was looking at the shelves that contained forensic books, a stack of professional journals, a density gradient instrument and...his single-malt scotch. The bottle of Glenmorangie had been placed within reach. Thom usually stashed it higher on the shelf—out of Rhyme's grasp, the way you'd keep candy away from a child, which pissed Rhyme off to no end.

But apparently the old mother hen had been distracted and screwed up.

He resisted temptation for the time being and maneuvered back to the evidence from Pam's apartment and the storeroom in the basement and Seth's clothing laid out on an examination table. For a half hour he and Cooper went through the finds—which weren't many. No friction ridges, of course, a few fibers, a hair or two, though they might have been Pam's or they might have come from a friend of hers. Or even from Amelia Sachs, who had been a frequent visitor. There was trace, but it was mostly trace identical to that of the earlier scenes. Only one new substance was discovered: some fibers on Seth's shirt, where the unsub had grabbed him. They were from an architectural or engineering blueprint. They had to come from 11-5, since Seth wouldn't use such diagrams in his work as an ad agency freelancer. And Pam would have no reason to come in contact with such plans either.

Mel Cooper filled a new evidence chart, which included the trace, the syringe, the pictures of the scene, the bootie footprints.

Rhyme glanced at the sparse info, displeased. No insights.

He circled away and headed for the shelf, thinking of

the peaty smell and taste of the whisky, tangy but not too smoky.

With another glance toward the kitchen, where Thom was laboring away, and toward Cooper, securing evidence from the scene, Rhyme easily picked the bottle off the shelf and deposited it between his legs. He was clumsier with the crystal glass, lifting that—careful, careful—and setting it on the shelf within pouring distance.

Then he returned to the bottle and, with careful manipulation, he eased out the cork and poured into the glass.

One finger, two fingers, all right, three.

It had been a difficult day.

The bottle landed safely where it had been and he turned the chair around and returned to the center of the lab.

"I didn't see a thing," Cooper said, his back to Rhyme.

"Nobody believes witnesses anyway, Mel." He eased up to the evidence chart and stopped.

Not spilling a drop.

CHAPTER 46

Amelia Sachs was sitting at a coffee shop in Midtown, one of those traditional delis you see fewer and fewer of, dying off in favor of corporate franchises with faux-foreign names. Here, stained menus, Mediterranean staff, unsteady chairs—and the best comfort food for miles around.

Fidgety. She dug a thumbnail into a finger, avoided blood. Bad habits. Unstoppable. Some things Sachs could control. Other things, not.

And stopping Pam's sojourn with Seth?

Sachs had left two messages for the girl—her limit, she decided—but had called once more and on the third ring Pam had picked up. Sachs had asked how Seth was doing after the attack: "The doctors at the hospital said he's okay. He wasn't even admitted."

Apparently he wasn't as mad as earlier; at least they were talking.

"And you?"

"Fine."

Quiet, once again.

Sachs had taken a figurative breath and asked if they could meet for coffee.

Pam had hesitated but then agreed, adding she had to be at work anyway. Suggesting this deli, which was across the street from the theater.

Sachs now toyed with her phone to keep from digging into flesh.

The Skin Collector...

What could she say to Pam to convince the girl not to quit school and go on the worldwide tour.

Well, wait. You can't think of her that way. *Girl.* Of course not. She was nineteen. She'd lived through kidnapping and attempted murder. She'd defied militiamen. She had the right to make decisions and the right to make mistakes.

And, Sachs asked herself, was her decision a mistake at all?

Who was she to say?

Look at her own romantic history. High school for her was, as for everybody, a time of exploration and exhilarating fumbling and false starts. Then she had hit the professional world of fashion. A tall, gorgeous model, Sachs had had to take the repel-all-boarders approach. Which was a shame because some of the men she'd met on photo shoots and at ad agency planning sessions had probably been pretty nice. But they were lost among the vast number of players. Easier to say no to everyone, slip into her garage and tune engines or go to the racetrack and work on lap times with her Camaro SS.

After joining the NYPD, things hadn't gotten much better. Tired of the relentless pressure to go out, the filthy jokes, the juvenile looks and attitudes offered up by fellow cops, she'd continued to be a recluse. Ah, that was the answer, the male officers understood, after she'd rejected their overtures. She was a dyke. Such a pretty one too. Fucking waste.

Then she'd met Nick. The first real love, true love, consuming love, complete love. Whatever tired adjective you wanted.

And, with Nick, it'd turned out to be betrayed love, too.

Not of the daily variety, no. But, to Sachs, perhaps worse. Nick had been a corrupt cop. And a corrupt cop who hurt people.

Meeting Lincoln Rhyme had saved her. Professionally and personally. Though that relationship was obviously alternative, as well.

No, Sachs's history and experience hardly qualified her to preach to Pam. Yet, like driving slowly, or hesitating before kicking in a door during a dynamic entry, Sachs was unable to stop herself from giving her opinion.

If the girl...the *young woman* showed up at all.

Which finally she did, fifteen minutes late.

Sachs said nothing about the tardiness, just rose and gave her a hug. It wasn't exactly rejected but Sachs could feel the stiffness rise to Pam's shoulders. She noted too that the young woman wasn't taking off her coat. She just tugged her stocking cap off and tossed her hair. The gloves too. But the message was: This'll be short. Whatever your agenda.

And no smiles. Pam had a beautiful smile and Sachs loved it when the girl's face curled into a spontaneous crescent. But not here, not today.

"How're the Olivettis?"

"Good. Howard got the kids a new dog for Jackson to play with. Marjorie lost ten pounds."

"I know she was trying. Hard."

"Yeah." Pam scanned a menu. Sachs knew she wasn't going to order anything. "Is Lon doing okay?"

"Still critical. Unconscious."

"Man, that's bad," Pam said. "I'll call Rachel."

"She'd like that."

The young woman looked up. "Look, Amelia. There's something I want to say."

Was this going to be good or bad?

"I'm sorry what I said, about you and my mother. That wasn't fair."

Sachs in fact hadn't taken the comment particularly hard. It was clearly one of those weaponized sentences that get flung out to hurt, to end conversations.

She held up a hand. "No, that's okay. You were mad."

The woman's nod told Sachs that, yes, she'd been mad. And her eyes revealed that she still was, despite the apology.

Around them couples and families, parents with children of all ages, bundled in winter sweaters and flannel, sat over coffee and cocoa and soup and grilled cheese sandwiches and chatted or laughed and whispered. It all seemed so normal. And so very far away from the drama of the table she and Pam sat at.

"But I have to tell you, Amelia. Nothing's changed. We're leaving in a month."

"A month?"

"The semester." Pam wasn't going to be drawn into a debate beyond that. "Amelia. Please. This is good, what we're doing. I'm happy."

"And I want to make sure you stay that way."

"Well, we're doing it. We're leaving. India first, we've decided."

Sachs didn't even know if Pam had a passport. "Look." She lifted her hands. The gesture smelled of desperation and she lowered them. "Are you sure you want to...disrupt your life like that? I really don't think you should."

"You can't tell me what to do."

"I'm not telling you what to do. But I can give advice to somebody I love."

"And I can reject it." A cool sigh. "I think it's better if we don't talk for a while. This is all...I'm upset. And it's pretty clear that I'm pissing you off totally."

"No. Not at all." She started to reach for the girl's hand but Pam had anticipated her and withdrew it. "I'm worried about you."

"You don't need to be."

"Yes, I do."

"Because to you I'm a child."

Well, if you're fucking acting like one.

But Sachs held back for a moment. Then thought: Knuckle time.

"You had a very hard time growing up. You're...vulnerable. I don't know how else to put it."

"Oh, that again. Naive? A fool."

"Of course not. But it *was* a hard time."

After they'd escaped from New York following the terrorist plot Pam's mother had orchestrated, the two of them had gone underground in a small community of militiamen and "their women" in Larchwood, Missouri, northwest of St. Louis. The girl's life had been hell—indoctrination into white supremacist politics and bare-butt whippings in public for being disrespectful. While militia-homeschooled boys learned farming, real estate and construction, Pammy, as a girl, could look forward to mastering only cooking and sewing and homeschooling.

She'd spent her formative years there, miserable but also resolute in defying the ultra-right, fundamentalist militia community. At middle school age she'd sneak out of the enclave to buy "demonic" Harry Potter books and *Lord of the Rings* and the *New York Times.* And she wouldn't put up with what many of the other girls were expected to. (When one of the lay ministers tried to touch her chest to see if "yer heart's beatin' for Jesus," Pam delivered a silent "hands off" in the form of a deep slash to his forearm with a box cutter, which she still often carried.)

"I told you, that's in the past. It's over. It doesn't matter."

"It *does* matter, Pam. Those were very hard years for you. They affected you—in ways you don't even know. It'll take time to work through all that. And you need to tell Seth everything about your time underground."

"No, I don't. I don't need to do anything."

Sachs said evenly, "I think you're jumping at the first chance for a normal relationship that's come along. And you're hungry for that. I understand."

"You understand. That sounds condescending. And you make me sound desperate. I told you, I'm not getting married. I'm not having his baby. I want to travel with a guy I love. What's the big fucking deal?"

This was going so wrong. How did I lose control?

This was the same conversation they'd had the other day. Except that the tone was darker.

Pam pulled her hat back on. Started to rise.

"Please. Just wait a minute." Sachs's mind was racing. "Let me say one more thing. Please."

Impatient, Pam dropped back into her seat. A waitress came by. She waved the woman away.

Sachs said, "Could we—?"

But she never got to finish her plea to the teenager, for just then her phone hummed. It was a text from Mel Cooper. He was asking her to get to Rhyme's town house as soon as she could.

Actually, she noted, the message wasn't a request at all.

It never really is when the word "emergency" figures in the header.

CHAPTER 47

Upon examining the back door to Rhyme's town house, a gowned and gloved Amelia Sachs decided: The son of a bitch sure can pick locks.

Unsub 11-5 hadn't left more than a minute scratch when he'd broken into the town house to doctor a bottle of scotch on Rhyme's shelf—insidiously leaving it within the wheelchair-bound criminalist's reach. Sachs wasn't surprised the unsub had some skill at breaking and entering; his talent at skin art attested to his dexterity.

The sleet spattered and the wind blew. By now any evidence in the cul-de-sac and around the back door had probably been obliterated. Inside the door, where footprints would have been visible, she discovered nothing other than marks left by his booties.

The strategy behind the assault was now clear: 11-5 had called in a false alarm—an attempted rape in Central Park, near the town house. When Rhyme and the others inside went to the front door to see what was going on, the unsub had snuck through the back and found an open bottle of whisky, poured some poison inside, then escaped silently.

Sachs walked the grid on the route from the back door up the stairs, through the hall from the kitchen to the parlor. Rhyme had an alarm system, which was turned off when the town house was occupied, as now. Video cameras covered the front and back doors but they were real-time monitoring only; the images weren't recorded.

A sense of violation filled Sachs. Somebody had breached the castle, somebody stealthy and adroit. And deadly. Thom had already arranged for the locks to be changed and a drop bar put on both doors but once someone has intruded into your living area, you're never completely free from the taint of desecration. And from worry that it might happen again.

Finally she arrived at the main floor and handed the bagged trace off to Mel Cooper.

Lincoln Rhyme turned his Merits wheelchair around from the table where he'd been reviewing evidence and asked, "Well? Anything?"

"Not much," Sachs told him. "Not much at all."

Rhyme wasn't surprised.

Not with Unsub 11-5.

Sachs looked him over carefully, as if he'd actually sipped some of the poisoned whisky.

Or maybe she was just troubled that the unsub had gotten inside, spiked the bottle and gotten out without anybody's knowing.

Lord knew Rhyme himself was. Actually more pissed off than troubled—because he hadn't deduced that the whisky was tainted, even though, looking back, he should have. It was obvious that Thom would never leave a nearly full bottle of forty-proof liquor within his boss's reach. Combine that with the facts that Lon Sellitto and Seth McGuinn had been attacked and that a police action had unfolded right outside his town house, a perfect diversion, and, yeah, Rhyme should have guessed.

But, on the contrary, the salvation had come from a call to 911. A passerby on the cross street had seen someone slip into the service area behind Rhyme's and pocket a hypodermic. "Looking suspicious," the Good Samaritan had reported. "A drug thing, maybe going to break in, you know."

The dispatcher had called Rhyme, who understood immediately that the mis-shelved Glenmorangie was Snow White's apple.

He'd glanced at the glass in his hands and realized that he'd come an instant away from a very unpleasant demise, though less unpleasant to him than to others, given that most of his body would not have felt the excruciating pain the poison causes.

But he'd tucked this shadow of mortality away because he was a man for whom death had been an easy option—voluntary and otherwise—for years. His condition, quadriplegia, brought with it many accessories that could dump him into a coffin at a moment's notice: dysreflexia and sepsis, for instance.

So, an attempted poisoning? Good news, as far as he was concerned. It might reveal new evidence to lead them a bit closer to the man who was the spiritual heir to the Bone Collector.

CHAPTER 48

Something was up.

Ron Pulaski had been told that there was no memorial service planned for Richard Logan.

But apparently that had changed.

Six people stood in the room he'd been directed to in the Berkowitz Funeral Home, Broadway and 96th.

He hadn't gone inside yet. The patrol officer stood in the hallway, off to the side, peering in. He was thinking: Tough to blend comfortably when you're a stranger facing a half dozen people who know each other—one or all of whom might have a very good incentive to suspect you're an intruder and shoot you dead.

And the name of the place! Wasn't Berkowitz the Son of Sam? That serial killer from the 1970s or '80s?

Bad sign.

Even though Ron Pulaski tried hard to be like Lincoln Rhyme and not believe in signs or superstitions, he kind of did.

He started forward. Stopped.

Pulaski had been spending a lot of nerves on the idea

that he was going undercover. He was a street cop, a beat cop—he and his twin brother, also blue, used to say. He was thinking of a bad hip-hop riff the bros threw together.

A beat cop, a street cop, write you up a ticket and send you on your way.

Or let you know your rights and put your ass away...

In Rikers, the island, in the bay.

He knew next to nothing about the art of sets and covert work—so brilliantly played by people like Fred Dellray, the tall, lean African American FBI agent who could be anyone from a Caribbean drug dealer to a Charles Taylor–style warlord to a Fortune 500 CEO.

Man was a born actor. Voices, postures, expressions...everything. And apparently this Gielgud guy too (maybe Dellray worked with him). And Serpico. Even if he got shot.

Beat cop, street cop, walking through the sleet cop...

The rap riff skipped through his head, somehow stilling the uneasiness.

Why're you so damn nervous?

Not like he was having to pass with druggies or gangbangers. Richard Logan's family or friends, whoever these visitors were, seemed like your average law-abiding Manhattanites. The Watchmaker had moved in a different circle, a higher level than most criminals. Oh, he'd been guilty of murder. But it was impossible to picture Logan, the Watchmaker, the sophisticate, in a crack house or in the double-wide of a meth cooker. Fine restaurants, chess matches, museums had been more his thing. Still, he was aware that the Watchmaker *had* tried to kill Rhyme the last time they'd met. Maybe he'd left instructions in his will for a hit man associate of his to do just what Pulaski was doing at the moment: hang out in the funeral home, identify any nervous undercover cops, drag 'em into the alley afterward.

All right. Jesus. Get real.

There is a risk, he reflected, but not a bullet in the back of the head. It's that you'll fuck up and disappoint Lincoln and Amelia.

That damn uncertainty, the questioning. They never go away. Not completely.

At least he thought he looked the part. Black suit, white shirt, narrow tie. (He'd almost worn his dress NYPD tie but decided: Are you out of your fucking mind? It didn't have little badges on it but one of these people might've known cops in the past. Be smart.) He had scruffed up, per Lincoln Rhyme's request. A one-day growth of beard (a bit pathetic since you had to get close to see the blond stubble), shirt stained, shoes scuffed. And he'd been practicing his cold stare.

Inscrutable, dangerous.

Pulaski peeked inside the memorial service room again. The walls were painted dark green and lined with chairs, enough for forty, fifty people. In the center was a table, draped in a purple cloth; a simple urn sat on it. The visitors were four men, ranging in age from late forties up to their seventies, he judged. Two women seemed to be spouses or partners of two of the men. Wardrobe was what you'd expect—dark suits and dresses, conservative.

It was odd. He'd been told there was no viewing or service. Just someone to collect the remains.

Yeah, suspicious. *Was* it a setup?

Bullet in the head?

On the other hand, if it was legit, if plans had changed and it was an impromptu service for the Watchmaker, this'd be a real coup. Surely somebody here had known Richard Logan well and could be a source of info about the dead mastermind.

Okay, just go ahead and dive in.

Street cop, beat cop, goin' to a funeral in the sleet cop.

He walked up to one of the mourners, an elderly man in a dark suit.

"Hi," he said. "Stan Walesa." He'd rehearsed saying, and responding to, the name over and over (he'd had Jenny call him by it all last night), so he wouldn't ignore somebody's calling him "Stan" during the set. Or, even worse, glance behind him when somebody did.

The man identified himself—Logan was not part of his name—and introduced Pulaski to one of the women and another man. He struggled to memorize their names, then reminded himself to take a picture of the guest list with his cell phone later.

"How did you know him?" A nod toward the urn.

"We worked together," Pulaski said.

Blinks from everybody.

"A few years ago."

A frown from one of the younger men. Right out of *The Sopranos*. "You worked together?"

"That's right."

"Closely?"

Be tough. "Yeah. Pretty close." His gaze said, What's it to you?

Pulaski recalled everything he could about the crimes

that the Watchmaker had run. His plan wasn't to claim outright that he'd been a partner but to suggest that he'd had some mysterious dealings—to whet the appetite of anyone who might want to get a piece of the Watchmaker's ongoing projects after his death.

Containers, shipments, insider trading…

Less is more, more is less.

People fell silent. Pulaski realized that classical music was streaming from invisible speakers. He hadn't heard it earlier.

To get the conversation going Pulaski said, "So sad."

"A blessing, though," one woman offered.

Blessing, Pulaski reflected. He supposed that, yes, rather than spend most of your life in prison, a fast, relatively painless death was a blessing.

Pulaski continued, "A couple years ago, we were working, he seemed healthy." He could actually picture Logan from that time. He *had* seemed healthy.

Those present exchanged glances once more.

"And so young," the undercover cop added.

Something was wrong. But the oldest one of the mourners leaned close and touched Pulaski's arm. A smile. "To me, yes, he was young."

The visitors eased away. One, he noticed, had left the room.

To get his gun?

This isn't going well. He turned back to the older man but before he could speak another voice intruded. Soft but firm. "Excuse me, sir."

Pulaski turned to find a large man, in a dark suit, looking him over closely. He had silver hair and dark-framed glasses. "Could I speak to you for a moment?"

"Me?"

"You."

The man extended his hand—a very large, calloused hand—but not to shake. He pointed and directed Pulaski out of the room and up the hallway to the left.

"Sir," the man said, "you are?"

"Stan Walesa." He had a cheap ID that he'd hacked together himself.

But the man didn't ask for any identification. His eyes boring into Pulaski's, he rasped, "Mr. Walesa. You know some people occasionally come to services in hopes of getting something."

"Getting something?"

"It ranges from food at the reception afterward to selling insurance or financial programs. Attorneys too."

"That a fact?"

"It is."

Pulaski remembered he was supposed to be playing the tough guy. Instead of looking nervous and saying that was terrible, he snapped, "What's that got to do with me? Who are you?"

"I'm Jason Berkowitz. Associate director. The family in there thought your behavior was a little suspicious. You were claiming to know the deceased."

"What's suspicious? I did know him."

"You claim you worked with him."

"Not claimed. I did." Pulaski's heart was pounding so hard he was sure the man could hear it. But he struggled to play the wise guy.

"You don't seem like the sort who'd work with Mr. Ardell."

"Who?"

"Blake Ardell."

"And who's that supposed to be."

"Not supposed to be. He is, *was*, the man whose service you're crashing."

"Crashing? What the hell does that mean? I'm here about Richard Logan."

The assistant director blinked. "Mr. Logan? Oh. My. I'm so sorry, sir. That's Serenity."

"Serenity?"

"The name of the room across the hall. This room is Peace, Mr. Ardell's service."

Goddamn. Pulaski thought back. The fellow at the front door had told him to turn right. He'd turned left.

Shit, shit, shit. Fucking head injury. If this'd been a drug set, he might be dead now.

Think smarter.

But act the part. "One of your people, I don't remember who, sent me to that room."

"I'm so sorry. Please accept our apologies. Our fault entirely."

"And names? I've never heard of naming rooms in a funeral parlor. You ought to have numbers."

"Yessir, it's a little unusual. I'm sorry. I do apologize."

"Oh, all right." Pulaski grimaced. He nodded back. Then paused, recalling the curious expression on the faces of the mourners when he'd mentioned working with the deceased.

"One question. You said I didn't seem like the sort who worked with this Ardell. What'd he do for a living?"

"He was an adult film star in the seventies,"

Berkowitz whispered. “Gay. The family doesn’t like to talk about it.”

“I’d guess not.”

“That’s the room with Mr. Logan’s remains.” He pointed to a small doorway.

Serenity…

Pulaski stepped through it and into a small room, twenty by twenty. There were a few chairs, a coffee table, innocuous landscapes covering the walls. Also a bouquet of subdued white flowers. And on a velvet-draped table, similar to the one holding the urn of the late porn star, sat a brown cardboard box. This would, Pulaski knew, be the Watchmaker’s remains. Beside it stood a round, balding man in a dark business suit. He was making a mobile phone call. He looked at Pulaski briefly, with curiosity, and turned away. He seemed to speak more softly. Finally he disconnected.

Inhaling a steadying breath, Pulaski walked up to him. He nodded.

The man said nothing.

Pulaski looked him up and down—keep it blunt, keep it tough. “You were a friend of Richard’s?”

“And you are—?” the man asked in a soft baritone, with the hint of a Southern accent.

“Stan Walesa,” Pulaski said. The name almost seemed natural at this point. “I was asking, you’re a friend of Richard’s?”

“I don’t know who you are and I don’t know why you’re asking.”

“Okay, I worked with Richard. Off and on. I heard he was being cremated this morning and I assumed there’d be a service.”

"Worked with Richard," the man repeated, looking the officer up and down. "Well, there is no service. I've been retained to bring his remains back home."

Pulaski frowned. "A lawyer."

"That's right. Dave Weller." No hands were proffered.

Pulaski kept up the offensive. "I don't remember you from the trial."

"Mr. Logan was not my client. I've never met him."

"Just taking the ashes back home?"

"Like I said."

"That's California, right?"

The only response was: "What are you doing here, Mr. Walesa?"

"Paying respects." He stepped closer to the box. "No urn?"

"Not much point," Weller said. "Richard wanted his ashes scattered."

"Where?"

"Did you send those?"

Pulaski looked at the bouquet, which Weller was nodding at. The officer tried to look somewhat, but not overly, confused. "No." He stepped to the vase and read the card. He gave a bitter laugh.

Inscrutable.

He said, "That's pretty low."

Weller asked, "How do you mean?"

"You know who that is, who sent them?"

"I read the card when I got here. But I don't know the name. Lincoln Rhyme?"

"You don't know Rhyme?" Lowering his voice: "He's the son of a bitch who put my friend in prison."

Weller asked, "Police?"

"Works with the police."

"Why would he send flowers?"

"I think he's gloating."

"Well, that was a waste of money. Richard's hardly going to be offended now, is he?" A glance at the box of ashes.

Silence.

How to behave now? Man, this acting stuff was exhausting. He decided to shake his head at the unfairness of the world. He looked down. "Such a shame, really. When I talked to him last, he was fine. Or at least he didn't mention anything, like chest pains."

Weller now focused. "Talked to him?"

"Right."

"This was recently?"

"Yeah. In prison."

"You're here alone?" Weller asked.

A nod. Pulaski asked the same question.

"That's right."

"So there's no funeral?"

"The family hasn't decided." Weller looked Pulaski up and down carefully.

Okay, time to go with the less…

"Well, so long, Mr. Weller. Tell his family, or whoever your clients are, I'm sorry for their loss. I'll miss him too. He was an…interesting man."

"Like I said, I never met him."

Pulaski pulled on dark cotton gloves. "So long."

Weller nodded.

Pulaski was at the door when the lawyer said, "Why did you really come here, Mr. Walesa?"

The young officer stopped. He turned back. "'Really'? What's that supposed to mean?"

De Niro tough. Tony Soprano tough.

"There was never going to be a memorial service. If you'd called to see when I was picking up the remains—which you did, since here you are—you would have learned there was no service. So. What do I make of that?"

Pulaski debated—and made a show of debating. He dug into his pocket and produced a business card. Offered it to the man with a gloved hand. He said, "Give that to your clients."

"Why?"

"Just give it to them. Or throw it out." A shrug. "Up to you."

The lawyer looked at him coolly, then took the card. It had only the fake name and the prepaid mobile number on it.

"What exactly do you do, Mr. Walesa?"

Pulaski's gaze began at the lawyer's bald head and ended at his shoes, which were nearly as shiny. "Have a good day, Mr. Weller."

And, with an oblique glance at the box containing the Watchmaker's ashes, Pulaski headed for the door.

Pulaski, thinking: Yes, nailed it!

CHAPTER 49

The unsub, however, had not left as much evidence in the town house as Rhyme had hoped.

And there were no other solid leads. The phone call about the intruder had come from an anonymous source. A canvass of the area, to find witnesses who'd seen the intruder, had yielded nothing. Security video cameras in two nearby stores had recorded a thin man in dark coveralls, walking with his head down and carrying a briefcase. He'd diverted suddenly into the cul-de-sac. No image of his face, of course.

Mel Cooper had run an analysis on the bottle and found, naturally, only Rhyme's and Thom's fingerprints, not even those of a liquor store stocker or a Scottish distiller.

No other trace was on the bottle.

Sachs was now telling him, "Nothing significant, Rhyme. Except he's an ace lock picker. No tool marks. Used a pick gun, I'm sure."

Cooper was checking the contents of the evidence collection bags. "Not much, not much." A moment later, though, he did make a discovery. "Hair."

"Excellent," Rhyme said. "Where?"

Cooper examined Sachs's notes. "It was by the shelf where he spiked the whisky."

"And very good whisky it used to be," Rhyme muttered. "But a hair. Good. Only: Is it his, yours, mine, Thom's, a deliveryman's?"

"Let's take a look." The tech lifted the hair from the tape roller and prepared a slide for visual observation in the optical microscope.

"There a bulb?" Rhyme asked.

Hair can yield DNA but generally only if the bulb is attached.

But this sample, no.

Still, hair can reveal other facts about the perp. Tox and drug profiles, for instance (hair retains drug-use info for months). And true hair color, of course.

Cooper focused the microscope and hit the button that put the image on the high-def monitor nearby. The fiber was short, just a bit of stubble.

"Hell," Rhyme said.

"What?" Sachs asked.

"Look familiar, anyone?"

Cooper shook his head. But Sachs gave a soft laugh. "Last week."

"Exactly."

The hair hadn't come from the unsub but from the City Hall murder case of the week before, the worker killed fighting with the mugger. The beard stubble. The victim had shaved just before he'd left the office.

This happened sometimes. However careful you were with evidence, tiny samples escaped. Oh, well.

The mass spectrum computer screen came alive. Cooper focused and said, "Got the toxin profile: tremetol. A form of alcohol. Comes from snakeroot. There wasn't enough to kill you, unless you drank the whole bottle at once."

"Don't tempt me," Rhyme said.

"But it would have made you very, very sick. Severe dementia. Possibly permanent."

"Maybe he didn't have time to inject the whole dosage into the bottle. You know, it's the dosage that's deadly, not the substance itself. We all ingest antimony and mercury and arsenic every day. But not in quantities that do us any harm. Hell, water can kill you. Drink enough too quickly and the sodium imbalance can stop your heart."

That was it, Sachs reported. No fingerprints, no footprints, no other trace.

Nor had any leads been discovered at or near the Belvedere apartment building. No one had seen a man impersonating a fireman, handing out poisoned coffee. A team sent to check the trash cans in the area had found no other containers of tainted beverage. Security videos were not helpful.

Lon Sellitto was still in critical condition and unconscious—and therefore unable to give them any more information about the unsub, though Rhyme doubted that he'd have been so careless as to reveal anything about himself as he'd handed out the tainted coffee.

Mel Cooper checked with the research team that Lon

Sellitto had put together and learned they had not been able to find anything having to do with the numeric message. They did receive something, though. A memorandum had come in from other Major Cases officers Sellitto had "tasked," his verb, with researching the centipede tattoo.

> From: Unsub 11-5 Task Force
> To: Det. Lon Sellitto, Capt. Lincoln Rhyme
> Re: Centipede
>
> We have not had much luck in finding connections between specific perpetrators in the past and the unsub in this case, regarding centipede tattoos. We have learned this:
>
> > Centipedes are arthropods in the class Chilopoda of the subphylum Myriapoda. They have one pair of legs per body segment but don't necessarily have one hundred legs. They can have as few as two dozen, as many as three hundred. The largest are about a foot long.
> >
> > Only centipedes have "forcipules," which are modified front legs, just behind the head. These legs grab prey and through needle-like openings deliver venom that paralyzes or kills. They have venom glands on the first pair of legs, forming a pincer-like appendage always found just behind the head. Forcipules are not true mouthparts, although they are used in the capture of prey items, injecting venom and holding

> on to captured prey. Venom glands run through a tube almost to the tip of each forcipule.
>
> Culturally, centipedes are depicted for two purposes: One, to intimidate enemies. The image of a walking snake, armed with venom-delivering fangs, taps into root fears of humans. We came across this quotation from a Tibetan Buddhist: “If you enjoy frightening others, you will be reincarnated as a centipede.”
>
> Two, centipedes represent invasion of apparently safe places. Centipedes will make their homes in shoes, beds, couches, cradles, dresser drawers. The theory is that the insect represents the idea that what we think is safe really isn’t.
>
> Note that some people have tattoos based on *The Human Centipede*, a particularly bad gross-out film in which three people are sewn together to form what the title suggests. These tattoos have nothing to do with the centipede insect.

“Reads like a bad term paper,” Rhyme muttered. “Mumbo-jumbo but print it out, tape it up.”

The door buzzer sounded and he was amused to notice everyone else in the room start. Cooper and Sachs dropped their hands near their weapons—the aftershock of the attempted attack earlier today. Though he doubted their unsub would return, much less announce his arrival with the bell.

Thom checked the door and let Ron Pulaski into the town house.

He walked in, noticed everyone's troubled faces and asked, "What's up?"

He was told about the attempted attack.

"Poison you, Lincoln? Oh, man."

"It's okay, Rookie. Still here to torment you. How did the undercover job go?"

"I think I did okay."

"Tell us."

He explained how the trip to the funeral home had gone, meeting the lawyer, the man's reluctance to say much or reveal his clients.

A lawyer. Interesting.

Pulaski continued, "I think I won him over. I called you a son of a bitch, Lincoln."

"That work for you?"

"Yeah, felt good."

Rhyme barked a laugh.

"Then I did what you told me. I suggested—didn't say anything exactly—but I suggested that I'd worked with Logan. And that I'd been in touch recently."

"Did you get a card?"

"No. And Weller didn't offer. He was keeping his cards close to his chest."

"And you didn't want to overplay your hand."

Pulaski said, "I like that, what you just said. You slapped down my cliché with one of your own."

The kid was really coming into his own. "Anything you could deduce?"

"I tried to see if he was from California but he wouldn't say. But he was tanned. Looked healthy, balding, stocky. Southern accent. Name was Dave Weller. I'll check him out."

"Well, good. We'll see if he makes a move. If not, I'll talk to Nance Laurel in the DA's Office about getting a subpoena to scoop up the funeral home records. But that's a last resort; I want to keep you in play for as long as we can. Okay. Not a bad job, Rookie. We wait. Now: to the task at hand. Unsub Eleven-Five. He's still got his message to complete. 'the second.' 'forty.' 'seventeenth.' He's not through yet. I want to know where he's going to hit next. We have to move on it."

He wheeled closer to the chart. The answers are there someplace, he thought. Answers to where he would strike next, who he was, what his purpose in orchestrating these terrible attacks might be.

But those were answers as shadowed as the sleet-laden skies of New York.

582 E. 52ND STREET (BELVEDERE PARKING GARAGE)

- Victim: Braden Alexander
  - Not killed
- Unsub 11-5
  - See details from prior scenes
  - Six feet
  - Yellow latex mask
  - Yellow gloves
  - Possibly man in Identi-Kit image
  - Possibly coveralls
  - Probably from Midwest, West Virginia, moun-

tains—other rural setting
    — Had scalpel
— Sedated with propofol
    — How obtained? Access to medical supplies? (No local thefts)
— Potential Kill Zone
    — Underneath garage
    — Similar infrastructure to other scenes
        — IFON
        — ConEd
        — Metro-North Rail Emergency Communication Link
— Tattoo
    — Implants
    — "17th"
    — Loaded with concentrated nicotine
        — Nightshade family
        — Too many locations to source
— Handcuffs
    — Generic, cannot be sourced
— Trace from plastic bag
    — Human albumin and sodium chloride (plastic surgery in his plans?)
    — "No. 3" written on bag in red water-soluble ink
    — Hypochlorous acid
        — Generally used for water treatment but not in prior locations or here, so could be a poison for future attack (however too many sources to find)

SIDNEY PLACE, BROOKLYN HEIGHTS (PAM WILLOUGHBY'S APARTMENT)

— Victim: Seth McGuinn
 — Not killed, minor injuries
— Unsub
 — Red centipede tattoo
 — Confirmed had American Eagle tattoo machine
 — Fit general description from earlier attacks
 — Coveralls
— Sedated with propofol
 — How obtained? Access to medical supplies? (No local thefts)
— American Medical 31-gauge single-use hypodermic syringe
 — Used primarily for plastic surgery
— Toxic extract from white baneberry plant (doll's eyes)
 — Cardiogenic
— No friction ridges
— No footprints (wore booties)
— Handcuffs
 — Generic, cannot be sourced
— Trace:
 — Fibers from blueprint/engineering diagram
 — Cicutoxin trace, probably from earlier scene

RHYME TOWN HOUSE

— Unsub
 — No friction ridges

    — No footprints (booties)
    — Talented lock picker (used pick gun?)
— Hair
    — Beard stubble, but probably from prior scene
— Toxin
    — Tremetol from snakeroot

CHAPTER 50

Leaving the poisoned whisky for Rhyme had been as exhilarating as Billy Haven had expected. More, actually.

Part of this was the need to derail the criminalist's investigation. But part too was the thrill of the game. Sneaking inside, right under the man's nose, while he and his associates were in the front hall, watching the excitement in the park.

Dark-skinned male…

Making his way through the East Village, Billy was reflecting that the Commandments took into account nearly everything about the Modification. But some contingencies it didn't cover. Like poisoning the forensic expert who anticipated everything.

He was now on a similar mission.

Thou shalt be prepared to improvise.

The residents in this part of the city seemed frazzled, unclean, distracted, tense. After the abortive trip to the hospital in Marble Hill, escaping, he'd felt a certain contempt for those on the streets of the Bronx, but at least he'd observed plenty of families, shopping together, going into diners together, heading to or from school events. Here, everyone seemed on their own. People in their twenties mostly, wearing threadbare winter coats and ugly boots, protecting them from the gray-yellow slush. A few couples but even they seemed drawn together by either rootless infatuation or desperation. No one appeared really in love.

He pitied them but he felt contempt for these people too.

Billy thought, naturally, of Lovely Girl. But now he wasn't sad. Everything was going to be okay. He was confident. All would be made right. Full circle.

The Rule of Skin...

He walked a few blocks farther until he came to the storefront. The sign on the door reported *Open* but there was no one inside, not in the shop itself, though in the back he could see a shadow of movement. He looked over the art and posters and photos in the windows. Superheroes, animals, flags, monsters. Slogans. Rock groups.

A thousand examples of tattoos.

Mostly silly and commercial and pointless. Like TV shows and Madison Avenue advertising. He mentally sneered at the tackiness on display.

How skin art had changed over time, Billy reflected. Inking was, in ancient days, a serious affair. For the first thousand or more years of its existence, tattooing was not primarily about decoration. Until the 1800s body art was ritualistic and bound up with religion and societal structure. Primitive people tattooed themselves for a number of practical reasons: defining class or tribe, for instance, or sucking up to this god or that. The art served another reason too, vital: identification of your soul for entry into the underworld; if you were unmarked in life, you'd be rejected by the gatekeeper and wander the earth after death, weeping for eternity. Inking acted too as a barrier to keep your soul from migrating out of the body (the origin of the chain and barbed-wire body art so common nowadays on biceps and necks). And high on the list of reasons people inked themselves was to open a portal so evil spirits would flee the body, like wasps out an open car window—spirits that would, say, prod them to do something they didn't want to do.

Taking pleasure from blood, for instance.

The Oleander Room...

His reflections faded as Billy pulled on his jaundiced latex gloves and opened the door, which set off a buzzer.

"Out in a minute," the voice from the back called.

"No worries." Billy looked around the tiny shop. The chairs, the massage-style tables for tramp stamps and shoulders, the machines and tubes and needles. Good stuff. He looked at the pictures of satisfied customers and concluded that, even if most of the works the shop produced were crap, TT Gordon was a talented artist.

Extracting the hypodermic needle filled with propofol from his backpack, Billy flipped the hanging sign on the door to *Closed* and locked the latch. He made his way toward the shimmery curtain of beads separating the front room from the back.

FRIDAY, NOVEMBER 8

IV

THE UNDERGROUND WOMAN

CHAPTER 51

8:00 A.M.

There's a moment that occurs when you finish a complicated mod and you wonder: Is the work a success? Or have you ruined a perfectly good piece of skin and possibly someone's life for the foreseeable future?

This is what Billy Haven was thinking as he lay in bed in his workshop off Canal Street this morning. Recalling some of his more complex mods. You've just inked the last line (you're always temped to keep going but you have to know when to stop). And you set down your Freewire or your American Eagle or your Baltimore Street or Borg and sit back, edgy and nervous, looking over the finished job for the first time.

Initially a work is just an indiscernible mass of blood and Vaseline and, if it's big, a nonstick bandage or two.

Ah, but underneath, unrecognizable at the moment, is beauty, soon to be revealed.

You hope.

Like Doctor Moreau, unwrapping the bandages of his subjects and finding the successful creation of a beautiful Cat-woman, with almond-shaped eyes and flowing gray Siamese hair. Or a Bird-man, complete with yellow claws and peacock plumage.

The same thing with the Modification. On the surface—to the police, to the citizens of New York paralyzed at the thought of going into basements—the crimes appeared to be a mystery. Some murders, some torture, some curious messages, random locations, random victims, a killer obsessed with skin and poisons.

But underneath: the perfect design. And now it was time to lift off the bloody curtain of bandages and gaze at the Modification in all its glory.

He threw off the sheets and blanket and sat up, glancing again at the front of his thighs.

ELA

LIAM

He had good memories and sad memories, seeing the names. But, after today, he knew the bad ones would fade.

His parents, Lovely Girl.

His watch hummed. He glanced at it. A second vibration soon after.

Billy dressed and spent the next hour scrubbing the workshop: filling trash bags with clothes he'd worn to the sites of the killings, bedclothes, napkins, paper towels, plastic silverware, plates—anything that might be a nest for his DNA or fingerprints.

He carted the bags outside into the chill, sleety morning—his nose stinging with his first breath on the street—and set them on the curb. He waited. Three minutes later the noisy Department of Sanitation truck rolled to a stop and the workers leapt off the back, collecting the garbage along this short, dark street.

He'd noted the exact time the trucks arrived—to make sure that the trash wasn't on the street for more than a few minutes; he'd learned that the police had the right to go through your garbage on public streets.

With a grind of transmission and sigh of gassy exhaust, the truck vanished. The most incriminating evidence was gone. He'd return later—maybe in a week or so—and set fire to the place to destroy the rest. But for now, this was enough. It was very unlikely the police would find the subterranean lair anytime soon.

With this thought—about the police—he wondered about Lincoln Rhyme. He'd heard nothing about the man getting sick from the poison. Which reminded him that the plan to derail the great anticipator wasn't as efficient as it might've been. But he hadn't thought of any other way to get the poison into the man's bloodstream. Whisky seemed the best choice. Maybe something else would have been better.

Still, as he'd considered earlier: There'd been successful battles and unsuccessful ones. But in the war of the Modification, ultimately he'd win.

Billy returned to the apartment and continued packing.

He walked from terrarium to terrarium. Foxglove,

hemlock, tobacco, angel's trumpets. He'd developed a fondness for the plants and the toxins they produced. He flipped through some of the sketches he'd done.

He slipped them away in his backpack, along with the Modification Commandment notebook. Although he'd written at the end of the Commandments an instruction that amounted to: *Thou shalt destroy this holy book itself*, he couldn't bring himself to do so. He wasn't sure where this reluctance to shred the pages came from. Perhaps it was that the Commandments were the means to fix the pain he'd endured because of the loss of Lovely Girl.

Or maybe because it was simply a marvelous work of art, the sentences so carefully written in Billy's elegant script—as intricate as a ten-color mod on virgin white skin using a dozen different lining needles and six or seven shaders. Too beautiful to hide from the world.

He zipped up his backpack and then walked to the workbench and packed a half dozen tools and a heavy-duty extension cord into a canvas gear bag. He added a large, sealed thermos. Then pulled on a tan leather jacket and a dark-green Mets cap.

His watch hummed. Then, the second reminder.

Time to make right all the wrongs of this troubled world.

CHAPTER 5

Lincoln Rhyme was back in his parlor.

He'd awakened several times, wrestling with the puzzle of the tattoos. No insights had blossomed. Then he'd fallen back to a sleep filled with dreams as pointless as most were. He was fully awake at 6 a.m. and summoned Thom for an expedited morning routine.

Pulaski, Cooper and Sachs were back too and they huddled in the parlor, wrestling with the same mysteries that had refused to unravel when the hour hit midnight.

Rhyme heard the buzz of a mobile and looked across the room to see Pulaski pulling his phone from his pocket. It was the prepaid, not his own iPhone, that was humming.

Which meant the undercover operation.

The young man looked down at the screen. And that deer-in-the-headlights look formed. The officer had changed from his funereal outfit but had dressed undercover nonetheless: jeans, a T-shirt and a V-neck sweater, dark blue. Running shoes. Not exactly a Mafia thug attire but better than a Polo shirt and Dockers.

The inalist said, "It's the lawyer? From the funeral h ?"

P said, "Right. Should I let him leave a mes-

sa won't. Answer it. Everybody else, quiet!"

a moment Rhyme thought Pulaski was going to . But the young man's eyes grew focused and he the phone. For some reason he turned away from others so he could carry on a more or less private nversation.

Rhyme wanted to hear but he'd delegated the job of finding the deceased Watchmaker's associates—whether innocent or lethal—to Pulaski and it was no longer Rhyme's job to micromanage. It wasn't even his position to tell the officer what to do or how to do it. Rhyme was merely a civilian consultant; Pulaski was the official law enforcer.

After a few minutes Pulaski disconnected and turned back. "Weller wants to see me. One of his clients, too."

Rhyme lifted his eyebrow. That was even better.

"He's staying at the Huntington Arms. West Fifty-Sixth."

Rhyme shook his head. He didn't know the hotel. But Mel Cooper looked up the place. "One of those boutiques on the West Side."

It was just north of Hell's Kitchen, that neighborhood of the city—named after a dangerous 'hood in Victorian London—that had at one point been a thug-infested den of crime. Now it was gentrification personified, though occasional blocks of decrepit color remained. The hotel the man described, Cooper explained, was in a block in which were tucked overpriced restaurants and hotels.

Pulaski said, "We're going to meet in a half hour. How should I handle it?"

"Mel, what's the layout of the neighborhood and the hotel?"

The tech went to Google Earth on one computer and the New York Department of Buildings on another. In less than sixty seconds he slapped onto the main monitor an overhead view of the street and a blueprint of the hotel itself.

There was an outdoor patio, on 56th, which would have been a great place for surveillance if the weather had been less Arctic, but the meeting would take place inside today.

"Sachs, can we get a surveillance team in the lobby?"

"I'll call. See what I can do." After a few minutes on the phone, she said, "No time to go through channels. But I pulled some strings at Major Cases. There'll be two undercovers inside in twenty minutes."

"We'll need a bigger operation in place, Pulaski. You've got to buy time. A couple of days. What did he sound like? Did he make it seem urgent?"

Running a hand through his blond hair, the officer said, "Not really. He's got an idea he wants to pitch, I got the impression. He told me not to park in front of the hotel if I was driving. He was pretty, you know, mysterious. Wasn't going to say anything on the phone."

Rhyme looked him over. "You have an ankle holster?"

"Ankle—oh, for a backup piece? I don't even own one."

"Not for backup. Your *only* piece. You may be frisked. And most friskers stop at the thigh. Sachs?"

Sachs said, "I'll hook him up. A Smith and Wesson Bodyguard. A three eighty. It's got a laser built in but don't bother with that. Use the iron sights." She dug into a drawer and handed him a small, black automatic. "I put nail polish on the sights. Easier to seat a target in bad light. You okay with fiery pink?"

"I can cope."

She handed him a small cloth holster with a buckling leather strap. Rhyme recalled she never liked Velcro to secure her weapons. Amelia Sachs left very little to chance.

Pulaski lifted his foot onto a nearby chair and strapped on the holster. It was invisible. Then the officer examined the small, boxy gun. He chambered a round, took another bullet from Sachs and loaded it into the magazine. Six in the hallway, one in the bedroom. He snapped the mag back in.

"What's the pull?"

"It's heavy. Nine pounds."

"Nine. Well."

"And double-action only. Your finger's almost all the way back before it fires. But it's small as a minnow. Leave the safety off. I don't even know why they added one. With a pull like that."

"Got it."

Pulaski looked at his watch. "I've got twenty-five minutes. No time for a wire."

"No, there isn't," Rhyme agreed. "But the surveillance team'll have microphones up. You want body armor?"

Shaking his head. "They'll spot that faster than a piece. No, I'll go in clean."

"You sure?" Sachs asked. "Entirely up to you."

"I'm sure."

"You need to draw them out, Rookie. Tell them you want to meet again. Act coy and cautious but insist. Even if it's in a different state. We'll get Fred Dellray involved. Federal backup. They do spying right. And don't go anywhere with them now. We won't be able to keep tabs on you."

Pulaski nodded. He walked into the hallway and looked at himself in the mirror. He mussed his hair a bit. "Am I inscrutable enough?"

Rhyme said, "You are the epitome of unscrupulousness."

"Dangerous too," Mel Cooper said.

The officer smiled and pulled on his overcoat then disappeared into the front hallway of the town house.

The criminalist called, "Keep us posted."

As he heard the door open to the howling wind, Rhyme asked himself, And what kind of pointless request was that?

CHAPTER 53

You can do this.

Ron Pulaski was minding his steps on the sidewalk in the West 50s, which was encrusted with gray snow and grayer ice. His breath popped out as wispy clouds in the relentlessly cold air and he realized he was having trouble feeling his fingers.

A trigger pull of nine pounds? Thinking of the Smittie Bodyguard pistol on his ankle. His standard weapon, a Glock 17, had a pull of one-third that. Of course, the issue wasn't the effort to pull the trigger. Nine pounds of effort were easily handled by anybody over the age of six. The problem was accuracy. The harder to pull the trigger, the less accurate the shot.

But it wasn't going to come to a shootout, Pulaski reminded himself. And even if it did, the backup team would be positioned in the hotel, ready to, well, back him up.

He was—Jesus! The street spun. He nearly ended up on his ass, thanks to a patch of ice he hadn't seen, inhaling hard in surprise, taking in air so cold it burned.

Hate winter.

Then reminded himself it wasn't even winter yet, only the sinkhole of an autumn.

He looked up, through the sleet. Three blocks away—long blocks, crosstown blocks—he could see the hotel. A red neon disk, part of the logo.

He increased his pace. Just a couple of days ago, he and Jenny and the kids had spent the night in front of the fireplace because there'd been a problem with the gas line for the block. The cold had seeped in and he'd gotten a fire going, real logs, not Duraflames, the kids in PJs and sleeping bags nearby, and he and Jenny on an air mattress. Pulaski had told the worst jokes—children's jokes—until the youngsters had fallen asleep.

And he and Jenny had cuddled fiercely, until the caress of chill went away under their combined bodies. (No, not that, of course; they were in pajamas as chaste and comical as the children's.)

How he wanted to be back with his family now. But he pushed aside those thoughts.

Undercover. That was his job. His only job. Jenny was married to Ron Pulaski, not Stan Walesa. The kids didn't exist.

And neither did Lincoln Rhyme or Amelia Sachs.

All that mattered was finding the associates of the late and not very lamented Watchmaker. Who were they? What were they up to? And most important: Did the killer have a successor?

Ron Pulaski had a thought on this topic, though he'd decided not to say anything to Lincoln or Amelia, for fear that he'd look stupid if proven wrong. (The head injury again. It plagued him every day, every day.)

His theory was this: The lawyer *himself* was the main associate of the Watchmaker. He'd been lying about never meeting the man. He appeared to be a real lawyer—they'd checked that out. And had a firm in LA. (The assistant who answered the phone said Mr. Weller was out of town on business.) But the website looked dicey—bare bones—and it gave only a P.O. box, not a street address. Still, it was typical of an ambulance chaser's site, Pulaski supposed.

And what was Weller's plan here?

The same as Pulaski's maybe. After all, why come to New York to collect ashes when it would have been far easier and cheaper simply to FedEx them to the family?

No, Pulaski was now even more convinced that Weller was here on a fishing expedition himself—to find other partners of the Watchmaker, who had been the sort of master planner to have several projects going on at the same time, without telling one set of colleagues that the others even existed. He guessed that—

His phone vibrated. He answered. It was an NYPD officer from the team at the hotel. He and his partner were in position in the lobby and bar. Pulaski had relayed the details on Weller's appearance but the undercover reported that there was nobody fitting that description in the lobby yet. It was, however, still early.

"I'll be there in five, six minutes."

"K," said the man with a serenity that Pulaski found reassuring. They disconnected.

A gust of wind slashed. Pulaski pulled his coat more tightly around him. Didn't do much good. He and Jenny had been talking about getting to a beach, any beach. The kids were in swimming class and he was really looking forward to taking them to an ocean. They'd been to a few lakes Upstate but a sandy beach, with crashing waves? Man, they would love—

"Hi, there, Mr. Walesa."

Pulaski stopped abruptly and turned. He tried to mask his surprise.

Ten feet behind him was Dave Weller. What was going on? They were still two blocks from the hotel. Weller had stopped and was standing under the awning of a pet shop, not yet open for business.

Pulaski thought: Act cool. "Hey. Thought we were going to meet at the hotel." A nod up the street.

Weller said nothing, just looked Pulaski up and down.

The officer said, "Hell of a day, hm? This sucks. Been sleeting like this off and on for almost a week." He nearly said, "You don't get this in LA." But then he wasn't supposed to know that the lawyer had his office—or un-office—in California. Of course, maybe it would've been *less* suspicious and *more* inscrutable to let Weller know he'd done some homework on the man. Hard to tell.

Hell, this undercover stuff, you really had to think ahead.

Pulaski joined Weller in front of the pet store, out of the sleet. In the window, just behind them, was a murky aquarium.

A beach, any beach...

Weller said, "Thought this'd be safer." That faint Southern accent again.

But, of course, Stan Walesa might be wondering why safety was an issue. He said, "Safer?"

But Weller said nothing in reply. He didn't wear a hat, and his bald head was dotted with moisture.

Pulaski gave a shrug. "You were saying you have a client who might want to meet with me."

"Maybe."

"I'm into import-export. Is that what your client needs?"

"Could be."

"And what specifically you have in mind?"

"Exactly" would've been better than "specifically." Tough guys wouldn't use the S word.

Weller's voice dipped, hard to hear over the wind. "You know that project that Richard put together down in Mexico?"

Pulaski's gut thudded. Getting even better. The man was referring to an attempted hit of a Mexican anti-drug officer a few years ago. Logan had orchestrated an elaborate plan to kill the *federale*. This was great. If Weller knew about that, he wasn't quite who he claimed to be.

My theory…

"Sure. I know it. He told me that that asshole fucked it up, Rhyme."

So the lawyer did know about the criminalist, after all.

Pulaski offered, "But Richard came up with a good plan."

"Yeah, it was." Weller seemed more comfortable now that Pulaski had given him some details not known in public about Richard Logan. He eased closer. "Well, my client might be interested in talking to you about that situation."

Your client or you? Pulaski wondered. He kept his eyes locked on Weller's. This was hard but he didn't waver.

"What's there to talk about?"

Weller said evasively: "Could be renewed interest in an alternative approach to the situation. In Mexico. Mr. Logan had been working on it when he died."

"I'm not sure what we're talking about," Pulaski said.

"A new approach."

"Oh."

"If it's to everybody's advantage."

"What kind of advantage?" Pulaski inquired. This seemed like a good question.

"Significant."

That didn't seem like a particularly good answer. But he knew you had to play games like these—well, he supposed you did, since what he'd learned about undercover work was mostly from *Blue Bloods* and movies.

"My client is looking for people he can trust. You might be one of those people. But we'd need to check you out more."

"I'll have to do some checking too."

"We'd expect that. And," Weller said slowly, "my client would need something from you. To show your commitment. Can you bring something to the table?"

"What sort of 'something'?"

"You have to spend money to make money," Weller said.

So, he was being asked to invest. Cash. Good. Much better than having to bring them the head of a rival drug dealer to prove his loyalty.

"That's not a problem," Pulaski said dismissively, as if he could jump in his private jet, fly to Switzerland and pluck stacks of hundreds from his private bank.

"What would you be willing to cough up?"

This was a stumper. It was tough to get buy-money for sting operations. The brass knew there was always a chance of losing it. But he had no idea what the limits were. What would they do on *Blue Bloods*? He shrugged. "A hundred K."

Weller nodded. "That's a good figure."

And it was then that Pulaski thought: How did he know I'd come this way? There were three or four possible approaches to the hotel. And, hell, for that matter, how did he know I'd be on foot and not take a cab or drive? Earlier Weller had referred to parking in front of the Huntington Arms.

One answer was that Weller, or somebody, had been following Pulaski.

And there was only one reason for that. To set him up. Maybe he'd seen him come out of Rhyme's and looked up the owner of the town house.

And here I am without a fucking wire and two blocks from the backup team and a gun on my ankle, a thousand miles away.

"So. Glad this is moving along. Let me see about that money and—"

But Weller wasn't listening. His eyes flickered past Pulaski, who spun around.

Two unsmiling men in leather jackets approached. One with shaggy hair, one with a shaved head.

When they noted Pulaski's gaze, they drew pistols and lunged.

The young officer turned and started to sprint. He made it all of two yards before the third killer stepped out from behind the truck where he'd been waiting, wrapped his massive arm around the patrolman's throat and slammed the officer against the window of the pet shop.

Weller stepped back. The hit man touched the gun muzzle to Pulaski's temple while, inside the store, a colorful toucan in a flamboyant Polynesian cage ruffled its feathers and watched with scant interest the goings-on outside.

CHAPTER 54

Rhyme phoned Rachel Parker and happened to get Lon Sellitto's son.

The young man had come to town from Upstate New York, where he was working after graduating from SUNY in Albany. Rhyme remembered the boy as being quiet and pleasant enough, though he'd had some anger issues and mood problems—common among the children of law enforcers. But that was years ago and now he seemed mature and steady. In a voice missing any of Lon's Brooklyn twang, Richard Sellitto told Rhyme that his father's condition was largely unchanged. He was still categorized as critical. Rhyme was pleased that the young man was doing everything he could to support Rachel and Sellitto's ex, Richard's mother.

After he disconnected, Rhyme gave Cooper the update—which was really no update at all. He reflected that this was one of the most horrific aspects of poisoning: The substance wormed its way into your cells, destroying delicate tissues for days and weeks afterward. Bullets could be removed and wounds stitched. But poisons hid, residing, and killed at their leisure.

Rhyme now returned to the chart containing the pictures of the tattoos.

What on earth are you trying to say? he wondered yet again.

A puzzle, a quotation, a code? He kept returning to the theory that the clues referred to a location. But where?

His phone buzzed once more. He frowned looking at the caller ID. He didn't recognize it.

He answered. "Rhyme here."

"Lincoln."

"Rookie? Is that you? What's wrong?"

"Yes, I—"

"Where the hell have you been? The team's at the hotel, where you're meeting Weller. Or were *supposed* to be meeting. They've been in place for an hour. You never showed up." He added sternly, "We were, you can imagine, a little concerned."

"There was a problem."

Rhyme fell silent. "And?"

"I kind of got arrested."

Rhyme wasn't sure he'd heard. "Say again."

"Arrested."

"Explain."

"I didn't get to the hotel. I got stopped before."

"I said explain. Not confuse."

Mel Cooper looked his way. Rhyme shrugged.

"There's an agent with the NYBI here. He wants to talk to you."

The New York Bureau of Investigation?

"Put him on."

"Hello, Detective Rhyme?"

He didn't bother to correct the title.

"Yes."

"This's Agent Tom Abner, NYBI."

"And what's going on, Agent Abner?" Rhyme was trying to be patient, though he had a feeling that Pulaski had screwed up the undercover set and ruined whatever chance they had to learn more about the associates of the late Watchmaker. And given the "I got arrested" part, the screwup must've been pretty bad.

"We've found out that Ron is an NYPD patrol officer in good standing, active duty. But nobody at headquarters knew about any undercover set he was running. Can you confirm that Ron was working for you on an operation?"

"I'm civilian, Agent Abner. A consultant. But, yes, he was running an op under the direction of Detective Amelia Sachs, Major Cases. An opportunity presented itself very fast. We didn't have time to go through channels. Ron was just making initial contact with some possible perps this morning."

"Hm. I see."

"What happened?"

"Yesterday, an attorney named David Weller, based in LA, contacted us. He was retained by the family of a decedent, Richard Logan—the convict who died?"

"Yes." Rhyme sighed. And the whole fiasco began to unfold before him.

"Well, Mr. Weller said that somebody had come to the funeral home and was asking a lot of questions about Mr. Logan. He seemed to want to meet the family or associates and suggested that he might want to participate in some of the illegal deals that Logan had started before he died. I suggested a sting to see what this fellow had in mind. Mr. Weller agreed to help. We wired him up and he mentioned some crime in Mexico that Mr. Logan had been involved in. Ron offered money to participate in another attempt to kill the same official. As soon as he mentioned a figure we moved in."

Jesus. Like the most common prostitution sting.

Rhyme said, "Richard Logan had orchestrated some pretty complicated crimes when he was alive. He couldn't have been operating alone. We were trying to find some of his associates."

"Got it. But your officer was really pushing the bounds of undercover ops."

"He hasn't done that kind of thing before."

"That doesn't surprise me. Attorney Weller wasn't too happy about the whole thing, as you can imagine. But he's not going to pursue any complaint."

"Tell him we appreciate that. Can you have Ron call me?"

"Yessir."

They disconnected and a moment later the parlor phone rang once more. It was Pulaski's undercover phone.

"Rookie."

"I'm sorry, Lincoln. I—"

"Don't apologize."

"I didn't handle it very well."

"I'm not so sure it worked out badly."

There was a pause. "What do you mean?"

"We learned one thing: Weller and his clients—the

Logan family—*don't* have any connection with any of the Watchmaker's associates or any planned crimes. Otherwise, they wouldn't've dimed you out."

"I guess."

"You're free to go?"

"Yeah."

"Well, the good news is we can let the Watchmaker rest in peace. No more distractions. We've got an unsub to catch. Get your ass back here. Now."

He disconnected before the young officer said anything more.

It was then that Rhyme's phone rang and he received the news that there'd been a fourth attack.

And when he heard that the killing had been in a tattoo parlor in downtown Manhattan, he asked immediately which one.

Upon hearing that—not surprisingly—it was TT Gordon's shop, Rhyme sighed and lowered his head. "No, no," he whispered. For a moment Views of Death Number One and Two vied. Then the first prevailed and Rhyme called Sachs to tell her she had yet another scene to run.

CHAPTER 55

Amelia Sachs returned from the most recent crime scene in the Unsub 11-5 case. TT Gordon's tattoo parlor in the East Village.

It turned out, though, that Gordon himself was not the victim. He'd been out of the parlor when the unsub snuck inside, locked the door and proceeded into the back room for the lethal tattooing session. The body was that of one of the artists who worked in the parlor, a man named Eddie Beaufort. He was a transplant from South Carolina who'd moved to New York a few years ago and was, Sachs had learned from Gordon, making a name for himself in the inking world.

"We should've had somebody on the tattoo parlor, Rhyme," she said.

"Who would've thought he'd be at risk?" Rhyme was truly surprised that the unsub had tracked the artist down. How? It seemed unlikely but possible that he'd followed Gordon from Rhyme's. But the tat community would be a small one and word must've gotten back to the killer that Gordon was helping with the case. The unsub would have heard and gone to the parlor to kill him. Finding he wasn't there, maybe he had just decided to make clear that it was a bad idea to assist the police and picked for a victim the first employee he found.

It was also time to send another message.

Sachs described the scene: Beaufort, lying on his back. His shirt was off and the unsub had tattooed another part of the puzzle on his abdomen. She slid the SD card from her camera and displayed the pictures on the screen.

the six hundredth

Ron Pulaski, back from his car wreck of an undercover assignment, stood in front of the display with his arms crossed. "They're not in numerical order: the second, forty, seventeenth and the six hundredth."

Rhyme said, "Good point. He could have gone numerically if he'd wanted to. Either the order is significant—or he wanted to scramble them for some reason. And we're ordinal again, not cardinal. 'Forty' is the only cardinal number."

Mel Cooper now suggested, "An encryption?"

That was a possibility. But there were far too many combinations and no common reference point. In breaking a simple code in which letters are converted to numbers, you can start with the knowledge that the letter "e" appears most frequently in the English language and preliminarily assign that value to the most commonly occurring numbers in the code. But here, they had far too few numbers—and they were combined with words, which suggested that the numbers did not mean anything other than what they appeared to, cryptic though that meaning was.

It could still be a location, but this number eliminated longitude or latitude. One or more addresses?

Pulaski said, "Beaufort wasn't killed underground."

Rhyme pointed out, "No, the unsub's motive was different here: to kill TT Gordon specifically or at least somebody in the parlor. He didn't need to follow his standard MO. Now let's look at what else you collected, Sachs."

She and Cooper walked to the examination table. Both donned gloves and face masks.

"No prints, finger or footwear," she said. "ME has the blood workup. I told him we needed the results yesterday. He said it was all hands on deck."

"Other trace?" Rhyme asked.

Sachs nodded at several bags.

The criminalist barked, "Mel, get on that."

As Cooper picked up and examined each one, then analyzed the contents, Sachs ran through the other pictures of the scene. Eddie Beaufort, hands cuffed behind him and lying on his back, like the others. It was obvious he'd suffered gastrointestinal symptoms and severe vomiting.

The phone rang with a familiar number.

Sachs gave a laugh. "That's as ASAP as it gets."

"Doctor, it's Lincoln Rhyme," he said to the medical examiner. "What do you have?"

"Odd, Captain." Using Rhyme's old title. It never failed to be both jarring and familiar.

"How? Exactly."

"The victim was killed by amatoxin alpha-amanitin."

"Death cap mushroom," Cooper said. "*Amanita phalloides*."

"That's it," the medical examiner said.

Rhyme knew them well. Amanitas are known for three things: a smell like honey, a very pleasant taste and the ability to kill more efficiently than any other fungus on earth.

"And the odd part?"

"The dosage. I've never seen a concentration this high. Usually it takes days to die, but he lasted about an hour I'd guess."

"And a pretty bad hour," Sachs said.

"Well, that's right," said the medical examiner, as if this had never occurred to him.

"Any other substances?"

"More propofol. Just like the others."

"Anything else?"

"Nope."

Rhyme grimaced and began to hit disconnect. Sachs called, "Thanks."

"You're—"

Click.

"Keep going, Mel," Rhyme said.

Cooper ran another sample of trace through the gas chromatograph/mass spectrometer. "This is—"

"Don't say 'odd,'" Rhyme snapped. "I've had enough odd."

"Troubling. That was the word."

"Go on."

"Nitrocellulose, di-ethylene glycol dinitrate, dibutyl phthalate, diphenylamine, potassium chloride, graphite."

Rhyme frowned. "How much?"

"A lot."

"What is it, Lincoln?" Pulaski asked.

"Explosives. Gunpowder, specifically. Smokeless—modern formulation."

Sachs asked the tech, "From a discharged weapon?"

"No. Some actual grains. Pre-burn."

Pulaski asked, "He reloads his own ammunition?"

It was a reasonable suggestion. But Rhyme considered this for a moment and then said, "No, I don't think so. Usually it's only snipers and hunters who reload. And our unsub hasn't left any evidence that he's either. Not much interest in firearms at all." Rhyme stared at the computer printout of the GC/MS. "No, I think he's using the raw powder for an improvised explosive device." He sighed. "Poison's not enough. Now he wants to blow something up."

537 ST. MARKS STREET

- Victim: Eddie Beaufort, 38
  - Employee at TT Gordon's tattoo parlor
  - Probably not intended victim
- Perpetrator: Presumably Unsub 11-5
- COD: Poisoning with amatoxin alpha-amanitin (from Amanita phalloides, death cap mushroom), introduced via tattooing
- Tattoo reads: "the six hundredth"

- — Sedated with propofol
    - — How obtained? Access to medical supplies? (No local thefts)
- — Handcuffs
    - — Generic, unable to source
- — Trace
    - — Nitrocellulose, di-ethylene glycol dinitrate, dibutyl phthalate, diphenylamine, potassium chloride, graphite: smokeless gunpowder
        - — Planning to use improvised explosive device?

CHAPTER 56

"You know how skeptical I am of motives."

Sachs said nothing, but a cresting smile told her reaction.

Easing his wheelchair up to the evidence boards, Rhyme continued, "But there's a time when it's appropriate to ask about them—particularly when we've built up a solid evidentiary base. Which we have. The possibility of a bomb—possibility, mind you—may take this out of psychotic-perp world. There's a rational motive at work possibly. Our unsub's not necessarily satisfying deep-seated yearnings to do the Bone Collector one better. I think he may have something more calculated in mind. Yes, yes, this could be good," he added enthusiastically. "I want to look at the victims again."

The team perused the charts. Rhyme said, "We can take Eddie Beaufort out of the equation. He was killed because he was in the wrong place at the wrong time. Lon and Seth and I were attacked to slow us down. There were four intended attacks as part of his plan: We ruined two of them—Harriet Stanton at the hospital and Braden

Alexander at the Belvedere Apartments. And two were successful. Chloe and Samantha. Why those four?" Rhyme whispered. "What about them beckoned?"

Sachs said, "I don't know, Rhyme. They seemed purely random...happenstance victims."

Rhyme stared up at the board in front of him. "Yes, the victims *themselves* are random. But what if—"

Pulaski blurted, "The *places* aren't? Did he pretend to be psycho to take attention away from the fact that there's something at the scenes he wants to blow up?"

"Exactly, Rookie!" Rhyme scanned the boards. "Location, location, location."

Cooper said, "But blow up what? And how?"

Rhyme scanned the crime scene photos again. Then: "Sachs!"

She lifted an eyebrow.

"When we weren't sure where the hypochlorous acid came from we sent patrolmen to the scenes, remember? To see if there were chlorine distribution systems there."

"Right. The boutique in SoHo and the restaurant. They didn't find any."

"Yes, yes, yes, but it's not the acid I'm thinking of." Rhyme wheeled closer to the monitor, studying the images. "Look at those pictures you took, Sachs. The spotlights and batteries. Did *you* set them up?"

"No, the first responders did." She was frowning. "I *assumed* they did. They were there when I arrived. Both scenes."

"And the officer who searched the tunnel for chlorine later said he was standing by the spotlights. They were still there. Why?" He frowned and said to Sachs, "Find out who set them up."

Sachs grabbed her phone and called the Crime Scene Unit in Queens. "Joey, it's Amelia. When your people were running the Unsub Eleven-Five scenes, did you bring halogens to any of them?...No." She was nodding. "Thanks." Disconnected.

"They never set them up, Rhyme. They weren't our lights." She then called a friend at the fire department and asked the same question. After a brief conversation she disconnected and reported, "Uh-uh. They weren't the FD's either. And patrol doesn't carry around spots in their RMPs. Only Emergency Service does and they didn't respond until later."

"And, hell," Rhyme snapped, "I'll bet there're lights in the tunnel under the Belvedere."

Sachs: "That's what the bombs're in, right? The batteries."

Rhyme looked over the images. "The batteries look like twelve-volt. You can run halogens on batteries that're a lot smaller. The rest of the casing's filled with gunpowder, I'm sure. It's brilliant. Nobody'd question spotlights and batteries sitting in a crime scene perimeter. Any other mysterious packages'd be reported and examined by the Bomb Squad."

"But what's the target?" Cooper asked.

The brief silence was broken by Amelia Sachs. "My God."

"What, Sachs?"

"IFON." She dug what seemed to be a business card out of her purse. And walked fast to the crime scene photos. "Hell, I missed it, Rhyme. Missed it completely."

"Go on."

She tapped the screen. "Those yellow boxes with *IFON* printed on the side? They're Internet cables, owned by International Fiber Optic Networks." She held up the card. "And the building directly over the Samantha Levine crime scene was IFON's headquarters. She worked for them. I interviewed the CEO just after she died." Sachs then called up the photos of the Chloe Moore scene. "There. The same boxes."

And there was another box visible in the tunnel beneath the parking garage in the Belvedere Apartments.

Sachs said, "In the hospital, in Marble Hill, where Harriet Stanton was attacked, I didn't go underground to look for any tunnels. But I'll bet there're IFON routers or whatever they are somewhere."

Pulaski said, "Somebody wants to blow up the boxes." His face finally grew inscrutable. "Hey—think about it—the Internet outages? The rumors of the traditional cable companies sabotaging the new fiber-optic systems? I'll bet that's it."

Sachs said, "Our Skin Collector may feel like he's the Bone Collector's heir but, bottom line? That's just a cover. He was hired to smuggle bombs underground to take out International Fiber Optic's routers."

Pulaski asked, "What would happen if they detonated?"

"Assume the entire Internet in Manhattan would go down," Cooper said.

"Banks," Rhyme muttered. "And hospitals, police, national security, air traffic control. Call Dellray and have him alert Homeland Security. I'm guessing hundreds of deaths and billions of dollars in losses. Get our computer man, Rodney Szarnek, on the phone. Now."

CHAPTER 57

Harriet Stanton was returning with her husband, Matthew, from Upper Manhattan Medical Center in Marble Hill.

They were in a cab, which was—so far—about seventeen dollars in fare.

"Look at that," Matthew muttered, eyeing the meter. "Can you believe it? It'll be thirty by the time we get to the hotel. Subway would've been cheaper." Matthew had always been a bit of a curmudgeon. Now, after the brush with death—or with New York City health care—his mood hadn't improved.

Harriet, in her yes-dear mode, replied that given the neighborhood they'd been driving through—the Bronx and Harlem—wouldn't it be better to spend the money? "And look at the weather."

Where they lived, in downstate Illinois, the weather could be just as cold and sloppy. It didn't seem, though, so *dirty* cold and sloppy. "Tainted" was the word that came to mind.

Mathew took her hand, which was a way of saying, You're right, I suppose.

His bill of health was, if not clean, then not as bad as it might've been. Yes, the incident had been a heart attack—or the ten-dollar phrase, myocardial infarction—but no surgery was called for. Medication and a slow, steady increase in the amount of exercise should do the trick, the doctor had told them. Aspirin, of course. Always aspirin.

She called their son, Josh, back at the hotel, and told him to collect Matthew's prescriptions, which the doctor had called in to a nearby pharmacy. Matthew sat back silently in the seat of the taxi and stared at the sights. The people were what interested him, she judged, from the way his eyes danced from one cluster of passersby to another.

The cab dropped them in front of their hotel. The place had been built in the 1930s or so, Harriet guessed, and clearly hadn't undergone a renovation for years. The colors were gold and yellow and gray. The scuffed walls and over-washed curtains had brash, geometric designs, ugly. The place reminded her of the Moose Lodge at home.

The decor, along with the persistent scent of Lysol and onions, set her on edge. But maybe that was just the disappointment about her husband's heart attack, the disruption of their plans. They rode the elevator to the tenth floor and stepped out, walked to their room.

Harriet felt like she should help her husband into bed or, if he chose to stay up, help him on with his slippers and into some comfortable clothing and order some food. But he waved her off—though with a faint smile—and sat at the battered desk, going online. "See. I was saying. Fifteen dollars a day for the Internet. At Red Roof it's free. Or Best Western. Where's Josh?"

"Getting your prescriptions."

"He probably got lost."

Harriet placed a load of dirty clothing into the room's dry-cleaning bag, which she'd take to the guest self-serve laundry room in the basement. This was one thing that she would not pay for, hotel valet service. It was ridiculous.

She paused to look at herself in the mirror, noting that her tan skirt needed no pressing and the brown sweater, clinging to her voluptuous figure, was largely hair-free. Largely but not completely. She plucked off several strands and let them fall to the floor; they had three German shepherds at home. She wound together stray strands of her own hair, milking to white, and pinned them into her severe bun.

She noted that in her haste to get to the hospital she'd hooked her silver necklace on backward and she fixed it now, though the design appeared abstract; no one would have noted the mistake.

Then a grimace; don't be so vain.

Leaving Matthew, she walked into the hallway with the laundry and took the elevator to the lobby. It was crowded. She waited in line at the front desk, to get change. A gaggle of Japanese tourists clustered around their suitcases like pioneers protecting their women. A couple that appeared to be honeymooning stood nearby, adoring each other. Two men—gay, she could see—chatted enthusiastically about some plans that night. Young, leather-jacketed musicians lounged, their feet up on battered instrument cases. An obese couple pored over a map. The husband was in shorts. In this weather. And with those legs!

New York. What a place.

Harriet suddenly had a sense that somebody was watching her. She looked up quickly. But didn't see anyone. Still, she was left with an uneasy feeling.

Well, after the close call at the hospital, it was natural for her to be a little paranoid.

"Ma'am?" she heard.

"Oh, sorry." She turned back to the desk clerk and got change for a ten.

She took the elevator to the basement and followed signage down two corridors to the laundry room, a dim space, dusted with spilled detergent and smelling of dryer exhaust and hot lint. Like the hallways, the room was deserted.

She heard the click and then the rumble of the elevator going up. A moment later there came the sound of a car returning to this level. If it was the same one, it had only traveled to the main floor.

Two dollars for a one-use container of detergent? She should have had Josh pick up a bottle of Tide at the drugstore. Then reminded herself: Don't be like Matthew. Don't worry about the petty things.

Were those footsteps coming from the direction of the elevator?

She glanced toward the doorway, the shadowy corridor. Heart thudding a bit faster, her palms dampening.

Nothing.

She added the clothing to the least-dirty machine and shoved in the six quarters.

Then footsteps again, growing louder.

She turned, staring at the young man in the tan leather jacket and green NY Mets cap. He carried a backpack and a canvas work bag.

Silence for a moment.

Then she smiled. "Billy."

"Aunt Harriet." Billy Haven looked around to make certain they were alone and then stepped inside the room. He set down the bags.

She lifted her hands, palm up. Like summoning a child.

Billy hesitated then came to her and let himself be drawn into her arms, which closed around him, enwrapping him tightly. They were about the same height—she was just under six feet herself—and Harriet easily maneuvered her face to his, kissing him hard on the mouth.

She sensed him resist for a moment but then he gave in and kissed her back, gripping her lips with his, tasting her. Not wanting to but unable to stop.

It had always been this way with him: reluctant at first, then yielding . . . then growing commanding as he pushed her down on her back and wrestled off clothing.

Always this way—from the very first time, more than a decade ago, when she'd pulled the boy into the study above the garage, the Oleander Room, for their afternoon trysts, while Matthew was busy with—aunt and nephew sometimes joked—God knew what.

CHAPTER 58

Typically—and irritatingly—Rodney Szarnek was listening to some god-awful rock when he picked up the call from Rhyme's parlor.

"Rodney, you're on speaker. It's…Can we lose the music?"

If you could call that head-banging crap music.

"Hey, Lincoln. That's you, right?"

Rhyme turned to Sachs and rolled his eyes.

The cyber detective was probably half deaf.

"Rodney, we have a situation."

"Yep. Go on."

Rhyme explained about the bombs and where they'd been set—near key International Fiber Optic Networks routers and under the company's headquarters.

"Man, that's tough, Lincoln."

"I have no idea what the detonator timing situation is. It's possible we can't render-safe before one or maybe all of them go off."

"Are you evacuating?"

"Under way right now. They're gunpowder bombs,

not plastic explosives—that we know—so we don't think there's a risk of major casualties. But the infrastructure damage could be significant."

"Oh."

The detective didn't sound concerned. Was he checking his iPod for a new song list?

"How can I help?" he finally asked, as if his sole purpose was to fill the growing silence.

"Whom should we call, what precautions should we take?"

"For what?" the computer cop asked.

Jesus Christ. What was the disconnect? "Rodney. If. The. Bombs. Go. *Off*. The Internet—what precautions should we take?"

More silence. "You're asking if bombs take out a couple of the fiber-optic routers."

A sigh from Rhyme. "Yes, Rodney. That's what I'm asking. And the IFON headquarters."

"There's nothing to do."

"But what about security services, hospitals, Wall Street, air traffic control, alarms? It's the Internet, for God's sake. Some cable company's hired industrial saboteurs to blow it up."

"Oh, I get it." He sounded amused. "You're thinking like some Bruce Willis movie thing? The stock markets crash, somebody sticks up a bank because the alarms are off, kidnaps the mayor, since the web's out?"

"Well, along those lines, yes."

"Look, the cable syndicate versus the fiber-optic outfit? That's way old news. Used chewing gum."

I don't need two fucking clichés in a row. Get to the point. Rhyme fumed, but silently.

"They don't like each other, IFON and the traditional cable providers. But nobody's going to sabotage anything. In fact, in six months International Fiber Optic will've bought out or signed licensing agreements with the other cable companies."

"You don't think they'd try to blow up IFON routers?"

"Naw. Even if they did, or *anybody* did, you'd have a five-, ten-minute interruption in service in isolated parts of the city. Believe me, Chinese and Bulgarian hackers cause more problems than that every day."

Sachs asked, "You're sure that's all that would happen?"

"Hey, hi, Amelia. Okay, maybe twenty minutes. ISPs've thought of this before, you know. There's so much redundancy in the system, we call it dedundant."

Rhyme was irritated both at the bad joke and that his theory was in the toilet.

"At the very worst, signals'd be rerouted to backup servers in Jersey, Queens and Connecticut. Oh, traffic'd be slower. You couldn't stream porn or play *World of Warcraft* without the signals' breaking up but basic services'd keep running. I'll call the providers and Homeland Security, though, and give them a heads-up."

"Thanks, Rodney," Sachs said.

The music rose in volume and the line went to blessed silence.

Rhyme parked in front of the evidence boards and photos. He had another thought, discouraging. He snapped, "Sloppy thinking—speculating that Samantha Levine, from IFON, was the target. How would the unsub know she'd go to the bathroom at just that time, and be waiting for her? Careless. Stupid."

The idea of the syndicate of traditional cable Internet providers taking down the fiber-optic interloper had seemed good—sheep ranchers versus cattle barons. Like most conspiracy theories, it was sexy but ultimately junk.

His eyes strayed to the tattoos.

the second

forty

17th

the six hundredth

Rhyme read them out loud.

Pulaski, next to him, leaned forward. "And those wavy lines."

"Scallops," Rhyme corrected.

"I don't know what a scallop is except a seafood thing that tastes pretty bland unless you put sauce on it."

"The shell that *seafood thing* comes in is shaped like that," Rhyme murmured.

"Oh. To me they just looked like waves."

Rhyme frowned. Then he whispered, "And waves that TT Gordon said were significant—because of the scarification." After a moment: "I was wrong. It's not a location he's giving us. Goddamn!" Rhyme spat out. Then he blinked and laughed.

"What?" Sachs asked.

"I just made a very bad joke. When I said, 'Goddamn.' "

"How do you mean, Lincoln?" Cooper wondered aloud.

He ignored the question, calling, "Bible! I need a Bible."

"Well, we don't have one here, Lincoln," Thom said.

"Online. Find me a Bible online. You're on to something, Rookie."

"I am?"

CHAPTER 59

Leaning against the wall, his arms crossed, Billy watched his aunt Harriet—his mother's sister—add soap to the washer.

She asked, "Did you see anybody in the lobby? I was worried the police were watching me. I felt something."

"No. I checked. Carefully. I've been up there for an hour."

"I didn't see you."

"I was watching," Billy said. "Not being watched."

She lowered the lid and he glanced at her breasts, her legs, her neck. Memories...

He always wondered if his uncle knew about their time in the Oleander Room.

In one way it seemed impossible that Uncle Matthew had been oblivious to their affair, or whatever you wanted to call it. How could he miss that the two would disappear for several hours in the afternoon on the days when she wasn't homeschooling neighborhood children?

And there had to be shared smells, smells of each other's bodies and of perfume and deodorant.

The smell of the blood too, even though they would shower meticulously after every afternoon liaison.

All the blood…

The American Families First Council had a religious component. The tenets didn't allow members to use birth control any more than they sanctioned abortion and so Harriet "invited" Billy to the studio above the garage only at that time of month when they could be absolutely certain there'd be no pregnancy. Billy could control his repulsion, and, for some reason, the sight of the crimson smears inflamed Harriet all the more. Oleander and blood were forever joined in Billy Haven's mind.

Uncle Matthew might not even have known about that aspect of women's bodies. Wouldn't surprise Billy.

Then too, when it came to what she wanted, Harriet Stanton could look you in the eye and make you believe just about anything. Billy didn't doubt that whatever story she spun for her husband he bought pretty much as-is.

"This will be your art studio," she'd told thirteen-year-old Billy, showing him for the first time the room she'd decorated above the detached garage of their compound in Southern Illinois. On the wall was a watercolor he'd done for her of an oleander—her favorite flower (a poisonous one, of course). "That's my favorite picture of yours. We'll call this the Oleander Room. *Our* Oleander Room."

And she'd tugged at his belt. Playfully but with unyielding determination.

"Wait, no, Aunt Harriet. What're you doing?" He'd looked up at her with horror; not only was there a strong resemblance to his mother, Harriet's sister, but Harriet and Matthew were his de facto foster parents. Billy's mother and father had died violently, if heroically. Orphaned, the boy had been taken in by the Stantons.

"Uhm, I don't think I want to, you know, do that," the boy had said.

But it was as if he hadn't even spoken.

The belt had come off.

And so the bloody years of the Oleander Room began.

On the trip here to New York, there'd been one liaison between the two of them: the day of Billy's escape from the hospital—where he'd gone not to mod another victim but simply to visit his aunt, ailing uncle and cousin Josh. Billy had hardly been in the mood to satisfy her. (Which is what sex with Aunt Harriet was all about.) But she'd insisted he come to the hotel—Matthew was still in the hospital and she'd sent Joshua out to run some errands. Josh always did what Mommy asked.

Now, with the washer chugging rhythmically, Billy asked, "How is he? Josh said he looks pretty good. Just a little pale."

"Damn it," Harriet said bitterly. "Matthew's going to be fine. He couldn't be courteous and just die."

"Would have been convenient," the young man agreed. "But it'll be better the way you planned it originally."

"I suppose."

Better in this sense: After they had completed the Modification here in New York, they'd return to their home in Southern Illinois, murder Matthew and blame it on some hapless black or Latino plucked at random from a soup kitchen in Alton or East St. Louis. Matthew would be a martyr and Billy would take over the American Families First Council, building it into the finest militia in the country.

Billy would be king and Harriet queen. Or queen mother. Well, both really.

The AFFC was one of dozens of militias around the country all joined in a loose alliance. The names were different but the views virtually identical: state or municipal or—best of all—clan rights over federal, ending the liberal media's lock on propaganda, complete cessation of aid to or intervention in foreign countries, a ban on homosexuality (not just gay marriage), outlawing mixed marriage and supporting separate (and not necessarily equal) doctrines for the races, kicking all immigrants out of the country, a Christ-inspired government, homeschooling. Limitations on non-Christian religious practices.

Many, many Americans held these views or some of them but the problem such militias faced in expanding membership wasn't their views, but that they were run by people like Matthew Stanton—aging, unimaginative men with no appeal whatsoever except to aging unimaginative men.

There was no doubt that Uncle Matthew Stanton had been effective in his day. He was a charismatic lecturer and teacher. He believed to his core in the teachings of Christ and of the founding fathers—the devout Christian ones, at least. But he'd never had a win like the Oklahoma City bombing. And his proactive approach to fighting for the cause was the mundane killing or maiming of an abortion doctor occasionally, firebombing a clinic or IRS office, beating up migrant workers or Muslims or gays.

Harriet Stanton, though, far more ambitious than her husband, knew that the militia would die out within the next decade unless they brought new blood, new approaches to spreading their political message and appealing to a younger, hipper audience. The Modification had been her idea—though spoon-fed slowly to Matthew to make him believe that he'd thought of it.

As Harriet and Billy had lain on the settee in the Oleander Room several months ago, she'd explained her vision to her nephew. "We need somebody in charge who can appeal to the new generation. Excitement. Enthusiasm. Creative thinking. Social media. You'll bring the young people in. When *you* talk about the Rule, they'll listen. The boys will idolize you. The girls'll have crushes. You can get them to do *anything*. You'll be the Harry Potter of the cause.

"After Matthew's dead your stock'll be through the roof. We can bring hundreds, thousands of young people into the fold. We'll take over Midwest Patriot Frontier." This was a legendary militia not far from the AFFC hometown, headed by two visionary leaders. "And we'll keep going, spread around the country."

Harriet believed there were vast swaths of the American people who hated the direction the country was going and would join the AFFC. But they needed to know what dangers were out there—terrorists, Islamists, minorities, socialists. And they needed a charismatic young leader to protect them from those threats.

Harriet and Billy would save them all.

There was another reason for the coup. Harriet had limited power in the AFFC as it existed now—since she was, of course, merely a woman, the wife of the founder of the council. Billy and the new generation believed that discrimination against women deflected from the important issues—of racial segregation and nationalism. As long as Matthew or his kind—the hunting and cigar-smoking sort—were in charge, Harriet would be marginalized. That was simply not acceptable. Billy would empower her.

Now, in the laundry room, he felt her gaze and finally looked back. This locking of eyes was as he'd remembered it for years. When he was atop her, every time he would press his face into the pillow but she would grip his hair and draw him back until they were pupil-to-pupil.

She asked, "Now, what are the police leads like?"

"We're okay," Billy said. "The cops're good. Better than predicted but they bought your description—the Russian or Slav, thirty, round head, light blue eyes. The opposite of me."

When Amelia Sachs had "rescued" Harriet in the hospital, the woman had come up with a false description for the Identi-Kit artist, to lead the police away from her nephew, who'd come to the hospital not to ink another victim to death but merely to visit Matthew.

Billy asked about his cousin, was he handling everything all right?

"Josh is Josh," Harriet said distractedly. Which pretty much described the mother-son relationship in a nutshell. Then she was laughing like a schoolgirl. "We're having quite a trip to New York, aren't we? Didn't turn out the way we'd planned but I do think it's for the best. After the heart attack, Matthew'll be seen as weak. Easier for him to...go away when we get back home. God works in mysterious ways, doesn't He?"

His aunt stepped forward, gripping his arm, and with her other hand brushed fingers across his smooth cheek.

A light flashed on the washer and it moved to a different portion of the cycle. Harriet looked at the machine with a critical eye. Billy recalled that at home she let clothing dry naturally on lines. He pictured them now, slumped body parts, swaying in the breeze. Sometimes she would bring lengths of clothesline to the Oleander Room.

He now saw that Harriet's hands were at her hair and the pins were coming out. She was smiling at him again. Smiling a certain way.

Now? Was she serious?

But why did he even bother to wonder? Aunt Harriet never kidded. She walked to the laundry room door and closed it.

The hypnotic rhythm of water sloshing was the only sound in the room.

Harriet locked the laundry room door. Then snapped out the overhead light.

CHAPTER 60

Bomb Squads are rolling," Pulaski called.

"Good. So, did you find it, Mel?"

Cooper had a Bible pulled up on the main monitor. He was reading. "Just like you said, Lincoln. In the book of Genesis."

"Read it."

" 'In the six hundredth year of Noah's life, in the second month, on the seventeenth day of the month, on the same day were all the fountains of the great deep broken up, and the windows of heaven were opened. And the rain was upon the earth forty days and forty nights.' " Cooper looked up. "We've got 'the six hundredth,' 'the second,' 'seventeenth' and 'forty.' They're all there."

"The other book! I need the other book!"

"*Serial Cities*?" Cooper asked.

"What else, Mel? I'm hardly in the mood for Proust, *Anna Karenina* or *Fifteen Shades of Grey*."

"It's *Fifty*," Pulaski said and received a withering glance in exchange. "I'm just saying. It's not like I read it or anything."

Amelia Sachs found the true crime book and flipped the slim volume open. "What should I look up, Rhyme?"

Rhyme said, "The footnote. I'm interested in the footnote about our investigation of Charlotte, Pam's mother, and her right-wing militia cell."

The bombing in New York that Charlotte had planned out.

Sachs read the lengthy passage. It detailed how Rhyme, the NYPD and the FBI had investigated the case.

Rhyme blurted, "Okay, our unsub maybe does have some affection, if you will, for the Bone Collector. But that's not why Eleven-Five was looking for the book—he wanted to see our techniques in tracking down domestic *terror cells.* Not psychotics. That was an assumption I made," Rhyme said, spitting out the noun as if it were an obscenity.

"A cell hired him to do this?" Pulaski asked.

"Maybe. Or maybe he's part of the group himself. And the target?" Rhyme gestured at the pictures of the underground crime scenes: "See the pipes. The ones stamped with *DEP*. Environmental Protection. Water pipes."

Sachs said, "Waves, the biblical flood. Of course. They want to blow the city's water mains."

"Exactly. The crime scenes are in places where the flooding would cause the most damage if the pipes blew."

Rhyme turned to Pulaski. "Thanks, Rookie."

"You're welcome. I'm still not sure what I did."

"You thought those scars around the numbers were

waves, not scallops. And they were. Waves! That put me in mind of the flood and Noah. Now we've got an apocalyptic theme going. This changes everything." Rhyme scanned the evidence chart. His thoughts fell hard, clattering like the sleet outside. "Good, good. Moving along."

Mel Cooper asked, "How would the unsub know where the vulnerable spots would be, though? The water grid charts're classified."

It was then that Rhyme's mind made one of its unaccountable leaps. They didn't happen often; most deductions are inevitable if you have enough facts. But occasionally, rarely, an insight gelled from the most gossamer of connections.

"The bit of beard—the one you found here, by the shelf when Eleven-Five ruined my favorite single-malt."

Eyes bright, Sachs said, "We thought it was cross-contamination. But it wasn't. The beard came from Unsub Eleven-Five himself when he broke in here. Because *he* was the one who killed the worker last week."

"To get the keys to his office," Rhyme said.

"Why? Where did he work?" From Ron Pulaski.

"Public works, specifically, Environmental Protection," Rhyme muttered. "Which runs the water supply system. The unsub broke in and stole the water grid charts to know where to plant the IEDs. Ah, and the blueprint fiber that the perp left at the scene in Pam's apartment, when he attacked Seth? That was from the plans."

Rhyme looked again at the map of the city. He pointed to massive Water Tunnel 3, the biggest public works project in the history of the city. It was one of the most massive sources of water in the world. The tunnel itself was too far underground to be vulnerable. But there were huge distribution lines running from it throughout the city. If they were to blow, billions of gallons of water would gush through Midtown and lower Manhattan. The results would be far worse than any hurricane could produce.

"Call Major Cases," Rhyme ordered. "And Environmental Protection and the mayor. I want the water supply shut down now."

CHAPTER 61

How are you feeling, Uncle Matthew?"

"All right," the man muttered. "In the hospital you could count on one hand the number of people who spoke English. Lord have mercy."

That, Billy was sure, wasn't accurate. And was typical of exactly the attitude that the AFFC had to guard against. The issue wasn't that the hospital workers didn't speak English; of course they did. It was that they spoke it with thick accents, and not very well. And that, like the color of their skin, was proof that they came from cultures and nations that didn't represent proper values. And that they hadn't bothered to assimilate.

"Well, you're back and looking good." He sized up the older man—190 pounds, slightly damaged cardiac system, but healthy otherwise. Yep, it seemed he'd live forever…or until Billy put a bullet in his uncle's head and then propped the gun in the hand of some hapless day laborer, whom Billy and a half dozen others had already clubbed to death in "self-defense."

"He's doing just fine," Harriet said, her voice light as

mist as she stowed freshly washed and folded laundry. "Back to normal."

"Hey, bro." Joshua Stanton joined them from the bedroom in the small suite. When Joshua heard voices from nearby he tended to appear quickly, as if he couldn't stand the thought that a conversation was occurring without his presence. He may also have worried that people were saying things about him, though really there was very little to say about Joshua, except that the thirty-two-year-old was a competent plumber's assistant whose main talent was killing birds and deer and abortion doctors.

Still the solidly built man, strawberry blond, was dependable to the point of irritation, doggedly doing what he'd been told and reporting regularly in great depth about his progress. Billy wasn't quite sure how he'd found a wife and managed to father four children.

Well, dogs and salamanders were capable of the same. Though then he had trouble dislodging the image of Josh as a lizard.

Joshua hugged his cousin, which Billy would have preferred he not do. Not germs; that transfer-of-evidence matter.

I try, M. Locard.

No, Joshua wasn't the brightest bulb. But he'd been key in the Modification. After Billy had killed the victims, and the bodies had been discovered, Joshua, dressed in medical coveralls and face mask, had quickly appeared, carting into the tunnels the lights and batteries containing the bombs, set them up and vanished. Nobody thought twice about him. An emergency worker.

The young man now prattled on about his success in

the masquerade, smuggling the devices into the crime scenes. He kept looking Billy's way for approval, which his younger cousin gave in the form of a nod.

Harriet glanced at her son with a dip of eyelid, which Billy knew meant Quiet. But Joshua missed it. And kept talking.

"It was pretty close at the Belvedere. I mean really. There were cops everywhere! I had to go through a different manhole than was in the plan. It added another six minutes but I don't think it was a problem."

The look from Aunt Harriet again.

Matthew didn't need the patience that women in the AFFC were required to display. He snapped, "Shut up, son."

"Yessir."

Billy was troubled by his uncle's and aunt's treatment of his cousin. Matthew was just plain mean and it was pathetic how Josh simply took it. As for Harriet, she largely ignored him. Billy sometimes wondered if she ever took her own son to the Oleander Room. He'd concluded no. Not because that would be too perverse. Rather because Josh probably didn't have the stamina to meet his mother's needs; even Billy could manage only three times an afternoon and Harriet occasionally seemed disappointed by that low sum.

Billy liked Joshua. He had fond memories of the years spent with him, his de facto brother. They'd tossed footballs and played catch because they thought they ought to. They'd flirted with girls for the same reason. They'd tinkered with cars. Finally in a moment of adolescent candor they admitted they didn't really like sports or cars and were lukewarm about dating. And took up more enjoyable activities—stalking faggots and beating the crap out of them. Illegals, too. Or legals (they still weren't white). Graffiti'ing crosses on synagogues and swastikas on black churches. They'd burned an abortion clinic to the ground.

Billy's watch hummed. "It's time." A few seconds later, another vibration.

Uncle Matthew looked at the backpack and gear bag. He announced, "We'll pray."

The family got down on their knees, even unsteady Matthew, and Harriet and Joshua took positions on either side of Billy. They all held hands. Harriet was gripping Billy's. She squeezed his once. Hard.

Matthew's voice—a bit weak but still powerful enough to split open sinners' hearts—intoned, "Lord, we thank You for giving us the wisdom and the courage to do what we are about to do, in Your name. We thank You for the vision You put into our souls and for the plans You've delivered into our hands. Amen."

"Amen" echoed through the room.

CHAPTER 62

Rhyme wheeled back and forth before the white-boards in his parlor.

He glanced at the water main grid chart, which the DEP had just sent them via secure server, then back to the evidence. Water Tunnel 3 and all the branches were clearly diagrammed.

Ron Pulaski called, "We've got our Bomb Squad at the boutique and the restaurant. The army has their people at the third site—the Belvedere."

"Are they making a big scene?" Rhyme asked, half-attentive. "Are all the lights and sirens going?"

"I—"

Rhyme cut him off. "Is there any evacuation from downtown? I wanted the mayor to order an evacuation."

"I don't know."

"Well, put on the news and find out. Thom! Where the hell—?"

"I'm here, Lincoln."

"The news. I need the news on! I asked you."

"You didn't ask. You *thought* you asked." The aide lifted a chastising eyebrow.

"Maybe I didn't ask," Rhyme grumbled. The best "sorry" the man was going to get. "But turn the fucking thing on now."

In the corner the Samsung clicked to life.

Rhyme stabbed a finger at the screen. "Breaking News, News Alert, This Just In, We Interrupt This Program. Why aren't I seeing *those*?...I'm looking at a fucking commercial for car insurance!"

"Don't use your arm for useless gestures." Thom changed the channel.

"...press conference ten minutes ago the mayor told citizens of Manhattan and Queens that an evacuation would not be necessary at this time. He urged people—"

"No evacuation?" Rhyme sighed. "He could at least have cleared Queens. They can go east. Plenty of room on Long Island. Orderly evacuation. He could've arranged for that."

Mel Cooper said, "It wouldn't be orderly, Lincoln. It'd be chaos."

"I recommended announcing an evacuation. He ignored me."

"DEP's calling," Pulaski said, nodding at the caller ID box on the main monitor over a worktable.

Rhyme's mobile rang too. The area code was 404. Atlanta, Georgia.

"It's about goddamn time," he muttered. "You take the water people, Rookie, and coordinate with Sachs. I'll talk to our friends in Dixie. Let's move, everyone! We've only got minutes!"

And he hit the answer button on his keypad hard, drawing another admonishing look from Thom.

CHAPTER 63

In his Department of Environmental Protection coveralls and hard hat, Billy Haven stepped into a cross street in Midtown, the East Side, and lifted a manhole cover with a hook, then descended partway and muscled the disk back in place.

He climbed down to a metal floor and began walking through the tunnel, under the shadow of a water main pipe glistening with condensation. This huge conduit ran from Water Tunnel 3's main valve room, in central Midtown, to the three submains that supplied water throughout Manhattan and to parts of Queens. Approximately eighteen thousand households and businesses received water that passed through this pipe.

He switched the heavy gear bag from one hand to the other as he walked. It weighed forty-eight pounds. The contents were what he'd removed from the workshop on Canal Street: the drill, portable welding kit, electric cord and other tools, along with the bulky steel thermos. He didn't have his American Eagle with him now. That part of the Modification was over with. No more inking with poison.

Though the Rule of Skin was still very much at work, of course.

He checked his GPS, made an adjustment and kept walking.

The plan for the Modification was complex, as befit a scheme delivered through an intermediary whom God Himself had picked.

The Commandments...

At the last scene, at TT Gordon's tattoo parlor, the police would have found trace of explosives he'd intentionally planted and Lincoln Rhyme would immediately wonder about this anomaly. Explosives and poison? What was the relationship?

The Commandments speculated that Rhyme would then think: What if the poisoned tattoos were about something other than random killings by a psychotic?

They'd analyze the numbers in the tattoos and would come up with the flood in Genesis. He'd intentionally inked the tattoo artist in the Village with "the six hundredth" last, because it would have been too easy to find the flood passages in the Bible if he'd given them in proper order.

> In the *six hundredth* year of Noah's life, in *the second* month, on the *seventeenth* day of the month, the same day were all the fountains of the great deep broken up, and the windows of heaven were opened. And the rain was upon the earth *forty* days and forty nights...

So domestic terrorists had returned to plant bombs to re-create the flood and wash away the sin of this Sodom.

Rhyme and Sachs would brainstorm about where the bombs might be and realize that, yes, of course, they were in the batteries for the crime scene lights. Since they might go off at any time and it would take awhile for the Bomb Squad to break through the sealed cases and render-safe, or extract the IEDs, the Department of Environmental Protection would take the drastic but necessary step of shutting the massive gates of Water Tunnel 3's Midtown valve, squelching the supply of water flowing to the pipe Billy was now walking beside.

As soon as that happened the pressure in the pipe would drop to nearly nothing.

Which would allow him to drill a one-thirty-second-inch hole through the iron—a feat impossible when the line was active because the pressure would force the water out of the hole at the speed and with the cutting force of an industrial laser.

With the pressure off he could then inject into the water supply pipe what he'd brought with him here, in the metal thermos. The last poison of the Modification.

Botulinum, a neurotoxin produced by the bacterium *Clostridium botulinum*, is the most poisonous substance on earth. A half teaspoon could easily kill the entire population of the United States.

While it is generally very difficult to come by the more toxic substances in the world—say, radioactive poisons such as polonium and plutonium—botulinum is surprisingly available.

And we have vanity to thank for that.

The bacteria are the basis for Botox, a muscle relaxant to relieve spasticity. It's mostly known, though, for cosmetic treatments to smooth skin (its toxic qualities inhibit a neurotransmitter that creates wrinkles).

The stockpiles of the spores are carefully guarded but

Billy had located a source and broken into a cosmetic surgical supply company in the Midwest. In addition to a good selection of drugs and medical gear, he'd managed to steal enough spores to create a botulinum factory, which had been silently—and airlessly—producing a stockpile of the bacteria and the toxin and more spores.

The idea of weaponizing such a delightfully deadly substance was hardly original, of course. But no one had ever done so before—for a very simple reason. Delivery was nearly impossible. The toxin must be ingested or inhaled or enter the body through mucous membranes or open wounds. Contact with skin alone is not enough. Since it is very difficult to deliver a large amount of aerosol toxin, that meant an attack would have to be via food or water.

But salt, heat, alkaline substances and oxygen can kill the bacteria. So will chlorine, which is added to New York City's water supply, along with the anti-tooth-cavity additive fluoride, orthophosphate to counterbalance lead contamination and hydroxide to increase the alkalinity of the supply.

Billy, however, had learned to grow a concentrated form of botulinum that was resistant to chlorine. Yes, some of the toxin he injected into the water supply would be destroyed, or its deadly effects dimmed, but the estimate was that enough would survive and be carried to households throughout Midtown and lower Manhattan and much of Queens. The death toll would probably be four thousand or so; the sick and severely injured would be many times that.

One group would be particularly hard hit: children. Infant botulism poisoning occurred with some frequency (often children younger than twelve months who'd eaten honey in which spores naturally resided). Billy had considered their deaths and he didn't feel troubled by them. This was a war, after all. Sacrifices had to be made.

The city would react quickly, of course, with the Health Department and Homeland Security racing to find the source of the illness. There'd be some delay as officials thought chemical nerve agents—the symptoms are similar—and with some luck medical workers would start injecting atropine and pralidoxime, which actually increase botulism's lethal strength. Some would diagnose myasthenia gravis. But then would come the serum and stool tests and finally mass spectrometry would confirm what the disease truly was.

By then, of course, the damage would be done.

A secondary consequence, which would cause even more extensive, if less lethal, damage, was also predicted by the Modification: The city would soon find the source of the toxin but wouldn't know how far-flung the poisoning was. Was the Bronx in danger next? New Jersey or Connecticut?

The only thing the authorities could do—the utterly incompetent city, state and federal governments—was shut down the entire water system. New York City, not a drop to drink, not a drop to carry away sewage. Or clean. Or generate electricity (most of the city's power came from electric generator plants whose turbines used steam). The East River and the Hudson would become a Ganges, a source of bathing, waste and drinking water...and disease.

A plague, not a flood, would destroy the city.

But the plan's success depended on the one remaining key factor: closing the Midtown valve to allow Billy to inject the poison. If that didn't happen, the Modification would fail. The upstream reservoirs and aqueducts—easily accessible—were monitored in real time for any kind of toxins; the plan required that the poison had to be introduced into the supply here, south of Central Park, where it was theoretically impossible to taint the system and was therefore not guarded.

Billy now checked his location. Yes. He was close to the best spot to drill into the pipe.

But he needed confirmation that the water supply had been shut down.

Come on, he thought, come on...

Impatient.

Timing was everything.

Finally his phone hummed with a message. He looked down. Aunt Harriet. She'd sent him a link. He tapped the screen and turned the phone sideways to read the article. The story was time-stamped one minute ago.

TERROR ALERT IN NEW YORK
Water Supply Targeted
By Unknown Bombers

Officials in New York City are shutting down the largest mains supplying water to Manhattan south of Central Park and much of Queens, to prevent the risk of flooding, in response to an apparent terrorist plot.

Spokespersons for the New York City Police

Department, the Department of Homeland Security and the FBI reported in a joint press conference that they have uncovered a plot to detonate improvised explosive devices underground, meant to destroy portions of the water system.

Bomb Squad officers have discovered the locations of three devices and are evacuating people in the immediate vicinity around the IEDs. They are about to begin dismantling the bombs, a process called "rendering-safe."

It is anticipated that the water supply will be shut off for no more than two hours. Officials are telling residents that there's no need to stockpile water.

Good. Time to finish up and say goodbye to New York City.

CHAPTER 64

Amelia Sachs was pounding her Ford Torino toward Midtown.

She'd blown seven red lights after leaving Rhyme's. Only one slowed her down. The angry horn blasts and stabbing fingers were not even memories.

Times Square was around her, the huge planes of high-def video billboards, the preoccupied locals and the marveling tourists, the timely Thanksgiving decorations and the premature Christmas ones, the bundled-up vendors, rocking from foot to foot to jump-start the circulation.

Bustling innocence.

She sped east to Lexington Avenue, then skidded to a stop as blue smoke from the tires wafted around her. It was here that she'd been instructed to pause and await further instructions.

Her phone rang and a moment later Pulaski's voice was pumping through her earbud. "Amelia. I've got DEP on the other line. They're checking...Hold on. The tech's back." She heard some mumbling as he turned away from the speaker to a second phone. Then his voice rose. "The hell does that mean, 'The sensors aren't that accurate'? What does that even *mean*? And anyway it's not my problem about the sensors. I want the location. Now!"

She laughed. Young Ron Pulaski had come into his own under Rhyme's tutelage. A moment later he was back with her. "I don't know what the problem is, Amelia. They're— Wait. I'm getting something now." The voice faded again. "Okay, okay."

Looking around the streets. Innocence, she thought again. Businesspeople, shoppers, tourists, kids, musicians, hawkers, hustlers, street people—the astonishing, unique mix of humanity that is New York City.

And under their feet, somewhere, one of the worst terror attacks in New York City history was being carried out.

But where?

"Okay, Amelia, DEP has something for us. They've cross-referenced flow rates—I don't know. Anyway, I have a location. An access room a quarter mile south of the Tunnel Three valve station. It's at Forty-Four and Third. There's a manhole about fifty feet to the east of the intersection."

"I'm close."

She was already popping the clutch and skidding away from the parking space in the same way she'd arrived, though this time leaving the blue smoke behind her. She cut off a bus and a Lexus. They might have collided, avoiding her. She kept right on moving, headed south. Insurance issue, not her issue.

"I'll be there in one minute." Then corrected: "Okay,

two." Because she was forced up onto the sidewalk again and braked to nudge a falafel cart out of the way.

"Fuck you, lady."

Unnecessary, she thought, since he'd escaped light; she might've knocked the cart on its ass. Had considered it.

Back on the street with a grind of metal versus curb. Then she was speeding on once again.

After Lincoln Rhyme had concluded that the unsub and his domestic terror group were planning on blowing up the water mains, he'd grown thoughtful. Then dissatisfaction bloomed in his face.

"What?" Sachs had asked, noting his eyes straying out the window, his brow furrowed.

"Something doesn't feel right about this whole thing." He zoned in on her. "Yes, yes, I detest the word 'feel.' Don't look so shocked. The conclusion's based on evidence, on facts."

"Go on."

He'd considered further, in silence, and then said, "The battery-bombs are packed with gunpowder. You know guns, Sachs, you know ammunition. You think that'd blow up iron pipes the size of the water mains?"

She'd thought about this. "True. If they'd really wanted to rupture the pipes they'd use shaped charges. Armor piercing. Of course they would."

"Exactly. He *wanted* us to find the bombs. And—with the Bible verses—wanted us to believe the target was the water mains. Why?"

They'd answered nearly simultaneously. "To shut down the supply."

Shutting off the water flow by closing the main valves would be only temporarily disruptive.

"Who cares? That couldn't be the motive," Rhyme had said.

Then he'd offered: But what *would* make sense was to trick the city into shutting off the supply to lower the pressure. Which would allow their unsub to drill into the pipe and introduce a poison into the line. He'd then plug the hole; Rhyme had reminded the team about the welding material evidence found at the Chloe Moore crime scene.

And the poison, Rhyme had concluded, would be botulinum—since they'd found traces of the material from cosmetic surgical supply houses and the Botox syringes. Rhyme had thought the plastic surgery evidence meant their unsub was planning on changing his appearance. But it was possible too that the purpose of the break-in was to steal botulinum, whose spores were maintained by medical operations specializing in plastic surgery products and supplies. He'd decided botulinum had to be the poison; no other toxin was powerful enough to cause widespread devastation.

Rhyme had called his FBI contact, Fred Dellray, and City Hall and explained what he suspected. The mayor and police chief had in turn ordered the DEP to announce that it was shutting down the water supply for a few hours. In fact, they kept the system fully operational—which because of the pressure would prevent anything from being introduced into the pipes. The DEP would use the grid sensors to pinpoint any leaks, telling the NYPD exactly where the unsub had cut into the line.

As she sat impatiently behind the wheel of her car,

the engine growling, Sachs's phone rang once more. It was Rhyme. "Where are you, Sachs?"

"Almost at the spot DEP gave us."

"Listen to me."

"What else would I be doing?" she muttered. And concentrated on avoiding an idiot of a bicyclist.

Rhyme continued, "I've just been on the phone with the Centers for Disease Control in Atlanta. We conferenced—forgive the verb—with Homeland Security and the bio-chem weapons people at Fort Detrick. It's worse than I thought. Don't go into the access room. We're getting a tactical hazmat team together."

"I'm *here*, Rhyme. Now. I can't just sit around and wait. The unsub's right underneath me."

She pulled the muscle car up on the sidewalk, scooting pedestrians out of the way. They complied; she looked far too fierce to argue.

Rhyme continued, "I just realized that this isn't ordinary botulinum."

"Now, that's a phrase you don't hear every day, Rhyme."

"It's been modified to be chlorine-resistant. That's why we found the undiluted hypochlorous acid—what he was using to alter the strain. We have no idea how potent it is."

"I'll be wearing face mask and coveralls." She ran to the back of her car, popped the trunk and yanked out her crime scene kit.

"You need full biohazard gear," he protested.

She hit speaker, set the phone down and called, "The unsub knows we haven't cut the supply yet—the water'll still be spurting out of the hole he drilled. He's waiting for the valves to close but he's not going to wait very long. He'll rabbit, with who knows how much of that shit."

"Sachs, listen. This isn't arsenic or snakeroot. You don't have to drink it or eat it. One ten-thousandth of a gram in a mucous membrane or wound'll kill you."

"Then I won't pick my nose or scrape my knee. I'm going in, Rhyme. I'll call when I've cleared the scene and got him in metal."

"Sachs—"

"For this one I need to go in quiet," she said firmly and clicked disconnect.

CHAPTER 65

Amelia Sachs easily found where the unsub had gone underground: the manhole on 44th Street, near Third, which Pulaski had told her about.

She dug the tire iron out of the trunk of her Torino and used it to muscle the heavy metal disk up and then managed to push the cover to the side. She aimed her Glock into the pitch-black hole. She peered down, hearing a powerful hissing noise—the leaking pipe, she assumed. She holstered her weapon.

Well, let's get to it. Go and go fast.

When you move, they can't getcha...

Thanks to the recent medical procedures, she now felt lithe as a thirteen-year-old as she turned and began down the ladder.

Thinking: I'm in bright white coveralls, lit from above and behind.

A perfect shooting solution for him.

One way to put it. The other was: sitting duck.

Climbing into hell. Practically sliding down the rails

as she'd seen sailors do on some TV submarine movie, going from deck to deck.

She hit the floor of the spacious tunnel—open and without any cover whatsoever. Natch. Drawing her gun fast, she lunged to the side, where at least it was darker and their unsub would have a harder time placing a lethal shot. There she crouched and spun the muzzle 180 degrees, squinting to spot threats.

That she hadn't pulled any fire didn't allay her concern; he might still be near, aiming her way and waiting for any other officers to enter the target zone before he began squeezing off rounds.

But as her eyes grew accustomed to the dark, she noted that this portion of the tunnel was unoccupied.

Heart tapping, breath loud through the mask, Sachs peered in the direction of the hiss, which was now a piercing sound. She moved up to the wall on the other side of which was the access chamber where he'd drilled the hole in the pipe. She glanced in fast, low, in case he was aiming head or chest toward the doorway. All she could see in the one-second look was mist roiling in shifting curtains, pastel colors, like the northern lights. It was backlit by a muted white lamp—maybe one the unsub had set up to illuminate his drilling. The hypnotic swirls, beautiful, would be from the particulates of streaming water flowing from the pipe.

Sachs was reluctant to do a typical one-person dynamic entry, look high, go in low, two pounds' pressure on a three-pound trigger. Shoot, shoot, shoot.

Not here. She knew she had to take him alive. He wasn't operating on his own, not with a plan this elaborate. They needed to collar his co-conspirators, too.

Also, any weapons discharges might mean she'd end up shooting herself; the pipe and the concrete surfaces of the tunnel would easily send the copper-jacketed slugs and fragments zipping in unpredictable directions.

Not to mention what a 9mm parabellum round would do to a vial containing the deadliest toxin on earth.

Closer, closer.

Peering into the wall of mist, looking for shadows moving, shadows in position to fire a weapon. Shadows charging out with a hypodermic syringe loaded with propofol.

For his final skin art session.

But nothing other than the shimmering particles of water vapor, refracting light so beautifully.

Into the chamber, she told herself. Now.

The cloud rolled closer and withdrew, surely from the breeze created by the stream of water. Good cover, she thought. Like a smoke screen. Sachs gripped the Glock and, with her feet in a perpendicular shooting position, not parallel, to minimize his target area, she moved fast into the room.

A mistake, she realized quickly.

The spray was much thicker inside and soaked the filter of the mask. She couldn't breathe. A moment's debate. Without the protection, she'd be susceptible to the botulinum toxin. With it, she'd pass out from lack of air.

No choice. Off came the mask and she flung it behind her, inhaling the damp air, which, she hoped, contained only New York city drinking water and not poison powerful enough to kill her in all of five seconds.

Breathing, breathing...

But so far, no symptoms. Or bullets.

She continued forward, swinging the gun from side to side. To her right she could see the dark form of the massive pipe; the puncture was about fifteen feet in front of her, she guessed; from a vague image of a thin white line—the stream of water—shooting up to the left and hitting the far wall about ten feet off the ground. The hiss grew louder with every step.

The whistle made her ears throb with pain and threatened to deafen; the good news was that it would also deafen him, so he wouldn't sense her approach.

Smells of moist concrete, mold, mud. The sensation took Sachs back to her childhood, father and daughter at the zoo in Manhattan, one of the houses, reptile. "Amie, see that? That's the most dangerous thing here."

She'd peered inside but couldn't see anything other than plants and rocks covered with moss. "I don't see anything, Daddy."

"It's a *leeren Käfig*."

"Wow. What's that?" Snake, she'd wondered. Lizard? "Is it dangerous?"

"Oh, the most dangerous thing in the zoo."

"What is it?"

"It means 'empty cage' in German."

She'd laughed, tossing her tiny red ponytail as she'd looked up at him. But Herman Sachs, a seasoned NYPD patrol officer, wasn't joking. "Remember, Amie. The most dangerous things are the ones you *can't* see."

And now too she saw nothing.

Where was he?

Keep going.

Ducking and, with as deep a breath as she could take yet not choke on the mist in the air, she stepped through the cloud.

And she saw him. Unsub 11-5.

"Jesus, Rhyme," she whispered, stepping closer. "Jesus."

Only after some moments of hearing nothing but the wail and hiss of the water did she remember that the mike and camera were off.

The experts from Fort Detrick had helicoptered into town in all of forty-five minutes.

When the poison in question is sufficient to kill a high percentage of the population of a major U.S. city, the national security folks don't fool around.

Once it was clear that the unsub was not going to be shooting anyone, Sachs was politely but emphatically ordered out of the tunnel while eight men and women in elaborate self-contained biohazard suits went to work. It was clear from the start that they knew what they were doing. Fort Detrick, in Frederick, Maryland, was home to the U.S. Army's Medical Research and Materiel Command and its Medical Research Institute of Infectious Diseases. In effect, if the prefix "bio" and the words "warfare" or "defense" were linked in any project of any kind, Fort Detrick was involved.

Rhyme's voice clattered through the radio. "What, Sachs? What's going on?" She was standing, freezing, on the slushy sidewalk near Third, where she'd parked her Torino.

She told him, "They've secured the botulinum. It was in three syringes in a thermos. They've got them in a negative pressure containment vehicle."

"They're sure none got into the water?"

"Absolutely positive."

"And the unsub?"

A pause. "Well, it's bad."

Rhyme's plan to have the city falsely announce that the water supply was going to be shut down had had one unexpected consequence.

Unsub 11-5, wearing nothing more protective than Department of Environmental Protection coveralls, had been standing right in front of the hole he was drilling. When he'd broken through the main, the stream of water, like a buzz saw, had cut straight through his chest, killing him instantly. As he'd dropped to the floor, the water had continued to slice through his neck and head, cutting them apart.

Blood and bone and tissue were everywhere, some blasted onto the far wall, many feet away. Sachs had known she should get the hell out and let the bio team secure the scene but she'd been compelled, out of curiosity, to perform one last task: to tug the unsub's left sleeve up. She had to see his body art.

The red centipede stared out at her with probing, human eyes. It was brilliantly done. And utterly creepy. She'd actually shivered.

"What's the status of the scene?"

"Army's sealing it—about a two-block radius. I got prints and DNA from our unsub and pocket litter and bags he had with him before I got kicked out."

"Well, bring back what you have. He's not working on his own. And who knows what else they have in mind?"

"I'm on my way."

CHAPTER 66

The TV news was frantic but ambiguous.

A terrorist attack on the water supply in New York, improvised explosive devices...

Harriet and Matthew Stanton sat on the couch in the suite at their hotel. Their son, Joshua, was beside them in a chair, fiddling. One of those bracelets the kids wore nowadays, even boys. Colored rubber. Not normal. Gay. Matthew tried to frown his son to stillness but Joshua kept his eyes on the TV. He sipped water from a bottle; the family had brought gallons with them. For obvious reasons. He asked questions that his parents didn't have the answers to.

"But how could they know? Why isn't Billy calling? Where's the, you know, poison?"

"Shut up."

The simple-minded commentators on the media (the liberal cabal *and* the conservative in this case) were offering nonsense: "*There are several types of bombs and some are calculated to do more damage than others.*" "*A terrorist could have access to a number of types of ex-*

plosives." "The psychology of a bomber is complicated; basically, they have a need to destroy." "As we know from the recent hurricane, water in the subways can cause serious problems."

But that was all they could say because apparently the city wasn't releasing any real information.

More troubling, Matthew was thinking, was what Josh was stewing over. Why *hadn't* they heard from Billy? The last word from him: After they'd reported that the city had shut down the valves, he was going to start drilling. The botulinum was ready to go. He'd have the toxin in the water supply within a half hour.

The talking heads kept droning on about bombs and floods...which would be like some teenager's pimple, when the true attack would be a cancer. Poison to destroy the poisoned city.

The stations kept repeating the canned purée of info over and over again.

But no word of people getting sick. Nobody retching to death. No word yet about panic.

Stealing the thought from her husband, Harriet asked, "He couldn't've gotten the poison on him, could he?"

Of course he could. In which case he'd die an unpleasant if brief death. But he'd be a martyr to the cause of the American Families First Council, strike a blow for the true values of this country and, not incidentally, solidify Matthew Stanton's role in the underground militia movement.

"I'm worried," Harriet whispered.

Joshua looked her way and played with his homosexual bracelet even more. At least he'd fathered children, Matthew reflected. A miracle, that was.

He ignored both wife and son. It seemed inconceivable that the authorities had figured out the plot. The elaborate scheme—crafted and refined over months—had been as detailed as a blueprint for a John Deere tractor. They'd executed it exactly as planned, each step at precisely the right moment. Down to the second.

And thinking of time: Now it passed like a glacier. Whenever a new anchor appeared, a new man in the street began talking into an obscene microphone, Matthew hoped for more information. But he heard the same old story, recycled. No news of thousands of people dying in horrific ways dribbling from the predatory journalists' lips.

"Joshua?" he asked his son. "Call again."

"Yessir." The young man fumbled the phone, dropped it and looked up, apologizing with a fierce blush.

"That's your prepaid?" Matthew asked sternly.

"Yessir."

No testy retorts from Josh, ever. Billy was respectful but he had a backbone. Joshua was a slug. Matthew waved a dismissing hand to the boy, who rose and stepped away from the noise of the TV.

"Water Tunnel Number Three is the largest construction project in the history of the City. It was begun—"

"Father?" Joshua said, nodding at the phone. "Still no answer."

Outside the windows, sirens made up the soundtrack of the bleak afternoon. All three in the room fell silent, as if plunged into icy water.

Then an anchor girl was speaking crisply: "...have an announcement from City Hall about the terrorist plot...Investigators are now reporting that it was not a bombing that the terrorists had planned. Their goal was to introduce poison into the New York City drinking water. This attempt failed, the police commissioner has said, and the water is completely safe. There's a massive effort under way to find and arrest the individuals responsible. We're going to our national security correspondent, Andrew Landers, to learn more about the domestic terrorism movement. Good afternoon, Andrew—"

Matthew shut the TV off. He slipped a nitroglycerin tablet under his tongue. "Okay, that's it. We leave. Now."

"What happened, Father?" Joshua asked.

As if I know.

Harriet was demanding, "What happened to Billy?"

Matthew Stanton waved her quiet. "Your phones. All of them. Batteries out." He popped the back off his while Harriet and Joshua did the same. They threw them into what the Modification Commandments called a burn bag, even though you didn't really burn it. You pitched it into a Dumpster some distance from your hotel. "Now. Go pack. But only the essentials."

Harriet was saying again, "But Billy—?"

"I told you to pack, woman." He wanted to hit her. But there was no time for corrections at this point. Besides, corrections with Harriet didn't always go as planned. "Billy can take care of himself. The story didn't say he was captured. It just said they've uncovered a plot. Now. Move."

Five minutes later Matthew had filled his suitcase and was zipping up his computer bag.

Harriet was wheeling her luggage behind her into the living room. Her face was a grim mask, nearly as unsettling as the latex one Billy had showed them, the one he'd been wearing when he attacked his victims.

"How did it happen?" she asked, fuming.

The answer was the police, the answer was Lincoln Rhyme.

Billy had described him as the man who anticipated everything.

"I want to find out what happened," she raged.

"Later. Let's go," Matthew snapped. Why was it God's will that he ended up with a woman who spoke her mind? Would she never learn? Why had he stopped with the belt? Bad mistake.

Well, they'd escape, they'd regroup, go underground once more. Deep underground. Matthew bellowed, "Joshua, are you packed?"

"Yessir." Matthew's son twitched into the room. His sandy hair was askew and his face was streaked with tears.

Matthew growled, "You. You act like a man. Understand me?"

"Yessir."

Matthew reached into his computer bag, shoved aside the Bible and extracted two pistols, 9mm Smith & Wessons (he wouldn't think of buying a foreign weapon, of course). He handed one to Josh, who seemed to relax when he took hold of it. The boy was comfortable with weapons; they seemed to offer a familiarity that soothed. At least there was that about him. Guns, of course, weren't a woman's way and so Matthew didn't offer one to Harriet.

He said to his son, "Keep it hidden. And don't use it unless I use mine. Look for my cue."

"Yessir."

The weapons were merely a precaution. Lincoln Rhyme had stopped the plan but there was nothing that would lead back to Matthew and Harriet. The Commandments had taken care to insulate them. It was like what Billy had explained: the two zones in a tattoo parlor, hot and cold. They should never meet.

Well, they'd be in their car and out of the city in thirty minutes.

He surveyed the hotel suite. They had not brought much with them—two suitcases each. Billy and Joshua had moved all the heavier equipment and supplies ahead of time.

"Let's go."

"A prayer?" Joshua offered.

"No fucking time," Matthew snapped.

Clutching and wheeling their satchels, the three of them stepped into the corridor.

The good news about using a hotel as a safe house for an operation of this sort was that you didn't have to sweep it down afterward, Billy's Commandments had reported—the hotel politely and conveniently supplied a staff of folks to do that for you, disgusting illegals though they undoubtedly were.

Ironically, though, having had that thought, Matthew noted that the two women on the cleaning staff near the elevators, chatting beside their carts, were of the white race.

God bless them.

With Joshua behind them, the husband and wife

walked down the corridor. "What we'll do is head north," Matthew explained in a whisper. "I've studied the map. We'll avoid the tunnels."

"Roadblocks?"

"What would they be looking for?" Matthew snapped, pushing the elevator button. "They don't know us, don't know anything about us."

Though this turned out not to be the case.

As Matthew stabbed impatiently at the elevator button, which refused to illuminate, the two God Bless Them They're White maids reached into their baskets, pulled out machine guns and pointed them at the family.

One, a pretty blonde, screamed, "Police! Down! Down on the floor! If we don't see your hands at all times, we will fire."

Josh began to cry. Harriet and Matthew exchanged glances.

"On the ground!"

"Now!"

Other officers were moving in from the doors. More guns, more screaming.

My Lord, they were loud.

After a moment, Matthew lay down.

Harriet, though, seemed to be debating.

What the hell is she doing? Matthew wondered. "Lie down, woman!"

The officers were screaming at her to do the same.

She looked at him with cold eyes.

He raged, "I command you to lie down!"

She was going to get shot. Four muzzles were pointed her way, four fingers were curled around triggers.

With a look of disgust, she lowered herself to the carpet, dropping her purse. Matthew lifted an eyebrow when he noted a gun fall out. He wasn't sure what disappointed him the most—that she had been carrying a gun without his permission, or that she'd bought a Glock, an okay weapon, but one that had been made in a foreign country.

CHAPTER 67

Mention the word "terrorism" and many Americans, perhaps most, think of radicalized Islamists targeting the country for its shady self-indulgent values and support of Israel.

Lincoln Rhyme knew, though, that those fringe Muslims were a very small portion of the people who had ideological gripes with the United States and were willing to express those views violently. And most terrorists were white, Christian card-carrying citizens.

The history of domestic terrorism is long. The Haymarket bombing occurred in Chicago in 1886. The *Los Angeles Times* offices were blown up by union radicals in 1910. San Francisco was rocked by the Preparedness Day bombing, protesting proposed involvement in World War One. And a horse-drawn wagon bomb outside J. P. Morgan bank killed dozens and injured hundreds in 1920. As the years went by, the political and social divisiveness that motivated these acts and others continued undiminished. In fact, the terrorist movements grew, thanks to the Internet, where like-minded haters could gather and scheme in relative anonymity.

The technology of destruction improved too, allowing people like the Unabomber to terrorize schools and academics and to evade detection for years, and with relative ease Timothy McVeigh manufactured a fertilizer bomb that destroyed the federal building in Oklahoma City.

Presently, Rhyme knew there were about two dozen active domestic terror groups being monitored by the FBI and local authorities, ranging from the Army of God (anti-abortion), to Aryan Nations (white, nationalist neo-Nazis), to the Phineas Priesthood (anti-gay, anti-interracial-marriage, anti-Semitic and anti-taxation, among others), to small one-off, disorganized cells of strident crazies called by police "garage bands."

Authorities also kept a watchful eye on another category of potential terror: private militias, of which there's at least one in every state of the union, with a total membership of more than fifty thousand.

These groups were more or less independent but were joined by common views: that the federal government is too intrusive and a threat to individual freedom, lower or no taxes, fundamentalist Christianity, an isolationist stance when it comes to foreign policy, distrust of Wall Street and globalization. While not many militias put it in their bylaws, they also embrace certain de facto policies like racism, nationalism, anti-immigration, misogyny and anti-Semitism, anti-abortion and anti-LGBT.

A particular problem with the militias is that, by definition, they're paramilitary groups; they believe fervently in the Second Amendment ("*A well regulated Militia, being necessary to the security of a free State, the right of the people to keep and bear Arms, shall not be infringed*"). Which meant that they were usually armed to the teeth. Admittedly some militias aren't terrorist organizations and claim their weapons are only for hunting and self-defense. Others, such as Matthew Stanton's American Families First Council, obviously felt otherwise.

Why New York City should be a particularly juicy target Rhyme had never figured out (the militias, curiously, pretty much left Washington, DC, alone). Maybe it was the other trappings of the Big Apple that appealed: gays, a large non-Anglo population, home of the liberal media, the headquarters of so many multinational companies. And maybe they felt the Rockettes and *Annie* were thinly veiled socialist propaganda.

If Rhyme totaled the number of perps he'd been up against over the years, he supposed he'd rank anti-social personality disorder doers first (that is, psychos) and domestic terrorists second, far more numerous than foreign plotters or organized crime perps.

Like the couple he was about to speak to: Matthew and Harriet Stanton.

Rhyme was now on the tenth floor of the Stantons' hotel, along with officers of the NYPD Emergency Service operation. ESU had cleared the building and found no other co-conspirators. Rhyme and Sachs hadn't expected any. The hotel records indicated that only the Stantons and their son were staying here. Clearly there was one other perp—the deceased Unsub 11-5—but there was no evidence of anyone else in New York.

After Rhyme and Sachs had determined that the Stantons had been involved in the terror attack they and Bo Haumann had put together a tactical op to nail them.

The hotel manager had arranged for the elevators to bypass the tenth floor and had moved his staff elsewhere while the police evacuated the floor's legitimate guests. Then woman ESU officers donned cleaning jackets, tossed their MP-7s into laundry carts and hung around the elevator until the family showed up.

Surprise...

Not a shot fired.

The Bomb Squad had cleared the room—no booby traps; in fact not much of anything left. The terrorists had traveled light. Sachs was presently running the scene there.

Lincoln Rhyme was now scrolling through his iPad, reading reports sent to him over the past half hour from the FBI based in St. Louis, the closest field office to the Southern Illinois home of the Stantons and the AFFC. The group had been on the Bureau's and the Illinois State Police's radar—members were suspected in attacks on gays and minorities and of other hate crimes but nothing could ever be proven. Mostly, it was felt, they were bluster.

Surprise.

The authorities in the Midwest had already arrested three others within the AFFC for possession of explosives and machine guns without federal licenses. And the search there continued.

No longer in her crime scene coveralls, Amelia Sachs joined him.

"Anything left behind?" He looked at the milk crate

she carried. It was filled with a half dozen paper and plastic bags.

"Not much. Lot of bottled water."

Rhyme grunted a laugh. "Let's see if our friends'll be willing to have a tête-à-tête." A nod toward a linen room, where the Stantons were being held until the FBI showed up; the feds were taking point on this one.

They walked and wheeled into the room, where the prisoners sat handcuffed and shackled. The parents and son—their only child, Rhyme had learned—gazed back with a hesitant resolution. They were flanked by three NYPD officers.

If the Stantons were curious as to how Rhyme had figured out they were the associates of the unsub and that this was their hotel, they didn't express any desire to learn the answer. And that answer was almost embarrassingly mundane, involving no subtle analysis of the evidence whatsoever. Unsub 11-5's backpack, recovered beside his body near the water main pipe, contained a notebook called *The Modification*, a detailed list of steps in the plot to get poison into the New York drinking water. Inside that was a slip of paper with the address of the hotel. They knew the Stantons were staying there; Harriet had told Sachs this fact. So the couple and the unsub knew each other. The "attack" at the hospital wasn't that at all. The unsub had probably gone there to visit his ailing colleague, Matthew Stanton, in the hospital's cardiac care ward.

On reflection, there *were* clues they'd discovered that might have led to the conclusion that the Stantons were connected. For instance, the writing on the bag at the Belvedere holding the implants said *No. 3*, suggesting that the attack on Braden Alexander was the third one. But if the assault on Harriet Stanton had been legitimate, the bag notation would have read *No. 4*.

Similarly, they'd found trace evidence of Harriet's cosmetics in places where the unsub had been. Yes, he'd grabbed her in the hospital and there might have been some transfer of the substance, but it would have been minimal. More likely he'd picked the trace up by spending time in her company. Also, Rhyme recalled the back-and-forth of the bootied footprints at the crime scenes; that suggested that an accomplice had brought in the lights and batteries after the tattoo killings. A check with the hotel here revealed that the Stantons had been accompanied by their son, Josh, a young, muscular man who could easily have carted the heavy equipment in after his cousin had finished his lethal inking.

But sometimes fate short-circuits.

A slip of damn paper with an address—found in the perp's possession.

"You know your rights?" Sachs asked.

The officer behind Harriet Stanton nodded.

His long face pale and with a matte texture, Matthew Stanton said, "We don't recognize any rights. The government has no authority to grant us anything."

"Then," Rhyme countered, "you won't have any problem talking to us." He thought this logic was impeccable. "The only thing we need at this point is the ID of your colleague. The one with the poison."

Harriet's face brightened. "So he got away."

Rhyme and Sachs shared a glance. "Got away?" Rhyme asked.

"No, he didn't escape," Sachs told the Stantons. "But

he didn't have any ID on him and his fingerprints came back negative. We're hoping you'll cooperate and—"

Her smile vanished. "But then you arrested him?"

"I thought you knew. He's dead. He was killed by the stream of water after he drilled the hole. Because the pressure was never shut off."

Absolute silence descended. It was shattered only a few seconds later when Harriet Stanton began to scream uncontrollably.

CHAPTER 68

It's over," Pam Willoughby said, practically leaping into Seth McGuinn's arms.

He was at the front door of her apartment building in Brooklyn Heights. He stumbled back, laughing. They kissed long. The sky finally was clear and the incisive sunlight, ruddy from the afternoon angle, poured onto the façade of the building. The temperature, though, was even colder than in the past few days, when sleet pelted from the gray sky.

They stepped inside the hallway and then walked into her apartment on the first floor, to the right. Even a glance at the basement stairs, at the bottom of which Seth had nearly been killed, didn't dampen her joy.

She was buoyant. Her shoulders were no longer knots, her belly no longer tight as a spring. The ordeal was over. She could return home, at last, without worries that that terrible man who'd attacked Seth would come back. According to Lincoln Rhyme's message, the unsub was dead and his colleagues had been arrested.

Pam had noted immediately that Amelia wasn't the one delivering the news.

Fine with her. She was still angry and wasn't sure she could ever wholly forgive Amelia for trying to break up her relationship with her soul mate.

In the living room Seth pulled off his jacket and they dropped onto the couch. He cradled her head and pulled her close.

"You want anything?" she asked. "Coffee? I've got some champagne or, I don't know, bubbly wine. I've had it for a year. It's probably still good."

"Sure, coffee, tea. Anything warm." But before she rose Seth took her by the arm and studied her carefully, looking her over with a face of both relief and concern. "You all right?"

"I am. How about *you*? You're the one was going to get a tattoo from that crazy guy."

Seth shrugged.

She could see he was troubled. She couldn't imagine what it had been like to be pinned down like that, knowing you were about to be killed. And killed so painfully. The news reported that the poisons the killer had used were picked because of their agonizing symptoms. At least he didn't seem to blame her for the attack any longer. She'd been cut deeply to see him pulling away afterward. Walking away from her, not looking back…that was almost more than she could stand.

But he'd forgiven her. That was all in the past.

Pam walked into the kitchen and put water on to boil, readied the drip coffeemaker.

He called, "And what exactly *did* happen? You talk to Lincoln?"

"Oh." She stepped into the doorway. Her face was grave and she brushed her static-clinging hair from her face, twined it into a rope and let it fall on her back. "It was terrible. That guy? Who attacked you? He wasn't a psycho at all. He'd come here to poison the water supply in New York."

"Shit! *That* was it? I heard something about water."

"One of those militia groups, like my mother was in." She gave a wry smile. "Lincoln thought that the killer was obsessed with the Bone Collector. But, get this, it wasn't that at all; he was interested in the attack my mother planned here years ago. He was trying to figure out how Lincoln and Amelia would conduct an investigation. Oh, he wasn't very happy he missed that. Lincoln, I mean. He gets pretty mad when he makes mistakes."

The kettle whistled and Pam ducked back into the kitchen and poured the boiling water into the cone. The crisp sound was comforting. She fixed his the way he liked it—two sugars and one dash of half-and-half. She drank hers black.

Pam brought the cups out and sat beside him. Their knees touched.

Seth asked, "Who were they exactly?"

She tried to recall. "They were with, what was it called? The American Family Council. Something like that. Doesn't sound like a militia." Pam laughed. "Maybe they had a public relations team work on their image."

Seth smiled. "You ever hear of them when you and your mom were hiding out in Larchwood?"

"Don't think so. Lincoln said the people doing this

were from Southern Illinois. It wasn't far away from where my mother and I were. And I remember my mother and stepfather would meet with people from the other militias sometimes but I never paid any attention. I hated them all. Hated them so much." Her voice faded.

"But the tattoo guy, the killer, he's dead and the others got arrested."

"Right. A husband and wife and their son. They still don't know who the guy in the tunnel was, who was killed. The tattoo artist."

"You're still not talking to Amelia?"

"No," she said. "I'm not."

"For now."

"For a *long* time," Pam said firmly.

"She doesn't like me."

"No! That's not it. She's just protective. She thinks I'm this fragile doll. I don't know. Jesus."

Seth put down the coffee. "Okay if we talk about something serious?"

"Sure, I guess."

All right, what was this?

He laughed. "Relax. I've decided we need to hit the road sooner. Right away."

"Really? But I don't have my passport yet."

"I was thinking we could stick to the U.S. for a while."

"Oh. Well, I just thought we were going to see India. And then Paris and Prague and Hong Kong."

"We will. Just not now."

She considered this but then looked at his intense brown eyes, staring into hers. And she said, "Okay.

Sure, baby. Wherever you are, that's where I want to be."

"I love you," Seth whispered. He kissed her hard and she kissed back, embracing.

Pam sat forward, sipped coffee. "Munchies? I could use something. A pizza?"

"Sure."

She rose and walked into the kitchen again, opened the freezer door, pulled out a pizza and set it on the counter.

And sagged against the wall, feeling her gut churn, heart rate pound.

Thinking: How the hell did Seth know about Larchwood? She desperately thought back to their time together. No, I never mentioned it. I'm sure.

You need to tell Seth everything about your time underground.

No, I don't.

Think, think...

"Need a hand?" his voice called.

"Nope." She made noise, ripping the pizza box open, banging the oven door down.

This can't be happening. There's no way he could be involved with those people.

Impossible.

But Pam's instincts, honed by years of survival, took over. She eased to the landline phone and picked it up. Held it to her ear.

Hit 9. Then 1.

"Making a call?"

Seth stood in the doorway of the kitchen.

Keeping a smile on her face, she turned, forcing herself to move slowly. "You know, we were talking about Amelia. I was just thinking. Maybe I will apologize. I think that'd be a good idea, don't you? I mean, wouldn't you, if you were in my place?"

"Really?" he asked. Not smiling. "You were calling Amelia?"

"Yeah, that's right."

"Put the phone down, Pam."

"I..." Her voice faded as his steely dark eyes bored into hers. The same shade of brown. Her thumb hovered over the 1 button on the phone. Before she could hit it Seth stepped forward and pulled the phone from her hand, hung it up.

"What are you doing?" she whispered.

But Seth said nothing. He took her firmly by the arm, pulling her back to the couch.

CHAPTER 69

Seth walked to the front door, put the chain on and returned.

He smiled ruefully. "I can't believe that I mentioned Larchwood. I knew you and your mom stayed with the Patriot Frontier there. But you never mentioned it. Stupid of me, a mistake like that."

She whispered, "It was one of the things Amelia and I argued about. She asked if I'd told you about my life there. I said it didn't matter. But really? I was afraid to tell you. And now... You're one of them, aren't you? You're working with the people who tried to poison the water."

He picked up the remote to turn the TV on, presumably to see the news. Pam took the chance to leap from the couch, shoving him back hard. When he stumbled back she sprinted for the door. But she got no more than two steps before he tackled her. She went down hard, her face bouncing on the wood. Pam tasted blood from a split lip. He grabbed her by the collar and dragged her roughly back to the couch, virtually tossing her onto it.

"Never do that again." Leaning close, he dipped his finger in her blood and drew something on her face.

Whispering, he told her, "Body markings're windows, you know. Into who you are and what you're feeling. In some Native American tribes using paint—which is just a temporary tattoo—was a way to tell everybody what you were feeling. Warriors couldn't express emotion through words or facial expressions—not part of the culture—but they could use painted mods to show they were in love or sad or angry. I mean, even if you lost a child, you couldn't cry. You couldn't react. But you could paint your face. And everyone knew how sad you were.

"On your face, just now? I wrote the marks that mean Happy in the Lakota tribe."

Then he reached into his backpack and took from it a roll of duct tape and a portable tattoo gun.

When he did this, his sleeve tugged up and Pam found herself staring at a tattoo. It was red. She couldn't see it all but the portion exposed was the head and upper body of a centipede, whose all-too-human eyes stared at her just as Seth's did now: The look was of hunger and disdain.

"You're the one tattooing those people," Pam said, her voice a frail whisper. "Killing them."

Seth didn't respond.

"How do you know that couple? The terrorists?"

"I'm their nephew."

Seth—but no, not Seth; he'd have a different name—was assembling his tattoo gear. She stared at his arm, the tattoo. The insect eyes stared back.

"Oh, this?" He tugged his sleeve all the way up. "It's

not a tat. It's just a drawing—water-soluble ink. The sort some artists use to do outlines." He licked his finger and smeared it. "When I was the Underground Man—out on the prowl—I'd draw it on my arm. Took ten minutes. When I was your friend Seth, I'd wash it off. It only had to be good enough to let witnesses see it and for your police friends—and you—to be happy that the new man in your life, me, wasn't the killer."

Pam was crying.

"Lip hurt? You tried to run." He shrugged. "A busted lip is nothing compared with—"

"You're insane!"

His eyes flared and he slammed a fist into her belly. The room burst yellow and she whimpered under the pain. Controlled the nearly overwhelming urge to vomit.

"Do not speak to me that way. Do you understand?" He grabbed her hair and brought his mouth inches from her ear. He shouted so loud that her ears stung. "Do you?"

"Okay, okay, okay! Stop please," she cried. Then, "Who, who are you?" she whispered, but tentatively, afraid of another blow. He seemed capable of murder; his eyes were possessed.

He pushed her away. Pam collapsed on the floor. He pulled her roughly onto the couch, duct-taped her hands behind her and rolled her over on her back.

"My name is Billy Haven." He continued to set out some jars and assemble his tattoo gun. He glanced at her and noted the look of utter confusion.

"But I don't understand. I talked to your mother on the phone, she... Oh, yes, yes: It was your aunt."

He nodded.

"But I've known you for a year. More."

"Oh, we've been planning the attack for at least that long. And I've been planning to get you back into my life forever. My Lovely Girl."

"Lovely Girl?"

"Stolen from me. Not physically. But mentally. You'd been kidnapped by Amelia and Lincoln. By the wrong thinkers of the world. You don't remember me. Of course you don't. We met a long time ago. Ages. We were young. You were living in Larchwood, the militia run by Mr. and Mrs. Stone."

Pam recalled Edward and Katherine Stone. Brilliant radicals who'd fled Chicago after advocating a violent overthrow of the federal government. Pam's mother, Charlotte Willoughby, had fallen under their sway after her husband, Pam's father, died in a UN peacekeeping operation.

"You were six or so. I was a few years older. My aunt and uncle came to Missouri to meet with the Stones about an anti-abortion campaign. A few years later my uncle wanted to solidify the connection between the Larchwood militia and the American Families First Council, so Stone and my uncle arranged our marriage."

"*What?*"

"You were my Lovely Girl. You'd grow up to be my woman and the mother of our children."

"Like I was some kind of cow, some kind of fu—"

Striking like a snake, he jabbed his fist into her cheek, bone-to-bone. She inhaled at the pain.

"I won't warn you again. I'm your man and I'm in charge. Understand?"

She cringed and nodded.

He raged, "You have no idea what I've lived through. They took you away from me. They brainwashed you. It was like my world ended."

That would be when Pam and her mother and stepfather came to New York a few years ago. Her parents had another terror plot in mind but Lincoln and Amelia stopped it. Her stepfather was killed, her mother arrested. Pam was rescued and went into foster care in the city.

She thought back to the day when she and Seth had met. Yes, she'd thought he seemed too familiar, too nice, too infatuated. But she'd fallen hard anyway. (All right, Pam now admitted—maybe Amelia was right that, thanks to her early years, she was desperate for affection, for love. And so she'd ignored what she should have noticed.)

Pam stared at the tattoo gun, the vials of poison. Recalled that his victims had died in agony.

What delightful toxin had he picked for her?

That's what was coming next, of course. He'd kill her because, Lincoln had said, she might have to be a witness in the trial against the Stantons. And he'd kill her because their plan had failed and his aunt and uncle would be in jail for the rest of their lives.

He wanted revenge.

He now looked once more at the design he'd painted on her cheek in her own blood.

Happy . . .

She thought of the time they'd sat on this very couch one rainy Sunday, a rerun of *Seinfeld* on TV, Seth kissing her for the first time.

And Pam, thinking: I was falling in love.

A lie. All a lie. She recalled the months he'd spent in London, in a training program for an ad agency opening an office here. Bullshit. He was back with his aunt and uncle planning the attack. And, after he'd supposedly returned from the UK, she hadn't thought anything of his odd behaviors. Assignments that kept him out all hours, phone calls he never took in her presence, having to leave for meetings at a minute's notice, never taking her to meet his co-workers, never inviting her to the office. How they'd communicate through brief texts, not phone calls. But she hadn't been suspicious. She loved him, and Seth would never have done anything to hurt her.

She forced the crying to stop. This was easier than she'd thought. Anger froze the tears.

Seth... *Billy* began filling the tube with a liquid from a bottle.

She couldn't imagine what it would be like to die that way. Pain. Nausea, fire in her belly, stabbing up to her jaw, puking, puking, but finding no relief. Her skin melting, blood from her mouth, nose, eyes...

He was musing, "Feel bad about my cousin. Josh, poor Josh. A shame about him. The others? No worries there. My uncle was going to die soon. That was on the agenda. I was going to kill my aunt too as soon as we got back to Illinois. Blame them both on some homeless guy, an illegal probably. But once I saw the pressure in the pipes hadn't been shut off, I knew Lincoln Rhyme had figured the plan out and I had to give them up. I left a note with the address of the hotel at the scene. That's how Lincoln found them."

He worked meticulously, filling the tube with the care

of a surgeon, which he was, in a way, she reflected. The battery-powered tattoo gun was spotless. After he assembled the device he sat back and tugged her shirt up to below her breasts. He looked over her body, obsessed, it seemed, with her skin. She recoiled when he stroked her below the navel. As if the contact were not via his fingers but with the centipede's crimson legs.

But there seemed nothing sexual about the touch. He was fascinated only with her flesh itself.

She asked, "Who was it? That you killed in the water tunnel?"

"Hey, hold on there!" Billy said.

Pam winced. Was he going to hit her?

"*I* didn't kill him. Your friend did. Lincoln Rhyme. He's the one who made the announcement that the water pressure was shut off. But I was suspicious. So I got some insurance. I met a homeless man underground a few days ago. Nathan. One of the mole people. You ever heard about them? I thought it'd be helpful to use him. I gave him a pair of coveralls and did a fast tattoo of a centipede that matched mine, on his left arm. I knew where he hung out—near the Belvedere—so before I drilled into the pipe I found him.

"I offered him a thousand dollars to help me drill a hole to help me test the water. He agreed. But"—Billy shook his head—"I was right. The city was bluffing about cutting down the pressure. As soon as he drilled through the pipe, the stream of water cut him in half." He shivered. "There was nothing left of his head and chest. It was pretty tough to see."

At least he had a spark of sympathy.

"Knowing that that might've been me."

Or maybe not.

"That told me it was time to bail. The police'll find out soon enough it wasn't me but I've bought some time. Okay, time to bleed..." Then he said something else. She couldn't quite hear. It seemed to be "Oleander."

He rose, looked her over. Then he bent down and gripped the button of her jeans. *Pop*, it opened and the zipper came down.

No, no, he wasn't going to take her. She'd rip his precious skin off with her teeth before he got close. Never.

With a fast sweep, down came the denim.

She tensed, ready to attack.

But he didn't touch her there. He brushed the smooth flesh of her thighs. He was interested only in finding an appropriate part of her body on which to tattoo his deadly message, it seemed.

"Nice, nice..."

Pam recalled Amelia talking about the code the killer was tattooing onto his victims. And she wondered what message he was going to leave on her body.

He picked up the gun and turned it on.

Bzzzz.

He touched it to her skin. The sensation was a tickle.

Then came the pain.

CHAPTER 70

The point of the American Families First Council attack was now clear.

Among the documents in the dead unsub's pocket, in addition to the name of the Stantons' hotel, Sachs had found a rambling letter.

It reminded Rhyme of the Unabomber's manifesto—a diatribe against modern society. The difference, though, was that the unsub's screed didn't offer up the AFFC's own racist and fundamentalist views; just the opposite, in fact. The document, intended to be found by the police after the citywide poisoning, purported to be written by the *enemy*—some unnamed coalition of black and Latino activists, affiliated with Muslim fundamentalists, all of whom were taking credit for the poisoning of New York City to get even with the white capitalist oppressors. The statement called for an uprising against them, proclaiming that the poison attack was just the start.

Characterizing the attack in this way was rather clever, Rhyme decided. It would take suspicion off the AFFC and would galvanize sentiment against the council's enemies. It would also cause immeasurable damage to the Sodom of New York City, bastion of globalization, mixed races and liberalism.

Rhyme suspected there was more at work as well. "Power play within the militia movement? If word gets around that AFFC pulled this off, their stock would rise through the roof."

A call came in from the federal building in Manhattan.

"The Stantons are *not* doin' the talkie-talkie, Lincoln," said Fred Dellray, the FBI agent who was running the federal side of the attempted attack. The couple and their son were now in federal custody but apparently not—to translate Dellray's distinctive lingo—cooperating at all.

"Well, sweat 'em or something, Fred. I want to know who the hell our unsub was. Prints came back negative and he wasn't in CODIS."

"I saw those pictures of your boy in the tunnel, after the run-in with the H two Oh. My, my, that was a *Breaking Bad* moment, no? How fast they think that water was going?"

He was on speaker and, from a nearby evidence table, Sachs called, "They don't know, Fred, but after it cut him in half it also cut through a concrete wall and a steam pipe on the other side. I had to haul ass out of there 'fore I got scalded."

"You catch anything helpful in the tunnel?"

"Got a few things, not much. It was pretty much toast. Well, more oatmeal than toast, what with the steam and water."

She explained about the letter, intended to start a race riot.

The agent sighed. "Just when you think the world's a-changin'..."

"We'll work up the evidence, Fred, and be in touch."

"Thanks mightily."

They disconnected and Sachs returned to helping Mel Cooper analyze the trace and isolate and run the friction ridges from the Stantons' hotel suite. Regarding the prints, though, only one set was on file, though they knew the perpetrator's identity already: Joshua Stanton had a prior in Clayton County for assaulting a gay man. Hate crime.

Rhyme glanced up at the crime scene pictures, immune to the gruesome images. He looked once more at the stark tattoo, the centipede in red on the left arm. The eyes eerily human. It was, as Sachs had told him, very well done. Had he inked it himself? Rhyme wondered. Or was it painted by a friend? The unsub probably. Point of pride.

Sachs took a phone call.

"No, no," she whispered, drawing the attention of everybody in the room. Her face revealed dismay.

What now? Rhyme wondered, frowning.

She disconnected. Looked at them all.

"Lon's taken a turn for the worse. He went into cardiac arrest. They've revived him but it's not looking good. I should be with Rachel."

"You go on, Sachs. We'll take care of this." Rhyme hesitated. Then asked: "You want to give Pam a call and see if she wants to go with you? She always liked Lon."

Pulling her coat off the hook, Sachs debated. Finally she said, "Naw. Frankly, I don't think I could handle any more rejection."

CHAPTER 71

Apparently, though, Billy wasn't going to kill her.

Not yet, at any rate.

It was ink, not poison, he'd loaded into the tattoo gun.

"Stop fidgeting," he instructed. He was on his knees in front of the couch she lay on.

Pam said, "My hands hurt behind me. Please. Undo the tape. Please."

"No."

"Just tape them in front of me."

"No. Stay still." He glared and she stopped squirming.

"What the fuck are—"

Another fierce slap. "We have an image to maintain. Do you understand me? You will never use the F word and you will never take that tone!" He gripped her hair and shook her head like prey in a fox's mouth. "From now on your role is to be my woman. Our people will see you by my side. The loyal wife."

He returned to the inking.

Pam thought of screaming but she was sure he'd beat the crap out of her if she tried. Besides, there was no one else in the building. One unit was empty and the other tenants were on a cruise.

He was speaking to her absently. "We'll have to go deep underground for a while. My aunt and uncle won't give me up. But my cousin, Joshua? It's just a matter of time until he gets tricked into telling them everything he knows. Me included. We can't go back to Southern Illinois. Your friend Lincoln will have the FBI picking up all the senior people at the AFFC now. And he'll suspect the Larchwood crowd again, so Missouri's out. We'll have to go someplace else. Maybe the Patriot Assembly in Upstate New York. They're pretty much off the grid." He turned to her. "Or Texas. There're people there who remember my parents as martyred freedom fighters. We could live with them."

"But, Seth—"

"We'll lie low for a few years. Call me 'Seth' again and I'll hurt you. I can do tattooing work for cash. You can teach Sunday school. Little by little we can reemerge. New identities. The AFFC's over now, but maybe it's just as well—we'll move on. Start a new movement. And do a hell of a better job. We'll do it the right way. We'll place our women into schools—and I don't just mean church schools. I mean public and private. Get the kids young. Break them in. We men will run for office, low level, cities and counties—at first. We'll start local and then move up. Oh, it's going to be a whole new world. You don't think that way now. But you'll be proud to be part of it."

He lifted the machine off her leg, looked over the work and returned to inking her.

"My uncle was backward in a lot of ways. But he had one moment of genius. He came up with the Rule of Skin. He'd lecture about it all over the country—at other militias, at revival meetings, at churches, at hunting camps." Billy's eyes shone. "The Rule of Skin... It's brilliant. Think about it: Skin tells us about our physical health, right? It's flushed or pale. Glowing or dull. Shrunken or swollen. Broken out or clear... And it tells us our spiritual development too. And intellectual. And emotional. White is good and smart and noble. Black and brown and yellow are subversive and dangerous."

"You can't be serious!"

He made a fist and Pam cringed and fell silent.

"You want proof. The other day I was in the Bronx and this guy stopped me. A young man, I don't know. About your age. Black. He had keloids on his face—scars, like tattoos. They were beautiful. A real artist had done them." His eyes looked off slightly. "And you know why he stopped me? To sell me drugs. That's the truth about people like that. The Rule of Skin. You can't fool it."

Pam laughed bitterly. "A black kid tried to sell you drugs in the Bronx? Guess what? Go to West Virginia and a white kid'll try to sell you drugs."

Billy wasn't listening. "There's been an argument about Hitler: whether he genuinely hated Jews and Gypsies and gays and wanted to make the world a better place by eliminating them. Or whether he didn't actually care but thought that German citizens hated them, so he used that hate and fear to seize power."

"You're holding up Hitler as a role model?"

"There are worse choices."

"So? What is it for you, Billy? Do you believe in the Rule of Skin or are you using it for power, for yourself, your ego?"

"Isn't it clear?" He gave a laugh. "You're smarter than that, Pam."

She said nothing and he dabbed the tears of pain off her cheeks. And she did know the answer. Something occurred to her, hit her like one of his blows. It had to do with the blog she and Seth had worked on together. She whispered, "Our blog? That's the opposite of everything you're saying. What…what did you create the blog for?"

"What do you think? Everybody who posts a favorable comment is on our list. Pro-abortion, pro–food stamps, pro–immigration reform. Their day of judgment's coming."

There were probably fifteen thousand people who'd posted something on the site. What was going to happen to them? Would Billy's followers track them down and kill them? Firebomb their houses or apartments?

Billy set the tattoo gun aside, smeared Vaseline on the ink on her thighs and blotted.

He smiled and said, "Look. What do you think?"

Reading upside down, she saw two words on the front of her thighs.

PAM WIL

What the hell was he doing? What did he mean?

And he pulled his jeans down. She read similar tattoos on his thighs, in matching type fonts.

ELA LIAM

When read together:

PAM ELA

WIL LIAM

"We call them splitters. Lovers get parts of their names tattooed on each other. They can only be read when they're together. It's us, see? Separately, we're missing something. Together, we're whole." What passed for a smile crossed his sallow face.

"Lovers?" she whispered. Looking at his inking—it'd been done years ago.

He was gazing at her confused face. He pulled up his pants, then hers, and zippered and buttoned them.

"I knew someday I'd get you back." Billy was gesturing at the tattoos. "'Pamela,' 'William.' Nice touch, don't you think? Our names will be whole when we lie together to make our children."

He noted her expression of dismay. "What's that look

about?" As if speaking to a daughter upset about a bad day at school.

"I loved you!" she cried.

"No, you loved somebody who was part of the cancer of this country." His eyes softened and he whispered, "What about me, Pam? The woman I've loved all my life turns out to be the enemy? They took your mind and heart away from me."

"Nobody changed me. I never believed what my mother did. What you believe."

He stroked her hair, smiling, murmuring, "You were brainwashed. I understand that. I'll fix you, honey. I'll bring you back into the fold. Now let's go pack."

"All right, all right."

He pulled her to her feet.

She turned and looked into his eyes. "You know, Billy," she said in a soft voice.

"What?" He seemed pleased to note her smile.

"You should've checked my pockets."

Pam swung her right arm toward his face as hard as she could, holding tight, fiercely tight, to the box cutter she'd used to cut through the duct tape—the same as she'd carried in her hip pocket ever since those terrible days in Larchwood.

The blade connected with Billy's cheek and mouth. Not like the slush sound of a stabbing in movies. Only the silent cutting of flesh.

As he howled and gripped his face, spinning away, Pam leapt over the coffee table and headed for the front door, calling, "Okay, *there's* a mod for you, asshole."

CHAPTER 72

Pam's hands were slick with Billy's blood, but she got the door open and stumbled into the front hallway of the building.

She'd get outside onto the street and start screaming her head off. Maybe there was no one to hear her pleas for help in the building. But there were plenty of neighbors.

Ten feet, five feet…

Yes! She was going to—

But then fingers grabbed her ankles and she was falling to the lobby floor, with a cry. Her head bounced on the hardwood.

The knife went flying. Pam squirmed around and faced Billy, kicking furiously toward his groin.

His face was a mess—the image both pleased and shocked her. The gash began below his eye and continued to the middle of his cheek. She'd hoped to blind him but he could see all right, it seemed. Still, blood poured from his cheek and bubbled from his lips and she knew the blade had cut clean through to the inside of his mouth. She couldn't understand what he was saying. Threats, of course. Rage.

Blood flecked her jacket, her arm, her hand. The spray spattered her face.

The horrific expression revealed the pain he'd be feeling.

Good!

She gave up fighting. He was weakened but still much stronger than she was. Escape, she told herself. Just get the hell out!

Clawing at the floor, she managed to move a foot or so away from him, closer to the door.

But he stopped her and spun her onto her back, landing a blow in her solar plexus, knocking the air from her lungs again and doubling her over. She broke away momentarily—thanks to the slick blood, he'd lost his grip. She made it up on her knees. But fury possessed him. Billy planted his foot against the hallway wall and lunged forward, wrapping his sinewy hands around her throat. On her back again, gasping for air.

She kicked upward once more and connected, knee to groin. He gasped, inhaling hard, and began coughing blood. He reseated himself on top of her. His grip relaxed and he drew back and pounded her own cheek and jaw, sputtering words she couldn't understand, flecking her with more blood.

She tried to kick again, tried to punch, but she could get no leverage.

And all the while she was gasping, trying to draw air into her lungs and cry for help.

But nothing. Silence only.

The gash on his face was ghastly but the flow of blood was slowing, coagulating around the wound, dark and crisp as maroon-colored ice. Now she could hear: "How could you do that?" More words but they snapped and sputtered and grew unintelligible once more. He spat blood. "What a fool, Pam! You're beyond saving. I should have known."

He leaned down and fixed his grip around her neck and began to tighten.

Pam's head throbbed even more, the agony increasing, as she struggled for breath. Trapped blood pulsed in her temple and face.

The hallway began to grow dark.

It's all right, she said to herself. Better this than going back to the militia. Living the way Billy would insist she live. Better than being "his woman."

She thought briefly of her mother, Charlotte, speaking to Pam when the girl was about four.

"We're going to New York to do something important, honey. It'll be like a game. I'm going to be Carol. If you hear somebody call me Carol, and you say, 'That's not her name,' I'll whip you within an inch of your life. Do you understand me, honey? I'll get the switch out. The switch then the closet."

"Yes, Mommy. I'll be good, Mommy."

Then Pam knew she was dying because all around her was light, brilliant light, ruddy light, blinding light. And she nearly laughed, thinking: Hey, maybe I got that God stuff wrong. I'm looking at the glow of heaven.

Or hell, or wherever.

Then she felt weightless, light as could be, as her soul began to rise.

But, no, no, no . . . It was just that Billy was getting off her, rising, grabbing the box cutter and lifting it.

He was going to slash her throat.

He was mouthing something. She couldn't hear.

But she clearly heard the two, then three, huge explosions from the front doorway of the apartment building. She saw that the sun was the source of the light: the sun pouring onto her west-facing building. And saw two silhouettes, men holding guns. Looking then toward Billy she watched him stagger back, stumbling, clutching his chest. Torn mouth opening wide.

He looked down at her, dropped the box cutter, settled awkwardly into a sitting position, then eased to his side. He blinked, surprised, it seemed. He whispered something. His hands twitched.

Then the officers pushed into the hallway and had her by the arms, lifting her to her feet and pulling her toward the front door. Pam shook them off, though, apparently surprising them with her strength. "No," she whispered. She turned back and kept her eyes locked on Billy's until his gaze went unfocused and the pupils glazed. Inhaling hard, she waited a moment longer and then turned and stepped outside, while the officers advanced to Billy's body, pistols forward and ready—which was, she guessed, procedure, even though it was clear, unquestionably clear, he was no longer a threat.

CHAPTER 73

The medics had finished tending to Pam Willoughby, who walked outside her town house onto the chill, bright street.

From a spot on the curb, where he sat in his rugged Merits wheelchair, Lincoln Rhyme noted that Amelia Sachs started to step forward, arms extending slightly—to embrace her—but then slowed to a stop. She eased back, lowering her hands, when Pam gave no response, other than a formal nod of greeting.

Rhyme asked, "How are you feeling?"

"Getting by," said the somber-faced young woman—Rhyme could no longer think of her as a girl. He heard how she'd fought the unsub and he was proud of her.

For some reason Pam kept brushing at her legs—the front of her thighs. It reminded him of the compulsive way Amelia Sachs sometimes touched or scratched her own body. She noted him looking and stopped. "He tattooed me. But it wasn't poison. It was a real tat. He had part of his name and mine on his legs, he did the other part on mine."

Splitters, Rhyme recalled TT Gordon telling them. Lovers who mark portions of their names on each other.

"I'm..." She swallowed. "I feel pretty creepy."

"I know somebody who can get them removed. I've got his number."

If TT Gordon knew how to ink he'd surely know how to de-ink.

Pam nodded and rubbed compulsively again. "He was telling me all these terrible things. He was, it sounded like he was planning to be a new Hitler. He was going to kill his aunt and uncle and start his own militia movement. You know, Mom wasn't really all that smart. She'd ramble on and on and you couldn't take her seriously. But Billy, he was in a different league. He'd been to college. He was going to start schools and indoctrinate kids. He talked about the Rule of Skin. I could see he was obsessed with it. Racism, pure and simple."

"Rule of Skin," Rhyme mused. It certainly jibed with the manifesto they planned to leave at the site of poisoning at the water pipe. He thought back to what Terry Dobyns had told them.

If you can find out why he's so fascinated with skin, that's key to understanding the case...

Pam continued, "And he'd been obsessing about me all these years." She explained about the betrothal, about Billy's coming here a year ago to start planning his attack on the city—and his seduction of her. Pam shivered.

"Do you want to get in the van?" Rhyme asked, nodding toward the accessible vehicle Thom had driven here. Her place was sealed for the crime scene search and Pam was clearly cold; her nose and eyes red, fingertips too.

"No," Pam said quickly. She seemed more comfortable with the sunlight, despite the frigid air. "You caught them all?"

"Everybody who was here in New York, it seems," Rhyme explained. "Matthew and Harriet Stanton. Their son, Joshua."

The search team had found a real ID on the unsub's body. William Haven, twenty-five. A tattoo artist who lived in South Lakes, Illinois.

Rhyme continued, "We have people going through all of their documents now, notes, phones, computers. We've got a few conspirators in Southern Illinois but there'll be others. The bombs weren't set to detonate but they were real: gunpowder, detonators and cell phone triggers. Somebody who knew what they were doing put the IEDs together."

"If they were anything like my mother's underground group, the Patriot Frontier, there'd be dozens of people involved. They were always meeting late at night, sitting in kitchens, drinking coffee, making their fucking little plans...Lincoln?" Pam asked.

He raised an eyebrow.

"How did you know? About Seth? To send the police here?"

"I didn't *know*. But I suspected it when I got the idea when it occurred to me: How did the unsub know about TT Gordon?"

"Who?"

"The tattoo artist that you and Seth met in my lab."

"Oh, the guy with the weird beard and the piercings."

"That's him. Billy broke into his shop, killed one of his associates. I think he wanted to kill TT but he was out. He might've found out about the tattoo artist some other way but that was the simplest explanation—seeing TT in my town house.

"Since we learned that the motive for the group was domestic terrorism and that there was a tentative connection with you, Pam, and your mother—the Bone Collector—I just wondered if it wasn't too much of a coincidence that Seth had appeared in your life.

"Of course, the unsub had the tattoo of the centipede. Seth didn't seem to have any inkings; I'd seen him in a short-sleeve shirt. What to make of that? And then I remembered the waterproof ink—red ink—on one of the evidence bags. TT told us that some artists use washable pens like that to outline a tattoo first. Maybe that's what he'd done—a temporary tattoo on his arm to trick us."

Pam nodded. "Yes, exactly. He told me he'd draw it to make people think he was somebody else. Then wash it off when he was playing the role of Seth. It was a homeless man he tattooed with the centipede and paid to drill the hole. He was the one who died in the tunnel. He said he didn't trust you to turn off the water pressure. He wanted to be cautious."

"Ah, so that's who it was." Rhyme continued, "Then he broke into my town house and tried to poison me. We thought he was an expert with lock picks; there was no sign of jimmying the lock. But of course—"

"He took the key to your town house off my keychain," Pam said, grimacing. "Had a copy made."

"That's what I was thinking, yes. Was he the unsub? I couldn't say for sure, of course, but I wasn't going to take any chances. I called Dispatch and had some patrolmen get over here right away."

Sachs said, "And the attack here yesterday. He faked it."

"Injected himself with a bit of propofol, then cuffed himself. He dropped the bottle of poison and the syringe on the floor and lay down to take a nap until the police showed up."

"Why?" Pam asked.

Sachs added, "Wanted to keep suspicion off him. What better way than becoming a victim himself?"

Rhyme said, "And, I have to admit, our profilers contributed. Did some research that said centipedes in art and fiction represent an invasion of a safe, comfortable space. They lie in wait, invisible. That was Seth. Well, Billy."

"Sure was." Pam's still eyes swiveled back to her apartment. She frowned, pulled a tissue from her pocket and licked it. She scrubbed away a smear of blood on her cheek.

Sachs, the lead investigator on the case, now that Lon Sellitto was out of commission, spent about twenty minutes debriefing the girl, with Rhyme nearby. They learned that Billy, with Pam in tow, had planned to escape to a militia group in Upstate New York, the Patriot Assembly, which Rhyme and Sachs had tangled with before.

Ron Pulaski finished walking the grid in Pam's apartment—even if you stop the perp in the most absolute sense possible, as here, you still go through the formalities. When he was finished he bundled up the evidence, signed the chain-of-custody cards and told Rhyme he'd get everything to the town house. The ME team carted away the body. With eyes cool as the air, Pam watched the gurney wheeled to the van.

Rhyme, then, was concentrating on Sachs. When she and Pam had been talking about what had just happened, the policewoman had occasionally tried to joke or offer words of sympathy. Pam responded with a formal smile that might as well have been a sneer. The expression cut Sachs deeply, it was clear.

A pause as Sachs stood, hands on hips, looking over the town house. She said to Pam, "The scene's clear. Help you clean up, you want."

Rhyme noted that she was hesitating, and the tone in her voice told him that she regarded this question as perilous.

"Think I'll just head over to the Olivettis, you know. And maybe sometime this week I'll borrow Howard's car, come over to the town house and pick up what's left. That okay, Lincoln?"

"Sure."

"Wait," Sachs said firmly.

Pam regarded her defiantly.

The detective continued, "I want you to see somebody about this. Talk to them." She dug into her purse. "This's Terry Dobyns. He works for the NYPD but he can hook you up with somebody."

"I don't—"

"Please. Do it."

A shrug. The card disappeared into her back pocket, where her cell phone rested.

Sachs said, "You need anything, give me a call. Anytime." A whiff of desperation that was hard to hear.

The girl said nothing but walked inside and returned

with a backpack and a computer bag. White wires ran from ears to iPod and were tucked up under a bulky hat.

The girl waved in the direction of Rhyme and Sachs but to neither in particular.

Sachs stared after her.

After a moment Rhyme said, "People hate to be proven wrong, Sachs, even when it's for their own good. *Especially* then maybe."

"So it seems." In the cold she was rocking back and forth, watching Pam disappear in the distance. "I broke it, Rhyme."

It was moments like this when Rhyme detested his disability the most. He wanted nothing more than to walk up to Sachs and wrap his arms around her shivering shoulders, hold her as tightly as he could.

"How's Lon?" Rhyme asked.

"He came out of the crisis. But still unconscious. Rachel's in bad shape. Lon's son is there."

"I talked to him," Rhyme told her.

"He's a rock. Really came into his own."

"Headed back to the town house?"

Sachs replied, "In a bit. I've got to meet with a witness about the Metropolitan Museum investigation."

Sellitto's other case, the break-in at the museum on Fifth Avenue. With the detective in the hospital, other Major Cases officers were taking over. Now that the AFFC terror plot had been stopped, it was time to resurrect the politically important, if mysterious, case.

Sachs walked to her Torino. The engine fired up with a blast of horsepower and she peeled away from the curb, raising smoke whose blue tint turned violet in the red light from the low sun.

CHAPTER 74

Lincoln Rhyme wasn't happy he'd missed the deduction about the identity of the unsub; it was a search of the body and Pam's explanation that were the source of information about Billy Haven.

"I should've guessed it, though," he said to Cooper and Pulaski.

"What?" Pulaski set down the plastic bag from which he'd been tweezing evidence and turned to Rhyme.

"That Billy was somebody close to the Stantons. Harriet's reaction? When Amelia told her he was dead? She got hysterical. Which should have told me she knew him well. *Very* well. The son too, Joshua—I thought he was going to faint when he heard. I could have deduced that even if the unsub wasn't part of the immediate family, he was in the extended. We know he's the nephew, we know his name. But get the rest of the details on Mr. William Haven, Rookie. Stat."

"Latin, from *statim*, meaning immediately," Pulaski said.

"Ah, yes, that's right. You're a student of the classics. And, I remember, a student of crime films in which digressive banter is used to distract from faulty plotting and character development. E.g., those grammatically correct hit men you were referring to. So shall we get going on the task at hand?"

"*Exempli gratia*," Pulaski muttered and began typing fast on his keyboard.

A few minutes later, he looked up from the computer screen. "*Negotium ibi terminetur*," he said with a tone of finality.

"The job is finished," Rhyme translated. "More elegant to say, '*Factum est*.' Has a nicer ring. That's the problem with Latin. It sounds like you're chewing on rocks. Bless the Italians and Rumanians for pulling the language out of the fire."

Pulaski read from the screen. "Matthew Stanton was an only child. But Harriet had a sister, Elizabeth. Married Ebbett Haven. They had a son, William Aaron. Ebbett was an elder with the AFFC but he and his wife died when the boy was young." He looked up. "In the Branch Davidian standoff. They were there to sell guns to the Davidians and got caught inside during the siege.

"William went to live with Aunt Harriet and Uncle Matthew. Went by Billy mostly. He's got a record—juvie, so there are no prints on record; it was sealed. The case was an assault charge. Hate crime. Billy beat up a Jewish boy at school. Then used an ice pick and ink to tattoo a swastika on the kid's forearm. He was ten. There's a picture. Check it out."

The tattoo was pretty well done. Two-color, shaded, razor-sharp lines, Rhyme noted.

"Then he studied art and political science at the University of Southern Illinois. Then, for some reason, opened a tattoo parlor."

In Billy's backpack were receipts for two apartments in town. One was in Murray Hill, in the name of Seth McGuinn—Pam's boyfriend. The other, under the pseudonym Frank Samuels, was near Chinatown, off Canal Street. Crime Scene had searched both. Billy had largely scrubbed them but in the second place—a workshop—the teams had recovered equipment and a number of terrariums filled with the plants from which Billy had extracted and distilled the poisons he'd used in the murders.

These boxes and their eerie lights now sat in Rhyme's parlor, against the far wall. Well, all but one. That was the sealed terrarium that had housed the botulinum spores. The bio-chem folks from Fort Detrick had decided it was best to take control of that one. Normally possessive of evidence, Rhyme had not made an issue of that particular box being handed off.

The criminalist finished logging the plants into evidence—noting the hemlock was particularly lovely—and rang up Fred Dellray, the FBI agent, who would be handling the federal side of the investigation. He explained what they'd found. The eccentric agent muttered, "If that don't beat all. I wondered where Hussein's WMDs got themselves to. And we finally found 'em about two blocks from my favorite Chinese restaurant. Happy Panda. The one on Canal. No, not the

Happy Panda on Mott or the Happy Panda on Sixth. The original one and only Happy Panda. Yu-um. The jellyfish. No, no, 's better'n you think. Okay, call me when you got the report ready to go."

After he disconnected, Rhyme heard a laugh across the room.

"That's pretty good," Mel Cooper said, staring at a computer screen.

"What?" Rhyme asked.

Pulaski laughed too and turned the screen: It was the *New York Post* online edition. A headline over the story about the Stantons was *Poison Pen.*

Referring to Billy Haven's murder weapon.

Clever.

As Cooper and Pulaski continued to analyze and catalog the evidence from both Pam's apartment and Billy's workshop and safe house, Rhyme motored back to the evidence table. "Glove," he called.

"You want—?" Thom asked.

"Glove! I'm about to fondle some evidence."

With some difficulty the aide slipped one onto Rhyme's right hand.

"Now. That." He pointed to the slim notebook titled *The Modification*, which contained pages of details on the poison plot: timing, victims to choose, locations, police procedures, quotations from *Serial Cities*, the true crime book about Rhyme and directions on how to "anticipate the anticipator." The notes were written in Billy's handsome cursive. Not surprisingly, given his artistic skill, the handwriting resembled that in an illuminated manuscript inked by scribes.

Rhyme had skimmed the booklet earlier but now he

wanted to examine it in depth to search for other conspirators.

Thom arranged it on the arm of his wheelchair and, in a gesture at times awkward, at times elegant, but ever confident, Lincoln Rhyme turned pages and read.

SATURDAY, NOVEMBER 9

V

REUNION

CHAPTER 75

5:00 P.M.

The stocky, balding man, in a short gray overcoat, strolled along the wide sidewalk with feet pointed outward. He carried a battered briefcase. Few people on the street noted his physique or gait. He was as nondescript as could be. Businessman, accountant, ad agency executive. He was a Muggle. He was a Prufrock.

He liked this place. Greenwich Village was less chic than, say, SoHo or TriBeCa but more of a neighborhood; Little Italy had come and gone but the Village remained a bastion for old-school Manhattanites, the quirky ones, the artistic, the descendants of European immigrants. The 'hood was populated by the families of, yes, stocky, balding husbands and stolid wives, ambitious yet modest sons, clever daughters. He blended here.

Which was good. Considering his mission.

The sun was down and the temperature low but at least the sky was clear and the sleet of the past few days had ended.

He walked to the window of the Café Artisan and

perused the stained menu. It was a real coffeehouse. Italian. This place had been steaming milk before Starbucks was even a gleam in the eye of whatever Seattlian, not Sicilian, had created the franchise.

He gazed through the early deployment of Christmas decorations in the fudgy window and studied the scene at a table against the far wall: A redheaded woman in a burgundy sweater and tight black jeans sat across from a man in a suit. He was lean and looked like a lawyer on the verge of retirement. The woman was asking the man questions and jotting responses in a small notebook. The table, he noted, rocked a bit; the wedge under the north-by-northeast leg was not performing.

He studied the man and the woman carefully. Had he been interested in sex, which he was not, the woman would certainly have appealed.

Amelia Sachs, the woman he'd come here to kill, was quite beautiful.

Since the weather was cold, it wasn't conspicuous for this man to be wearing gloves, which was fortunate. The ones covering his hands were black wool, since leather gives a print nearly as distinctive as one's own friction ridges. Traceable, in other words. But cloth? No.

He was now noting where Amelia's purse sat—on the back of her chair. How trusting were people here. Had this been São Paulo or Mexico City, the purse would have been fixed to the back of her chair with a nylon tie, like the sort used to bind garbage bags and prisoners' wrists.

The purse was latched but this didn't trouble him. Several days ago he'd bought a bag just like hers and practiced, practiced, practiced slipping something inside silently (he'd studied sleight of hand for years). Finally he'd honed the technique sufficiently so that it took all of three seconds to open the bag, slip a small object inside and refix the clasp. He'd done this a hundred times.

He now reached into his pocket and palmed a bottle of an over-the-counter painkiller. It was identical in brand to those that Amelia Sachs preferred. (He'd learned this from her medicine cabinet.) She'd had osteoarthritis problems in the past and though she didn't seem to be too troubled recently, he'd observed, she still popped the pills from time to time.

Ah, the trials our bodies put us through.

The capsules in this bottle looked identical to the ones she bought. There was one difference, however: Each of his pills consisted of compressed antimony.

Like arsenic, antimony is a basic element, a metalloid. The name is from the Greek for "banishing solitude." Antimony had been used in the past to darken the eyebrows and lids of promiscuous women, including Jezebel in the Bible.

It's a ubiquitous and useful element, employed frequently even today in industry. But antimony, Sb, atomic number 51, has also been the cause of thousands of excruciatingly painful deaths throughout history. Wolfgang Amadeus Mozart was perhaps the most famous victim. (The question remains: intentional or not? We'd have to ask Antonio Salieri.)

At a jab of pain from her reconstructed knee, which she'd feel sooner or later, Sachs would pop two pills.

And instead of relief she'd be hit with a fierce headache, vomiting, diarrhea, numb extremities.

She'd be dead in a few days—according to the media,

yet another victim of Billy Haven, who'd managed to slip the tainted drugs into her purse before he and his terrorist relatives were stopped.

Although in truth the Stantons had nothing to do with this impending murder.

The man outside the Café Artisan, preparing to kill Sachs, was Charles Vespasian Hale, his birth name, though he was known by many others too. Richard Logan was one. And most recently: David Weller, the indignant attorney who'd contacted the New York Bureau of Investigation about the upstart young officer Ron Pulaski.

The only name that he truly liked, however, was the one that described him best: the Watchmaker—echoing both his skill in crafting intricate criminal plots and his passion for clocks and watches.

He now regarded one of these, a Ventura SPARC Sigma MGS, a digital wristwatch that cost five thousand dollars. Hale owned 117 watches and clocks, the majority of which were analog, even if powered by electronics and batteries. He had Baume & Merciers, Rolexes and TAGs. He'd had a chance to steal a six-million-dollar Patek Philippe Calibre 89, the famed commemorative pocket watch created to honor the company's 150th anniversary. It had more complications—those windows and dials giving information in addition to the present time—than any other watch ever created. The eighteen-karat masterpiece offered such data as the phase of the moon, power reserve, month, temperature, date of Easter, constellations, sunset and split second.

And yet Hale had chosen not to steal the masterpiece.

Why? Because the Patek was a relic. It was a new

era now. The way of analog was gone. It had taken Hale some time to accept this but his arrest by Lincoln Rhyme some years ago had shown him that the world had changed.

And Hale had risen to greet the dawn.

The Ventura on his wrist represented this new face—so to speak—of timekeeping. Its unparalleled accuracy gave him great pleasure and comfort. He looked at the watch once again.

And counted down.

Four...

Three...

Two...

One...

A blaring fire alarm screamed from the back of the café.

Hale pulled on a wool cap over his shaved head and stepped into the offensively hot coffee shop.

He was unseen by everybody—including Amelia Sachs and her interviewee—as they stared toward the kitchen, where he'd left the device twenty minutes ago. The stand-alone smoke detector, sitting on a shelf, appeared old (it wasn't) and greasy (it was). The workers would find it and assume it had been discarded and left on the top shelf accidentally. Soon someone would pull it down, pluck the battery out and throw the thing away. Nobody would think twice about the false alarm.

Amelia looked around—as did everyone—for smoke but there was none. When her eyes returned to the kitchen door behind which the blare persisted, Hale sat in a chair behind Amelia and on the pretense of setting his briefcase on the floor, slipped the bottle into her purse.

A new record: two seconds.

Then he looked around, as if debating whether he wanted to enjoy a latte in a place that was potentially on fire.

No. He'd go someplace else. The man rose and headed out into the chill.

The sound stopped—battery-plucking time. A glance back. Sachs returned to her coffee, to her notes. Oblivious to her impending death.

The Watchmaker turned toward the subway entrance at West 4th Street. As he walked along the sidewalk in the brisk air an interesting thought occurred to him. Arsenic and antimony were metalloids—substances that shared qualities of both metals and non-metals—but were rigid enough to be crafted into enduring objects.

Would it be possible, he wondered, to make a timepiece out of these poisons?

What a fascinating thought!

And one that, he knew, would occupy his fertile mind for weeks and months to come.

CHAPTER 76

"Go with it," Lincoln Rhyme said. The criminalist was alone in his parlor, talking through the speakerphone as he gazed absently at a website featuring some rather classy antiques and fine arts.

"Well," said the voice, belonging to a captain at the NYPD, presently in police headquarters. The Big Building.

"Well, what?" Rhyme snapped. He'd been a captain too; anyway, he never took rank very seriously. Competence and intelligence counted first.

"It's a little unorthodox."

The fuck does that mean? Rhyme thought. On the other hand, he himself had also been a civil servant in a civil-servant world and he knew that it was sometimes necessary to play a game or two. He appreciated the man's reluctance.

But he couldn't condone it.

"I'm aware of that, Captain. But we need to run with the story. There are lives at risk."

The captain's first name was unusual. Dagfield.

Who would name somebody that?

"Well," Dag said defensively. "It has to be edited and vetted—"

"I wrote it. It doesn't need to be edited. And *you* can vet. Vet it now. We don't have much time."

"You're not asking me to vet. You're asking me to run what you've sent me, Lincoln."

"You've looked it over, you've read it. That's vetting. We need to go with it, Dag. Time's critical. Very critical."

A sigh. "I'll have to talk to somebody first."

Rhyme considered tactical options. There weren't many.

"Here's the situation, Dag. I can't be fired. I'm an independent consultant that defense attorneys around the country want to hire as much as the NYPD does. Probably more and they pay better. If you don't run that press release exactly, and I mean exactly, the way I sent it to you, I'll hang out my shingle for the defense and stop working for the NYPD altogether. And when the commissioner hears that I'll be working *against* the department, your job'll be in the private sector and I mean fast food."

Not really satisfied with that line. Could have been better. But there it was.

"You're threatening me?"

Which hardly required a response.

Ten seconds later: "Fuck."

The slamming phone made a simple, sweet click in Rhyme's ear.

He eased his wheelchair to the window, to look out over Central Park. He liked the view more in the winter than the summer. Some might have thought this was because people were enjoying summer sports in the fine months, running, tossing Frisbees, pitching softballs—activities forever denied Rhyme. But the reality was that he just liked the view.

Even before the accident Rhyme had never enjoyed that kind of pointless frolic. He thought back to the case involving the Bone Collector, years ago. Then, just after his accident, he'd given up on life, believing he'd never exist in a normal world again. But that case had taught him a truth that had endured: He didn't *want* that normal life. Never had, disabled or not. His world was the world of deduction, of logic, of mental riposte and parry, of combat with *thought*—not with guns or karate blows.

And so looking out at the stark, leaf-stripped vista of Central Park, he felt wholly at home, comforted by the lesson that the Bone Collector had taught him so many years ago.

Rhyme turned back to the computer screen and waded once more into the world of fine arts.

He checked the news and discovered that, yes, Dag had come through. The unvetted, unedited, unchallenged press release had been picked up everywhere.

Rhyme glanced at the clock face on his computer and returned to browsing.

A half hour later his phone rang and he noted the caller ID report: *Unknown.*

Two rings. Three. He tapped the answer button with his right index finger.

He said, "Hello there."

"Lincoln," said the man he knew as Richard Logan, the Watchmaker. "Do you have a moment to talk?"

"For you, always."

CHAPTER 77

I've seen the news," the Watchmaker said to Rhyme. "You released my picture. Or the artist's renderings of me as Dave Weller. Not a bad job. An Identi-Kit, I assume. Both fat and slim, hair, no hair, mustache, clean-shaven. Aren't you *so* impressed with the confluence of art and computer science, Lincoln?"

A reference to the press release Rhyme had pressured the NYPD brass into going with. "It was accurate then?" the criminalist asked. "My officer wasn't sure when he worked with the artist if he had the cheek structure right."

"That young man. Pulaski." The Watchmaker seemed amused. "He observes two-dimensionally and draws conclusions from the preliminary. You and I both know the risks of that. He's a better forensic cop than undercover, I'd imagine. Less improvisation in crime scene work. I deduce a brain injury?"

"Yes. Exactly."

The Watchmaker continued, "He's lucky that when I set him up, it was with the Bureau of Investigation, not some of my real associates. He'd be dead otherwise."

"Possibly," Rhyme said slowly. "His instincts are good. And he's quite the shot apparently. Anyway, he's all I could spare under the circumstances. I was busy trying to stop a psychotic tattoo artist."

Now that he knew the Watchmaker had escaped from prison and was alive, Rhyme thought back to the man's appearance from several years ago, when he'd last seen him face-to-face. Yes, there were similarities, he now reflected, between the lawyer Pulaski had described to the Identi-Kit operator and the Watchmaker from several years ago—attributes that Rhyme could now recall, though some key factors were different. He now said, "You had non-surgical work done. Like packing silicone or cotton into your cheeks. And the hair—thinning shears and a razor—a good job duplicating male-pattern baldness. Makeup too. Most movie studios get it wrong. The weight—your size—that was a body suit, right? Nobody could gain fifty pounds in four days. The tan would be from a bottle."

"That's right." A chuckle. "Maybe. Or a tanning salon. There are about four hundred in the metropolitan area. You might want to start canvassing. If you're lucky, by Christmas you could find the one I went to."

Rhyme said, "But you've changed—modded, if you will—again, right? Since we've run the picture."

"Of course. Now, Lincoln, I'm curious why you released my information to the media. You ran the risk that I'd go to ground. Which I have."

"The chance that somebody might've spotted you. They'd call it in. We were ready to move fast."

"All-points bulletin."

The press announcement Rhyme had just coerced

the brass into releasing reported that a man known as Richard Logan, aka the Watchmaker, aka Dave Weller, had escaped several days ago from federal prison in Westchester. The Identi-Kit pictures were given, along with the hint that he might be feigning a Southern accent.

"But no takers," the Watchmaker pointed out. "No one dimed me out. Since I'm still... wherever I am."

"Oh, and by the way, I'm not bothering to trace this call. You're using cutouts and forward proxies."

This wasn't a question.

"And we've raided Weller's law firm."

A chuckle. "The answering service, post office box and website?"

"Clever," Rhyme said. "The wrongful death specialty seemed a bit cruel."

"Pure coincidence. First thing I thought of."

Rhyme asked, "Oh, a point of curiosity? You're not really Richard Logan, are you? That's one of your pseudonyms."

"Yes."

The man didn't offer his real name and Rhyme didn't bother to push.

"So how *did* you figure out that I'd escaped?"

"Like so much about what I do—what we *both* do—there was a postulate."

"A hunch," the Watchmaker said.

Rhyme thought of Sachs, who often chided his derision of the word, and he smiled. "If you will."

"Which you then verified empirically. And what gave rise to that postulate?"

"In Billy Haven's backpack we found a notebook,

The Modification, a how-to guide for getting botulinum toxin into the New York City water supply. Elegant in the extreme. It was like an engineering schematic, every step outlined, timed down to the minute. I doubted the Stantons and Billy would've been able to come up with something that elaborate: a serial killer to misdirect from a plot to target the water supply with bombs, which was in turn meant to cover up the real plot to poison the water. And you learned how to weaponize the toxin. Resistant to chlorine. Quite a coup, that was."

"You found the notebook?" The man sounded displeased. "I told Billy to transcribe it into an encrypted digital file on a computer with no Internet access. Then destroy the original." A pause. "But I'm not surprised. That whole gang from Southern Illinois seemed rather analog. And, yes, not particularly brilliant. Like the toxins Billy decided to use? I recommended commercial chemicals but Billy had this affection for plants. He spent a lot of time by himself in the woods, I gathered, sketching them when he was young. Tough childhood when your parents are killed by the federal government and your moral compass is a neo-Nazi militia."

"The Modification? You coined the word?"

"That was mine, yes. Though I was inspired by Billy's avocation. Body modifying. It suited their apocalyptic views. I was embarrassed actually. Too on the nose. But they liked the sound."

"You dictated it to Billy, the whole plan?"

"That's right. And his aunt. But Billy wrote it down. They came to visit me in prison. The cover was that Billy was writing a book about my life." He paused. "There's a story I've been dying to tell but haven't found the appropriate listener. I think you'll appreciate it, Lincoln. When I was finished giving him the plan and he'd written it all down, I said, 'It's all yours, Moses. Go forth.' Billy and Harriet didn't get it. I know you're familiar with the theological concept of God as a watchmaker."

When contemplating the origin of the universe, Isaac Newton, René Descartes and others of the Scientific Revolution in the seventeenth and eighteenth centuries argued that design requires a designer. If something as complex as a watch could not exist without a watchmaker, by analogy human life in the universe—far more complicated than a timepiece—surely could not exist without a God.

"I had to explain that, given my nickname, dictating *The Modification* was as if I were God, handing down the Ten Commandments to Moses. I meant it as a joke. But they took it seriously. They started to refer to the plan as the Modification Commandments." He clicked his tongue. "I feel sorry for those who don't appreciate irony. But to get back to the issue: how you found out about me...If you're willing to share."

"Of course."

"You had the notebook. But it wasn't in my handwriting; that was Billy's. No fingerprints or DNA. I never touched it. And, yes, there were a lot of references to critical timing—when to administer the poison and where, the diversionary attacks, when to have Joshua, Billy's cousin, get the batteries and lights in the underground passages where the crimes occurred, how many minutes after someone had called nine one one could the police be counted on to arrive. It's all in the timing, of course. But leaping from that to my escape from prison?"

Rhyme wondered where the man was standing, what his posture was. Was he outside, cold? Or outside, hot, in balmy weather? "Nemesis" was an imprecise term, not to mention melodramatic. But Rhyme allowed himself to think of the Watchmaker this way. He said, "Evidence."

"That doesn't surprise me, Lincoln. But what?"

"The tetrodotoxin. We found traces." The super poison from the fugu fish.

"Oh, my..." A sigh from the other end of the line. "I told Billy to destroy any residue."

"I'm sure he tried. There was just a minuscule amount of trace at one of the scenes." Rhyme, of all people, knew how difficult it was to banish all whispers of a substance. "We didn't find any in his safe house, so where had it come from? I checked VICAP and nobody had used it in any crimes that had been reported in the last few years. So what could Billy have been doing with tetrodotoxin? Then it occurred to me: A clue was its nickname, the zombie drug. To induce the appearance of cardiac arrest and death."

"That's right," the Watchmaker admitted. "Billy delivered some, smuggled in the pages of a book. In prison they check for shivs and heroin, not milligrams of fish ovary. I used it to fake the heart attack and get transferred to the hospital in White Plains."

Was that a seagull cawing in the background? And then, a ship's horn? No, a foghorn. Interesting. They were little used in this day of radar and GPS. Rhyme took note. A flare on his computer screen. It was a message from Rodney Szarnek, the computer crimes expert. It reported that the analysis of the Watchmaker's call to Rhyme had been unsuccessful; it had skidded to a stop at an anonymous proxy switch in Kazakhstan.

Rhyme had lied about the phone trace.

He gave a mental shrug—nothing ventured, nothing gained—and returned to the conversation. "What finally convinced me, though, was a mistake you made."

"Really?"

"When you were on the street with Ron Pulaski, you referred to the attempted hit in Mexico on the federal police official. The project you'd put together a few years ago."

"Right. I wanted to mention something specific. For credibility."

"Ah, but that case was sealed. If you were a legitimate lawyer who'd never met Richard Logan, like you claimed, you'd have had no idea about the Mexico City job."

A pause. Then: "Sealed?"

"Apparently the State Department and the Mexican *Gabinete Legal* were not happy that you—an American—had come minutes away from killing a high-ranking Mexican law enforcer. They preferred to act as if the incident had never happened. There was no press about it."

"Oh." He sounded bitter.

Rhyme said, "Now answer *me* a question."

"All right."

"How did you get the gig? For the Stantons and their AFFC?"

"It was time to get out of prison. I got in touch with the people who'd been involved in the domestic terror incident a few years ago when you and I went head-to-head. Remember?"

"Of course."

"They set me up with the AFFC—another white supremacist militia. I told them I could put them on the map. Harriet and Billy came to visit me in prison and I laid out a plan. By the way, did you ever see them together, those two, aunt and nephew? Uneasy dynamic there. Gives a whole new meaning to the name American Families First."

Rhyme demurred. The observation, true or not, didn't interest him.

The Watchmaker continued, "They wanted to make a name for themselves. So we brainstormed. I came up with the idea of botulism in the drinking water. I learned that Billy was a tattoo artist. We'd tattoo victims with an Old Testament message. Apocalypse, I was saying. They just love that kind of rhetoric. Striking a blow for their idiotic values. They loved it too when I suggested they use poisons as the murder weapons. Justice for the minority and socialist values that were *poisoning* society, et cetera, et cetera. Oh, they just lapped that up. Well, Matthew did. Billy and Harriet seemed a bit more tempered. You know, Lincoln, the small-minded are the most dangerous."

Not necessarily, the criminalist reflected, considering the man he was conversing with at the moment.

CHAPTER 78

"So," Rhyme continued, "in exchange for your plan they slipped you some of the tetrodotoxin. And arranged to bribe medical personnel and prison guards, so you'd be declared dead and smuggled out of the lockup. And found some homeless corpse to be shipped to the funeral home for cremation."

"More or less."

"Must have been pricey."

"Twenty million cash total."

"And the funeral home charade? With you as Weller. Why that?"

"I knew you'd send somebody to see who was collecting the ashes. I had to make you believe in your heart that the Watchmaker was dead. The best way to do that was to have the family's indignant lawyer come to town to collect his ashes... and report your undercover officer to the authorities. That was a wonderful turn. Didn't anticipate that."

Rhyme then said, "But one thing I don't understand: Lon Sellitto. *You* poisoned him, of course. You borrowed a fireman's outfit at the site of the Belvedere Apartment attack and gave him the laced coffee."

"You figured that out too?"

"Arsenic is metalloid poison. Billy used only plant-based toxins."

"Hm. Missed that. *Mea culpa.* Tell me, Lincoln, were you one of those boys who read children's puzzle books and could always spot what was wrong with this picture?"

Yes, he had been, and, yes, he could.

Rhyme added, "And you slipped the doctored painkillers into Amelia Sachs's purse."

A dense pause. "You found those?"

The minute Rhyme had deduced the Watchmaker was still alive and was probably behind Lon's attack, he'd told Sachs, Pulaski and Cooper to be on the lookout for any attacks. She'd recalled that someone had sat near her in a coffeehouse where she'd been meeting with a witness in the Metropolitan Museum case. She'd found a second bottle of painkillers in the bag.

Rhyme asked, "Arsenic as well? The results aren't back yet."

"I'll tell you, since you've figured it out. Antimony."

Lincoln Rhyme said, "See, that's what I don't follow: trying to kill Lon and Amelia and blame the deaths on the Stantons? It was *you* dressed up like Billy Haven at the scenes? Looking at her through the manhole cover on Elizabeth Street? Outside the restaurant in Hell's Kitchen? In the building near the Belvedere?"

"That's right."

"So why...?" His voice faded. The thoughts were coming fast, exploding like firecrackers. "Unless..."

"Catching on, are you, Lincoln?"

"Twenty million dollars," he whispered. "To buy your freedom. There is no way the Stantons and the AFFC could have gotten you that much money to bribe the guards and medics. No, no—they're a shoestring operation at best. Someone *else* financed your escape. Yes! Somebody who needed you for another job. You used the AFFC as a cover for something else."

"Ah, that's my Lincoln," said the Watchmaker.

The voice was condescending and a moment's anger burst. But then the thought landed and Rhyme laughed out loud. "Lon. Lon Sellitto! *He* was the whole point of this. You needed him killed or out of commission and you used the AFFC as a scapegoat."

"Exactly," the man whispered. And the tone of his voice taunted: Keep going.

"The case he'd been working on. Of course. The break-in at the Metropolitan museum. He was getting close to finding out what it was all about and your employer needed to stop him." He considered other facts. "And Amelia too. Because she'd taken over the Met case...But you're admitting it all now," Rhyme said slowly, troubled. "Why?"

"I think I'll let it go at that, Lincoln. Probably not good to say much more. But I will tell you that nobody is at risk anymore. Amelia's safe. The only reason to poison her or Ron or your brilliant nerdy assistant, Mel Cooper, would be to shift the blame to the AFFC. And obviously that's pointless now. Besides, I've changed tack."

Rhyme pictured the man shrugging.

"You're safe too, of course. You always have been."

Always have been?

Rhyme gave a laugh. "The anonymous phone call about somebody's breaking into my town house through the back door. When Billy snuck in to poison my whisky. That was you."

"I was keeping tabs on him. The night he went to your town house, I was following. He wasn't supposed to kill you, hurt you in any way. When he changed into a workman's uniform and got a needle ready, I knew what he was up to."

This made no sense at all.

Until a moment later another deduction. Rhyme whispered, "You need me for something. You need me alive. Why? To investigate a crime, of course. Yes, yes. But which one? One committed recently?" What open major cases were there? Rhyme wondered. Then realized. "Or one that's *going* to happen? Next week?"

"Or next month or next year," the Watchmaker offered, sounding amused.

"The Metropolitan museum break-in? Or something else?"

No word.

"Why me?"

A pause. "I'll just say that the plan I've put together needs you."

"And it needs me to be aware of it," Rhyme shot back. "So my knowing is a gear or a spring or a flywheel in your timepiece."

A laugh. "How well put. It's so refreshing to talk to somebody who gets it...But now I should be going, Lincoln."

"One last question?"

"Of course. Answering may be a different matter."

"You told Billy to find that book, *Serial Cities*."

"That's right. I needed to make sure he and the Stantons appreciated how good you were—and how much you and Amelia had learned about the militias and their tactics."

Rhyme said ruefully, "You had no particular interest in the Bone Collector? I got that wrong."

"I guess you did."

A laugh and Rhyme said, "So the connection I found between the Bone Collector and you wasn't there at all?"

A pause.

"You found a connection between us?" The Watchmaker sounded curious.

"There's a famous watch on display here in Manhattan. It's made entirely out of bone. Some Russian, I think. I wondered if stealing that was on your agenda."

"There's a Mikhail Semyonovitch Bronnikov in town?"

"I think that was it. And you didn't know?"

The Watchmaker said, "I've been rather... preoccupied lately. But I'm familiar with the piece. It's quite astonishing. Mid-1860s. And you're right: made entirely of bone, one hundred percent."

"I suppose it wouldn't make sense for you to risk getting caught—and waste the time, so to speak—trying to break into a Manhattan antiques store to steal a watch."

"No, but it was creative thinking, Lincoln. Just what I'd expect of you." Another pause. Rhyme imagined that he was checking his own timepiece. "Now I think it's best to say goodbye, Lincoln. I've been on the line a little too long. Sometimes those proxies and phone switches *can* be traced, you know. Not that you'd ever try." A chuckle. "Till we meet again…"

Next week, next month, next year.

The line went dead.

TUESDAY, NOVEMBER 12 VI

SKIN AND BONE

CHAPTER 79

1:00 P.M.

Ron Pulaski had assumed the job of scouring the Berkowitz Funeral Home for evidence and witnesses, searching for any clues that might lead to the Watchmaker.

He seemed to take the failure of his undercover mission to heart, though he could hardly be blamed; the Watchmaker had recognized him immediately. He'd seen the young officer as part of his project in New York a few years ago.

Moreover, Rhyme knew, even if it had been a righteous set, the kid *was* a pretty bad actor. The best thespians didn't play characters; they *became* them.

Gielgud…

So the young officer had collected trace from the documents at the funeral home that Richard Logan—or whatever his real name might be—had signed and where he'd collected the box containing the ashes of the unidentified homeless man from the city morgue. He'd interviewed everyone who'd been at the parlor when the Watchmaker had, including the relatives of someone named Benjamin Ardell, also known as Jonny Rodd, whoever he was. But he'd uncovered no leads.

Nor were there any among the New York Bureau of Investigation agents, who'd also been scammed by the Watchmaker. The agents hadn't had much contact with "Dave Weller," other than phone calls. And the mobile he'd contacted them on, diming out Pulaski, was, of course, long gone. Batteries in one sewer, snapped-in-half handset in another.

Sachs was handling a different portion of the case, tracking down the insiders who'd helped Logan escape, medical workers, an attendant in the New York City morgue and various prison guards. To Rhyme it seemed they'd taken an astronomical risk. If it was discovered that the Watchmaker was alive, then the ring of suspects would be quite small; they were sure to be detected. But, Rhyme supposed, it wasn't the Watchmaker's problem if they didn't hide the bribes he'd paid them or had failed to come up with credible alibis after they'd faked the medical reports and death certificate.

You have to be smart to earn a few million bucks illegally.

One or two had skipped town but it was only a matter of time until they were tracked down. Not a good idea to use your real credit card when you're on the lam. Natural selection applies to criminal activity, as well as to newts and simians.

Rhyme was handling part of the investigation too, though not the evidentiary part, curiously. The criminalist had made some meticulous plans of his own.

Probably nothing would come of them but he couldn't afford to pass up any opportunity.

He now gazed out the window, examining the clime—overcast again, white and gray—and he wondered, Where are you? And what are you up to? Why did you break into the Met? And what part of that plot do you need me alive for?

Thom appeared in the doorway. "I talked to Rachel. Leave in an hour?"

"That'll do," Rhyme replied.

The journey he was referring to would take them to the medical center. Lon Sellitto had regained consciousness. Even in his frail state, the detective remained true to his nature. Rachel reported that his reaction upon swimming into a waking state had been to look down at his belly and mutter, smiling, "Fuck, I musta lost thirty pounds."

Only then had he inquired about the Unsub 11-5 case.

But there were still many questions about his recovery. He had been, and would continue to be, treated with chelation drugs, which bind and deactivate toxins. Recovery is better with patients who've had chronic exposure, such as industrial workers (or victims of patiently homicidal spouses), but problematic with acute attacks, as in Sellitto's case. The jury was still out on the detective's long-term improvement. Nerve damage, liver and renal issues were possibilities.

Maybe even permanent paralysis.

Time would tell.

Amelia Sachs walked into the parlor. "Lon?" she asked.

"Leave here in about an hour."

"Should we get flowers?" she asked.

Rhyme muttered, "I've arranged for flowers once this week. I'm not doing it again."

Just at that moment the lab phone rang. Sachs, in a position to view caller ID on a monitor, said quickly, "Rhyme. I think it's going down."

He wheeled closer.

"Ah."

Then punched *accept call.*

"Yes?"

"Mr. Rhyme, it's Jason? Jason Heatherly?" The unnecessarily interrogative words were fast, the voice flummoxed. "I'm—"

"I remember you, Mr. Heatherly."

How could Rhyme not? They'd spoken at length only a week ago.

"Well, it's—I don't know how to explain this—but what you said might happen happened."

Rhyme and Sachs shared a smile.

"It's gone. Impossible but it's gone. The alarms were set when I left last night. They were set when I got here this morning. Nothing was disturbed. Not a thing out of place. Not. A. Thing. But it's gone."

"Really."

The "it" the worked-up jeweler was referring to was a watch. The Mikhail Semyonovitch Bronnikov timepiece made entirely of bone.

Contrary to what he'd told the Watchmaker, Rhyme had not believed the man had any connection with the Bone Collector whatsoever. He'd told the Watchmaker that simply to dangle bait.

And how better to snare a man whose strength—and weakness—was time and timepieces than by using a rare watch?

Rhyme had found out that a Bronnikov, one of the

few in existence, was in London, though not for sale. But he'd charmed the owner into changing his mind (charm plus twenty thousand dollars, that is) and spent another ten thousand to fly the watch to New York. Ron Pulaski had been the courier.

Rhyme had called Fred Dellray and learned that there was an art dealer under indictment for tax evasion, Jason Heatherly. Dellray got the U.S. attorney to drop a few of the charges if Heatherly cooperated; the feds wanted the Watchmaker back in the slammer as much as Rhyme and the NYPD did.

Heatherly agreed and the watch was delivered to him and put on display in a case in his Upper East Side antiques store/art gallery.

In his conversation with the Watchmaker a week ago Rhyme had brought up the Bone Collector and then casually segued to the Bronnikov watch, mentioning that it was in a gallery in Manhattan. He'd tried to be nonchalant and hoped his delivery was more fluid than Ron Pulaski's.

Apparently it was.

Several days after the conversation, Heatherly reported that a man had called, inquiring about any watches the gallery might have for sale—though asking nothing specific about the Bronnikov. Heatherly had told him the inventory, including a mention of the bone watch, and the man had thanked him and hung up. Caller ID was *Unknown.*

Rhyme and a task force had debated how to handle it. The bureau wanted surveillance and a take-down team near the gallery, ready to move in as soon as somebody came in to buy or steal the watch. Rhyme said no. The

Watchmaker would spot them instantly. They should take a different approach, more subtle.

So FBI and NYPD surveillance experts had installed a miniature tracker in the metal fob of the watch. The device would remain powered down, undetectable by any radio wave sensors, most of the time. Every two days, it would—for a millisecond—beam its location to the ICGSN, the International Consolidated Geopositioning Satellite Network, which blanketed nearly every populated area on earth. Then go quiescent.

The positioning data would be sent directly to the task force's mainframe. If the Watchmaker was on the move, they could narrow down the country and region he was traveling through and alert border authorities. Or, if luck was with them, they might find him stationary, enjoying a cool wine on a beach and admiring his stolen bone watch.

Or maybe he'd immediately separate the watch from its duplicitous fob, which he'd mail to Sri Lanka and go on with his plans for whatever heist or murder he was plotting.

So my knowing about this is a gear or a spring or a flywheel in the timepiece of your plan…

The gallery owner continued to be exercised about the break-in. He said breathlessly, "It's impossible. The alarms. The locks. The video cameras."

Rhyme had insisted that there be no lapses in security to make it easier for the Watchmaker to steal the bait; the man would have grown suspicious in an instant and balked.

Heatherly continued, "There's simply no way anybody could have gotten inside."

But we aren't dealing with just *anybody*, Rhyme reflected, and without comment he muttered goodbye to the gallery owner and disconnected the call.

Now, we wait.

A day, a month, a year…

He wheeled away from the examination tables, glancing at another watch—the Breguet that the Watchmaker had given to Rhyme some years ago.

Rhyme now said to Sachs, "Call Pulaski. I want him on the grid at the art gallery."

She spoke with the officer and sent him to run the scene at Heatherly's. Rhyme didn't hold out many hopes of getting any evidence from the theft. Still, the j's needed to be dotted.

"Thom," Rhyme said, "before we go to visit Lon, I'll have one for the road—a double, if you please."

He braced for defense. But, for some reason, the aide didn't object to the consumption of fine, aged—and poison-free—single-malt whisky. Perhaps he was sympathetic to the fact that, while the criminalist had prevented a terrorist attack, the Watchmaker had slipped away. And Rhyme would probably lose a slick thirty grand in the process.

A glass appeared in the cup holder.

Rhyme sipped the smoky liquor. Good, good.

He sent and answered several emails, to and from tattoo artist TT Gordon, whom Rhyme had taken a liking to. The man was coming over to hang out with the dude in a wheelchair next week. They'd talk about grammar and Samoan culture and life in hipster New York. And who knew what other topics, and projects, might arise?

Mt. Everest and falcons perhaps.

He cocked his head. A crunch of feet on the ice outside. Then a click, the front-door lock, more footsteps.

Rhyme took another sip. The sound told the story. Sachs, however, didn't interpret the sonic evidence and remained wary... until Pam Willoughby turned the corner and paused in the archway.

"Hey." The teen nodded to everyone, unwrapping an impressive scarf from her neck. The day was wind- and sleet-free but must've been cold. Her pretty nose was pink and her shoulders hunched.

Amelia Sachs's shoulders, on the other hand, sagged but she managed a smile. She'd be recalling that Pam was going to borrow her foster father's car to pick up the last of her possessions in the bedroom upstairs.

Silence for a moment. Sachs seemed to take a deep breath. "How's it going?"

"Okay. Good. Play opens officially next week. Busy. Victorian costumes. They weigh a ton. The dresses."

Small talk. Pointless talk.

Silence. Sachs said, "I'll help you get your things." Nodding toward the stairs.

Pam glanced around the parlor, avoiding eyes. "Well, actually, I mean, do you think it'd be okay if I moved back? Just for a while, till I can find someplace new? Didn't really want to go back to my place in the Heights. Just, you know, everything that happened there. And the Olivettis—they're great. Only." She looked at the floor. Then up. "Would that be okay?"

Sachs strode forward and hugged her hard. "That's a question you never need to ask."

Thom said, "You've got some things outside to bring in?"

"In the car. Yeah, I could use some help, sure."

Thom suited up, donning his own scarf and a faux-fur Russian Cossack hat. He followed Pam out to the car.

Sachs pulled on her coat and gloves and followed. She got as far as the arched doorway separating the parlor from the hall. She turned to Rhyme. "Wait a minute."

"Wait?" he asked.

She walked closer, tilted her head as if she were gazing at a gangbanger she'd just collared, and looked down. In a soft voice: "Thom changed the locks last week. After Billy broke in."

Rhyme shrugged. A sip. "Uhm."

"Well?"

"Well what?" he muttered.

"Pam didn't knock just now. She let herself in. That means she had one of the new keys."

"New keys?"

"Why are you repeating what I say? How did Pam get a new key? She hasn't been here for over a week."

"Hm. I don't know. That's a mystery."

She shot him a coy glance. "Rhyme, if I were to look over your phone log would I find any outgoing calls to Pam recently?"

"When would I *possibly* have had time to chat with anybody? Anyway, I'm hardly a chatterer. Do I seem like a chatterer to you?"

"That's evading the question."

"If you looked at my log, no, you wouldn't find any calls to Pam. Recently or unrecently."

This was true; he'd deleted them.

Of course, he'd forgotten that Sachs might pick up on

the conspiracy after he'd messengered Pam the new key a few days ago, after their, all right, "chat."

Sachs gave a laugh, leaned forward and kissed him hard, then headed out the door to help with the move.

Leaving Rhyme to do what he'd been looking forward to for some hours. He wheeled back to the examination table.

On a sterile tray sat a small bit of off-white resin or plastic or clay, which had been discovered lodged in the wristwatch band of a banker murdered last night on the Upper East Side. The murder itself wasn't remarkable—Rhyme was solidly in View of Death Number One mode here—but what struck him as unusual was that the body was found near a construction site between Madison and Park Avenues: The western wall of the foundation was about ten feet from an underground tunnel that led, after some maze-like twists, directly to the Metropolitan Museum of Art's underground archives.

The crime scene indicated that there had been a fierce struggle. It seemed likely that the source of the beige evidence in the watchband had been the killer and that it could tell reams about the man or woman who'd taken the victim's life.

But until the material was identified and its source determined, that tentative conclusion was a mere wisp of supposition. It had to be either proven valid and recorded on a whiteboard, or proven false and discarded like the autumn leaves now largely stripped from the trees outside his window. Rhyme prepared a sample for the chromatograph and wheeled to the humming machine, to see which of those two alternatives might prove to be the case.

Acknowledgments

With undying gratitude to: Will and Tina Anderson, Sophie Baker, Sonya Cheuse, Jane Davis, Julie Deaver, Jenna Dolan, Cathy Gleason, Jamie Hodder-Williams, Mitch Hoffman, Kerry Hood, Emma Knight, Carolyn Mays, Claire Nozieres, Hazel Orme, Michael Pietsch, Jamie Raab, Betsy Robbins, Lindsey Rose, Katy Rouse, Marissa Sangiacomo, Roberto Santachiara, Deborah Schneider, Vivienne Schuster, Madelyn Warcholik. You're the best!

About the Author

A former journalist, folksinger and attorney, Jeffery Deaver is an international number-one bestselling author. His novels have appeared on bestseller lists around the world, including the *New York Times*, the *Times* of London, Italy's *Corriere della Sera*, the *Sydney Morning Herald* and the *Los Angeles Times*. His books are sold in 150 countries and translated into twenty-five languages.

The author of thirty-three novels, two collections of short stories and a nonfiction law book, he's received or been shortlisted for a number of awards around the world. His *The Bodies Left Behind* was named Novel of the Year by the International Thriller Writers Association, and his Lincoln Rhyme thriller *The Broken Window* and a stand-alone, *Edge*, were also nominated for that prize. He has been awarded the Steel Dagger and the Short Story Dagger from the British Crime Writers' Association and the Nero Wolfe Award, and he is a three-time recipient of the Ellery Queen Readers Award for Best Short Story of the Year and a winner of the British Thumping Good Read Award. *The Cold Moon* was recently named the Book of the Year by the Mystery Writers Association of Japan, as well as by *Kono Mystery Wa Sugoi* magazine. In addition, the Japanese Adventure Fiction Association awarded *The Cold Moon* and *Carte Blanche* their annual Grand Prix award.

He contributed to the anthology *Books to Die For*, which won the Agatha Award.

His most recent novels are *The October List*, a thriller told in reverse; *The Kill Room*, a Lincoln Rhyme novel; *XO*, a Kathryn Dance thriller, for which he wrote an album of country-western songs, available on iTunes and as a CD; and before that, *Carte Blanche*, the latest James Bond continuation novel, a number-one international bestseller.

Deaver has been nominated for seven Edgar Awards from the Mystery Writers of America, an Anthony, a Shamus and a Gumshoe. He was recently shortlisted for the ITV3 Crime Thriller Award for Best International Author. *Roadside Crosses* was on the shortlist for the Prix Polar International 2013.

His book *A Maiden's Grave* was made into an HBO movie starring James Garner and Marlee Matlin, and his novel *The Bone Collector* was a feature release from Universal Pictures, starring Denzel Washington and Angelina Jolie. And, yes, the rumors are true: He did appear as a corrupt reporter on his favorite soap opera, *As the World Turns.* He was born outside Chicago and has a bachelor of journalism degree from the University of Missouri and a law degree from Fordham University.

Readers can visit his website at
www.jefferydeaver.com.

Please turn the page for an exciting sneak preview of Jeffery Deaver's next Lincoln Rhyme thriller, *The Burial Hour.*

Mommy."

"In a minute."

They trooped doggedly along the quiet street on the Upper East Side, the sun low this cool autumn morning. Red leaves, yellow leaves spiraled from sparse branches.

Mother and daughter, burdened with the baggage that children now carted to school.

In my day…

Claire was texting furiously. Her housekeeper had—wouldn't you know it?—gotten sick, no, *possibly* gotten sick, on the day of the dinner party! And Alan had to work late. *Possibly* had to work late.

As if I could ever count on him anyway.

Ding.

The response from her friend:

Sorry, Carmellas busy tnight.

Jesus. A tearful emoji accompanied the missive. Why not type the goddamn "o" in "tonight"? And remember apostrophes? Did it save you a precious millisecond?

"But, Mommy." An eight-year-old singsongy tone.

"A minute, Whitnee. You heard me." Claire's voice was a benign monotone. Not the least angry, not the least peeved. Thinking of the weekly sessions: Sitting in the chair, not lying back on the couch—the good doctor didn't even have a couch in his office—Claire attacked her nemeses, the anger and impatience, and she had studiously worked to avoid snapping or shouting when her daughter was annoying (even when she did it intentionally, which, Claire calculated, was easily one-quarter of the girl's waking hours).

And I'm doing a damn good job of keeping a lid on it.

Reasonable. Mature. "A minute," she repeated.

Claire slowed to a stop, flipping through her phone's address book, lost in the maelstrom of approaching disaster. It was early but the day would vanish fast and the party would be on her like a nearby Uber. Wasn't there someone, *anyone* in the borough of Manhattan who might have some decent help she could borrow to wait a party? A party for ten friggin' people! That was nothing. How hard could it be?

She debated: Her sister?

Nope. She wasn't invited.

Sally from the club?

Nope. Out of town. And a bitch, to boot.

Whitnee had slowed and Claire was aware of her daughter turning around. Had she dropped something? Apparently so. She ran back to pick it up.

Better not be her phone. She'd already broken one. The screen cost $187 to fix.

Honestly. Children.

Then Claire was back to scrolling, praying for waitperson salvation. Look at all these names. Need to clean out this damn contact list. Off went another beseeching message.

The child returned to her side and said firmly, "Mommy, look—"

"Shhh." Hissing now. But there was nothing wrong with an edge, of course. It was a form of education. Children had to learn. Even the cutest of puppies needed collar-jerk correction from time to time.

Another ding of the iPhone.

Another no.

Goddamn it.

Well, what about that woman that Terri from the office had used? Hispanic, or Latino...Latina. Whatever those people called themselves now. The cheerful woman had been the star of Terri's daughter's graduation party. Cooking—or at least reheating—and sweeping plates away the minute they were empty and stacking the dishwasher like a pro. She even spoke English.

Claire found Terri's number and dialed a voice call, rather than texting. Terri wasn't invited tonight, either, but she'd finesse that.

"Hello?"

"Terri! It's Claire. How are you?"

A hesitation then Terri said, "Hi, there. How're you doing?"

"I'm—"

At which point Whitnee interrupted yet again, snapping, "Mommy!"

Claire spun around and glared down at the petite blonde, hair in braids, wearing a snug pink leather Armani Junior jacket. She raged, "I am on the phone! Are you blind? What have I told you about that? When I'm on the phone? What is so f..." Okay, watch the language, she told herself. Claire offered a chill smile. "What's so damn important?"

"I'm trying to tell you. This man back there?" Nodding up the street. "He came up to another man and hit him or something and pushed him in the trunk."

"What?"

Whitnee tossed a braid, which ended in a tiny bunny clip, off her shoulder. "He left this on the ground and then he drove away." She held up a cord or thin rope. What was it?

Claire gasped. In her daughter's petite hand was a miniature hangman's noose.

Now it was Whitnee's face that curled into an icy smile. "That's what's so fucking important."

"Greenland."

Lincoln Rhyme was staring out the parlor window of his Central Park West town house. Two objects were in his immediate field of vision: a complicated Hewlett-Packard gas chromatograph and, outside the large nineteenth-century window, a peregrine falcon. The predatory birds were not uncommon in the city, where tasty and oblivious pigeons were plentiful. It was rare, however, for them to nest this low. Rhyme, as unsentimental as a scientist had to be—especially the criminal forensic scientist he was—nonetheless took a curious comfort in the creature's presence. Over the years he'd shared his abode with a number of generations of peregrines. Mom was home at the moment, a glorious thing, sumptuously textured brown and gray, beak and claws glistening gunmetal.

A man's calm, humorous voice filled the silence. "No. You and Amelia cannot go to Greenland."

"Why not?" Rhyme asked Thom Reston, an edge to his voice. The slim but sturdy man had been his caregiver for about as long as the line of falcons had resided outside the old residence. A quadriplegic, Rhyme was largely paralyzed south of his shoulders, and Thom was his arms and legs and considerably more. He had been fired as often as he'd quit, but here he was and, both knew, here he would remain.

"Because you need to go someplace *romantic*. Florida, California."

"Cliché, cliché, cliché. Might as well go to Niagara Falls." He scowled.

"What's wrong with that?"

"I'm not even responding."

"What does Amelia say?"

"She left it up to me. Which was irritating. Doesn't she know I have better things to think about?"

"You mentioned the Bahamas recently. You wanted to go back, you said."

"That was true at the time. It's not true any longer. Can't one change one's mind? Hardly a crime."

"What's the real reason for Greenland?"

Rhyme's face—with its prominent nose and eyes like pistol muzzles—was predatory in its own right, much like the bird's. "What do you mean by that?"

"Could it be that there's a practical reason you want to go to Greenland, a *professional* reason? A *useful* reason?"

Rhyme glanced at the single-malt scotch bottle sitting just out of reach. He was largely paralyzed, yes. But surgery and daily exercise had returned to him some ability to move his right arm and hand. Fate helped too. The beam that had tumbled upon his neck from a crime scene many years ago had severed and crushed some nerves, yes, but had left a few outlying strands intact, if injured and confused. He could grasp objects—like single-malt scotch bottles—but he could not rise from his complex wheelchair to fetch them if Thom, playing nursemaid, kept them out of reach.

"Not cocktail hour yet," the aide announced, noting the arc of his boss's vision. "So, Greenland? 'Fess up."

"It's underrated. Named 'Greenland' while much of it's barren. Not the least verdant. Compare Iceland. Quite green. I like the irony."

"You're not answering."

Rhyme sighed. He disliked being transparent and hugely disliked being caught being transparent. He would appeal to logic. "It seems that the Rigspolitiet, the Danish national police, have been doing some rather important research into a new system of horticultural spectrographic analysis. A lab in Nuuk. That's the capital, by the way. You can situate a sample in a much narrower geographic area than with standard systems.

Imagine." Rhyme's brows rose involuntarily. "We think all plants are the same—"

"Not a sin of mine."

Rhyme groused, "You know what I mean. This new technique can narrow down a target area to three meters!" He repeated, "Imagine."

"I'm trying to. Greenland—no. And has Amelia actually deferred to you?"

"She will. When I tell her about the spectrograph."

"How about England? She'd love that. Is that show on still, the one she likes? *Top Gear*? I think the original is off the air but I heard there's a new version. She'd be great as a guest. She's always talking about driving a hundred and eighty miles an hour on the wrong side of the road."

"England?" Rhyme mocked. "Greenland and England offer the same degree of romance."

"You'll find some disagreement there."

"Not from the Greenlanders."

Lincoln Rhyme did not travel much. The practical consequences of his disability added a layer of complication to journeys. But his uncharacteristic willingness to head off to a romantic spot, or a practical one, was buoyed by a very practical consideration: access to a private jet. This indulgence had come about thanks to a case Rhyme and Sachs had worked on recently. Their tidy forensic work resulted in a successful verdict—and a huge recovery for the victim's wife. Her grateful lawyer had not only paid a consulting fee but offered the use of a client's private jet, when it was available. They would pay only for fuel and the crew's fee.

And the jet would definitely be put to use. You cannot honeymoon in your hometown.

But choosing the exact destination would have to wait, it seemed. The door buzzer sounded. Rhyme glanced at the security video and thought: Well.

Thom rose and returned a moment later with a middle-aged man in a mahogany-colored suit, which he might have slept in, though he probably hadn't. He moved slowly but was steady, and Rhyme thought that soon he'd be able to discard the cane, which was, however, a pretty nifty accessory.

The man looked around the lab. "Quiet."

"Is. A few small private jobs recently. Nothing fun. Nothing exciting. Nothing since the Steel Kiss killer."

A recent perpetrator had taken to sabotaging household items and public conveyances—with tragic and occasionally disgusting results.

NYPD detective Lon Sellitto, in the Major Cases Division, had been Rhyme's partner when he himself was on the force—before he moved up to captain and took over the forensic unit. Nowadays Sellitto would occasionally hire Rhyme to consult on cases in which special crime scene expertise was needed.

"Where's Amelia?"

Rhyme replied, "In court. Testifying in the Gordon case. Then she was going shopping. For our trip."

"Buying herself a trousseau? What is that anyway?"

Rhyme had no idea. "Something about weddings, clothing. I don't know. But she's got a dress already. Something frilly. Blue. Or maybe pink. No, red. She's shopping for me. What's so goddamn funny, Lon?"

"Picturing you in a tuxedo."

"Just some sweats and a shirt. Maybe a tie. I don't know."

For all her edge and edginess, her need for speed and sleek firearms, her passion for tactical solutions, Sachs had a splinter of teen girl within her and she was enjoying the game of wedding planning. This included a whatever-the-hell-it-was trousseau and a honeymoon, and if that pleased her, by God, Rhyme was more than happy to accommodate.

Though he really hoped he could convince her about Greenland.

"Well, tell her to shop later. I need her to run a scene. We've got a situation."

A ping resounded within Rhyme the way a submarine's sonar detects something unexpected off the port bow.

Ah, interesting...

He texted Sachs and received no response. "Maybe on the stand, testifying. Tell me more."

Thom appeared in the doorway—Rhyme hadn't realized he'd left. The aide said, "Lon, some coffee? Cookies? I've been baking. I've got a couple of different kinds. One is—"

"Yes, yes, yes." It was Rhyme answering. "Bring him something. Make a decision yourself. I want to hear his story."

Sit-u-a-tion...

"Proceed."

"Anything chocolate," Sellitto called to Thom's back.

"You got it."

"Kidnapping, Linc. Upper East Side. Apparently one white male snatched another one."

"Apparently? What requires interpretation?"

"The only wit was a schoolgirl, eight years old."

"Ah." A scowl.

"Perp grabs vic, tosses him into a trunk. We think the nappee was a thirty-two-year-old businessman, Michael Kellerman."

"Think?"

"Deducing that from a phone found about two blocks away, pitched out of a vehicle, generally matching the one in question. Kellerman lives in Philly. In town for business. Respondings called the last dialed number and it was an ad agency where he was supposed to be at ten. He never showed."

"The girl is sure? Not a figment of imagination, stoked by too much television, reading too many Hello Pony stories."

"Hello Kitty. Ponies are a different book. Or TV show. Rachel's grandkids could tell you. But I think it's legit. Whitnee, the girl, found a calling card he'd left behind." Sellitto held up his phone and displayed a photo.

At first Rhyme couldn't make out the image. It was a picture of a dark shape, thin, sitting on concrete, apparently sidewalk.

Sellitto: "It's a—"

"Noose."

"Yep."

"Made out of?"

"Not sure. She picked it up but the responding set it back in the same place he'd left it, more or less."

"Great. I've never worked a scene contaminated by an eight-year-old."

"Relax, Linc. They're house-trained at that age. All

she did was pick the noose up. She didn't hopscotch through the scene. And the responding wore gloves. Scene's secure, waiting for somebody to run it. Somebody, as in Amelia. The wit's still there. With Mommy. She's gotta keep Whitnee out of school, so she isn't very happy."

Neither was Rhyme. An eight-year-old girl with the observational skills and perception of a . . . well, eight-year-old girl.

"This vic? Rich, politically active, connected with OC, record?"

Sellitto said, "None of the above. Nada remarkable. Consultant. A few Google hits is all. Pays his taxes. Not even a traffic ticket. Perp might just be a psycho. And Kellerman was WTWP."

"What?"

"Wrong time, wrong place."

Rhyme scowled once more. "Lon?"

"It's going around the department."

"Flu viruses—not viri, by the way—go around the department. Idiotic expressions do not. Or should not, at least."

Sellitto used the cane to rise to his feet and aimed his bulky form toward the tray of cookies that Thom was setting down, like a Realtor seducing prospective buyers at a condominium open house. He ate one, then two, then another, nodded approval. Sellitto poured a cup of coffee from a silver pitcher and spilled in some sweetener, his concession to the battle against calories being to sacrifice refined sugar for pastry.

"Good," he announced through a mouthful of cookie. "You want one? Some coffee?"

The criminalist's eyes swiveled instinctively toward the Glenmorangie, sitting golden and alluring on the high shelf.

But Lincoln Rhyme decided: No. He wanted his faculties about him. He had a feeling that the girl's observations were all too accurate, that the kidnapping had occurred just as she described it and that the macabre calling card was a taunting message—of a death soon to be.

"We've gotta move on this, Lon. I don't think the vic has much time."

And he texted Sachs once more.